Bad Boy

Olivia Goldsmith is the author of the international bestsellers *The First Wives Club*, also a major Hollywood film, *Flavour of the Month*, *Fashionably Late*, *Bestseller*, *Marrying Mom*, *The Switch* and *Young Wives*. Also, with Amy Fine Collins, *Simple Isn't Easy*, a practical guide to stylish dressing. She divides her time between her homes in upstate New York and Manhattan. For more about Olivia Goldsmith, visit her website at www.theoliviagoldsmith.com.

Acclaim for Olivia Goldsmith:

'Fizzing with acerbic dialogue and high-level sexual slapstick, this is a very funny romantic comedy'   *Good Housekeeping*

'More sassy, razor-sharp, laugh-out-loud wit from the bestseller - and some characters so real you'll want to hug them' *Evening Telegraph*

'A bubbly, fizzy story'   *Daily Mail*

'Olivia Goldsmith's forte has always been the writing of revenge novels with great good humor … Plenty of awful people get their comeuppance and there's more satisfactory coupling at the end than in a Shakespeare comedy.'   *Washington Post*

'Goldsmith hands out her characters' rewards and comeuppances like Jane Austen dealing blackjack … You keep licking your fingers and reaching for the next page as if it were another potato chip.'

Newsweek

Also by Olivia Goldsmith

FICTION

The First Wives Club
Flavour of the Month
Fashionably Late
Bestseller
Marrying Mom
The Switch
Young Wives

NON FICTION

Simple Isn't Easy

OLIVIA GOLDSMITH

BAD BOY

HarperCollins*Publishers*

HarperCollins*Publishers*
77–85 Fulham Palace Road,
Hammersmith, London W6 8JB

www.**fire**and**water**.com

This paperback edition 2001
3 5 7 9 8 6 4 2

First published in Great Britain by
HarperCollins*Publishers* 2001

ISBN 0 00 651437 5

Printed and bound in Great Britain by
Omnia Books Limited, Glasgow

To Nunzio Nappi

As long as I can sit in the front seat

Acknowledgments

A special nod to all the natural-born bad boys who helped with their contributions: Nick Ellison, Ivan Reitman, Tom "My-Sister-Bought-Your-Apartment" Pollack, Michael Chinich, Dan Goldberg, Joe Medjik, Jeff "Ice" Berg, Cliff Gilbert-Lurie, Skip "Bait-and-Switch" Brittenham, Paul "No Coast" Mahon, Bert Fields, Lenny Gartner, Dwight "The-Mean-One" Currie, Jim "Lincoln-Logs" Ragliamo, Tom LaPoint, Jerry "Rat-on-Acid" Balargeon, Carl "CJ" Benenati, Philip "Frisky" Kain, Justin Levy, Andy Fisher, Paul "Hang-'Em-High" Toner, not to mention Miracle Relocators—Nissim, Keith, and Patrick.

And thanks as well to all the bad boy wannabe men: Bob "You-Keep-the-Money" Levinson, Ross "She-Called-Me-a-Dick" Cantor, Alan "The Sweetie" Ladd, Jr., Lewis Allen, Jerry "Let's-Do-It" Offsay, John Moser, Harold "Just-One-More" Sokol, Tony the Line Dog, Jeff Kreutziger, Paul "The Dozer" Rothmel, Ed Harte, Michael "Hatrick" Elovitz, Peter "Overshoes" Davis, Ben Dower, Lenny Bigelow, Michael "The-Nice-One" Kohlmann, Charlie "You-Write-'Em-I-Buy-'Em" Crowley, Mohammed Rahman, Eric Breitbart, Howard "Just-One-More-Bill" Schwartz, David "Oh-That-Ginkgo!" Gandler, Louis "Editors! I-Hate-Editors!" Aronne, all the guys from James Lee Construction, Kami Ashrafi, Efrain Butron, and Herb Gruberger, my drivers from Mirage, Rob "Temple Bar" Hundley, and Anthony "Just-a-Little-Longer" Susino at Louis Licari.

An extra special nod to all the women in my life that have put up with or do put up with bad boys. Sherry Lansing, Barbara "Returning-My-Call" Dreyfus, Nancy Josephson, Ann Foley, Jacki Judd, Barbara Howard, Laurie Sheldon, Jay Presson Allen, Rachel Dower, Ali Elovitz, Susan "Slugmeister" Jedren, Lorraine "Marysue" Kreahling, Sara "The Equalizer" Pearson, Lynn "Have-I-Got-a-Guy-for-You" Phillips, Linda Grady, Jane Sheridan, Deborah Levitt, Kathy Isoldi, Lisa

Olivia Goldsmith

* * * * * * * * * *

Welti, The Bitch of Perkinsville, Rosie Sisto, Carol Sylvia, Robinette Bell, Debbie, Katie, and Nina LaPoint, Nancy Lee Kingsbury-Robinson-Delano, Rita Benenati, Pat Rhule, Judy Aqui-Rahim, Freeway, Mary Ann Chiapperino, Gladys, Rebekah, and Sarah Ashrafi, Lynn Goddel at Louis Licari, Edith Cohen at Marc Tash, and Mary Ellen "Bring-It-on-Home" Cashman. Special thanks to Martine Rothblatt who can put herself into any of the above categories that she chooses to. Last but not least, Louise and both Margarets.

Thanks also to the Canine Americans in my life: Mish "The Fish" Dubinofsky-Romanoff, Spice "The Rack" Escobar, New Baby "Jelly Roll" Levinson, Lexie Elovitz, and Max "Sergeant Ryan" Delano.

A very special acknowledgment must go to Pat Handly for introducing Nan to Rose Marie Jones, an endless resource for native Seattle lingo and sights. Thanks to the Seattle-King County Convention and Visitors Bureau for the tourist maps, to Jason Stamaris a special hello and thanks for identifying the location for exchange 807. Thanks to Jeff Cravens at REI for helping me with my rock climbing terminology and for the layout of the REI store in Seattle. Another big thanks to Margaret Santa Maria of Eastern Mountain Sports in Manhattan. I'm still not going to use a fefe hook, but that's a good thing.

Finally, kudos to my new friends at Dutton: Laurie Chittenden, Carolyn Nichols, Brian Tart, Louise Burke, Lisa Johnson, Michael McKenzie, and Carole Baron. Here's to all of you!

Bad Boy

Chapter 1

The sky was the same gray-white as the skim milk Tracie poured into her coffee. But that was what she loved about Seattle. It definitely wasn't Encino, where the sky was always a glorious blue, as empty of clouds as her house had been empty of people. As an only child with parents in "The Industry," Tracie had spent too many hours staring at that sky. No more empty blue for her. It made her feel as if she should be happy when she wasn't. Here in Seattle, any happiness against the overcast arc above seemed a reward.

Before Tracie had come here to college, she'd considered East Coast schools, but she wasn't brave enough for them. She'd read about Dorothy Parker, Sylvia Plath, and the Seven Sisters. Uh-uh. She knew, though, that she wanted out of California and far enough away from home that weekend visits wouldn't be possible. Unlike the heroine in a fairy tale, she couldn't say that her stepmother was wicked. Just passive-aggressive. So she'd picked the University of Washington, and the bonus had been that, aside from a pretty good journalism school, she'd made good friends, gotten a decent job, and fallen in love with Seattle. Not to mention that when the music scene got hot, she'd found a string of drop-dead-sexy guys. Of course, Tracie admitted to herself as she took her first sip of morning caffeine, Seattle was famous for its bad boys, good coffee, and Micro Millionaires. And, staring up at the cloud-filled sky, Tracie Leigh Higgins considered herself an aficionado on all three.

Sometimes, though, she thought she had them in the wrong positions: Maybe she ought to quit the bad boys completely, cut back on the coffee, and start dating the Micro Millionaires. Instead, she got serious with bad boys, guzzled lattes, and only interviewed and wrote about Micro Millionaires.

Tracie looked up at the sky once more. Her boyfriend, Phil, was giving her problems again. Maybe I should quit coffee, date the Micro and Gotonet guys, and write novels about the bad boys, she thought, and considered the idea as she stirred a little skim milk into her brew. She considered one of the chocolate and yellow-cake muffins, but then she scolded herself because they were addictive and she was off them for good. Somewhere in the back of her mind, Tracie realized it was either the thought of giving up Phil or writing a book that made her so upset she craved comfort. Did she have the courage to quit her day job to write books? And what did she have to write about? Too embarrassing to write about her ex-boyfriends, she decided. Tracie loved the quiet time she spent each morning reading out-of-town papers and staring out the coffeehouse window, but she'd be late if she didn't get moving. She had another Nettie profile to write. Boring.

She took another sip from the cup and glanced at her watch. Wait. Maybe I should quit bad boys and write about coffee. . . . It was all too confusing this early in the morning. She was a night person. She couldn't sort out life issues this early in the day. She'd wait until next New Year's to make some resolutions. Today, she had a deadline. She had to finish the article about one more Seattle TechnoWunderkind.

Then she'd see Phil.

Tracie tingled at the last part of her thought and picked up the coffee, which was now an almost-undrinkable temperature. She took a last gulp anyway and wondered if she could leave work early to get her hair done before seeing Phil.

She pulled out a Post-it notepad and wrote, "Call Stefan for a c,w & bd," then gathered her purse and backpack and walked to the door.

But as Tracie walked down the *Times* hallway, she was stopped by Beth Conte, eye-roller extraordinaire. "Marcus has been looking for you," Beth hissed. Even though Tracie knew Beth was a drama queen, her stomach took a little dive, and the coffee in it didn't like the plunge. The two of them kept walking toward Tracie's cubicle. "He's on the warpath," Beth added unnecessarily.

"Is that term politically correct?" Tracie asked Beth. "Or would it be considered a slur on Native Americans?"

"Putting Marcus in any ethnic group would be a slur on them. What is he, anyway?" Beth asked her as the two of them hurried along the corridor. "He's not Italian-American. I know that," she added, putting up her hands as if to defend her own ethnic background.

"He sprang from Zeus's forehead," Tracie conjectured as they turned the last corner and entered her cubicle at last.

" 'Zeus's forehead'?" Beth echoed. "Is Marcus Greek? What are you talking about?"

Tracie took off her raincoat, hung it on the hook, and stowed her purse under the desk. "You know, like Diana. Or was it Athena?"

"Princess Diana?" Beth asked, wrong and one beat behind, as usual.

This was what happened if you talked Greek mythology with Beth before 10:00 A.M. (or after 10:00 A.M.). Tracie took her sneakers off, threw them under her desk, and rooted around for her office shoes. She was about to explain her joke when the doorway to her cubicle was darkened by Marcus Stromberg's bulky form. Tracie pulled her head out from under her desk and hoped he hadn't had more than a few seconds look at her butt. She pushed her feet into her pumps. Facing Marcus barefoot was more than she could bear.

"Well, thanks for the lead," Beth squeaked, and slipped out of the cubicle.

Tracie gave Marcus her best I-graduated-cum-laude smile and sat down as coolly as she could. She refused to be cowed by Marcus. He wasn't so tough. He was a much smaller bully than all the men that her dad worked with back in L.A. He wasn't even as big a bully as her father. Just because Marcus had hoped one day to be Woodward or Bernstein and had wound up only being Stromberg was no fault of hers.

"How kind of you to drop in," Marcus said, looking down at his wristwatch. "I hope it didn't interfere with your social schedule."

Marcus had a habit of acting as if she considered herself some kind of debutante. "You'll have the profile by four," Tracie told him calmly. "I told you that yesterday."

"So I recall. But as it happens, I also need you to do a feature today."

Shit! As if she didn't have enough work to do. "On what?" Tracie asked, trying to appear unconcerned.

"Mother's Day. I need it good and I need it by tomorrow."

Tracie's beat included interviewing high-tech moguls and moguls-to-be, but, like everyone else, she was occasionally given other assignments. To make matters worse, Marcus had an uncanny knack of assigning the very story that would ruin your day. To Lily, an overweight but talented writer, he'd always assign stories about gymnasiums, anorexia, beauty pageants, and the like. To Tim, who tended to be a hypochondriac, he'd assign stories on new hospital wings, treatments. Somehow, he always found their weakness, even when it wasn't as obvious as Tim's and Lily's. Since Tracie rarely saw her family and didn't particularly like holidays, she was usually stuck covering the special occasions. And Mother's Day!

Her mother had died when Tracie was four and a half. Her father had long ago remarried, divorced, and remarried. Tracie could barely remember her mother and tried to forget her current stepmom. She considered Marcus's square jaw and the beard, which, to be accurate, should be called "10:00 A.M. shadow." "What's the angle?" Tracie queried. "Or can it be a sensitive essay on how I plan to spend Mother's Day?"

Marcus ignored her. "How Seattle celebrates its mothers. Mention a lot of restaurants, florists, and any other advertiser you can stuff into it. Nine hundred words by tomorrow morning. It'll run on Sunday."

God! Nine hundred words by tomorrow would kill any chances of fun with Phil tonight. Tracie looked at Marcus again, his curly dark hair, his ruddy skin, his small blue eyes, and wished, not for the first time, that he wasn't good-looking as well as totally obnoxious. Looks aside, Tracie made it a policy that she'd never give Marcus the satisfaction of knowing he'd upset her. So in keeping with her policy, she merely smiled. She knew that would bug him, so she tried to make it a debutante smile.

" 'As you wish,' said Wesley to the princess," she added.

"You're the only princess around here," Marcus grumbled as he turned and took himself off to darken the cubicle of some other poor journalist. Over his shoulder, he added, "And would you please try to get that Gene Banks profile fluff-free? I don't want to hear about his schnauzer."

"He doesn't have a schnauzer," Tracie called after him. Then, in a lower voice, she added, "He's got a black Lab." It was true she mentioned the Micronerds' pets and hobbies in her pieces, but that was a humanizing touch. Anyway, she liked dogs.

The phone rang, and it reminded her she'd have to call Phil about tonight, but at five after ten, it couldn't be him. He never got up before noon. She lifted the receiver. "Tracie Higgins," she said in as brisk and upbeat a voice as she could manage.

"And for that I am eternally grateful," Jonathan Delano teased. "What's wrong?"

"Oh, Marcus just had an aneurysm," Tracie told him.

"Isn't that a good thing?" Jon asked.

Tracie laughed. Jonathan always made her smile, no matter what. He had been her best friend for years. They'd met in a French class at the university. Jonathan had the biggest vocabulary and the worst accent that Tracie had ever heard. Her accent was pure Paris, but she couldn't conjugate a verb. She'd helped Jon with pronunciation and he'd helped her with grammar. They'd both gotten A's, and the partnership had thrived ever since. Only Jon or her girlfriend Laura could tell from four syllables that she was upset.

"I have a huge new assignment and I wanted to go out tonight. Plus, Laura is threatening to visit, so I gotta clean up my place."

"Famous Laura, your friend from Sausalito?"

"Sacramento, actually, but what's the dif? Yeah. She broke up with her freak boyfriend and needs some recovery time."

"Don't we all? What kind of freak was he?"

"Oh, just the usual 'I'm-sorry-I-didn't-call-you-can-I-borrow-three-hundred-dollars?-and-I-didn't-mean-to-sleep-with-your-best-friend' kind of freak."

"Oh. A freak kind of like Phil."

Tracie felt her stomach drop as if she were in the Needle elevator. "Phil's not like that. He's just having a hard time working on his writing and his music. Sometimes he needs help getting by, that's all."

Actually, Tracie more often felt Phil didn't need her help at all. While she always asked him to read her pieces, he rarely shared what he wrote. She still couldn't tell if it was because he was too sensitive to criticism, or if he didn't respect her opinion. Either way, Tracie felt attracted to that in him. His self-containment was so unlike her too-eager hunger for acknowledgment. He was cool. She was not.

Jon snorted. "Phil's a distraction from things that matter."

"Like what?"

"Um. Like the story of your mother's early death. Your complicated relationship with your father. Your *real* writing."

"What writing?" Tracie asked, playing dumb, though she'd been thinking the very same thing over coffee that morning. Jon meant well. He believed in her, but sometimes he . . . well, he went too far. "I don't do any *real* writing."

"Sometimes it creeps into the middle of a puff piece," Jon said. "Your real stuff is good. If they give you a column—"

"Ha! It will be forever before Marcus lets me have a column." Tracie sighed. "If he'd just stop cutting them and I got a few features published the way I wrote them . . ."

"You'd be a great columnist. Better than Anna Quindlen."

"Come on. Quindlen won a Pulitzer."

"So will you. Tracie, your stuff is so fresh that you'd blow everyone away. Nobody is speaking for our generation. You could be that voice."

Tracie stared at the receiver of the phone as if hypnotized. Neither one of them said anything for a moment and Tracie put the phone back to her ear. Then the spell broke. "Come on. Marcus doesn't even let my punch lines stay in my features. I'll be writing holiday features until I'm old and gray."

Jon cleared his throat. "Well, maybe if you focused more on your job . . ."

Tracie's other line rang. "Hold a minute, would you?" she asked Jon.

"I'll hold for Marcus but not for Phil," Jon said. "I have my pride."

Tracie punched the button, glad to hear Laura's soprano. "Hey ho, Tracerino. I phoned because I'm actually getting on the plane now."

"Get out. Right now?" Tracie asked. "I thought you were coming on Sunday."

"Face it. You thought maybe I wasn't coming at all. But I am. I really am. I'm just calling to say I packed up all my stuff and left my pots and pans with Susan."

"So that's it? You've told Peter?"

"I don't think I had to tell him. He saw the look on my face when I caught him going down on our next-door neighbor in our bedroom. Plus, he told me Quincy was an asshole."

Back in high school, Laura'd had a tremendous crush on Jack

Klugman. Tracie could never understand why, but sometimes the two of them drove through Benedict Canyon and staked out the house where somebody had told Laura he lived. They'd never seen him, but there wasn't an episode of *Quincy* that Laura didn't know by heart.

Tracie's eyes widened. "He didn't like *Quincy?*" she asked in mock horror. "And he went down on your neighbor?" she continued. "Was your neighbor a man or a woman?"

At least Laura laughed at that; it was better than tears. By Tracie's count, Laura had cried fifteen gallons' worth over Peter already. "So what's your flight number and what time should I meet you?" While Laura fumbled for the info, Tracie thought of her deadline and her date, but Laura had been her best friend for years. "I'll meet you at the airport," Tracie said, trying to assuage her guilt.

"You don't have to do that. I'm a big girl," Laura said, and laughed. Laura was six feet tall, and not skinny. "I'll just take the bus to your place," she offered.

"Are you sure?" Tracie asked.

"Yeah. I'll be fine. Besides, you've got work to do. You still get *Quincy* reruns in Seattle, don't you?" Laura added.

Tracie smiled. "Yup."

"Great. So hang up. I don't want to hold you up," Laura said.

That reminded her. "Oh no! I've got Jon on hold!" Tracie exclaimed.

"Don't worry, he's still there waiting for you. Hey, I'll get to meet the nerd at last." Laura laughed. "See you later," she said, and then hung up.

Tracie pushed the button for line one and, sure enough, Jon was still on the other end. "What's up?" he asked.

Chapter 2

"You're sure this isn't going to be inconvenient?" Laura asked, her sizable butt in the air, her head in the bottom drawer of the bureau Tracie had cleared out for her. She was putting away her T-shirts. Tracie had always marveled at how neatly Laura folded her shirts. Of course, once she put one on, it became as messy as her wild dark hair.

As she watched Laura, Tracie realized that she'd been really lonely for a girlfriend. She was pals with Beth and a few of the other women at work, but they were just work friends. Jon was her close pal, and though she adored him, it was nice to have Laura back again.

"I'm sure this *is* going to be inconvenient. Living in a one bedroom with a friend, not to mention a boyfriend as a frequent guest, is going to be very inconvenient, but it doesn't mean it's not going to be *fun*. I'm thrilled that you're here." Tracie squealed the way she had back in high school and opened her arms.

Laura gave great hugs. Sometimes, Tracie thought it was Laura's patient, listening ear and her great hugs that got her through. They had met in the seventh grade and for the next six years had spent less time apart than most married couples. In all that time, they'd never had one fight or disagreement—unless you counted the time Laura wanted to buy a dress with a fake fur bolero jacket for the junior prom. Tracie had absolutely forbidden it because (although she couldn't say so) it made Laura look almost exactly like a gorilla.

Tracie thought that they'd grown so close because they both were so needy at the time and yet so different. Laura was as tall as Tracie was short. Laura was big (God alone knew her weight) and Tracie was thin (104, but no more bulimia since she'd promised Laura not to throw up). Tracie was boyish, had almost no chest, and wore her hair short and streaked with blond. Laura was a brunette earth mother, had huge breasts and an unruly mane. Laura had always loved to cook; Tracie wasn't sure there'd been a kitchen in her Encino house.

"You can stay here as long as you want. As long as you don't bake farm cakes," Tracie told her girlfriend as they ended their hug. "I think you should move to Seattle permanently. But you do whatever you want as long as you don't go back to Peter."

"Peter, Peter Woman-eater. Hadda neighbor, hadda eat her," Laura sang.

"Was that really what he was doing when you walked in on them?" Tracie gasped.

"Sure was. Somehow, it was a lot worse than if they'd been fucking," Laura said. She stopped unpacking and sat down on the edge of Tracie's bed. "A guy can fuck a girl he doesn't even like, but he doesn't . . ." She paused and then shook her head. "Jesus, he hardly ever went down on *me*." She sighed, diving back into her bag to take out yet another perfectly folded T-shirt.

"Well, it doesn't matter," Tracie told her. "You're just never going to see him again. He's going to miss you."

"I don't know about me, but I do know he's going to miss my short ribs with braised cabbage and mango-apple-cranberry coulis." Laura laughed. "But enough about Peter. I can't wait to meet the famous Phil."

Tracie waggled her eyebrows in a poor imitation of Groucho Marx. "Well, you're not going to have to wait long. You finish unpacking while I work on this stupid feature. Then we'll get something to eat. After that, I'll take you to meet Phil at Cosmo."

"What's Cosmo?"

"It's easier to take you there than to explain it," Tracie told her friend. "You'll see tonight."

Cosmo was jammed by the time Tracie and Laura walked through its black glass double doors. It was enormous—three separate dance floors—with neon lights running along the black-painted walls and strobes and black lights picking up the slack, as if there was any. Laura eyed the scene. "An epileptic's nightmare," she quipped as they made their way to the crowded bar.

"Wait till you see the computerized light show," Tracie yelled above the din.

"They make it snow in here?" Laura yelled back.

"Light show—SHOW!" Tracie yelled, then saw by Laura's grin that she'd gotten her. "Yeah, yeah." Tracie grinned back.

Cosmo was bustling with habitués, all under thirty, thinking they were terminally hep. Personally, Tracie always thought there was something weird about the jeunesse dorée of Seattle. They had a lot more money and a lot less style than people in L.A. or other places Tracie had been, but she liked them for it. They either looked like they had forgotten to dress up before they went out or as if they'd put themselves together for some convention. In fact, the majority of Seattle young people seemed like Trekkies who had recently transferred their manic interest to some other sphere. Now a swing band was playing and couples danced, many of them in forties zoot suits and period dresses. Tracie thought the dresses were kind of cool actually, but otherwise, she just didn't get it.

"Me, neither," Laura said, as if Tracie had spoken her thoughts aloud.

Tracie picked up her drink, tossed it back, and tried to order another. Phil was late, as usual.

"Hey, how many of those did you have? And it's not even midnight yet," Laura commented.

"I'm just . . . uptight. You know, Mother's Day weekend always bothers me," Tracie admitted. And the story. And Marcus. And Phil being late. And . . .

"Look, take it from me: Having a mother can suck, too," Laura told her, and put her arm around Tracie's shoulder.

Tracie stood on a rung of the bar stool to look over the crowd. Her hair fell in her eyes and that, along with the lights, made it impossible to see. No Phil. Instead, Tracie motioned for another drink, and this time the bartender saw her. "I'd just like to know that I'm going to go home with Phil tonight and cocoon tomorrow in bed."

"While I quietly weep on my cot," Laura said, then added, "Hey, you deserve it, working so hard on that Mother's Day story. Marcus shouldn't have assigned it to you. It's totally harshed your buzz."

"Newspaper editors are rarely noted for their sensitivity. And my roommates always have big mouths."

"I'm not a roommate," Laura interjected. "I'm only visiting till I get over Peter."

"God! That'll take years."

"No. It took years to get over *Ben*." Laura stopped, considered, and continued. "It'll just be months to get over Peter. Unless he calls and begs."

"Tell him to drop dead."

"What?"

"Tell him to forget it."

"Regret it?" Laura yelled.

Tracie pulled out a Post-it notepad—she was never without one—and scribbled on it. She slapped it on the bar. It read *"Just Say No."* In a corner, a group of die-hard punk rock musicians sat in a booth. They were sucking down beers. "The Swollen Glands," Tracie said, and indicated to Laura. "Phil's band."

"Well, they don't look like my type, but it's better than sitting

* * * * * * * * *

here. Let's join 'em," Laura suggested. "Maybe they'll buy us a drink."

"Yeah, maybe they'll win a Congressional Medal of Honor, too." The two girls made their way through the crowd and over to the group in the corner.

"Hi, guys," Tracie said. "Glands, this is Laura. Laura, the Glands." Tracie sat down next to Jeff.

"This music sucks," Jeff, the regular Glands bass player, said.

"Yo, Tracie. Doesn't this suck?" Frank, the drummer, asked as Laura took the seat beside him. There was a silence until a beautiful blonde walked by.

"Yum, yum. Come to papa. I've got something for ya," Jeff said.

"Forget her. She works with me at the *Times*. She's a barracuda."

"Well, I've got something I'd like to hook her with," Jeff said.

"Now I know which Gland you are," Laura said. She turned to Frank. "And you? Lymph, perhaps?"

There was a commotion at the door. Tracie brightened as Phil entered. She gave Laura a look, and Laura turned her head. "God. He *is* tall. And good-looking." Tracie nodded. Her guy had a lot of grace and charm—when he wanted to use it. In his hand was a bass guitar, but she was disturbed to see that beside him was an extremely thin, pretty woman. The two made their way through the crowd and approached the corner table. "He doesn't walk," Laura said. "He swaggers. And who's the skank? Heavenly Host, he's worse than Peter."

"You haven't even met him yet," Tracie protested, though she was already nervous about the so-called skank herself. "Give me a break."

"Hey, girl. I got out late from rehearsal." Phil put his arm around Tracie.

"Phil, this is Laura," Tracie said, introducing them. Uh-oh, one look at Laura's face and Tracie recognized her mood. It was overly protective. She was staring at Phil as if instead of being late and accompanied by this nobody he had thrown acid on her face. Laura tended to overreact in situations like this. On the other hand, Tracie had the same tendency when Laura was being mistreated.

"Hi, Phil. Nice to meet you, too. Oh! And what have you brought us? Your tuning fork?" Laura asked. Tracie gave Laura a discreet kick in the ankle. When Laura had gone too far with Tracie's wicked stepmother (known to them always as W.S.M. and never Thelma), Tracie had used the same editing system. No one hated her stepmother as much as Laura—not even Tracie herself.

As if dealing with Laura, Phil, and the skank wasn't enough, Allison drifted over, too. Just because she had to work with Allison at the *Times* didn't mean she had to introduce her to anyone.

"Hi, Tracie," Allison said.

It was the first time Tracie could remember Allison saying hello to her or anyone. She wasn't even nice to Marcus, and he never gave *her* deadlines.

In a way, Tracie knew she should feel complimented and she did. Phil was so attractive and had so much presence. His height, his clothes, his hair, and his attitude all worked. Hey, they had worked on her, and she had snagged him, and she was thrilled every time she looked at him. But, other women were constantly being snagged as well and she had to be ever vigilant regarding her potential rivals and Phil's attitude toward them. Luckily, he was so used to female attention that he usually ignored it. Tracie sighed. She would have to introduce them. "Laura, Frank, Jeff, Phil, this is Allison." And even though she knew she shouldn't, Tracie looked at Phil and said, "And this would be . . ."

"This is Melody," Phil said. "She needed a ride over here."

"From where? Your apartment?" Tracie asked, and then wanted to bite her tongue.

Laura shifted slightly in her seat, so there was no room for anyone else at the banquette. Tracie had to hand it to her friend. Phil still ignored Laura as he tightened his embrace around Tracie's shoulder. "You look like a warm stove on a cold night," he whispered into her ear. "See you later, babe," he said to Melody, who was then forced, albeit reluctantly, to melt into the crowd.

Tracie eyed the girl's back as she left.

"Unchained Melody," Laura muttered with satisfaction.

"Righteous Brothers. 1965. Phillies label," Jeff said.

Best to just ignore her and what might have gone on, put it away, like a sweater at the back of the closet in summer. Not that she wouldn't hear all about it from Laura later. "So, are you playing tonight?" she asked Phil.

"Yeah. Bob is letting me do the second show."

Bob led the Glands, but not for long, if Phil had his way. "Great!" Tracie said, distracted. She looked back into the crowd to see if Melody was hanging around. She didn't seem to be, which was a relief. Tracie trusted Phil, but only within certain parameters. She'd better stay the whole night, then. When you mixed music, alcohol, and Melody, you were outside the parameters. "When is Bob arriving?"

"Well, there's the question," Phil said with a frown.

"Which Gland is he?" Laura asked. "The adrenal? The pituitary?"

"The asshole," Phil said.

"Oh. Then that would more properly be called 'the anal gland,' " Laura said smoothly.

Though Phil was the newest member, he was already jockeying to be leader. But why he would want it, Tracie could not fathom. It seemed like a lot of work: begging for unpaid jobs with club owners, making endless phone calls about rehearsals, begging vans from friends to schlep equipment—all just to pick the lineup of songs. Big deal. She supposed picking the lineup would be fun, but she couldn't imagine Phil organizing everything else. She thought, There must be a responsible side to him after all.

"You know," Jeff said for what had to be the three hundredth time, "I'm not so sure about our name." Tracie looked up to the ceiling and sighed. When the guys weren't fighting with one another or rehearsing or drinking, they spent their time arguing over the band's name. Tracie had managed to do a feature about them—overcoming a lot of resistance from Marcus—and she'd used the latest name that they had agreed upon: Swollen Glands. But now, once again, Jeff voiced an objection. "I saw this sign, and it was really cool," he continued. "Up in the mountains. They had them everywhere. It just said FROST HEAVES. Great name, huh? And, like, free advertising. Cool, huh?"

"How about Watch for Curves?" Laura joked.

"Nah," Jeff said, serious. "Too limp."

"Well, there's always Yield to Pedestrians," she suggested.

"There's nothing wrong with Swollen Glands," Phil said. "I thought of it, and anyway, the name's in the paper. We don't want to stop the swell of publicity that's building. Right, Tracie?"

Tracie didn't have the heart to mention that one article was more a pimple than a swell and that tomorrow there'd be another band in the paper. "Right," she said, and caught Laura rolling her eyes. She hoped Phil hadn't seen it.

Luckily, Phil was trying to get the bartender to fix him a drink. He then nuzzled closer and whispered into Tracie's ear, "I'm happy to see you."

Sometimes, Phil was a jerk. And Tracie knew he probably wasn't ready to make a commitment, but there was something about his wild good looks, the way his hair brushed across his cheek, the way his fingers hardly tapered, but instead came to an end in flat, smooth nails. Phil was heat to her coolness and passion to her planning, and sometimes he made her forget all of the bad. Tracie responded to his whisper with a blush.

Laura picked up on Tracie's blush and shook her head. "I think I'll try to buck the trend and do something socially responsible, like picking up a merchant seaman. Later," she said as she boogied off into the crowd.

"What's up her ass?" Phil asked Tracie.

She just shrugged and sighed. It was too much to expect her friend to like her boyfriend and vice versa. She turned to her laptop. She'd completed her profile at work and begun the Mother's Day feature, but she still had some polishing to do on it.

One of the things Tracie really liked about Phil was that he was also a writer. But, unlike her, he didn't write commercially. He was an artist. Phil wrote very, very short stories. Some less than a page. Often Tracie didn't get them, but she didn't admit that to him. There was something about his work that was so personal, so completely contemptuous of an audience, that she respected him.

Although Phil had roommates, and had always had a girlfriend, Tracie knew he was essentially a loner. He could probably spend five years on a desert island and when a ship landed to rescue him he'd look up from his writing or his guitar and say, "This is not a good time for me to be interrupted." He'd certainly said that enough to her, and she respected his integrity.

Sometimes she thought that journalism school and her job had spoiled her talent. After years of being told, "Always consider who might be reading your work," she found Phil's commitment refreshing, even if he looked down on writers like herself who took on commercial subjects.

Now she knew exactly who would be reading her feature: suburbanites over morning coffee; Seattle hipsters munching bagels at brunch; old ladies at the library. Tracie sighed and bent her head to get closer to the screen.

After just a minute or two Phil nudged her. "Can't you put that down and enjoy the scene?"

"Phil, I told you I have to finish this feature. If I don't get it in on time, Marcus will pull me off features altogether. He'd love the excuse. Or I could lose my job," she snapped.

"That's what you say about every story," Phil snapped back. "Stop living in fear."

"I mean it. Look, this feature is really important to me. I'm trying to do something unusual about Mother's Day."

"Hey, you don't even have a mother," Jeff announced.

Tracie turned to Jeff as if he was a child. "Yes, Jeff, it's true that my mother died when I was very young. But, you see, journalists don't always write about themselves. Remember, I wrote an article about you guys? Yet I'm not a Swollen Gland. Not even a mammary.

Sometimes, journalists write about current events. Or they report on other people's lives. That's why they call us 'reporters.' "

"Wow. The irony is so heavy in here, it's breaking my drumsticks," Frank said.

"Man, what time do we go on?" Jeff asked.

"Not till two, man," Frank told them.

Tracie kept herself from groaning. Two! They wouldn't be out of here until dawn.

"God. Was that the best Bob could do?"

"I hope these jerks clear out by then and we get a decent crowd," Phil said.

"I'm sure you will. The Glands are really building a following," Tracie assured him. She herself felt no such thing. In fact, the crowd could turn ugly if you cut off their supply of big-band standards.

Laura emerged from the dance floor, a short guy dressed like a forties bookie close behind her. Tracie noticed that a lot of small men went for Laura. The attraction was definitely not mutual. "Mind if we join you all? Or do you turn into rats and pumpkins at midnight?"

"Rats and Pumpkins. That would be a good name," Frank commented.

Tracie looked at her watch. "Oh God. I've got to get this in." She turned back to the laptop.

The band members were still giving one another glum looks. More dead soldiers littered the tabletop. Tracie snapped her laptop shut.

"This music sucks, man," Frank repeated to the uninterested table.

"Yeah, it sucks," Jeff echoed.

"Thank you for this introduction to Seattle. The conversation here really is a lot more sophisticated than in Sacramento," Laura quipped.

Tracie looked up. "It all gets better when my work is done and the guys play," she promised. She started to stand up.

"Where ya going?" Phil asked.

"I have to fax this to Marcus at home," Tracie explained.

"Hey, don't leave the table," Phil said, catching her hand. "You're making the band look bad. Don't you realize other girls would die to sit here with us?"

Tracie shrugged and laughed. It wasn't easy to find modem service in a bar. It would be hard enough to find a Yellow Pages, listing a twenty-four-hour copy center. Phil was being cute but difficult, and she couldn't afford to get Marcus in an uproar. She'd have to do what was necessary to get her piece in and hope Phil would relax. If she could leave, she'd get back before the band's performance. There'd be hell to pay with a pouting Phil for the rest of the night if she didn't get back in time.

When she finally returned twenty minutes later, a swing-dance girl was in her seat. "I made it in just under the wire," Tracie said, standing beside the table.

"Congratulations," Jeff said, handing her a beer.

"So what's new since I left?" Tracie said directly to Phil.

"Well, I hear the music still sucks, and I think there's a new mascot," Laura told her.

Tracie tapped the girl on her shoulder to get her seat back, shooting Phil a dirty look because he should have told the girl to move. "Hey, it's not my fault," Phil protested as the young woman walked away.

"I don't know why these bitches want to dress up like Betty Crawford anyway," Frank said.

"What assholes," Phil agreed.

Laura leaned across the table to Frank. "It isn't Betty Crawford."

"What?" he asked.

"There's no 'Betty Crawford,' " Laura informed him. "You must be the drummer, right?"

"Huh?" Frank grunted.

"There was Betty Grable and there was Bette Davis. There was also Joan Crawford. But I don't think Joan Crawford ever danced to swing," Tracie explained.

"Whatever," Jeff said.

"Yeah. Who cares? Whatever, man," Phil said to Laura.

The band began to play "Last Kiss." "Pearl Jam," Jeff said. "Epic Records. 1999."

"That was just a cover," Laura said. "It's an old fifties song."

"It is not. Pearl Jam writes all their own material," Jeff said.

"Wanna bet?" Laura asked, raising her brows in a dare.

"Why don't we bet each other a dance?" Jeff said. "Then I'll win either way." Tracie looked back at Laura, whose eyes had widened to match her brows. Wordlessly she extended her hand, and Jeff, who had to be less than half her size, took it and pulled her out onto the dance floor. God knows, Tracie thought, I'd rather give my jewelry to Allison than dance with Jeff.

"Where's Bob?" Phil asked.

"Yeah. Where is he?" Frank echoed, obviously disgusted by Jeff's departure. He and Laura were really getting into the music. Tracie had forgotten how well Laura danced. "I ask myself what would Guns N' Roses do if they were here?" Frank continued.

"Pull out an automatic weapon," Phil told him. Tracie had to laugh.

"Man, Axl Rose would turn over in his grave if he saw this," Frank added.

"Is Axl Rose dead?" Tracie asked.

The band members turned to look at her as if she was crazy. "What are you talking about?" Frank asked.

"You said he'd turn over in his grave. I just . . ."

Phil put his arm around her. "She's not smart, but she sure is beautiful," he told Frank by way of excuse, then gave Tracie a long, wet kiss.

Chapter 3

Jonathan Charles Delano rode his bicycle through the morning fog on Puget Sound. The road wound along the misty shore. He wore his Micro/Connection jacket—only given to founding staff with more than twenty thousand shares—and a baseball cap. The wind caught him broadside as he made a turn and then, as he swung into it, the wind inflated his open jacket as if it were a Mylar balloon. Riding was good therapy. Once he hit a rhythm, he could think—or not think, as he required. This morning, he desperately wanted not to think of last night—a night he'd spent standing in the rain getting stood up—or of the exhausting day ahead. He was actually reluctant to get to his destination, but he pedaled his heart out as if participating in the Tour de France. Mother's Day was always tough for him. For years now, he had been following this tradition, one he had invented out of unnecessary guilt and compassion. He figured that as Chuck Delano's son, he owed something. And anyhow, as an only child, these visits were the closest he got to extended family. Anyway, that's how he rationalized the visits.

As he pulled around the next curve of the coast road, the fog cleared all at once and a breathtaking view across the Sound opened.

Seattle appeared as green-fringed and magical as the Emerald City—and he noticed that Rainier was out, the towering mountain that reigned majestically over the city when visibility was good.

As one of the four actual natives of Seattle—it seemed everyone else had moved to the city from somewhere "back east"—he'd seen the sight a thousand times, but it never failed to thrill him. Now, though, he could only take a moment to enjoy it before he continued pedaling across Bainbridge Island and finally up to a shingled house. Jon jumped off his bike, pulled a bouquet out of the basket, and ran his fingers through his hair. He looked at his watch, cringed, and bolted up the path to the front door. The name plate on it read MRS. B. DELANO.

He knocked on the door. A heavyset middle-aged blonde in a zippered sweat suit opened the door. Jon couldn't help noticing Barbara was even bigger than last year. She had an apron on over her sweats. That made Jon smile. It was so . . . Barbara.

"Jon! Oh, Jon. I didn't expect you," she lied in the sweetest way as she hugged him. Barbara was his father's first wife, only slightly older than Jon's own mother, but somehow from a different generation.

Jon tried to be all the things he should be: in touch with his feelings, a good son, an understanding boss, a loyal employee, a good friend, a . . . Well, the list went on and on and made him tired. Being a dutiful stepson was the part that made him depressed, as well.

Something about the first Mrs. Delano really saddened him. It was her relentless cheerfulness. She seemed happy in her little cottage in Winslow, but Jon imagined that the moment he left, she'd begin to pine. Not for him—Jon knew no one pined for him—but for Chuck, Jon's father, the man she had loved and lost.

There was no reason for Jon to feel responsible, but he did, and he guessed he would always feel it, so he'd prepared in advance for this day. He brought the flowers from behind his back. "Not expect me?" he asked, as cheerful as she was. "How could you not? Happy Mother's Day, Barbara." Jonathan presented the bouquet with a flourish.

"For heaven's sake. Roses *and* gladiolus. My favorites! How did you remember?"

Jon figured this wasn't the time to tell her about his automated calendar, tickler file, or his Palm Pilot.

Barbara hugged him again. He could feel her soft bulk. She obviously didn't use the track suit on the track. "You're such a good boy, Jon." She stepped to the side to let him have access to the foyer. "Come on in. I'm making biscuits for breakfast."

"I didn't know you could bake," he lied, reluctantly. He didn't want breakfast and . . . well, once she got started, Barbara could really talk. And there were two questions he dreaded: the overly casual "Heard from your father lately?" and the even worse "Are you seeing someone special?" Though Chuck rarely communicated with Jon and though Jon almost as rarely had a date, Barbara never tired of asking. But that was probably because she was lonely. She and his father had no kids and she'd never remarried. She seemed isolated, not just on the island but in her life.

"You have to have coffee," Barbara said.

"Maybe just coffee. I don't have a lot of time. I really ought to . . ."

Barbara extended her hand and drew him into the house. "So, are you seeing anyone special?" she asked.

Jon tried hard not to flinch. If he didn't already know that the little time he spent on his personal life was a fiasco, last night would have been proof enough. He and Tracie, his best friend, had spent years trying to determine whose romantic life was less romantic. This week, he'd finally be the definitive winner. Or maybe that would make him the definitive loser. As he followed Barbara into the kitchen, he knew that whichever one it was, it wasn't good.

An hour later, Jon pushed his bicycle, careful not to skin the heels of anyone as he followed a crowd of people disembarking the Puget Sound ferry on the city side. Everyone but him seemed coupled up. Sunday morning and arm in arm with their sweeties. Except him. He sighed. He worked all the time—relentlessly as all the whiz kids. Seattle loomed over the waterfront, with its silly Space Needle and the newer towers gleaming. He mounted the bike, quickly passed the crowd, and pedaled wildly onto Fifteenth Avenue Northwest.

In less than ten minutes, Jon stopped abruptly outside a luxury apartment tower. He checked his watch, took another bouquet out of his basket—this one all tulips—and locked his bike against a parking meter. He entered the lobby of the building, an overdone mirrored space he used to visit when his dad took him for weekends. He pressed the elevator button, the door slid open, and he entered, pressing the number 12. Though it was only seconds, it seemed like a long ride.

The elevator stopped and the bell beeped as the door slid open. Jon sighed again, walked out of the elevator, and paused to gather himself. Then he knocked on an apartment door where the name below the brass knocker read MR. & MRS. J. DELANO, with the MR. & crossed out. A woman—almost middle-aged but younger and far better preserved than Barbara—opened the door. She was dressed (or even overdressed) in what Jon guessed was considered "a smart suit."

"Jonathan," the woman cooed as she took the tulips from his hand as if they were expected. "How nice."

"Happy Mother's Day, Mother," Jon said to Janet as he kissed her the way she'd taught him to: carefully on each cheek, being sure not to smudge her beautifully applied makeup.

"You don't have to call me 'Mother.' I'm hardly old enough for that," Janet replied with a little laugh. There was something about Janet's voice that had always made him feel uncomfortable. When he was younger, he'd felt that she was gently mocking him. More recently, he'd realized that she was actually flirting. "Let me just put these in water," she said. She opened the door wider to let him inside. He'd never felt comfortable with Janet.

The apartment was as overdecorated as Janet was herself. She wore way too much gold jewelry and had way too many gold buttons. The apartment had too many gold frames and too much cut glass.

When he was twelve years old and had visited his father here, she'd spent most of her time cautioning him not to touch anything.

Nothing had changed since last year except his flowers. It was frozen in time, like Janet's face or the palace in *Sleeping Beauty*. But no prince was making it up here for Janet's wake-up call. Jon liked Barbara, but he couldn't actually feel anything but pity for Janet. Now she played with the flowers in the little sink of the tiny kitchen. "Have you heard from your dad?" she asked, trying to sound casual.

"No," Jon said quietly. It was the question he most hated hearing. It made his father's exes seem vulnerable. Now he felt even more sorry for Janet and he'd have to stay longer.

"No? No surprise," she said, and her flirty voice changed and became hard. She pushed the last tulip into the vase too hard and broke the stem, though she didn't notice. "And how's *your* social life?" she asked, and Jon felt she might already know the answer wasn't good. She eyed him up and down, taking in his baggy khakis, his old sneakers, his T-shirt. Then she sighed. "Well, where shall we go for brunch?"

Jon's heart sank. "You know," he said uncomfortably, "I thought maybe we'd just have coffee here. I mean, I could afford to lose a few pounds. . . ."

"You mean *I* could," Janet said, smiling and using that flirtatious voice again. "I'm always on a diet. But since it's Mother's Day, any brunch calories I eat are exempt. Even for a stepmom."

Jon gave up and gave in. Until he left her, Jon's dad had always given in to Janet, too.

In less than ten minutes, Jon found himself standing in front of a chic Seattle café. Thank God there was no line yet, but by the time they'd finished and he'd waved good-bye to his second stepmother, more than two dozen people were waiting. Jon consulted his watch, panicked, and hopped on his bike. He pedaled like a madman, out of downtown, past the park, through the wealthier part of Seattle, and into his old neighborhood.

At Corcoran Street, Jon pulled his bike into the driveway of a brick bungalow. The house was covered in creeper and surrounded by flower beds. He ran past a well-tended bed, which reminded him to double back to the bike for yet another bouquet, the largest one.

He grabbed it and ran up to the door. There under the buzzer, the brass name plate read J. DELANO. Before he could knock, the door was thrown open by an attractive dark-haired woman who actually looked a lot like Jon.

"Jonathan!" his mother exclaimed.

"Happy Mother's Day, Mom!" Jon embraced her warmly, crushing the flowers between them.

"Right on time!" his mother said. She took the flowers and patted his cheek with obvious deep affection. "Oh, honey. Peonies! God, they're way before season. They must have cost you a fortune."

"It's okay, Mom. My allowance is bigger than it used to be."

She laughed. "But how's your appendix?" she asked.

"It's still missing—but I'm good," he said. He'd had an emergency appendectomy three years ago and it had frightened the hell out of her. She still asked about it, but it had come to mean his health in general.

"Did you see Rainier today?" she asked.

"Yes. And Mount Baker," he told her.

They went through the living room and into the kitchen. "You came alone?" she asked.

"Yes. Why?" Jon asked.

"I thought maybe you'd bring Tracie."

Jon smiled. Though he and Tracie had been close friends from the time they met, his mother still hinted or hoped they were more. Or that he'd bring some other girl—a real girlfriend—home. While all of Chuck's ex-wives focused on who Chuck's new girlfriend was, his mom focused on who Jon's girlfriend was. He knew she wanted him to be happy, and that she wanted grandchildren for herself and for him. It wasn't that Jon wouldn't love to meet a woman and settle down, it was just that women he met seemed to want to settle down with someone other than him. In his social life he was a disappointment to himself and others. He sighed. He'd have liked to oblige, but . . .

". . . This holiday's always hard on her," his mother was saying as she put the flowers in a vase.

Jon didn't bother to tell his mom that he'd thought of Tracie—sometimes he thought he thought of Tracie too much—but that she was booked up with the latest loser and her old friend from San Bernadino or somewhere.

"She was busy. But I'll see her tonight. You know, our midnight brunch."

"Well, give her my love," she told him.

"Sure," he agreed as he reached into the pocket of his jacket and pulled out a small wrapped box. He put it on the counter between them.

"Oh. A present? Jon. It's not necessary."

"I know that traditionally on Mother's Day you're supposed to steal your mom's bank card and go on a spree. I just thought this once we'd be untraditional."

Jon made a lot of money. Well, it was not a lot of money compared to what the four initial founders of his firm made, but it was a lot of money for a guy his age. And he didn't spend it on much, since he was usually too busy working to have time to shop. Plus, he didn't want anything. He had all the toys—stereos and laptops and video equipment—he could possibly want and very little time to listen, play with, or watch them. When he wasn't working, he was thinking about work or sleeping. So, for him to spend some bucks on his mother was no big deal. It was deciding what she might like that was difficult. In the end, he had let Tracie pick something out. She was great at shopping.

"You're so thoughtful. You sure didn't get that from your father." There was an uncomfortable pause, just for the tiniest moment. His father was the one subject Jon had asked that they not speak about. His mother laughed and unwrapped the gift. She held up the jade earrings. "Oh, Jonathan! I love them!" And it was clear she really *did*.

Tracie always knew stuff like that. His mother went to the hall mirror and held them up, then preened for a moment. It made Jon happy. "So, are we going to Babbette's for lunch?" she asked as she at last put the earrings on.

"Don't we always?" Jonathan responded without hesitation, despite the protests that Barbara's breakfast and Janet's brunch were making in his stomach.

"Let's capture the moment," his mother said as she grabbed her Polaroid and led Jon outside to the wisteria bush. "All I have to do is figure out the automatic timer and we're all set." She took about half an hour doing it, while he waited as patiently as he could. Then she scurried from the camera to him before the timer went off.

And, with a flash, the moment was over.

Jon was exhausted. He was only twenty-eight, but he wondered how many more Mother's Days he could survive before they killed him. He had three more stepmothers to get through, despite the three meals distending his gut. But tea, an early dinner, and a late supper were all on the agenda before he could meet Tracie at midnight. Grimly, Jon climbed on his bike and pedaled off into the Seattle rain.

Chapter 4

Tracie raised her head, trying to see the clock. She could, but that didn't help, as it clearly had been unplugged so that Phil could use the one overburdened outlet to plug in his guitar. No wonder he was always late.

Phil's apartment was a typical poet/musician's hellhole. He shared the space with two other guys, and it seemed that none of the three of them had heard of power strips, extension cords, vacuums, or the advent of dish-washing liquid. Tracie closed her eyes, turned away from the squalor, and cuddled up against Phil's warm side. She knew she had to get up, get dressed, and go meet Jon—as she did every Sunday night—but this felt so good. And today was Mother's Day. A quick wave of self-pity washed over her. She told herself she only wanted a few more moments in the gray zone between sexual exhaustion and sleep. She dozed there for a while, then slept again, and when she next awoke, the streetlights had gone on and she knew it was getting late.

She began to untangle herself from the wrinkled sheets, trying not to wake Phil. But as she stood up, Phil, only half-awake, grabbed at her with his long, long legs and pulled her back to the bed. "Come here, you," he said, and kissed her. He smelled so good—like sleep and sex and bread dough—and she responded; then her mouth guiltily pulled away. "I'll be right back," she promised, and Phil mumbled and turned over.

Tracie crept out of bed, slipped into her clothes, and snuck out to get the Sunday paper. It was already quarter past nine! God! No wonder she was ravenous. She'd better pick up some coffee, eggs, and bread for toast. Then she thought of the state of Phil's kitchen and gave up that idea. Maybe just a couple of cheese Danishes. She'd leave the cooking to Laura. Tracie felt in her jacket pocket for money. She'd only need a few dollars. Most importantly, she wanted to get the Sunday paper and see what the Mother's Day article looked like in print.

It was funny: She'd been working at the *Times* now for four years, but she still got a thrill seeing her byline. Maybe that's what kept her a journalist. She knew she could probably earn a lot more money hiring on as a technical writer at Micro/Con or any of the other high-tech companies in Seattle. But she didn't have an interest in writing manuals or ad copy. There was something magical to her about the immediacy of newspaper work. The gratification of working on an article and seeing it—with her name at the top—just a day or two later kept her hooked.

She walked to the deli closest to Phil's place. It wasn't clean, and the food wasn't good, but, as they said about Everest, it was there. Across the door was a hand-lettered sign that said HAPPY MOTHER'S DAY. She ordered a couple of coffees, bought a pint of Tropicana juice, but couldn't manage to sink to the level of the stale-looking pastries in the smudged case in front of her. She just went for a paper and called it a day. Then, even before she could leave the store, she had to look at the feature. She opened to her section. It wasn't on the front page. She began to look through it. And kept looking. Not on page two or three. Not even on the following two. Then she found it. On the bottom of six. Truncated. Overedited. Sliced and diced. Trepanned. The thing had been cut up and then stitched back together as badly as Frankenstein's monster. She actually felt sick to her stomach. Goddamn it! Tracie scanned it again. It couldn't be as bad as she thought, but it was. It really was.

She threw the rest of the paper on the counter, turned, and walked out with the Sunday section still in her hands. She almost stuffed it into the first garbage pail she saw and did go as far as crumpling it up, but her outrage was so strong, she needed to hold on to it, just to share it with Phil and look at it again. She walked through the spring night, back toward the apartment. Why did Marcus do this to her? Why did he even bother giving her an assignment if he was going to rewrite it? She could swear he did it out of spite. What was the point? She could never use this as a clip. Potential employers would think she was a moron. What was wrong with Marcus? What was wrong with *her* for putting up with Marcus? Or why did she even bother to struggle over her work? Why not just hand in bad stuff and let him revise it as much as he wanted?

She was to Phil's door when she realized she'd forgotten both the coffee and the juice, but now she didn't care. She just wanted to crawl into bed and blot out everything. It was too bad that she had to see Jon later. Usually, she looked forward to their midnight meetings. But now she felt like being alone, crawling into a hole somewhere. She couldn't go home to her apartment because Laura was there and would be cheery and busy. Of course, when she showed her the paper, Laura would get even more upset then she was, and then she'd have to spend her time calming Laura down. Laura would tell her to quit, to get a new job, one where they appreciated her. But it wasn't so easy to get a job as a journalist writing features for what the *Superman* show used to call "a large metropolitan daily." Without a nice portfolio of well-written articles, her value had actually gone down since she had left school with her masters in journalism.

Tracie sighed as she walked up the dirty stairway to Phil's apartment. She wanted to be held like an infant. She walked in the door, then through the living room, trying to ignore the month's worth of accumulated dirty dishes, the piles of clothes, CD cases, and the assorted sordid detritus of three pathetically dirty man-boys. She walked into Phil's bedroom.

"Hey, where you been?" he asked. "You took so long that my feet are getting cold. And where's my coffee?"

She sighed. Sometimes, Phil was incredibly self-involved. " 'Hello, Tracie. How did you sleep? What's wrong? Mother's Day a little tough on you?' " she began, imitating his voice. " 'Oh! Marcus, your bully editor, cut your Mother's Day feature to shit? I'm so sorry. And you worked so hard on that story.' "

He didn't show any remorse, but he sat up in bed and opened his arms. "Hey, come over here, baby."

Tracie hesitated, but the newspaper crumpled under her arm made her feel so bad that she needed comfort more than pride just at that moment. When Phil gave her *that* look, everything seemed better. He needed her, and Tracie felt so desired that work seemed instantly unimportant. She crawled in beside him. He gave her a deep, hot kiss. Tracie melted into his arms.

"Life is always hard for the artist, baby," he said, holding her tighter and starting to rub her back. "You know, I just finished another story."

"Really?" Tracie knew Phil could write only if he was inspired. He didn't believe in deadlines. "They kill your creativity," he'd said. "That's why they call them deadlines." "What's the story about?" Tracie asked shyly. Secretly, she'd always hoped he'd write something about her. But so far, he hadn't.

"I'll show it to you sometime," he said, and pressed both of his hands on either side of her spine. It was soothing. He was so much bigger than she was. It felt great to be held against his wide chest, encircled by his arms. This was what she wanted. Not sex, not words, just dumb comfort. She nuzzled against him. Then he turned her to him. "Nobody kisses like you do. You love me?"

Tracie nodded and hugged him back. "And my ironing isn't bad, either," she said. "But I have to go. I'm meeting Jon."

"Fuck Jon," he said, then lowered his voice. "No, fuck me." He nuzzled her ear. "I want you," he whispered.

"Phil, I have to go or I'm going to be late. I have to meet—"

"The computer weenie." Phil shifted his weight so that his whole length was against her. "Why don't you stay here with my weenie instead?" he asked.

"Phil, I mean it. I *have* to—"

He grabbed her again and pulled her to him. "You look so sexy right now. . . ."

"You only say that when you're horny."

"I'm horny all the time, so you always look sexy to me."

They struggled with each other until Phil was on top of her. She gave him a deep kiss. Oh, she liked him to touch her so much. When he began to unbutton her shirt, she stopped struggling. He wasn't always hot for her. Tracie was smart enough to notice that Phil withheld sex sometimes. She thought it was one of his power plays: make her want it and then pretend to be bored.

The sick part was, when he teased her it made her hotter for him. Most of the men Tracie's age were only too happy to grab her and stuff their thing inside her. Phil was the first man she'd known who knew how to hold off until she was almost ready to beg for it. She shivered just a little, but he was close enough to feel it. "I know you like me," he whispered. "You can't help it, can you?"

"No," she murmured, and he lifted her at the hips and pulled off her jeans as if she were no heavier than an infant. He ran his tongue from her knees all the way up to her breasts.

"So pink and so pretty," he said, and she felt a little thrill run from the back of her neck directly to her groin. He hooked his thumb under the elastic. "These always remind me of those frilly paper things that cupcakes come in." He kissed her again. "Come to me, my little cupcake." For an insane moment, Tracie thought about the farm cakes she craved, but when Phil moved his thumb elsewhere, she was right back to business.

And business was good.

Tracie's eyelids fluttered open. She hadn't meant to fall asleep again, but the sex had been so good, and being held by Phil and slipping off to sleep after a really satisfying orgasm had been too hard to resist. Not a bad way to spend Mother's Day, or any day, for that matter.

She remembered Jon again. She sat up and began to gather her clothes. Phil groaned, rolled over, and grabbed her back. He put the side of his face in the crook of her neck so that his mouth was just at her ear. "If you didn't have to leave," he whispered in her ear as he caressed her arm, "I'd be tempted to start kissing you right here." He was quiet while he kissed the nape of her neck, then her shoulder. His breathing was getting heavier. "I'd move my way down to your nipples and then I'd . . ."

Tracie felt Phil's erection against her leg. "Still playing hard to get?" Tracie asked.

"Hard, anyway. And you know why? Because of you, baby."

Tracie reached down to the inside of Phil's leg. "Oh, yes," she cooed. She took one hand and began to kiss his fingers. But then she stopped. "What is this?" She held up his hand. They both looked at it. A phone number was scrawled in blue pen across his palm.

"Uh." There was a tiny pause, the shortness of which only an experienced girlfriend could interpret. Was it the pause to remember or the pause to make up a plausible lie? "One of the guys' new phone numbers. From the band," Phil said.

"An 807 exchange? You're telling me this is a Gland's phone number?" she asked. "Frank's? Jeff's? I don't think so. Since when did they move to Centralia?" She looked at Phil, hoping to see truth in his eyes.

"Jeff moved awhile ago," he said, pulling away from her. He swung his long legs over the side of the mattress, sat up, and reached over to the night table for a cigarette. "I have to call him about rehearsal tomorrow," he told her.

"Whose number is it, Phil?" Tracie asked. She picked up the phone, prepared to dial.

"Jeff's," he said, his back still to her. He lit a match, sucked in a deep lungful of smoke.

She hated him right then. She wasn't stupid, after all. It was probably the phone number of that skinny little girl from Friday night. She should have known! She began to dial. "Phil, if I dial this number and I don't get Jeff, I'm going to cut off your hand, so your penis never has a friend again."

"Go ahead, baby," Phil said calmly as he did a French inhale. "Of course, you'll look like a psycho bitch and I'll look like an asshole, but hey, I don't mind."

Tracie paused. Was he being casual or just acting as if he was? She couldn't tell. And did she really want to know? Phil took a deep puff, then exhaled. "I mean, I can't help it if Jeff's old lady answers the phone and gets mad. She hates him to get calls there. Especially from women. And so late."

"Late? It's only ten-thirty." God! She'd be late for Jon!

"Why don't you stop fussing and come here and get what you really want?" Phil asked her. Sometimes she hated him. He put his cigarette down and opened his arms again to her.

"I miss you already and you're not even gone," he said, and rolled on top of her and kissed her again. His long body wasn't heavy enough to really pin her against the bed, but she liked the sensation of almost being pinned. His mouth tasted sharply of tobacco, but his tongue was so warm and alive. It searched hers like a friendly little vole looking for a home. Tracie dropped the phone and reached for the water bottle she kept on her bedside table.

"I'd like some of that, too," Phil said, and started to get up on his elbows.

"It's all yours," Tracie replied, and doused him with it. Just in case he was a liar. He yelped, but she paid no attention. She had no time to find out—and maybe she didn't want to know. She'd be hellishly late for Jon. She pulled on her clothes, slipped into her shoes, and crossed the floor. "I'm outta here," she called from the door, laughing. Her last look at Phil was of him untangling the wet gray sheet from his lanky body.

Chapter 5

Jon's office was impressive in size and location, occupying the corner of a building on the low-rise Micro/Con campus, with a view of the topiary garden. But instead of the usual corporate chairs and sofa he had been offered, Jon had used his decorating budget to buy vintage beanbag chairs upholstered in leatherlike Naugahyde. A lot of Naugas must have died, 'cause there were at least half a dozen shapeless mounds of chairs spread around the room. In the center of them, there was a coffee table actually made of coffee beans suspended in a clear acrylic. Jon particularly liked the coffee table. Narrow shelves lined one wall—not for books, or even software CDs, but for the vast collection of action figures he had acquired for work (he had a huge annual budget for them). They shared space with his numerous Pez dispensers (his own private collection). Jon had more than four hundred, including the rare Betsy Ross, the only Pez dispenser ever created based on a real person.

He more than liked the nonsense of his office. There was a method to his madness. It put people at ease, and encouraged playfulness, hence creativity. But there was no nonsense on his desk. Only three photographs were set at the corner of the shining (renewable) teak surface: a picture of his mother, a picture of Tracie and him at college graduation, and a picture of a much younger Jon standing with his mom next to his father, just after they'd planted the wisteria around the doorway of their house and just before Chuck had split.

Now he pulled out the Polaroid his mother had taken earlier in the day and inserted it into the corner of that frame. He stared at the picture: Jon Delano, twenty-eight years old, embracing his mother, and for a moment, it changed before his eyes. It turned black and white and suddenly there was no mature blooming wisteria nor a mature Jon. Instead, a very young Jon and his young mom were embracing while Mr. Delano walked past them, struggling with two suitcases. Jon blinked and the actual Polaroid returned. Spooked, he got up and walked away from the desk.

Well, he was really tired. Not to mention stuffed. Thank God Toni, his last stepmom but one, had canceled at the last minute, or his stomach would probably have burst. He looked out the window to the lit garden and the darkness beyond. It was almost 10:00 P.M., but that didn't stop people from working on Sunday at Micro/Con. All the staff prided themselves on the incredibly long hours they put in. Sunday was just another workday, and even now the parking lot was almost half-full. Jon patted his belly and sank into a beanbag, wiggling his butt until it assumed the position. There was something about Mother's Day that depressed him, and it wasn't merely surveying the trail of human wreckage his father had left behind.

Jon had grown up listening to the women's complaints. It wasn't only his father's various wives, though; it was also the women who gathered for coffee at his mother's house. Other women had even worse stories about their exes, stories that he'd listened to, hiding behind the couch, when he was seven, nine, and fourteen. His mother's friends seemed incapable of ditching their husbands or finding ones who treated them well. Why'd they stay? he still wondered. He thought of Barbara and her baking. After the biscuits had come the inevitable question: "Hear from your father?" He thought of Janet's skinny shoulders when she turned her back on him, pretending to arrange the flowers, and asked, "Have you heard from your father?"

It wasn't Mother's Day, Jon decided. Not for him. For him, it had been Heard from Your Father Day and Have You Got Anyone Special Day. He shook his head, closed his eyes, and, with his right hand, removed his glasses so that he could massage the reddened flesh under the nosepiece. Jon had almost two hours before his customary midnight date with Tracie and, although he had piles and piles of work to do, if he just kept his eyes closed and napped for just a minute, ten minutes at the most . . .

Jon was eleven and sitting in a leatherette booth across from his father. A plate of untouched eggs, their whites runny, the yolk congealing, sat undisturbed in front of him, while his father was busy tearing pieces of the running egg albumen with a side of his fork, then pushing the nasty stuff onto a burned corner of toast and popping it into his mouth. Jon was aware that he was asleep, yet the man in front of him was so real, so perfectly reconstructed in his dream, that it was impossible to believe the guy was not there. Jon could have counted each bristle of his father's five o'clock shadow. Chuck finished the last bit of egg, wiped the plate with some of Jon's toast, and began to chew it up. He leaned forward. "Just remember this, son," he said. "There's not a woman in the world who won't buy a lie she wants to believe."

Jon jerked his eyes open. He was losing it. Weeks of endless toil on the Cliffhanger project and a lousy Friday and Saturday night, topped off by this Sunday, bloody Sunday had given him the willies. He looked at his watch: 10:31. If he could just get out of the beanbag chair, he could get in at least a solid hour of work before meeting Tracie and reviewing what a lousy weekend they'd both had. Jon might have a surfeit of mothers to entertain, but on this weekend, he was careful to be extra attentive to Tracie. Without a mother, the day hit her hard. Not to mention her holiday article. God! He'd forgotten the article! She had E-mailed the draft to him and it was really good, but you never knew what it would look like when it was published in the *Times*. He'd been so busy today, he hadn't had a chance to get the paper or even to look at a copy. He'd better do it on his way over to Java, The Hut.

Actually, work was the only part of his life he had under control. Unlike Tracie, he had a successful career, liked and respected his boss, a wild woman who'd been in on the start-up of UniKorn. Bella was great, his staff was great, his job was great, and the money was great. Now he'd been given control of the Parsifal project, and if he made it happen, well, the sky was the limit. And he *could* make it happen. Parsifal was the code name for the project Jon had fought for since he'd joined Micro/Con almost six years ago. He was trying to bring together convergent wireless technology for a laptop/TV/ phone product so advanced, he wasn't allowed to let his right department know what his left department was doing. It would make him or break him, and it was certainly taking up every minute of his time. But if Parsifal worked, no one would ever buy a TV or phone from Panasonic again.

It was just that in the last three or four years, there'd been no time for a social life, and when there was . . . well, it was safe to say it was very definitely less than great. He thought again of his bad Friday night, followed by a worse Saturday evening, and winced. Maybe his reasoning was faulty. He rationalized his lousy social life because of his demanding career. But perhaps one of the reasons he worked all the time was because it was easier than going out. When he tried, as he had this weekend, look what happened.

Jon groaned aloud and sank deeper into the chair—such as it was. The beanbag cupped him at just the right tilt. He didn't feel like thinking anymore, nor did he want to sign on and see how many urgent E-mails he'd gotten in the last twenty-four hours while he bombed out with women and took care of his mothers—both step and natural. There would be mounds of work. Jon took a deep sigh. Every one of his employees thought that their problems were the most difficult and impossible for them to solve without either his help or his praise. He sighed again. He loved his work and he'd do the E-mail now, for half an hour. One less thing to do tomorrow morning. But he'd be sure to leave by eleven-thirty. Seeing Tracie was the high point of his whole week.

Chapter 6

Java, The Hut was just one of the 647 coffee shops in Seattle, but to Jon it seemed different from all the others. It was suffused with memories of the hundreds of Sunday-night "breakfasts" that he and Tracie had shared, fifty-one weeks a year for seven years. From the time they met in French class and crammed together until today, the two of them had bitched, studied, laughed, chewed each other out, and even cried (he briefly only once, she at great length more than a dozen times) over mochaccino at Java, The Hut. Jon sat there now, finished with all work and all mothers for the time being. He waited for Tracie to show up.

He had the *Seattle Times* spread in front of him and was shaking his head as he read the hatchet job that Marcus had made of Tracie's article. "You look like my Lab when 'e's got water in 'is ears," Molly, their usual waitress, said to Jon. Molly was a tall, slender blonde in her early thirties. A transplanted East Ender from London, she'd worked at the café since Jon and Tracie had begun coming there. Word was that she had been a rock bitch, one of those "successful groupies" who actually toured and slept with two important rock idols. Molly never spoke about it but Jon had heard she'd been with someone from INXS. Tracie claimed that after it Molly had made someone from Limp Bizkit hard. Whoever it was, it appeared that Molly had been dumped or had landed in Seattle and liked the town.

Rumors had run rampant that there might be a room or even a whole wing dedicated to Molly in the Experience Music Project, and that her first diaphragm was among the museum's eighty thousand rock artifacts. Jon had never believed any of it, and the opening of the museum last June had proved the rumors false, but even if they had been true, it wouldn't have changed Jon's feelings for Molly. She was acerbic, witty, and warm—at least to him. If she wasn't exactly a friend, she was a long-standing acquaintance and every time he rode by the blowsy, shimmering EMP, twenty-one thousand metallic shingles and the flapping, bright colors made him think of Molly.

"On your own, then, luv?" she asked now, though she knew the answer. Jonathan still shook his head as she indicated the empty seat with a jerk of her head. "The usual, then? Adam and Eve on a raft? Or are you going to wait for Little-Miss-Sorry-I'm-Late?" Molly asked sarcastically.

"I'll wait," Jonathan replied.

"Loyal, just like my Lab." Molly left the table briefly, then returned with his favorite drink. "One mochaccino light while she takes you for granted."

Jon looked up at her. "You really don't like Tracie, do you?"

"Bingo! What insight. That must be why Micro/Con pays you the big bucks."

"But why?" Jon asked innocently. "She's so nice."

"She's so stupid. Thick as two short planks," Molly said matter-of-factly as she placed his coffee in front of him, then straightened the place mat and silverware opposite.

"Hey! She is not," Jonathan answered defensively. "In college, she had a four point oh in everything—except maybe calculus. She graduated with honors."

"Oh. Summa cum stupid," Molly said as she turned around, only to see Tracie looking in through the window advertising the Mother's Day special. "I'll leave you to it."

A glowing Tracie entered and hurried toward Jonathan. Of course all the other guys' eyes followed her, but she acted oblivious to that. Jon sometimes wondered whether or not she knew the effect she had on men. He quickly crumpled the newspaper and tried to hide it, pulling out the latest *Little Nickel*. He smiled when she sat opposite him in the booth.

"Sorry I'm late," she said. "Nice try, but I already saw the butcher job. Marcus always cuts my best parts. Could my editor be Edward Scissorhands' evil twin brother?" Tracie shrugged out of her coat, then picked up the menu. He knew her well enough to know she was upset, but also not to push it now. "I'm starving," she said, then looked at him as if for the first time. "God, you look beat!"

Jon smiled and shrugged. "Today was my annual Mother's Day Olympics."

Tracie moved the menu away from her face. "Oh God! I was so wrapped up in my article and . . . everything. I completely forgot! Did you see all the steps? And how did you squeeze in your actual mom?"

"I saw mine for lunch."

"Did she like the earrings?" Tracie's face lit up with hope.

"She loved them!" Jon assured her. "And I took all the credit. But she sends her love. I saw stepmoms one through five before or after."

"You actually visited the toad who wouldn't let your dad come to your high school graduation?"

"Oh, Janet's not so bad."

Tracie snorted. "You have way too much compassion and too many mothers. I've got neither."

Jon had to smile. "That's probably why we're such good friends— opposites attract. Did you miss your real mom this Mother's Day?" Jon asked gently.

"You can't really miss what you don't remember." Tracie repositioned the menu to avoid looking at him. In all the years they'd been friends, she'd never spoken of her mother's death. Jon felt awkward, and there was a momentary silence between them. "Anyway," Tracie said, "Laura's at my house baking enough empty carbohydrates to stock a kindergarten bake sale."

Just then Molly rejoined him. "So, luv. Poached eggs on toast?" she asked Jon.

"Yeah. Gotta have 'em."

"And for you?" Molly asked Tracie, arching her brows with what seemed to Jon a bit too much attitude.

Tracie looked searchingly at the menu. "I'll have . . . the waffles, with a side of bacon." Molly didn't write it down. Instead, she just stood there. Tracie closed the menu decisively. Molly still didn't move. Tracie looked pointedly over at Jonathan. Molly remained standing there.

"You shouldn't eat pigs," Jon told Tracie. "You know, they're more intelligent than dogs."

"Don't start," Tracie warned. "Next, you'll begin imitating the singing mice in *Babe*. So, you had the whole Mother's Day trial while I had the Mother's Day article fiasco. But that wasn't all. Get ready to end your winning streak, because I had the worst weekend of my entire life." She looked up at Molly, who was still standing there, looking as permanent as the red London phone booths. Tracie waited her out. "I'll have my coffee now, if you don't mind."

Molly finally started to walk away, but Tracie reached out and took hold of Molly's arm, as she always did. Jon restrained a laugh. "Wait. I think I'll have the pancakes. The pancakes and a side order of ham." She stared at Jon. "The hell with the pigs." She turned back to Molly. "I mean it this time."

Molly heaved a big sigh, obviously bored, and pulled up a chair and sat down.

"Excuse me?" Tracie said rudely. "I don't remember asking you to join us. And I think I placed my order."

"Admit it to yourself," Molly said. "You want scrambled eggs and you want them dry."

"I told you pancakes. . . ." But Tracie wavered and then gave in to herself. "Yeah. Okay. I'll have the eggs."

"No chips, slices of tomato on the side." Triumphantly, Molly showed Tracie the order was already written down, then sashayed off to the kitchen.

Tracie waited a minute to regain her dignity. Jon just looked at her. For years now, they'd been meeting every Sunday to discuss their romantic lives, such as they were. And Molly's eavesdropping meant she probably knew the facts as well as they did. "So, my weekend has to make me the winner," Tracie told him. "It was a social nightmare."

"Let me guess: On Friday, Swollen Glands never got to play and Phil was pissed off and got drunk. On Saturday, the Glands did get to play, but they didn't invite Phil, so he was pissed off and got drunk. Then he flirted with some girl; you walked out of the club and hoped he'd follow. He didn't, so you went home. But he came back very late to your place, where he passed out in the foyer."

"You think you know everything, don't you?" Tracie asked, sounding half-amused and half-annoyed. "You aren't always right." She paused, but Jon waited her out. "Well, he didn't pass out in *my* foyer," she protested at last. "But you got the rest right."

Jon sighed and shook his head. "Trace, why don't you give this guy the keys to the street?"

Just then, Molly returned and placed Jon's plate carefully on the table in front of him. She slung Tracie's across the table.

Tracie looked down at the scrambled eggs quivering on her plate. "I know it's stupid . . . but I really love him."

"It's not love; it's obsession," Molly told her as she refilled Tracie's coffee mug. "It's not even an interesting obsession."

Tracie tilted her head toward Molly but looked at Jon. "She doesn't like me," Tracie announced.

"That's not true," Jon said in what he hoped was a consoling voice.

"Yes it is, rather. I've been listening to your 'istory of bad boy-friends for dog's years. You 'ave one of these wankers after another. Frankly, you bore me." She walked to the next booth.

Jonathan called after her, "Molly! Don't be mean."

And then came the moment he was dreading. "So how was *your* weekend?" Tracie asked.

Chapter 7

Jon had a problem. He told Tracie everything, or almost everything, which was good. But looking like an idiot and a goofball and a pathetic excuse for a man was not so good. He needed her empathy and advice, but he was afraid of her pity. So, usually, he made a joke of his pain. Now Jon raised his hands and clasped them over his head. "The undefeated world champion with the worst social life in America . . ."

"Well, with Mother's Day, it would be—"

"No. It was the disasters *previous* to Mother's Day that hurt."

Tracie raised her eyebrows and scrunched up her eyes in an exaggerated move of remembrance. She was really cute when she did it. "Oh God! I'm so sorry! I forgot! The look-see didn't work out?" Tracie sighed. "What about the big date?"

Molly returned with coffee and poured it out for Tracie, then shook her head and left. Tracie leaned across the booth and lowered her voice. "What happened? What went wrong with the look-see?" Her face assumed a look of horror. "You didn't wear that plaid jacket, did you?"

"No," he assured her. "I wore my blue blazer."

Tracie, her mouth by now full of coffee, almost did a spit take. "You wore a *blazer* for a look-see?"

"Yeah, I—"

"*Never* get dressed up for a look-see. The whole *point* is to appear casual." Tracie sighed with frustration at him, not for the first time. "So . . . what happened?"

"Well, I walked into the bar; she waved. She was attractive in a skinny, redheaded way. So I went over to her and gave her the flowers. . . ."

"You brought flowers?" Tracie cried, her hands flapping in exasperation. "God, that stinks of desperation."

"Maybe that's why it lasted eleven minutes. We'd hardly begun to talk when she said she'd left clothes in the dryer and didn't want them to wrinkle."

"That's a new wrinkle in lame excuses," Tracie told him. They both let the horror of it sink in for a few moments. Then, as always, Tracie brightened. Jon was certain her optimism was genetic. "Oh, forget about it. I'm sure she wasn't a natural redhead anyway. The drapes never match the rug." Jon managed a grin and Tracie grinned back. "So what about Saturday night? You know, the date with that woman you work with? The one you yearn for with the lust of a thousand pubescent boys. What's-her-name?"

"Sam. Samantha," Jon reminded her. For a moment, he wondered why he always knew every friend and boyfriend of hers by given, middle, and nicknames but she . . . He sighed. "Actually, it was worse," he admitted.

"How could it possibly be worse than an eleven-minute look-see?"

"Well, for one thing, I was meeting her outside. For another, it was raining. And for a third, she never showed."

Tracie's lower lip dropped in real surprise. Then she exaggerated it, just to cover. "She *totally* stood you up? She wasn't just late? I mean, you waited long enough?"

"Two hours."

"Oh, Jon! You stood in the rain for two hours?"

"Yeah. I didn't mind that as much as the fact that I have to see her tomorrow at work."

"Ouch!" Tracie winced, his upcoming humiliation on her face, then tried to recover. "At least tell me she called and left a message with a plausible lie," she begged.

"Neither. No message at home, work, not even an E-mail. And I'd left messages for her on all three."

Tracie grimaced. Jon flushed, embarrassed again. "I wish you hadn't done that," she said.

Jon got defensive. "Well, what should I have done?"

Tracie narrowed her eyes. "It reminds me of the Dorothy Parker line: ' "Shut up," he explained.' "

"But how else could she know I was waiting?"

"Like she needed to? You weren't humiliated enough already?"

Now she was irritated with him. Jon saw something in her face that looked too much like pity. "Well. What else could I do?"

Before Tracie could answer, Molly returned to their table, obviously drawn by bits of the conversation she'd overheard. "Find girls who want to date you? An older woman, perhaps," Molly suggested as she batted her eyes at him. Tracie didn't even look up but Jon managed a wan smile. "Oh, I guess that's a dumb idea. But then I didn't go to college." She whisked their empty plates away and sashayed back to the kitchen.

Tracie sighed. "Okay, Jon, you win. Your weekend was worse. I think that's eighty-three consecutive weeks. A new world record." She scribbled on a Post-it pad she pulled from her purse and stuck it on Jon's shirt. It had a blue ribbon drawn on it.

"Great. Winner of the Losers."

Tracie stopped to consider him for a moment. "You know, it's not *all* your fault. Women tend to gravitate to . . . trouble. Men who are . . . challenges. You know, on Friday, my friend Laura arrived . . ."

"Laura? She finally came? Will I at last get to meet Laura?" Jon had been hearing about Laura for years.

"Sure, but the point is, she's come to stay with me since she broke up with Peter. She's nuts about him, but Laura calls him an IPPy—"

"And that would be?"

"An Intimacy-Phobic Prick. So I think maybe women prefer pricks until they give up on them."

"It's not fair; I try so hard."

"To be a prick?"

"No. Not to—"

"I know. That was a joke. But see, maybe that's the point: You try too hard and you're . . . too nice."

"How can you be *too* nice?"

"Jon, *you're* already too nice. *You're* too considerate. I mean, look at the data. Today, you visited your mom *and* all wicked stepmothers. You're too nice."

"That's ridiculous," Jon told her.

"I know it doesn't make sense to you," Tracie agreed. "It doesn't even make sense to us. And I don't think we like to suffer. But I know we hate to be bored. Take Phil, for example: He fascinates me. He keeps my life so interesting."

"He's a bass player, for God's sake," Jon said, totally exasperated. "Dumber than dirt. *And* self-involved. *And* selfish. You call *that* interesting?" he asked, then realized he'd probably gone too far and maybe hurt her feelings.

Tracie only smiled. "You have something against guys who play four-stringed instruments or something?"

Jon calmed himself. "Not all. Just him. He's not worthy."

"But he's so cute. And the sex!" She blushed.

Jon looked away. That was his punishment for going too far. There were some things he didn't need to know. He sighed. "I'd give anything to be able to land chicks the way guys like Phil do. If I could just learn to get dumb. Or pretend to be selfish . . ." He paused. "Hey, Tracie, I'm getting an idea."

"You *always* have ideas," she said, getting up. "That's why you're the Intergalactic Alchemist of Cosmology Development and Systems Conception Worldwide, or whatever it is you are over there in Micro Land."

"No. Not an idea like that," Jon said, getting up to join her. She couldn't leave yet. "I mean an idea about my *life*."

"Great. Can we discuss this next week? I need to go to the supermarket."

"For what? Panty hose?" Tracie hadn't been inside a supermarket in years.

"No. For baking soda. And flour."

"Are you doing a science project? Or is it something for your hair?"

"It's to bake," Tracie said, attempting a dignity she couldn't quite achieve with him.

"Since when do you bake? And why do you need to at midnight?" Jon knew Tracie well enough to know that she thought the black thing in her kitchen with the door in the front was where you stored extra shoes. And he hoped to God she didn't have buns in her oven. "Is this some trick to try to get Phil to turn over and play dead? Because your baking will kill him . . . not that that's a bad thing."

"I'm not going to dignify any of that with a response," Tracie said, rising.

Jon got up, too. He didn't want to show how desperate for company he was. And also he was interested in the mystery of Tracie's new domesticity. Then it came to him. "It's your friend, your friend Laura from San Antonio. Isn't Laura a chef?"

"So what?" Tracie said as she shrugged into her jacket. "It doesn't mean that I don't know how to do things, too."

"You know how to do a lot of things," Jon agreed. "You're a really good writer, a good friend, and you know how to dress. You're great at picking out gifts for mothers. But baking . . ."

Tracie gave him a look. "She's from Sacramento," she corrected him, which was her way of acknowledging he was right.

Jon smiled. "I'll help you grocery shop," he offered.

"What? Don't you have to work, or sleep? You always need to do one or the other. Anyway, it's the most boring thing in the world."

"Not to a man who offered to fold laundry and was turned down," Jon pointed out. "I can push the cart for you."

"If that's what you want." Tracie shrugged and started to walk away from the booth as Jon went through his pockets and hurriedly threw a twenty onto the table. Without turning around, Tracie spoke: "You're overtipping again. See, your problem *is* that you're just too nice." Tracie shook her head as she wound her way through the deserted tables. "Women don't want nice guys."

Jon's excitement was mounting. Exactly. Why hadn't he thought of this before? It was perfect, a conception that came to him complete from beginning to end, as the Parsifal project had. He had to get Tracie to understand, to agree, and to make his vision a reality. But he was good at that. "See you next week," Jon shouted to Molly, then caught up with Tracie as she walked through the door.

"So what's your idea?" Tracie asked as she pulled a shopping cart from the corral. "If you're planning another fake, on-line Girls of the Silicon Forest calendar, I'm out."

"Come on, Tracie. I'm serious. I gotta make a change before I need Viagra."

"Oh, don't be so overly dramatic," Tracie told him as they walked up the paper-goods and health-care products aisle. She looked him over with her peripheral vision as they panned the dairy counter. "Your sell-by date hasn't expired. You're good for another two or three years yet."

"I'm not being dramatic. I'm being realistic." He took a deep breath. He had to get her cooperation. "I want you to teach me to be a bad boy," he said.

Tracie was about to pass the hair-care products when she stopped and turned around to look directly at Jon. "Huh?"

He felt his heart actually thumping against his ribs. He gulped down a breath. "I want you to train me to be the kind of guy that girls always go for. You know, the kind of guy you're always going with. Phil. Before him, Jimmy. And you remember Roger? The skin-popper. He was *really* bad. And you were nuts about Roger."

"*You're* nuts," Tracie said, and pushed the cart forward, leaving him behind her. She grabbed a bottle of Pert—a shampoo she'd never select if she wasn't flustered—and Jon quickly caught up to her in the almost-deserted baking-supplies aisle.

"Please, Tracie. I really mean it." He had to both calm her and create a wave of enthusiasm. He reminded himself that he knew how to build project teams.

"Don't be ridiculous. Why would you want to be a bum? Anyway, it's impossible. You could never act—"

"Yes, I could. I could if you would teach me." Overcome objections, he told himself. Then enlist her talent. "Remember what a good student I was in school? Come on, Tracie. Look at it as a challenge, a way to use all the research you've gathered from those tattooed boyfriends of yours." He observed her interest. Now, create desirable opposition. "Otherwise," he said, as casually as he could, "Molly is right."

At the mention of the waitress's name, Tracie stopped again and turned to face him. "Right about what?" she asked, brusquely. Then she turned away to examine the flour.

"Repetition compulsion," he explained, his heart beating hard. He'd hooked her. "You've just been repeating yourself for no reason for the last seven years. Wasting time. But if you could become an alchemist . . ."

She crouched down, reading the label on one of the lower flour sacks. "Who would have thought there were so many different kinds of flour?" she asked, a mere distraction technique he'd simply wait out. "Do you think she wants sifted bleached or sifted unbleached or unsifted unbleached or unsifted bleached?"

Jon remembered Barbara's biscuits of fifteen hours earlier and grabbed the presifted bleached. "This kind," he said, handing her the package. She stood up and accepted the bag. "So how 'bout it? Will you teach me?"

She shrugged, placed the flour in the cart, and began to move down the aisle. "Okay," she admitted. "Maybe I can write a pretty good feature and blow-dry my hair on a rainy day in Seattle without getting frizz. But I can't bake, and no one could teach *you* to be bad. You can't be bad, so this can't be serious." She turned away.

Jon suddenly felt desperate. He imagined seeing Samantha at work the next morning and could hardly bear it. Plus, Tracie was right: It was much worse that he had called. What made him so un-utterably stupid at times?

But despite her disclaimer, Tracie could help him, if only she would. She held the key, but she wouldn't give it up. What kind of friend was that? He told himself he had to go for a strong close. He'd succeeded in getting million-dollar project allocations. He could do this. He grabbed her by the arm and spun her around, looking directly in her eyes. "I've never been more serious in my life. And you're the only one who can help. You know all my dirty little habits *and* you've got your Ph.BB. You majored in Bad Boys all through college and you're doing your graduate work at the *Seattle Times*."

"Well, it would be a challenge, that's for sure," Tracie said, smiling at him. With affection. Yes! he cried to himself, though he didn't let his victory show. Tracie raised her eyebrows and with them her last objection. "But why would any alchemist want to turn gold into lead?" she asked, and took his hand warmly.

"Because the gold really wanted to change," Jon told her. "What if the gold *begged* the alchemist?" He knew, right away, he'd gone too far.

She let go of his hand. "I don't think so, Jon. I love you just the way you are," Tracie said, sounding just like his mother.

"Yeah, but no one else does," he reminded her, but it was too late. She shrugged and again moved down the aisle.

"I couldn't do it. Hey, did I say baking soda or baking powder?" she asked, looking at dozens of each stacked neatly on the shelf.

"You said soda," he told her. "And you could make me over if you wanted to."

Tracie paused. He hoped she was considering the project, but after another minute she shook her head. "I think I have to get baking soda. But maybe it was baking powder."

Jon sighed. "What's the difference?" he asked, dispirited.

"You use them for different things."

"Duh. And what would those things be?" he asked. He was angry with her and he wasn't going to let her get away with anything. "And how are they different?"

"Baking powder makes cakes rise."

"I can read cans, too, Tracie," he told her. "So what about baking soda?"

"Well, you can brush your teeth with it and you put it in your refrigerator to deodorize it."

"And your friend from Santa Barbara forgot her Crest or was knocked over by the odor of your Frigidaire?"

Tracie gave him a look, then shrugged and threw both products into the cart. She turned toward the front of the store and marched away. Jon followed her. He wouldn't give up on this brainstorm. He hadn't gotten where he was at Micro/Con without persistence. Maybe humor would work. He crouched down, holding on to the cart handle, and began begging, the way kids beg their mothers for stuff in all stores. "Please? Please will you? Please? Come on. I'll do anything. I promise."

Tracie glanced around, clearly embarrassed. "Get up!" she hissed. He knew she hated public scenes and was counting on it. "Jon, you have a great apartment, a terrific job, and you're going to be rich—as soon as you cash in your Micro stock options." She tried to ignore the old woman with a basket over her arm and the tall young man with a cart full of beer. "Get up," she repeated. "There have been plenty of girls who liked you."

He didn't get up. "But not *that* way," he whined. "It's never *that* way. Women want me as a friend, or a mentor, or a brother." He tried to keep the bitterness out of his voice. Bitterness didn't sell projects. Anyway, Tracie was one of those girls, foremost among them, but he didn't need to say so.

"Come on. Stand up," she begged again. "People are looking." Actually, the two had wandered off and now there was only a clerk, who wasn't looking, because he was too busy affixing price labels directly onto grapefruits. Tracie left him. Fine. He'd use her embarrassment against her. He could make it work for him. Tracie pushed the cart to the checkout line at the front of the store. Good—there were lots of people around. Jon helped Tracie put the groceries on the conveyor belt. Still on his knees, he whined loudly, "I want interesting girls. The hot girls. But they all want bad boys."

"Get up," she hissed. "You're exaggerating." Unfortunately, it was too late for a crowd to gather. He'd have to use his trump card: her innate honesty.

"Come on, Tracie. You know it's true."

"Well . . ."

The cashier finally stared at the two of them. Then she shrugged and totaled the purchases. Tracie fished in her bag for the money. Jon sighed, stood up, and looked blankly at the rack of tabloids and women's magazines. His knees were hurting. Begging was hard work. Then he noticed a GQ magazine. Some young movie star was on the cover, one who had recently dumped his girlfriend, publicly, on TV, right before the Oscars. Jon looked back at Tracie and pointed at the magazine cover. "I want to look like one of *those* kind of guys," he said.

"It's not just about looks," Tracie told him, picking up her bag. "You're good-looking . . . in a nice-guy kinda way."

He took the bag from her and the two of them began to walk out. "Right. And that guy doesn't look nice. He looks hot. *He* didn't take his stepmoms out on Mother's Day." He turned back around and pointed to the guy on the cover. "What *did* he just do? You know."

Tracie glanced at the magazine and shrugged. "He just told his new girlfriend that he'd like to see other people," she told him, and walked out the exit.

Jon followed her. "I could do that! If I had a girlfriend. And if you'd help me," he pleaded. "Look at it as your dissertation." He ran back, grabbed the magazine as a reference point, threw a five-dollar bill on the counter, and raced after Tracie. "You're an expert," he told her. "Only you could distill all the rotten behavior that you found so adorable and inject me with it."

Tracie was at the door of her car, fumbling with the keys. She took the bag from him, opened her door, and got in. "Forget this, would you?" she requested. "You're just having a larger dose of your weekly Sunday self-hate than usual. You'll be fine tomorrow."

"Yeah. When I see Samantha," he agreed glumly. "That will make me feel real fine."

"Oh, Jon, just get on your bicycle and go home," Tracie told him, so he did.

Chapter 8

Tracie's one-bedroom apartment was sunny, long, and narrow. It wasn't exactly small, but the kitchen consisted only of a sink, a half-size refrigerator, and an old black gas oven—which she did keep her extra shoes in. Now, for privacy, a temporary screen concealed one end of the place, a "guest room," so that Laura could have some privacy. Other than the cot, screen, and sofa, the only other real piece of furniture Tracie had in the living room was a desk covered with notes and photos and Post-its for article ideas. In fact, the whole apartment was covered with Post-it notes stuck on various surfaces.

Now at almost 2:00 A.M., after her day of sex with Phil and weird late-night breakfast with Jon, she was exhausted. She entered the place as quietly as she could. But Laura was up, busy with mixing bowls and cookie sheets. And—to Tracie's complete surprise—Phil was there, too, lying on the sofa and strumming his bass guitar. He looked over at Tracie. "What took you so long? I blew off a rehearsal to be here. Plus, Bobby would have bought me free drinks because he just got his tax refund."

Before she could answer, Laura responded, protective as usual. "It sucks to be you," she told Phil cheerfully.

Tracie tried to ignore Phil. Phil was odd, and in some ways adorable. He showed his affection like this, by turning up because he missed her but not being able to admit it. Every time it happened Tracie got a kick out of it. He looked sexy, stretched out there, but he knew it, so she'd act cool. "What are you doing?" she asked Laura, who was cracking two eggs at a time into a bowl.

"Welding a crankshaft."

"You're cooking something, aren't you?" Phil said, as if he'd just discovered DNA.

"Not cooking. I'm *baking*," Laura told him. She smiled at Tracie. "Did you get the baking soda?" Tracie nodded. Back in Encino, a weekend had never gone by without both brownies and sugar cookies. Laura baked from scratch, even back then. Tracie's only contribution had been licking the bowl.

"My mother used to bake," Phil offered. "Chickens, hams."

Laura rolled her eyes, then took a tray of cookies out of the oven. She lifted up one and gestured toward Phil. "Stupid want a cookie?" she asked with a cheery smile.

Tracie couldn't believe it. She waited for Phil's scowl, but instead he merely held out his hand. Tracie watched, amazed. Maybe the way to a man's heart *was* through his stomach.

"Wow!" Phil said as he sucked down the sugar cookie. "These are *amazing*!"

"Yeah. Fat and sugar can be a really powerful mood elevator," Laura said. "I'm hooked." She patted her hip.

Tracie hated the way she put herself down. "Laura, what's the difference between baking soda and baking powder?" Tracie asked.

"I know that," Phil offered. "One's a liquid and one's not. Easy."

Laura snorted. "Oddly enough, baking soda is not fizzy and you do not drink it through a straw," Laura told him. She turned back to Tracie. "You know, baking soda is like cream of tartar. You don't have to use them often, but when you need them nothing else will do. Boy, at Easter, I could have sold my supply of cream of tartar for more than you'd get for crack cocaine. The housewives of Sacramento were frantic."

Tracie smiled. She'd forgotten how odd, how unique Laura's humor was. Who else but Laura would be able to create a sentence combining crack and cream of tartar together.

"Cleanup time!" Laura announced, but Phil just picked up another cookie. Tracie shrugged. Phil didn't clean up his own place. Laura began to wash dishes, so Tracie covered and finished putting away the last of the ingredients.

"What took you so long?" Phil asked her, wiping crumbs from his mouth.

Tracie moved Laura over by hitting her gently with her hip and washed her hands. "It was the weirdest night. Jon asked if I could do a makeover on him."

Phil laughed. "A makeover on Techno-Nerd? What did he want to be made into?"

"Somebody more like you," Tracie said as she sat down on the sofa and slipped out of her shoes.

"Mr. Micro T. Stock Option? Now, *that* is impossible," Phil said. "The guy was born to wear glasses and work a day job. Day jobs were invented for people like him." Tracie was about to jump to Jon's defense, but then she noticed that Laura had left a bowl at the side of the tiny kitchen counter. She was about to bring it to be washed when she realized what it was. Gratefully, she picked it up and began to wipe the glass with her finger, then inserted the finger in her mouth.

"Just how many shares does he have, anyway?" Phil asked.

"Somewhere around thirty thousand, I think," she said, shrugging as the sweetness hit her tongue.

"Wow! So he's really rich. You'd think he'd never be lonely," Laura said. "When do I meet him?"

"Forget it," Phil told her. "You're better off with Jeff, and his IQ is in the double digits. But at least he has rhythm. He's still talking about you."

"Jon just doesn't get opportunities with the kind of women he likes," Tracie said.

"Too much money and you can't get a honey," Phil said. "And the guy wanted to be like me?" He laughed.

"Maybe I'm his type," Laura observed.

Tracie ignored her. "And what makes you think you're so impossible to imitate?" she asked Phil.

"Nothing. But he's so fuckin' lame. Totally void."

"Yeah," Laura agreed. "Never like a guy under thirty with a day job and a fortune in stock. That's my motto."

Phil missed her sarcasm and nodded. "Well, anyway, it's hopeless. You couldn't do it," he told Tracie.

"*He* thinks I could do it," Tracie retorted. Why was Phil so cruel when he spoke of Jon?

"Oh, Techno-Nerd thinks you can do anything."

"She could do it if she wanted to," Laura snapped at Phil as she rinsed off the last cookie sheet and retrieved the now-clean bowl from Tracie.

"Yeah. He has more faith in me than you do," Tracie told him. "What if I did change him, make him a hottie?"

"You should, and maybe write a feature on it," Laura said. "You know, a kind of day-by-day diary. People love makeovers."

It was a good idea. Plus it would really antagonize Phil, and she was in the mood to do that now. "Yeah!" Tracie agreed.

"Yeah? What, are you crazy?" Phil asked. "Why would you want to waste time writing about crap as ridiculous as that?"

"Oh, I don't know," Tracie said. "Everyone is interested in transformations. It's archetypal. You know, like Jung." Phil worshipped Jung. "The old Cinderella story."

"But I thought you weren't interested in *old* stories," he said. "You're interested in *new* stories."

"Yeah," Laura said. "Phil showed me one of his new stories." She caught Tracie's eye. Her mouth curled into the **W** it made when she didn't want to laugh.

"Really?" Tracie asked. Despite Laura's contempt, she was hurt. Phil had rarely shown her any of his work. "What did you think?"

"I think it could have been improved by characters and a plot," Laura opined. "Otherwise, it was great."

"Thanks," Phil said, as if he hadn't just been insulted. "It's a collective unconscious kind of thing." Well, Tracie thought, he probably didn't care about what Laura felt about writing. But why had he even shown her anything? "Anyway, even if you wanted to write crap like that, you couldn't make it happen," Phil added. "Making him cool would be like trying to refrigerate the Amazon. Too big a job. Impossible."

"Wanna bet I could?" Tracie asked.

"Bet what?" He reached out a finger to wipe the edge of her mouth, but Tracie dodged away. None of that stuff now, and certainly not in front of lonely Laura.

But there was a wager here. A legitimate way to address her gripes, teach Phil a lesson, and maybe move their relationship forward—or end it. "Bet you household money," Tracie said, inspired.

"Whoa. I don't pay household money." He almost dropped the latest cookie he was conveying to his mouth.

"Exactly my point, Phil. You eat here and sleep here most of the time, but you don't pay rent, or even chip in on the groceries."

"You know I can't, baby." He looked over at Laura then put his arm around Tracie and walked her over to the screen. He lowered his voice. "I'm still paying off the amplifier, and right now I'm even behind on my share of the apartment rent," he told her, gently pushing her toward Laura's bed.

"Not here!" she said sharply. What was he thinking of? "Anyway, if you gave up your place . . ."

"I think this is the point in the conversation where I diplomatically withdraw to provide you with the privacy you so obviously require," Laura said as she wiped her hands on the pathetic excuse for a dishcloth that Tracie had dug up somewhere. "I need a good, long, loud shower," she told them, and disappeared into the bathroom.

Phil took Tracie by the arm, went into the bedroom, pulled off his boots, and pulled her onto the bed. "Come over here," he said, and reached out to her.

"Phil. Stop. Seriously! Listen to me for a minute," Tracie insisted as he took her by the shoulders and pulled her to him. "If you moved in . . ."

Phil removed his arm from her shoulder and slid it under the pillow. All at once the emotional temperature dropped fifty degrees. "Hey, I have to have my own space," he told her, and turned to the wall, obviously wanting her to end the subject, or, better yet, fall asleep.

"But you were so sure about Jon. You afraid to bet?" Tracie egged him on. "If I can turn Jon into someone cool, would you give up your place and pay half the rent here?"

"It's not going to happen," he insisted.

"But if it did?"

He turned around, looked at her, and then grinned wolfishly. "I'd do whatever you wanted. But what if you can't?"

Tracie thought about it some more. "Then you can use this place as a free hotel where you drop your laundry and eat your meals but never have to make the bed." She paused again. "Oh, wait. You're already doing that."

Phil sat up. "Look, I told you, relationships are tough for a musician. You knew that going in. Right?" She nodded. "Relationships are like baths: At first they're okay, but after a while they're not so hot."

"Is that what you think about us? That we're not so hot?" she asked, getting off the bed. She didn't want him if that's what he thought.

"No, baby," he said soothingly. "How can you ask that after this afternoon?" His voice got husky. He pulled her back to him, though she kept her body stiff and resistant. "Hey, I was just raggin' on you. Look. I brought you something." Phil held out his hand and opened his fist. In his palm was a black velvet ring box. Her heart jumped and she threw her arms around his neck. "Oh, Phil!" she breathed.

Tracie was in front of the mirror in the ladies' room of the *Seattle Times*. She was applying Great Lash mascara while Beth looked on. She had dark circles under her eyes. She and Phil had been up till four, fighting, making love, and then fighting again. God, I need a haircut, she thought. She'd have to call and beg Stefan for an appointment.

"Then what?" Beth asked.

"So he's like, 'I need my own space.'"

Beth sighed. "My mother told me she would rent a warehouse for all the guys in Seattle I've dated who needed their own space."

The ladies' room door opened. Allison, the tall blonde who'd been at Cosmo and who could easily win a young Sharon Stone look-alike contest, entered the ladies' lounge. Beth and Tracie eyed her hostilely. She joined them at the mirror.

"Hi," Allison said as she needlessly fluffed her already-perfect hair.

"Hi," Tracie and Beth said simultaneously, and with precisely the same lack of enthusiasm.

There was a moment of silence. Allison kept playing with her hair. "So," Tracie continued, "Phil said he wanted to get married, but I'm like, 'I don't really know you well enough. I'm not even sure you're right for me.' But I took the ring anyway," Tracie told the reflection of herself and Beth.

Beth stopped putting on her lipstick and almost dropped the tube. "He asked you?" she asked. "I mean, he popped the big one?" Tracie covertly eyed Allison in the mirror. She finished her hair.

"Bye," Allison said.

"Bye," Beth and Tracie echoed at the same time as Allison exited the bathroom.

"Phil gave you a ring?" Beth asked after the door closed completely. "For real?"

"No, for Allison. Phil gave me a ring *box*. With a guitar pick inside."

"A *guitar* pick?"

Tracie imitated Phil's voice from the night before to make a joke out of her disappointment. " 'It's my first one. I didn't know I wasn't supposed to use one with a bass.' " She paused the way he had when he'd seen her lack of enthusiasm. " 'Hey. It means a lot to me.' " She went back to her normal tone of voice. "Well, it *does* mean a lot to him. You know, he lives for his music and his writing. He just doesn't think about material things like rings." Beth didn't say a word. "Well, he *doesn't*," Tracie insisted, then showed Beth the pick, which Phil had had a jeweler drill a hole through, now on a chain around her neck. "Doesn't Allison just get on your nerves?"

Beth became animated again. "You have no idea. Last week, she started dating this new guy. He was calling the office about six hundred times a day. By Thursday, he was waiting outside for her at lunch *and* after work. On Friday, she actually got a restraining order."

"No shit," Tracie said as she slipped the mascara wand back into its base.

"No shit! And he's not a mental patient. He's a big orthodontist in Tacoma," Beth added. "I swear she has the power to cloud men's minds. And I think she's after Marcus."

With a worse-than-usual display of neurosis and bad taste in men, not to mention career suicide, Beth had started up an office affair with Marcus. Now she tortured herself over it daily. Tracie thought Beth might be right about the Allison-Marcus thing, but there was no sense admitting it. "Well, you should give him to her on a silver platter."

"Noooo," Beth keened. "I mean, I admit he's troubled. But I love him." She blotted her lips and stood up to go. "Anyway, he's not mine to give."

"So let her have him. They deserve each other."

"But I . . ."

Tracie couldn't believe that Beth was still hung up on the jerk. "Oh, Beth, he dated and dumped you! You should have him up on harassment charges." Tracie began to throw her makeup in her purse. "Why are guys like that? My girlfriend Laura with Peter? Me with

Phil? And you with that bastard Marcus? How come they're so immature and selfish?"

"They're a challenge." Beth sniffed as they walked down the hall. "I mean, if Phil and Marcus did what we wanted all the time, it would get boring."

Beth was, of course, insane, but Tracie had to admit she recognized what Beth meant.

"Let's face it. The difficult ones make us feel special. You know, with Marcus it was like if I got *him* to love me, I was really something."

Tracie thought of Phil and how difficult he was. Then she remembered Jon and his request. Maybe he was right. Could she do it? Would it work? She sighed. "Sometimes I think we're just masochists. But Marcus is definitely a sadist."

"Never mind Marcus," Beth told her. "Look at Phil! He's not good enough for you, Tracie. I admit he's cute, but he's no good. And he'll never make a commitment." She grabbed the pick swinging around Tracie's neck. "That is just pathetic," she added.

"I don't know," Tracie said, feeling the glimmer of an idea. "I may have a way to force him to. *And* simultaneously get a good feature out of it." They got to the corner where they had to part.

"Don't bet on it," Beth said.

Tracie smiled. "I just might," she told her friend.

Chapter 9

Just outside of Jon's office, there were dozens of carpeted cubicles filling a space almost the size of an airplane hangar. The noise of beeping phones, copiers, printers, and fingers tapping keyboards made a low but constant thrum. Jon was tired from having to deal with his mothers, working on Parsifal, being out late last night with Tracie while she shopped. But now, sitting here, he had to muster up enough strength to pay attention. After all, this was his department, his kingdom. A bunch of Micro/Con guys were deep in tech-development talk while he, the enlightened despot, listened, trying to keep his eyes open.

Jon looked up from the discussion group he was in and saw Samantha walking toward his office. His kingdom crashed around him faster than the "I love you" virus crashed the Filipino E-mail system. He remembered he was the Winner of the Losers. Humiliation was walking right up to him. There was something about Sam that Jon, or any other guy, for that matter, couldn't resist. She was one of those tiny freckled redheads, tough in her job, but she had a sweetness—no, an innocence—that was a total magnet. He wanted to catalogue every one of her freckles as if they were constellations in the night sky. And that wasn't taking her legs into consideration—so long, so lean, so perfectly proportioned.

Sam was in marketing at Micro/Con. Most marketing folk were empty suits, but she was a smart woman with a sense of humor, a lot like Tracie. He had first met her at last year's sales conference, when the Crypton-2 had been completed and was ready for public release. The auditorium was filled with three hundred people—most of whom were uptight salesmen—but Jon couldn't get over Sam as she stepped up to the podium and began her pitch with an insanely off-color joke about a midget and a washing machine. Not only had she made the guys roar, but she'd managed to be very ladylike at the same time. Even now, Jon chuckled at the memory. She had gusto. She had a certain aura about her that was magical. She was incredible. No one that Jon knew—not even Tracie—would be able to pull something like that off and get away with it. For months, he'd had her on his radar, always aware of where she was. At last, he'd gotten up the courage to sit next to her at a couple of meetings. He'd passed her funny notes; she'd laughed. He sat next to her in the cafeteria one day, and then he'd asked her out. She'd agreed, then stood him up.

Now, seeing her in the hallway, he wished he could get away with not having to speak to her. She was involved in a discussion of her own with some marketing gunslinger. They were all so damn slick. All style, no substance. Jon froze, then became visibly uncomfortable. He hoped the guys around him didn't notice. She couldn't pretend not to see him. He wished he could disappear or just push his head through the 100 percent natural fiber industrial carpeting beneath his feet and pull an ostrich, but there was no chance.

"Oh. Hi, Jon," Samantha said calmly. She continued down the hall without missing a beat, her long legs a receding dream.

"Hi, Sam," Jon responded in a voice about an octave too high. God, her casualness was worse than being ignored! Now he could tell he'd been totally forgotten.

Then Samantha stopped. "Oh, hey. Sorry about Saturday," she

said over her shoulder, as if she'd just remembered it. Well, maybe she just had.

"Saturday?" Jon asked, his voice under control. Hey, he could get amnesia, too.

"I wasn't sure if it was on or not, and then I got tied up and I was—"

"No problem," Jon said cutting her off. Then he separated from the group and entered his office. He could hear the staff murmuring outside his door. Dennis said, "Man, what did she do with Jon that made *her* sorry?" Someone else made another wisecrack, one he couldn't hear, and everyone laughed. He jumped when the phone began to ring. For a moment, he was tempted to ignore it, but he couldn't. It might be Bella, his boss, with new info on the Parsifal funding. He picked up the receiver.

"Do you like surprises?" Tracie's voice asked.

"Hit me with one." He sighed. Anything would be a good distraction from his current modality.

"What if I said this isn't Tracie? That it's Merlin and I've considered your proposal?"

Marlon? Brando or Perkins? He was so tired, he felt fuzzy-headed. What was she talking about? Had he been so desperate Sunday night that he'd gotten drunk and asked her to marry him? He was confused. Then it hit him. The tutoring. Jon flung the papers he was holding onto a chair and sat down. "Tracie, I'll do anything. *Anything.*"

"First of all, we'd have to buy you some decent clothes," she said.

Jon couldn't help thinking of Emerson—"Never trust an endeavor that requires new clothes." "My credit card is yours," is what he said to Tracie.

"You'll have to change your hair."

Hey, I'd like to change my whole head, he thought. But he just said, "Transplants, or just the color? I'll do either," he assured her.

Tracie giggled. She had a really cute giggle. "A good cut will do for starters. And you need to start working out."

"No problem. I can work out or in. All I do is work."

"You know I mean at a gym!" Tracie remonstrated. "Partly to be buff, partly to meet people. Okay. So . . . for a start, you'll have to get rid of your home answering machine. *And* your E-mail."

She'd gone crazy. He was director of an entire R & D division, working on a cutting-edge project. "What? . . . How would I get my—"

"That's the point. Rule Number One: Unavailability."

"To women maybe. But I do have business to transact."

"You've been doing nothing but work for the last six years. You're going to have to change some of your ways to get cuties."

He thought of Sam. "Okay. Okay," he said. "Just give me the rules."

"Rule Number Two: Unpredictability. Lose the watch."

He began to unfasten the band from his wrist. "It's not hip, right? I should wear a different one? A Swatch?"

She groaned. "God no. Bad boys just don't *need* watches. You're either fashionably late or inconveniently early, but *never* on time."

"Plus, no logos. No little alligators, no boomerangs. If people want to read, let them buy the *Times*, not stare at your chest. And forget your Micro/Connection wardrobe."

"I don't *always* wear Micro/Con stuff," he said defensively. He looked down at his chest. It said FROM FLOPPY DISK TO HARD DRIVE IN SIXTY SECONDS. Perhaps his argument was weak. Actually, he hardly ever noticed what he wore.

"Not if you sleep in the nude. But whenever *I've* seen you, you've been branded. And it is so *lame*."

Maybe she was right. "I'll put on a real shirt," he promised.

"So, your homework assignment: Tomorrow, you go to work without a watch and no Micro/Con. Then we'll meet at your place tomorrow at seven."

Jon was a good student. He'd always gotten the extra-credit points and the trick questions right in school. It was only in his personal life that he screwed up. "Is this a test? Am I supposed to be late? Or early?"

"On time," she told him in a stern voice. "Don't play those games with your alchemist."

Jon hung up, smiled, and swirled around in his desk chair. Yes! Soon he'd have the Samanthas of the world and all their freckles at his feet.

Chapter 10

Tracie walked into her apartment and nearly fainted from the scent of rosemary and thyme in the air. She began salivating immediately. She never had any food in the place, because she'd eat it if she did. This was . . . overwhelming.

"Hi, honey. You're home," Laura sang out. The table was set with Tracie's nice china, salads were already put out, and Laura opened the door enough for Tracie to see something really good seemed to be roasting in the oven. "I didn't know how you felt about duck, so I made chicken à l'orange," said Laura. Tracie frowned. She thought that took hours—though she'd never even read a recipe. And she was starved, but she was also getting concerned. As far as she knew, Laura hadn't been out of the apartment in the last three days. Plus, neither of them needed this many calories.

"Honey, you can't go on like this," Tracie said as she sat down at the table. Laura pulled a small dish from the oven. On it was a tiny bit of bread smeared with something and decorated artfully with a few leaves.

"Have a cheese savory," said Laura cheerfully, ignoring Tracie completely. She was already drinking a glass of red wine and poured some out for Tracie. Tracie couldn't resist, but she knew she'd hate herself in the morning. It was funny—after only a few days, the two of them were acting like a long-married couple.

"Laura, this is impossible," she said as she popped the savory into her mouth. Then she couldn't do anything except make animal noises because it was so delicious. All thoughts of dieting left her head. "Can't we have these for dinner?" she asked. Laura laughed. "Don't worry. Everything is that good."

Laura was telling the truth. Tracie only came back to her senses after the flan that her guest had made for dessert. Only then—replete with food and guilt—did she begin to shake her head. "We're getting fat. I can't take this rich food every night."

"Don't be silly," Laura said in her best Julia Child imitation. "What's rich about a little sour cream and truffles and foie gras and cheese?" She winked. "It's not like I'm baking farm cakes." But she might as well be. Laura's cooking was rich.

With some difficulty, Tracie got up from the table and dragged herself over to the sofa. She was stuffed. "Okay," she said. "That was it. I'm locking up the pans and from now on we're spending our lunchtimes at the gym."

"I am not friendly enough with gymnasiums to call them by their first names," Laura sniffed. "I don't *do* gymnasiums."

"You didn't do them in Sacramento. You *do* do them here," Tracie told her. "And you are way too talented not to be cooking. You've got to go out and find some catering jobs. Better yet, get a job as a chef. You always wanted to do that."

"Hey, babe, you're not doing your transformation on *me*," Laura said. "You're doing one on Jon, and even that's not a good idea. It'll end in tears, as my mother used to say."

"Your mother used to tell you sex felt bad," Tracie said as she attempted to find the place where her waistline had been only a few days before. Now it wasn't just the top button but the entire zipper of her slacks that had to be loosened. "Jon *asked* me to do this."

"Yeah? Well don't you see that every single thing you're going to do will be a criticism of him? At some point, he's really going to resent it. Maybe my mother lied, but there's an old Chinese saying: Why does he hate me so? I never did anything for him. That's based on truth."

"Don't be silly," Tracie said. "Jon will be grateful for anything I do to help him."

"Mmm? Remember when you used to try to do diet consulting for me?"

"You didn't ask me to! And I stopped!"

"Look," Laura explained, "if Jon doesn't resent it, *Phil* is going to start to. Too much attention paid to someone else."

"Are you kidding me?" Tracie asked, then wondered if Phil would drop by that night, as he said he might. "Phil doesn't notice anything I do. I'd *like* it if he was jealous."

"We shall see," Laura told her, and blinked like an owl. Tracie hated it when she acted wise.

"We shall see. And maybe we won't. But we will be at the gym," Tracie told her. "Beth and some of the girls from work go there three days a week. So are we." She got up and put her arm on Laura's much higher shoulder. "You're gonna look great on the StairMaster," Tracie predicted.

Seventies music blared in the background of Simon's Gym. A roomful of women were working the circuit. "Susan went out with a guy, and when they started making out, she found out he was wearing a toupee," Sara, one of the junior reporters at the *Times*, said.

"That's a pucker," Beth answered.

"What's a pucker?" Tracie asked, sitting at the rowing machine, her head bent between her knees. She was so tired, she thought she might puke.

"It's the female equivalent of a wilt," Sara explained. She held her finger up and indicated the loss of an erection. "So accountants are a pucker."

"What else?" Tracie asked, still breathing heavily.

"Shoe salesmen," Laura offered from the StairMaster, raising her left knee to her waist. The seventies album continued, "Let's all celebrate and have a good time."

"Brokers—stock or real estate. And security guards," Sara chimed in while doing a warm-up side stretch to the left.

"Did you ever date a security guard?" Laura asked Sara.

"As if," Sara said as she side-stretched to the right.

"Oh, computer guys," Beth added as she changed the weights on the new device she was about to mount. It looked frightening and maybe sexual. "Seattle is full of them. They're a bore. For some reason, they think you really care about their serial ports." The music stopped for a minute and so did all the women. Then Kool & the Gang started in.

Sara grabbed a sweat towel and wiped off her brow. "Yeah," she agreed. "Mothers always try to set you up with guys in the computer industry. But they're like lepers. I think they all ought to be forced to wear bells around their necks and yell 'Unclean, unclean' when they come at you."

"Mothers?" Tracie asked, remembering her article and wincing.

"No. Geeks," Sara explained. "Unless, of course, they're vested." Sara never quite got another person's joke, but she was sweet. Laura, who only liked sweet pastries, rolled her eyes. "I'm not into marrying for money, but I heard Allison talking, and she knows exactly how much every stock is worth. She said she's looking for some guy who's floated his own IPO, whatever that is."

"Allison," Tracie said dismissively. "As if a rich man would look at her."

"You don't think Allison's beautiful?" Sara asked.

"Nah," Tracie said. "She looks too much like Sharon Stone, but with a better ass."

"Hey, girls, speaking of asses," called Beth. "It's bicycle time."

"No, let's do the treadmill first."

"Let's eat lunch first," Sara suggested. "I'm starved."

"How about naptime first?" Laura asked, wiping the sweat off her upper lip.

They moved past the line of stationary bikes. The four of them each stepped onto a treadmill, punched in numbers, and started to walk. "So we know what we don't like, but what is it about challenging boys we do like? Why are we addicted to difficult men?" Tracie asked.

"They're such a big challenge," Sara said. "There're loads of them at the *Times*."

They were stepping in sync and their arms swung. "Yeah. It isn't easy to get a bad boy to love you, but you feel like if they did, it would really be an accomplishment," Beth added.

"I think they appeal to our maternal instinct," Laura responded.

"Get outta town!" Sara and Beth answered at the same time.

Tracie wished she had her Post-its.

"No. Listen," Laura continued. "It's like we get to practice on them. You know, they need attention like an infant."

"I think it's because they're easy," Beth said.

"Boy, are they *not* easy," Sara added.

"But they are in a way," Beth asserted. "You never get really close to them, so you never have to test your own ability to love."

All of them stopped, silent. For a moment, none of them wanted to meet one another's eyes. Even Tracie, the reporter, felt uncomfortable.

They all dismounted the treadmills and proceeded to the bicycles.

They were late getting back to the office from the gym. Beth was gathering her papers in a frenzy while also trying to brush her hair. Tracie entered her cubicle area. "Come on, you'll be late. Your hair looks fine. And Marcus will ignore you anyway."

"I just hate these meetings."

"Everyone does. But today I'm going to beard the lion in his den. I've got a really great feature idea."

Beth looked at her doubtfully as she exited her office and Tracie followed her down the hall. "You're crazy. Why discuss it in front of everyone and let him humiliate you?"

"Because I think I can get support from everyone. This is a really good idea. Funny. Cute."

"And we all know how Marcus loves funny and cute."

As the door to the conference room opened, Tracie could see that the meeting had been in progress for a while. She turned and shot Beth a look to tell her they were screwed. As she took her seat, she tried not to make eye contact with Marcus. He sat at the head of the table, an unlit cigarette jiggling in the corner of his mouth as he talked. "Nice of you to join us, ladies. Beth, did you get your piece on the new mayor finished?"

"Not quite, but I can get it in tomorrow."

"It better be good." He turned his attention to Tracie. "As for you, I want a feature on Memorial Day." Tracie tried not to show her excitement. It was the only holiday she cared about. She'd been hoping for this, and she had even planned to do some interviews with World War II veterans. She tried, though, not to show any enthusiasm. Marcus kept going around the table. "As for you, Tim, I'd like the indoor picnic story by Friday. And Sara, you get the author interview. I think this week Susann Baker Edmonds is in town," Marcus added, yawning.

Sara huffed as Allison tried getting Marcus's attention by flinging back her perfect blond mane. "Uh, Marcus? I thought I could cover the Radiohead concert."

"Forget it. You just want to sleep with them," Marcus said nonchalantly. "Well, if there aren't any more ideas or pitches, class is dismissed." He stood up.

"Actually, I have an—"

"Ah, the lovely Miss Higgins. Last Moment Higgins?" Marcus asked, and walked up behind Tracie.

"I'm sorry," Tracie said.

"I'm Sorry Higgins. I. S. Higgins. Don't Edit Me Higgins. Yes?" He put his hands on her shoulders.

She hated it when he did that. Though she really didn't like making eye contact with him, either. "I have this idea for a . . . well, for a makeover piece."

"What? Like those women's magazines do? The beauteous Allison tried to thrust one of those at me, and even *she* couldn't get me to bite. . . ." He must have smiled at Allison, because she had a look on her face that was like a child being noticed by her daddy. "Although I was very tempted. But not by the story. But as for you, Miss Higgins, the answer is no."

"Wait," Tracie snapped back, then twisted around in her chair to look at him. "I thought we could do it a little differently. I thought, well, there are so many computer nerds with money here that we could do a man—I mean watch a man get made over from a nerd to, you know, someone like you."

"Miserable and alcoholic," Tim murmured under his breath.

Marcus shot him a harsh glance. "I heard that." He looked down at Tracie. "What do you really mean, Tracie?"

She swallowed hard. "You know, sort of a spoof on those girlie makeovers. But also a real service article. Where a doofus could get a cool haircut, hip clothes. The dorky restaurants to avoid and the cool ones to go to. We could take a person and do a real *Pilgrim's Progress.*"

"Could be cute. But how would you find someone who would agree to do it?"

"It would make the guy look like a real meat loaf," Tim said, sharing his opinion with the group.

"That makes you a candidate," Marcus shot back at him as he went to the door to leave. He paused and turned back to the table. "But that reminds me of something. It's time we did a survey piece about the best meat loaf in Seattle. Tracie, you take it." Marcus looked at Tracie. "I want a big piece with a lot of local places described in a positive way."

Tracie couldn't believe it. "And do they all win for best meat loaf?" she asked. "We wouldn't want to make any of our advertisers mad."

Marcus didn't even blink. "Only one winner, but a lot of four-star meat loaves. And Allison, could I see you in my office?" He pulled the door handle and slid out of the room.

Chapter 11

Jon was straightening up, getting rid of the take-out containers, pizza boxes, and back issues of computer magazines he had piled up. In his vast living room, there was a dusty but complete home gym, a fabulous entertainment system, half a dozen computers, and a small sofa. Once he got his new laptop, he'd finally unhook all of these. The doorbell rang and he looked down at his wrist, then realized there was no watch. Was it seven already? He looked up at one of the computer consoles. It was 7:20. He chucked the boxes in his arms into the hall closet and went to the sofa and picked up the rest of the magazines, threw them in the closet, too, and then turned to the full-length mirror on the back of the door. He slid the door open.

Tracie walked in, looked around, and hit her head with her hand. "Do you live here, or is this where you perform surgery? And the least you could do is listen to music instead of the business station KIRO. Did your stock fall or something?"

"I didn't even hear that it was on," Jon said. "What's the matter?" he asked, unsuccessfully trying to keep the plaintive note out of his voice.

"I don't have time to begin the list," Tracie said. "It doesn't matter, though. Rule Number Three: Never show them where you live."

Jon pulled out a Wizard 2000 and started to enter Tracie's wisdom into it. He'd already memoed himself on her other commandments. He was almost ready to keyboard it, when—

"Put that down!" Tracie told him.

"I'm just using it for notes," he protested. Tracie took it from his hand and put it firmly on the aluminum coffee table.

"Not anymore." She took off her jacket and handed it to him. He was about to hang it in the closet, but then he remembered the pizza boxes and thought better of it, smoothing the suede, folding it, and putting it over the back of the sofa. Tracie put down her bag, walked to the window, and turned around to face him. "So, back to Rule Number Three: Never show them where you live. No girl is going to come over here. It would ruin everything."

"They don't come over here now," Jon admitted. And it was too bad. The view was spectacular. "Not even my mother." Not that he spent much time here. He was always working.

"Then again, you don't get to go to *their* places now, either. Follow my rules and you will. You know, you're really kind, and so good at what you do. You deserve to have a wonderful woman in your life."

"Well, I do, but I don't sleep with you."

"Right. But now you can have both." She paused. "It's funny. You manage to do so well in work, but you can't pull your private life together. I can't manage to break through with work."

"And your personal life is okay? Excuse me, but your career *and* your boyfriend need a shot in the arm."

Tracie gave him a murderous look. Jon shrugged and moved to the refrigerator. "You want a drink or something? I've got cranberry juice and cranapple. Good for your urinary tract, you know. I think I also have—"

"Stop!" She got up off the sofa and went toward him. "Rule Number Four: Never offer them *anything*. You make *them* offer. That's the key to the whole thing. And never use either 'urinary' or 'tract' unless you're a vet, a gynecologist, or a religious fanatic." She took him by the lapels of his jacket. For a moment—a very brief moment—Jon thought she was going to kiss him. That or head-butt. "They're going to be asking *you* to go to bed with *them*."

"Them? More than one?" he asked, and realized his voice had risen an octave.

Tracie just ignored him, pulled on his lapels, spun him around, and twisted his jacket right off him. "Well, not at first," she said. "That's the advanced class." With a flourish, she threw his jacket in the wastebasket.

"Hey!" he began to protest, then remembered her stricture.

"No sports jacket. Ever. And no checks or plaids. Solid colors only. And dark ones. In fact, to begin with, we're going with the Henry Ford approach: any color you want, as long as it's black."

"Black? But I don't— Every—" he stopped himself. "Fine," he said.

Tracie walked around him slowly, like an officer inspecting the troops. "Where did you get that haircut?" she asked.

"Logan's."

"Never go there again except to clobber him. Stefan will try to fix it. If I beg him." She looked down at his legs. "Forget khakis. And you don't wear anything from the Gap, Banana Republic, J. Crew, or L. L. Bean." Jon was desperately trying to remember what she was saying, wishing for his Palm Pilot, and attempting not to take offense, all at the same time. "Look, if you wear this stuff, you'll just create a pucker in women."

"What's a pucker?"

Tracie made her big eyes bigger. "It's the female equivalent of a wilt in a man. There are some looks that are so bad, they make us pucker up to be sure we would never carry any of that genetic material."

"More information than I require." He tried to think of what, if anything, in his wardrobe was left. "So where do I get my—" he began.

"You wear either cool stuff from thrift stores or really, really expensive Italian clothes," Tracie said. "And you mix them. Let's go through your closet." She stalked across the room and pulled open the door to Jon's walk-in. He followed her. The clothes were meticulously arranged by pattern. Checks on one side, plaids on the other, descending down the color scale from light to dark. Tracie moved down the middle of the aisle like a machine gun mowing down soldiers. She pulled the first sports jacket off a hanger and dumped it on the floor. "No." She pulled the next and dumped it, too. "No and no and—ecch! No!"

"What's wrong with madras?"

Tracie ignored him, except to give him a withering what's-right-with-it? look. She opened his bureau drawers one after the other and scrabbled through his stuff. Jon panicked for a moment and wondered if there was anything that he . . . Well, he had no time to think, because Tracie threw him a black crewneck sweater, jeans, and—in desperation—pulled off her own belt. Jon cringed.

"No! Not the strap! Are bad clothes a whipping offense?"

"No, but spending real money on this crap probably is. We definitely have to go shopping. I'm not sure I can pull more than one cool outfit out of this. Okay? So here's the point. You *are* going to change: what you wear, what you say, where you go, what you eat."

"What I eat? Maybe we're talking too much change," Jon said.

"Hey, you asked for this. You get it." Tracie raised her brows. Silently, she gave him the belt and pointed back to the closet. He headed over to strip off his clothes behind the door.

"Change now?" She gave him a look. "That was just a question," he said as he slipped into the straight-legged jeans.

"No questioning the alchemist," Tracie called from somewhere near the door. "Otherwise, the magic doesn't work."

Tracie was going through his coats and jackets again. She began to bundle all the rejected clothes together and stuff them into a plastic bag.

Jon stepped out from the closet. Now he felt meek and small, like the real Oz. Tracie dropped the bag and looked him over. "Well, that's better. Except the shoes. No more sneakers."

"No more sneakers? But . . ." Tracie raised her brow and spun on her heel. "That wasn't a *but*," Jon hastened to tell her. "It wasn't even a question. It was . . . a clarification. So what do I wear instead of Nikes? Sandals?"

Tracie turned back to face him. "Only if you think Jesus had a hot social life. Look, footwear is very important. Nice guys wear Nikes, or Top-Siders, Keds, or Converse. Boring! Sexy guys wear Doc Martens or boots." She squinted and looked him over again. It made Jon feel . . . peculiar. Surely she was taking this too far. "Look," she said with a sigh. "I have to tell you about the pants thing."

"What pants thing?"

Tracie seemed not to hear him. "I'm really trusting you by telling you this, but I feel you have to know. Most women have a pants thing."

"What?" Jon asked. He was afraid she was going to tell him that he had to stuff socks in his crotch and that women picked out their lovers and husbands based on bulge factor. He just didn't think he could bear it, but before he could tell her to stop, she began with a completely irrelevant question.

"Did you see *Out of Africa*?" she asked.

"The movie?" he replied.

"Yeah. With Robert Redford and Meryl Streep."

"No," he said.

"How about *Legends of the Fall*?"

"I don't know anyone over fourteen who saw that one."

"Well, there were some of us," Tracie informed him. "And it was all about the pants thing. A lot of women have the pants thing."

"What the hell is 'the pants thing'?" he asked.

She sighed. "It would be easier if you'd seen the movies. But it's all about a certain kind of pants. Not tight, tight ones . . ."

Relief flooded Jon like water on a service station's bathroom floor.

He wouldn't have to stuff his pants, though he wasn't sure what kind of pants he wouldn't have to stuff.

"But not those pleated pants, either. God, not those pleated khaki Docker things that make men look like throw pillows when they sit down. You want pants that are flat in the front. I mean, Robert Redford was already a middle-aged wrinkle bunny when he made *Out of Africa*, but he looked so damn good in those pants. My friend Sara says it's the swoopy hair thing, but most women I know admit it's the pants thing."

"Where do you get those pants?" Jon asked, mesmerized.

"I'll have to go with you. Because it's not just that they're flat in the front; it's also the way they hug your . . . back."

"How high do they come up?" Jon asked, imagining some kind of one-piece overall. "They cover my back?"

Tracie shook her head in despair. "I mean your butt. Sometimes, I admit, women look at men's butts."

"Not our crotches?" Jon asked.

"Don't be disgusting," she said dismissively. "Why do . . ." Then she looked up and was silent for a moment.

He couldn't imagine what she was seeing on the ceiling, but it was clear that she liked it. Maybe it was Robert Redford's butt. "It's a funny thing," she said. "It also has to do with the textiles. Nothing shiny. No. A man in shiny pants is . . ." She shook her head to get rid of the thought. "It has to be a smooth, firm fabric. See, it's about butts, but it's also not about butts. If you know what I mean."

Jon hadn't a clue. But he didn't want her to stop now. He felt as if he might be about to witness a biblical revelation.

"It's like most naked butts are not that cute, but one that's in a nice pair of pants, that's just sitting there kind of cupped by them, not too big, not too flat, just kind of narrow yet full . . ."

Forget this! "You are an embarrassment to yourself and others," Jon said. "Tracie, are you telling me responsible adult women make choices based on trousers and footwear? Details like that?"

Tracie opened her big eyes even bigger. "Jesus, Jon. In all these years, I never knew you were so ignorant. You know what they say: God is in the details. We—women—talk about details for hours. You guys are the big picture; we *are* details."

"But *I* am details. I was a computer analyst for four years. Nothing but details."

Tracie nodded, but not in a positive way. "Exactly. Wasn't that just the time your celibacy kicked in?" Jon tried to think back, afraid that Tracie might be right. "Look. Trust me on this one. It's not that there's anything wrong with your job. It just isn't sexy. Don't tell *anyone*."

Slightly hurt, Jon shrugged. "But what if they ask what I do?"

"And they will. Women want to know everything. You just be vague. Vague drives women out of their minds."

"In a good way or a bad way?"

"Both." She laughed. "It took me three months to find out if Phil was an only child. But the point is, they'll come back for more. Just clear your throat and tell them you're . . . in sales. Let *them* try and figure out if it's drugs or rebuilt engines."

"So let me get this contradiction straight: Women are driven crazy by vague and they go over details like monkeys on fur."

"Right. Beth from work spent an hour and thirty minutes today discussing the cable-knit fisherman's sweater that this guy she went out with wore on their first date and if it meant he was gay."

"Did it?" he asked. She picked up a black jacket and threw it at him. Jon struggled into it.

"Yeah, unless he's a fisherman," Tracie said, smiling at him. At seeing Tracie's pleased face, Jon struck a series of supermodel poses. "*Okay.* Now you're put together."

Jon went to the mirror and checked himself out. He had to admit he looked different—and improved. The crewneck sweater, one he only wore over a polo shirt, kind of hung off his shoulders in a sexy way. And the pants, though a little uncomfortable, were tight enough along the legs to make him look a little taller.

"Look at your buns!" Tracie said. "Wow! You've had hidden talent all this time."

He blushed, but it didn't stop him from half-turning to look over his shoulder. "Have I got the pants thing?" he asked, hoping it might be true.

"Well, the pants aren't perfect, but it's easier to fix that than the butt. Okay, this is what you're wearing from now on."

"You mean every day? How do I keep it clean?"

"The French only have one outfit and they wear it over and over."

"But they're used to body odor in France," he protested.

"Look, wash it out every night until we go shopping. It's worth the trouble."

"Can't we do it on-line?" he asked. "That's how I buy most of my stuff."

"Oh, that's why it looks that way. Do on-line shopping if you want to have on-line sex. If you want it up close and personal, we're going to have to feel the goods, babe." She looked him over. "You actually look really presentable."

He eyed himself in the mirror. He had to admit he looked a lot more like a man and less like a Salvation Army hanger. "I think this is a good look for me," he said.

"Meet me tomorrow night and we'll go shopping," Tracie told him. "It's something I'm very, very good at. And bring your cards."

Chapter 12

The first place Tracie dragged Jon to shop at was Secondhand Rose's, a hip vintage-clothing emporium north of the city. Jon looked around at the odd clerks and the rails stuffed with even odder clothes. "Tracie, this is used stuff," he said.

She didn't have time to explain. "No it's not. It's vintage," she told him, and started tearing through the first rack. She could get him shirts, sweaters, or even jeans that were new, but to replace that impossible Micro jacket, she'd need something that didn't look as if it came right out of the Gap. In her opinion, the key to really interesting dressing for a man was not to be *too* different from anyone else, except in a single particular: a fabulous jacket or a great pair of boots. And it had to be something that couldn't be ordered from a catalog or bought at a boutique—that showed no originality or interest. A Prada jacket cost big bucks, but any asshole with a platinum card could buy one. Tracie was looking for something unique, something that would fascinate.

Maybe that was why it was so hard to find something worn, unique, and appropriate. In a way, this would still be like being a billboard, but instead of advertising Bill Gates or Ben & Jerry's or Micro/

Con, you were advertising yourself—your inner self: "This is the kind of guy I am. One who bought this black lambskin jacket twenty years ago and wore it until it was the texture and thinness of baby's skin. And I love it." She looked at Jon appraisingly, her eyes partially closed.

Then she went back to the rack. Now, what jacket will tell people who Jon is—or, more to the point, who he wants to be? Tracie kept making the hangers squeal as she shoved them along the rack, past bowling jackets, polyester sports coats, and the tops of leisure suits. Nothing. Nothing. Then she stopped. A possibility. A long black frock coat with narrow lapels. She told him to hold it. Then she noticed the expression of horror on his face.

"This?" he asked, his voice almost matching the pitch of the hangers. "You want me to try it?"

"It's a start," she told him grimly, and began again to tear through the rack. A guy up ahead was also working it, and it looked as if he knew what he was doing. He was dressed well, cool, and was probably rich. He'd get all the good stuff.

Her nervousness made her hurry, and she almost missed a gem: a tight little black leather shirt hanging inside out. She looked at it and then eyed Jon, who was standing beside her, useless. He was watching her as if she had suddenly sprung a leak or something.

She searched and searched. At last, despite the guy ahead of them and the lack of decent material on the rails, she had accumulated a small pile of possibilities, which Jon was holding as if he was afraid of infestation. She'd even found a cool pair of trousers from a morning suit that might work. She took Jon to the corner where the dressing rooms were clustered and pointed to one. "Go ahead," she said. "Try these on." He stood there motionless.

"Did these come off dead people?" he asked.

"Who knows?" she asked. "Just put them on. The pants and long jackets first."

"Did you know the bubonic plaque was caused by fleas in people's clothes?" Jon asked her.

She ignored him and pushed him into a cubicle. "Put them on," she insisted. She waited. And waited. "What's taking so long?" Tracie called in to him.

The dressing room door opened very slowly. Jon stepped out wearing an outfit that looked a lot like the one Lincoln might have been shot in. The black frock coat was to his knees, and the long striped pants—well, he'd never be a Goth. Tracie snapped a photo, then gave him a thumbs-down. "Thank God," Jon muttered, obviously relieved, and disappeared back into the dressing room.

In a few minutes, the door opened again. This time, Jon was in an Austin Powers jumpsuit with a puff-sleeved shirt. Had she picked *that* out? Tracie was horrified. He looked like a gay space clown.

"That isn't for you," she said. "Where did you find it?"

"It was here on the rack," Jon said, shrugging.

She looked into the dressing room. There was also an orange overall and an aqua calf-length skirt. "Were you going to try *that* on?" she asked, hearing the same voice her stepmother had used when she inquired if Tracie would jump off the roof if her Encino friends did. God, there was something about shopping that brought out the bully in her.

She took the extra stuff out of the room and pointed to the garments she'd selected. "Only those," she told him. "This other junk must have been left behind by some circus carnies." Couldn't he tell the difference? If he couldn't, then he really *was* hopeless.

He tried on two more garments and she gave him another couple of thumbs-down. Jon shrugged each time and, in return, gave Tracie a grateful look. At least he went back into the dressing room. It was starting to look like a waste of time, until the door opened and Jon walked out in a pair of torn blue jeans and the supple black leather shirt. Now Tracie paid attention.

It wasn't perfect, but it was moving in the right direction. She walked around Jon appraisingly. She added the loden coat. Yes! He actually looked interesting. Maybe even good. She gave a high school cheer but then stopped in midjump. Now one of those sports jackets, the one near the end of the rack. She ran off and returned with a battered but stylish tweed sports jacket that she made him exchange the loden coat for. She regarded her living science project. Unbelievable. Now he actually looked hot.

Now that they were at the shoe store, Jon could at last sit down. He flopped back into the chair as if he'd been pushed. He'd never been so tired. Who knew shopping could be as exhausting as the Olympic decathlon? No wonder young women were so buff. Even Tracie—who once had held the Ms. Young Encino Shopper title—was tired from their bout with the stores. Jon, with none of her battle experience, must be absolutely dead, she thought. But there was one item still not crossed out on her Post-it list, and she was nothing if not thorough.

And who would have suspected that Tracie was such a shopping maniac? She was relentless. Some primal passion glinted in her eyes as she pounced on what looked to Jon like more useless and boring textiles. They'd been at it for hours, it seemed, and he'd spent more on clothes today than he had in the last two decades.

Now Tracie was holding up shoes for Jon's approval. These were suede, and awful. He contorted his face in an expression of distaste. Tracie pointed to another pair. Well, they weren't bad, if you liked pimp shoes. Jon sat up, trying to show some interest. Tracie handed him the left shoe. He picked it up gingerly.

"Not bad," he admitted, trying to muster some enthusiasm. Then he turned it over and looked at the price on the bottom of the shoe. He nearly fainted. You could support a Moldavian family for a decade on that amount.

"That's what good shoes cost," Tracie told him as if she could read his mind. He knew he better keep still if he wanted her help. He did as he was told, trying them on. Tracie flashed his credit card and forced Jon to buy them. At the counter, the owner smiled. Behind the head of the owner, written in Roman-style type, was a sign that proclaimed THE SOLES ARE THE SOUL OF THE BODY. Tracie pointed to it, nodded at Jon, and nudged him, as if to say, You see? Jon hunched his shoulders in defeat and put his feet into "de shoes."

Tracie stood beside Jon outside the shoe store. He was wearing the cool shoes, as well as the great jacket she'd found, but he'd begun to show his fatigue. Poor guy. Just another couple of stops.

"You're doing great," she said, and took his hand, leading him across the street toward a toiletries store. As they passed a young woman in the crosswalk, she turned to look back at Jon. Yes! Although Tracie noticed, Jon didn't even realize the girl was interested. What's wrong with his radar? Maybe he hasn't used it in so long, it's permanently broken, she thought.

She nudged him. "You're being checked out," she whispered.

Like a dork, he began to crane his head in every direction. Finally, he saw the girl. He returned her glance and then, to Tracie's horror, spun in a slow circle to show himself off.

"Are you nuts?" Tracie hissed, grabbing his arm and pulling him into the store. "Don't you know how to behave?" she asked him, as stern as a mom reprimanding a nine-year-old. "Never let them know you're looking back."

"But then how will they know I'm interested?"

"You're not supposed to be interested in them. They're supposed to be interested in *you*."

"But then how will we get together?" Jon asked. It was a reasonable-enough question, but somehow Tracie hadn't actually imagined that part. She'd thought of renovating him and about the before and after, but not about seeing him walk off with the girl in the crosswalk. But, of course, that was the whole point.

"We get to that later," she said, and took him to the men's cologne and aftershave counter. A group of bored saleswomen at the counter tried to glom on to them, but Tracie dismissed all but one—the oldest, most motherly one. The sales clerk proceeded to spray thirty different scents on various areas of Jon's body: his wrist, lower arm, upper arm, elbow, and neck. Tracie watched Jon twist with each spray and thought that ever since she'd met him back in college, he'd been dorky but kinda cute. Now, she noticed. Maybe he'd grown out of his dorky stage. When had that happened? Was it only now, with some cool clothes on, or was it earlier and she'd never seen it? "What do you think?" the saleswoman kept asking, and it wasn't in a motherly way at all.

In fact, a small crowd of saleswomen were gathering. Tracie looked at Jon. Once she had stripped off the ugly veneer of lameness, he was kind of cute, and there was something so sweet about the way he took the saleswoman and her advice seriously that it attracted the others. He was too inexperienced to know that fragrances were about hype more than anything else and that saleswomen would tell a size-fourteen customer in a size-ten skirt that she "really looks great." As her mean but shrewd stepmother used to say, "They lie like they breathe." Now the coterie consisted of two younger women, one blonde and one a horrible fake red, who began to flirt and bat their lashes at Jon.

"I think he's an Aramis man," the blonde who repped that line said.

"What's an Aramis man like?" Jon asked.

"Handsome. Important. And single." The blonde looked at Tracie. "Is she your sister?"

"No. I'm his mother," Tracie snapped, then looked at Jon, who appeared to be blushing. "We're looking for something a lot more subtle than you have to offer," she declared, and turned back to the older woman.

Meanwhile, the redhead had picked up Jon's left arm and was nibbling on it the way you might pick at corn on the cob. Jon smiled at the redhead with a kind of goofy look. Tracie yanked his arm away.

But by this time, the saleswoman had run out of available skin on Jon's wrists and arms. She picked up a crystal vial and smiled at him. "You might like this," she said. "It's very expensive, but I think it would suit you." She sprayed it on his neck and turned to the blonde. "What do you think, Margie?"

Margie immediately moved close to Jon and put her face up against his chest, nuzzling his neck. Tracie couldn't believe it! These women were without shame.

"It's got patchouli in it," Tracie said. "Nobody has worn that since 1974."

"It's coming back," Margie said, and then she looked at Jon. "I hope you do, too." Jon blushed again.

Tracie felt as if she was losing control of the situation, and she didn't like it. When the older saleswoman picked up another bottle and started to open Jon's shirt to spray some cologne onto his chest, Tracie slapped her hand away. "We've already got plenty to choose from," she told the woman. Jon kept sniffing like a beagle, while all three of the women gave him the eye but kept their hands off. Jon seemed to be enjoying the attention, until all at once he began to sneeze.

And it wasn't just one sneeze. It became three and then a dozen. In no time, he was spraying them all with bodily fluids. Even the blonde backed off. Tracie handed him a tissue. Freed of the fan club, she finally selected Lagerfeld. The saleswomen cheered and, despite his sneezing, Jon held the purchase over his head like a trophy. He grinned and, without being told, reached for his credit card.

Out on the street, Jon struggled with most of the bags. "I'm exhausted," he said.

"Yeah, shopping can wear a person out," Tracie agreed, but she was exhilarated. And when they passed a car stopped at the light, an older blond woman lifted her sunglasses to give Jon a better once-over. "You're ready," Tracie said.

"Ready for what? A couple of anti-inflammatories and a day of bed rest?"

In the safety of Java, The Hut, Jon, in some of his new regalia, and Tracie were seated at their regular table, packages piled around them. Molly approached, but Jon was too tired to raise his head to say hello. He pulled his feet out of his new boots. They already hurt.

"What are you doing 'ere? And where's Jon?" Molly asked Tracie. For a moment, Jon thought he might have disappeared from fatigue. But Tracie smiled, as if she knew what was happening.

"That's for me to know and you to find out," she told Molly, doing another Encino imitation.

Molly handed a menu to Tracie and then handed one to Jon. When Jon reached up to take the menu, she stopped, squinted at him, and did a double take. "Bugger all! That is you, isn't it?" She looked at Tracie with renewed respect. "You go, girl! Brilliant!" Then she turned to Jon. "Stand up, Cinderella." Molly took his hand, pulled him into the aisle, and then walked around him slowly. "My God! You look bloody marvelous. And you 'ave trouble written all over you."

"I do?"

"Big-time! Where did you get that fab jacket? And the excellent jumper?" Molly asked.

Since he had no idea what a jumper was, he only shrugged. "Tracie helped me," he said.

"Bloody marvelous! I love everything but the glasses. You going to get 'im some Elvis Costello ones?" she asked Tracie and gave her a look of something close to respect. "I take it all back. You're not useless," she told Tracie. She looked back at Jon with concern. " 'e looks tired."

Tracie shook her head. "No. His eyes are too good. He's going to get contacts."

Jon felt as if he had really disappeared from the table. Is this what women meant when they said men "objectified" them? Jon wasn't sure if he disliked it, but it felt odd.

"Tracie, I can't wear those things." Jon took off his glasses and rubbed the bridge of his nose.

"Wow!" Both Molly and Tracie exclaimed simultaneously.

"Is it because 'e can't focus 'is eyes?" Molly asked Tracie. "Or is it 'is eyes themselves that 'it you?"

"I don't know, but it works for me," Tracie cooed. "You've got to give them up," she told him.

"I'll be hitting walls and doors if I can't wear my glasses," Jon whined.

"Great! Scars are a real turn-on," Tracie said as she stood up, stepped back, and looked at him from a different angle.

"Why not? Did you ever try?"

"Call me crazy, but I can't stand the idea of pushing tiny bits of glass into my eyes."

"Well, it's either contacts or flying blind, because you can't wear these," Tracie said, twirling the glasses in her fingers. "You look like a newborn puppy, blinking like that."

"On 'im, it looks good."

Embarrassed, Jon felt himself blush, and he took his glasses back. Then Molly noticed the motorcycle helmet on the table. Oh, don't go there, Molly, he thought.

"Did you get a motorbike, too, luv?" she asked, as breathless as an original Beatles fan at Shea Stadium.

"No. Tracie said I just have to carry the helmet as if I have a bike."

"It was my one cost concession," Tracie told Molly, unusually chatty with the waitress for a change. "Plus, he'd probably kill himself on it and ruin all my work."

"Thank you for that compassionate expression of concern for my welfare."

"Is 'e tattooed? Or pierced?" Molly inquired.

Tracie took a disappointed breath and sighed. Jon knew that sigh. She'd be trying to talk him into a Suzuki GS 1100 before the end of the week. "He drew the line." She looked at Jon. "You know, I never noticed how heavy your beard is."

"Probably because I usually shave twice a day."

"For real?" Molly asked, raising her brows. "That's a lot of testosterone, darling."

Tracie stared at him, thinking. "From now on, you also can't shave—except once every three days," she pronounced.

"Oh. The old George Michael thing," Molly said, nodding in approval. "It would work."

"But I wouldn't," Jon told them. "I can't show up at work like that—looking hungover."

"Why not? It would make women wonder about your private life," Molly said, leering.

"Yeah. And then you might get one," Tracie added.

Molly crossed her arms then and looked down at both of them. "So, what are you two fashion victims 'aving? I've never served you dinner, so I'm curious."

"I'll just have a beer," Tracie told her.

"I'll have a mochaccino."

Tracie made a face.

Molly went off to fetch the drinks. Tracie leaned across the table. "You do look really good, Jon. And you were so patient. You didn't yell once. As a reward"—she paused for effect—"I'll buy you the mochaccino. It may be your last."

"Promises, promises." Jon sighed. Now that it was over, it seemed as if the episode had had a certain kind of charm. He imagined Tracie and himself years into the future, talking it over: Remember that time we shopped till you dropped? Back in the days when people didn't do all their shopping on-line?

Tracie got up from the table. "More lessons as soon as I come back from the ladies' room. . . ." She was off, and Jon sighed in relief.

Molly returned with their drinks. She slipped into the empty seat opposite Jon and looked him over again. "Bloody amazing," she said. Then she took his hand. "But Jon, don't you think this might be going a little too far? It might be fun to play fancy dress just once, if you got invited to the Oscars or something. But changing your whole persona . . . well, on some level, it must be scary."

"Especially when I look in the mirror, or at next month's Master-Card bill," Jon agreed. "But I've seen five or six women look at me tonight. That's never happened before."

"I've never 'ad cirrhosis of the liver before, but that wouldn't mean 'aving it now would be a good thing, now would it, luv?" Molly responded. "I mean, so what if a girl looks at you now? It's not the real you, is it?" She paused. "On some level, this is a betrayal of your-self." She waited for another moment, silent, letting that sink in. Jon was too tired for this. He just sat there, rubbing one foot with the other under the table. She looked around the restaurant, as if that would explain what she wanted to say. "I don't want to throw a span-ner in the works, but 'ave you been to Freeway Park?" she asked.

Freeway Park was built on the roof of a highway. It was beautiful, with waterfalls and big lawns and terraces. "Sure," he said. "I watched them build it."

"Well, I can never rest there," Molly said. "No matter 'ow lovely and serene the fountains and the grass look, underneath it, there's insane traffic going in both directions. What I'm trying to say is, it doesn't matter if you pave over yourself with good sod." She plucked at his arm. "You're still you underneath these clothes. Think about what you Americans call your 'inner child.' Isn't 'e weeping?"

"I don't have an inner child, Molly. I have an inner dweeb, and he's doing the mambo because he thinks he just learned the magic words: 'Open sesame.' "

Molly shook her head. "I predict that at some point your inner dweeb is going to start fighting with this outer wild one," Molly warned. "Mark my words."

"What a world! A girl goes to the bathroom for two minutes and her so-called waitress becomes a psychiatric aide," Tracie cried. She stepped up to the booth and used her hip to evacuate Molly. "Trai-tor! I thought you were being too nice! Jon doesn't need any bad pop psychology advice from you."

"You're right. 'e's getting more than necessary from you."

Tracie ignored Molly. "You know, I was thinking. You need a new name. Jon is weak and Jonathan is lame."

"Oh. Perfect! Now it's not just 'is wardrobe and personality. Even 'is name needs changing," Molly said.

Tracie continued to ignore her. "Have you ever had a nickname?"

"My dad used to call me Jason sometimes, but I think that was because he forgot what my name really was," Jon admitted. "And my second stepmom called me 'the pest.' "

"It doesn't quite convey the sense of danger and sexual urgency I had in mind," Tracie told him. "How about Eric? I always thought that was a sexy name."

"Look, get real. I can't just have a totally new name," Jon protested.

Molly began to laugh. " 'ow about Big Swinging Dick?"

"I like it," Jon chimed in with excitement. "Or Big Swinging Richard, if I go formal."

"As long as it's not Little Richard, luv." Molly added. "Although I always 'eard 'e was *very* well equipped." Whether it was from fatigue or nerves or humor, Jon joined in Molly's laughter.

Tracie ignored the two of them. "There's got to be something . . ."

"Tracie, I'm not changing my name," Jon insisted.

"How about Jonny?" she asked. "Guys named Jonny are cool. Johnny Depp, Johnny Dangerously, Johnny Cash. They wear black and they're intense. They're heartbreakers."

"Yeah, like Johnny Carson," Molly agreed. "Or Johnny 'oliday, the French wanker."

He calmed down. "Well, I always wanted to be called 'Bud.' "

"Bud?" Molly asked. "Like on a tree? You can't be serious."

"No, like on a TV show. *Father Knows Best*. An old sixties thing," Tracie told Molly. "I wanted to be 'Princess.' "

"Now, that's perfect for you," Molly said sarcastically.

"Enough of that," Tracie said to Molly. "So, it's Jonny. And now that you're cutened up enough, I want you to go out on your own and start trolling for skank."

Chapter 13

A warren of a thousand tiny shops stacked on a Seattle hillside, the main fresh-food market of Seattle was a hive of produce sellers and their customers. But the market had become a lot more than that. Well-dressed Yuppies walked through, selecting endive or frisée for their dinner salads as they sipped their lattes from paper cups marked Counter Intelligence. It was incredible how espresso had become the craze of Seattle. Espresso drinkers had a language all their own—Milky Way, grande, skinny, extra foamy, half-caf. Jon always asked for a McD's spill, which meant the temperature should be as close to boiling as possible. Though he had been born and raised in Seattle, he still didn't know the names of most of the special coffee drinks.

Like most natives of any city, Jon didn't take advantage of what Seattle had to offer. He had never taken the Bremerton ferry, just across from Pike Place, still hadn't gotten to the EMP, never hung out in Gas Works Park, and he'd avoided the market, partly because when he was younger it was tougher and navy guys often hung there—a draw for hookers. What with work and the few dates he had, he hadn't been to Pike Place in years. When he wasn't working, Jon hung out at the Metropolitan Grill, which was the favored place for all Micro/Con employees. Here, though, there were Asian women dressed in Gucci, naval officers, a few hippie chicks wearing clothes they might have gotten from their mother's closets, an African-American who was wearing a turban and had a parrot walking across his shoulders, as well as the usual tourists. Jon's head was spinning.

But he was here to "troll for skank," as per Tracie's order. He stood in front of a baked-goods stand. Well, no time like the present. A blond woman, short and thin and dressed all in gray, stood outside. She looked like a nice person, so he tried to catch her eye. She avoided his glances, though, so he gave up. Blondes were cold, anyway, Jon decided.

Looking across the way, he spotted a tallish brunette in jeans and a green sweater. She also looked like good company—until she smiled. Jon wondered, for a moment, how much lipstick the average woman ate in a year. A tubeful? Two? What was in that stuff, anyway? Red dye number two? Did he eat it when he kissed a girl? (Not that he was in any danger of being poisoned lately.) Lipstick on the teeth, he decided, was a definite turnoff, but she did smile at him. He pushed himself forward and approached her. Now what? For a moment, he panicked. Why hadn't he prepared a line, a hello, a speech. God, he was standing there with his mouth open like a guppy. *Think, Jon, think.* "Do you know what time it is?" he finally managed to ask.

The brunette's smile faded. She looked him up and down. "No," she said, turned around, and walked away.

Embarrassed, Jon cowered next to the candle shop entrance behind him. God, I'm such a loser! Then he wandered over to a third woman, this one a little older and maybe a little less attractive. "Do you have the time?"

"For what?" the woman asked, then winked and waggled her eyebrows in the same bad Groucho Marx imitation that Tracie did. Jon froze for a moment, not expecting the response. Then, when he was idiotically silent, she shrugged and walked away.

On the other side of the marketplace, Tracie, Laura, and Phil wandered into the crowd around the seafood section. "This place is a caterer's dream!" Laura exclaimed.

"Yeah, but it's a tired musician's nightmare. It's a tourist trap. If you know any schmuck with a straight job, you'll meet him here on a weekend morning," Phil said.

"Pay no attention to him," Tracie told Laura. "Just look at this food. Maybe you'll set up business in Seattle instead of going back." She giggled. "Wait till you see the fish."

"Oh God. Not the fish," Phil moaned. "Next it'll be the fountain."

"What fountain?" Laura asked.

"The one at the Seattle Center. The water is choreographed to music," Tracie explained. Just to punish Phil, she added, "We'll go there after the Underground Tour but before the Experience Music Project."

"Oh, goody, goody, Mom," Laura said. "But what's so great about the fish? Good selection?"

"It's all in the delivery," Tracie told her, taking Laura by the arm and moving her toward the center of the seafood stands.

Laura looked up at a sign that read WATCH OUT FOR LOW-FLYING FISH. "They're kidding, right?" Laura asked. Just then, a screaming vendor whipped a flounder across to the cashier at the center of the stall. It almost whapped Laura in the head. "Oh my God!" she cried out.

"Okay, she's seen the fish. Can we go home now?" Phil asked. "Let's go back to bed." He yawned.

Tracie could see that Laura was embarrassed. Tracie could have kicked Phil.

"Hey, listen," Laura said. "I don't want to be in the way. I can just wander around by myself and you two can have the apartment to yourselves for the afternoon."

"Don't be silly. I love doing this. If I need privacy, I can go to Phil's."

"No you can't." Phil yawned again. "Bobby brought a band over. They've crashed at my place."

"That's not the point," Tracie said. "The point is, we're showing you Pike Market and we're thrilled to have you here." Tracie emphasized the plural and shot Phil a warning look.

"Oh, yeah," Laura said. "A thrill for Phil. Look, I'm going to take a look at that candle shop again. Some dork tried to pick me up there. Maybe I'll get lucky twice."

"Fine. We'll see you in a minute," Tracie replied as Phil pulled her in the opposite direction.

"That was really rude," Tracie told him angrily.

"What?" Phil asked. "Yawning?"

"Saying you wanted to go home." How could she explain that acting romantic in front of Laura was unkind? God, it might make Laura miss Peter.

"Hey, I worked late last night," he reminded her, as if she didn't know it.

"Yeah, but she's my friend. And it's my apartment."

He put his arm around her and lowered his voice. "And it's your bed, but let's both get into it." She felt a shiver down her back. Then, as if he felt her weakening, he leaned in and nuzzled her ear.

"Phil, I have to work this afternoon. I really have to come up with a couple of original ideas."

Phil put his hands on either side of her face. She loved it when he did that. "I have some original ideas."

"Not ones I can write about for the *Seattle Times*," she said, and laughed. She couldn't help it.

Leading her by her shoulders, he maneuvered her into a doorway next to a lobster tank. Just then, Tracie looked up and, through the lobsters, spotted a Micro/Con jacket. She peered through the glass. Jon. She'd forgotten that she'd told him to "troll" for a date. He looked lonely and glum. She pulled out of the doorway. Jon saw her and brightened, coming up beside her and Phil. "Hey, guys!"

"Hi there!" Tracie exclaimed.

"Hi!" Jon repeated. Phil didn't bother with a greeting.

"Didn't I tell you to forget this Micro/Con stuff?"

"The jacket, too?" Jon asked. "But I love my Micro jacket!"

"Jon, honey, you got to make them believe that *nothing* about you is Micro," Tracie said in her Mae West voice. "Anyway, what are you? A man or a billboard?" she asked.

"What difference does it make?" he asked her in return. "The new clothes are too confusing. I'm still not sure what goes with what. And I saw Samantha at work yesterday, but in spite of my new outfit, she blew me off."

"Don't worry," Tracie said in a voice she probably meant to reassure him with. "In two weeks, she'll be begging to be seen with you. You'll have to . . ." There was a pause, as if even she—his fan and guru—actually couldn't imagine the scenario herself. But she was a true friend. "You'll have to get a restraining order to keep her away," Tracie predicted.

"Yeah. Just call me Tommy Lee Delano," Jon joked.

Phil laughed. "As if you could land a babe like Pamela Anderson. Look, I'm gonna bum a cigarette." Without waiting for a response, Phil wandered down the aisle. Tracie allowed herself a tiny withheld sigh as she watched Phil's receding back. So, she noticed, did another woman.

"He's a pain in the ass, but doesn't he have a cute butt?" she asked Jon.

"I'm not an expert, but that redhead seems to think so."

Tracie glared at Jon, shrugged as if she didn't care, and stopped at the produce in front of her and, with exaggerated concern, began to select tomatoes carefully.

Jon watched Phil, who'd begun effortlessly talking to the redhead who'd been eyeing him. Jon wondered whether Phil's butt looked a lot better than his own or if it was something else that attracted women's attention.

"How do people do it? It's hard for me, but for some people it's so easy," he said, still watching Phil.

"I wonder the same thing. But Laura's been cooking since she was a kid." Jon realized he'd been talking about Phil but that she was talking about Laura. Love was blind. "It isn't just an instinct; it's a learned skill. Her dad taught her. And she's willing to teach me. You want a ripe tomato but a firm one." Jon watched as the redhead took a cigarette out of her mouth and handed it to Phil. He took it and put it to his own lips. The redhead looked like a ripe tomato all right. "It's got to be really red, too. Because you want it sweet."

Jon came back from his reverie. "I didn't know there was so much to a tomato. What are you making?" he asked, not that he was interested in that.

"Spaghetti sauce. Phil doesn't like to eat anything canned."

Oh God. Couldn't she get it? "Phil! Forget Phil. Tracie, you're such an idiot. You deserve someone . . . well, someone so much better." Jon raised his voice and called out to Phil, who was just leaving the redhead, apparently to come back to Tracie. "Do you know what the bass player got on his IQ test?" he asked.

"Uh-uh," Phil grunted.

"Drool," Jon replied, and looked at Tracie for a reaction. She giggled but then covered it by putting the bag of tomatoes in the basket. "What do you call a bass player with half a brain?"

"Gifted," Phil snapped. "I've already heard all of these from the band."

"You haven't heard this one. I just made it up. What's the difference between a bass player and a pig?" Tracie gave Jon a raised eyebrow, but he wouldn't stop. He turned to Phil. "A pig won't stay up all night trying to fuck a bass player." Then he glanced at Tracie. "Present company excluded," he said, as if that would make everything all right.

Phil flipped Jon the bird. "I'm getting those smokes," he said, and walked away.

"Okay," Tracie said, and watched him stride down the aisle. Then she turned to Jon. "Please. Don't antagonize him," she begged. She paused for a moment. "You know, I've been wanting to talk to you about an idea that Marcus shot down. But I'm actually thinking of writing it freelance and sending it around."

"That's great," he said. "Anything I can do to help? I'll proofread it, edit it, or—"

"That's not exactly what I was thinking about," Tracie said. "It's more like I wanted to put you in it."

"What? Another one of those profiles? I'm not interesting enough . . . unless the Parsifal project comes together. Then I'll be on the front page of every tech section in the country. Don't worry, I'll give the exclusive to you."

His morning wasn't going well. Jon believed in facing reality, no matter how unpleasant. So first he'd gotten blown off by three women, his jacket had been dissed, he'd had to watch a jerk succeed where he'd failed, and now he'd pissed his best friend off. As if that wasn't enough, there was a new embarrassment in the making.

Jon looked down the produce aisle in horror. There, coming at them with a full basket, was the brunette from the candle store, the one who had leered at him. Now she smiled with such a friendly smile that for a moment she was very pretty. Then he realized she wasn't focusing on him. She was smiling at *Tracie*. God! She was a lesbian! That would explain—

"Hey, congratulations. You traded Phil in for a new model?" she asked Tracie.

Jon looked from her to Tracie. Tracie was looking back at the brunette attentively, but she certainly didn't act surprised. They must know each other, he thought. The brunette gave him the once-over. "He looks familiar," she said. "I think you once tried to play Twenty Questions with me." She smiled at Jon. "Well, I guess Tracie gave you the right answers. Congratulations. She's a great girl. Did you have to kill Phil to get her? Or just give him a buck?"

"What are you talking about?" Tracie asked, but Jon had a nauseated feeling that he knew. "Do you think he's a—"

"I don't think anything," the brunette said smoothly. "I hardly think at all. You just look cute together. But are you mute?"

Jon was worse than mute. He was speechless, frozen in the kind of embarrassment he'd only experienced in that dream when you're naked on-stage and you've forgotten your lines. Because, with growing horror, Jon realized he'd tried to pick up Tracie's best friend.

"Laura, Jon. Jon, Laura," Tracie said over the grocery carts.

"The famous Jon," Laura cooed, almost laughing.

Tracie could swear that Jon blushed. God, he was impossible! He couldn't even meet a friend of hers without acting as if it was a big deal. Tracie tried to remember if Jon had been so retarded back in college. "The infamous Laura. You're the Sacramento cook, right?" Jon murmured, his face still red.

"Caterer," Tracie corrected. She didn't need these two not getting along.

"I seem to have interrupted something again," Laura said in the silence.

"We were just talking about Tracie's writing. How great it could be."

"Ha! *Could* is the operative word," Tracie said, sighing.

"You can't help it if your stories are cut till they bleed to death," Jon said defensively.

"Well, I could quit."

Tracie began to push her cart to the next aisle. Laura shot a grin at Phil as he rejoined them, with yet another bummed cigarette in his mouth. "You'd be a great columnist. Better than Anna Quindlen," Jon said.

"Who's Anna Quindlen? Do I know her?" Phil asked.

"Just a Pulitzer Prize–winning journalist," Laura said. "Now she's moved on to novels."

Phil shrugged. "I don't read commercial stuff," he said.

"Tracie, you really should write something independently, something you could be proud of," Jon continued, as if the Phil/Laura interruption had never happened. "Your dad would write you fan letters and all the kids from journalism school would send you résumés."

Tracie stared at him. No matter what, Jon always spoke up for her.

"Give it a rest!" Phil exclaimed. Tracie was dumbfounded by Phil's anger, but she didn't want to push his button. She knew that he was depressed over a rejection he had just gotten from some literary magazine. Of course, his work was so different from hers. It was dense and indirect. But it was best not to talk too much about her writing. It just antagonized him. He couldn't take it seriously, and she couldn't, either, because it was just commercial nonsense, after all.

"Laura, do you use white or Bermuda onions in your tomato sauce?" Tracie asked to change the subject.

"I prefer red."

Phil wandered off again. Tracie couldn't help but sigh out loud. She moved to the onions. Jon and Laura followed her in silence. Tracie tossed the onions into her basket and, with Laura, headed down another aisle. "Look, I've got to get a few things. I'll see you later," Jon said.

Tracie was surprised, because he usually stuck to her side like glue. Sometimes she actually had to whisper to him that he should go home so she could spend some time alone with Phil.

"Well, see you," Jon said. "Nice to meet you, Laura."

"Same here," Laura called back over her shoulder. "Let me know what time it is sometime."

"If you see Phil, tell him I'm ready to go," Tracie called out to Jon's back. She watched him walk away, and Laura watched, as well.

"So that's Jon," she said. "I think he's kinda cute, in an R2D2 kind of way."

"Jon? Cute? Yeah, I guess he is," Tracie agreed. "But is he cute enough to get himself a date?"

"Well, he acts like a dork. How much work have you already done on him?"

"I've just made a start," Tracie admitted.

"Why doesn't he have more confidence?" Laura asked. "He's smart and he's got nice shoulders."

"He's too smart," Tracie said. "You know, in that too-smart-to-be-good-for-you kind of way. He didn't have a father," Tracie said. "I think that really screws guys up, being raised by their moms."

Laura looked over at her and raised her eyebrows. "As much as being raised by their dads screws up girls?" she asked Tracie.

Tracie waggled her head the way they used to do back in high school. "Okay. Point taken," she said. "I shouldn't generalize, but you get the drift."

"Oh yeah, I get the drift. But do you?"

Tracie shrugged. "What?" she asked.

Laura laughed, then shook her head. "You are a mystery unto yourself," she told her best friend.

Chapter 14

Tracie sat across the table from Jon, observing him the way an artist might stare at a blank canvas. Well, she thought, it would actually be easier if he were a blank canvas. His clothes were a lot better—a black Armani T-shirt, the vintage leather jacket, and a pair of Levis 501s—but it wasn't coming together. His dorky haircut, his glasses, even his posture still spelled doofus. She knew what he would order, the way he'd eat it. It definitely wasn't sexy. Maybe Phil is right, she thought. I'll never win the bet, let alone get a feature out of this project.

Well, she'd never been afraid of a challenge. It hadn't been easy to get into the master's program or to talk her way into a job at the *Seattle Times*. It wasn't going to be easy to do this, either. Tracie sighed. "Okay," she told Jon. "People dating go out to restaurants a lot, so you have to be prepared."

"How?" he asked. "I've got my AmEx Card."

"No, no. I mean prepared to be . . . appropriate. Women notice everything. You've got to be careful of what you eat." She wrote a note to that effect on a Post-it pad.

"What I eat?" Jon echoed. "What do you mean?"

Tracie sighed once more, then began in earnest. "You're never ordering poached eggs or a Cobb salad again. Poached eggs are *not* sexy."

"Look, the truth is I don't even *like* poached eggs," Jon admitted. "I just love it when Molly yells, 'Adam and Eve on a raft.' It sounds so romantic."

"Only to you," Tracie told him. "Poached eggs are for invalids or babies, not for men."

Jon stared up at the ceiling, as if someone would have written permission for poaching across it. Exasperated, he asked, "Well, what's wrong with Cobb salad? I don't even eat the chicken. And I *like* Cobb salad."

"But you'd like getting a second date better," Tracie murmured, leaning across the table.

He had to agree. "No argument there."

Tracie smiled. The guy was highly motivated, as well as respectful. Maybe with a strong dose of both the stick of her disapproval and the carrot of sex, she'd stop him from being such a donkey. "Okay, here's what you have to understand: What women *see* you eat is important, especially when they're first sizing you up." She leaned back against the banquette. "Eating is like sex: You want to give the impression of both strength and restraint. Spontaneity, but with some health awareness." Jon was staring at her; that all sounded good, but confusing. Tracie paused. She was as impressed with herself as Jon was. She jotted most of it down on another Post-it. Then she remembered who she was dealing with and looked up, a horrified look on her face. "And for God's sake, don't tell them you're a vegan."

"I'm *not* a vegan," Jon whined. "I've told you. Vegans don't eat dairy or eggs. I'm a *vegetarian*."

Tracie rolled her eyes. "Whatever. Just don't tell them." Then, knowing him as well as she did, she continued. "And don't point out the difference. Remember, you're not an educator; you're a sex machine." She nodded to herself and wrote, "Educator—No. Sex machine—Yes" on yet another Post-it.

"So what exactly does a sex machine order to eat?" Jon asked. "Raw meat?"

From the corner of her eye, Molly, who up until then had been sitting over at her own dinner at a table in the back, stood up, noticed them, and came their way. Tracie braced herself for the usual hostility. "Bloody 'ell," Molly said, raising her brows almost to her hairline. "You rock my world." Then, and Tracie knew she did it just to annoy her, Molly bent over and gave Jon a kiss on the lips. He smiled up at her. When he smiled, Tracie had to admit he was kind of cute, even with the dumb glasses.

Well, it was easier to join her than to lick her. "Molly, could you help out here?" Tracie asked. "Pretend you're a waitress."

"Sure, luv. If you'll stop pretending to tip." Molly stood up even taller, straightened her shoulders, and pushed out her sizable chest. In a tiny voice, she said, "My name is Molly. I'll be your waitperson this evening. Our specials are vegetable lasagna and veal Parmesan and our water is tap. Can I get you a beverage to start?"

Jon laughed. That irritated Tracie. After all, she was taking this on as a serious project. And why did Molly always flirt with Jon? And why did he seem to enjoy it so much? She was way too old and— men! Tracie just dismissed the whole unworthy thing. "I'll have a mochaccino, please," Jon said.

Tracie gave him a thumbs-down. "No. From now on, you drink only beer, bourbon, or coffee—black."

Molly's brows went up again.

"I hate black coffee!" Jon protested.

"Not as much as you hate being dateless," Tracie reminded him.

"Check and mate," Jon agreed, and he turned to look up at Molly, shrugged, and made a face. "I'll have a beer."

"Can we see your ID?" Molly asked, to Tracie's horror. Jon actually began to reach for his wallet when Molly added, "Just joking!"

Tracie felt ready to cry. Or laugh. Jon getting carded on a date, oh God! She looked at him. You know, it's possible. She sighed. "I'll have one, too. Need *my* ID?" she asked Molly.

"Dream on, darling. So would these be pretend beers or real ones?"

"I'll spring for real," Jon told her.

"As you like it," Molly said, and moved off toward the bar, to Tracie's relief. But she kept eyeing the menu.

"Now, on to menu etiquette," Tracie began. "You're at the table, looking over the menu." She demonstrated. "*She* orders veal Parmesan. What do *you* do?"

"Tell her how they actually raise veal?"

"No! None of your political rants," Tracie warned.

"Okay. Okay. That was a pop quiz, right? I failed," Jon admitted. "Let me try again." He paused, thought it over, and started by lowering his voice to a basso profundo. "I say, 'Sounds good. I'll have that, too.' "

Tracie looked at him, clearly frustrated. She shook her head. "No, you don't. You look at her hard, raise your eyebrows, and say, 'Geez, are you really going to get *that*? Isn't that a little . . . rich for you?' "

Jon stared at her blankly for a moment, as if waiting for a bell to ring. "Why would I say that?" he asked.

"To set the tone. To put her at the disadvantage. To tell her you've already thought of her thighs. To make her begin to think her thighs might not be good enough for you."

"All that happens when I say veal is 'rich'?" Jon asked, his voice almost a squeak.

"Sure," Tracie told him. "Women—all women in *this* country anyway—think they're too fat. Every mouthful they take is accompanied by guilt. Use it."

Molly arrived with two beers and two empty plates. "I've been listening to you two. Let me try to get this straight. Right now, I'm a real waitress bringing real beers, but I'm also pretending to be a waitress and I'm bringing pretend food, but not veal Parmesan." Molly put two empty plates in front of them. She looked at Tracie. "Kafka didn't 'ave a patch on you."

"Ignore her," Tracie commanded. "Now, what do you say to the waitress?"

Jon hesitated. "Nothing. You just told me to ignore her."

"I meant ignore *Molly*," Tracie said, totally frustrated. She wished Molly would stop with those flying eyebrows and go away. "This is what you do with the pretend waitress: You say, 'Wait a minute. Stand right there.' Then you say to your date, 'Doesn't she have the most beautiful eyes you've ever seen?'"

"It's 'igh time you noticed them," Molly agreed.

Jon stared at Tracie as if she'd just told him to go down on a duck or something. "Wait a minute. You're telling me to compliment my date's eyes to the waitress?"

Impatiently, Tracie shook her head. "No. No! I'm telling you to compliment the *waitress's* eyes to your *date*. This will either really irritate the shit out of her or fascinate her. Or both." She paused in her tutelage and thought about it for a moment. "Anyway, women often can't tell the difference between the two."

"I can," Molly volunteered.

Tracie slapped her forehead. "Okay. Molly can. But you're not dating Molly." Tracie wished Molly would go away once and for all. She wasn't as self-conscious about her advice when she was alone with Jon. But in front of Molly, it seemed absurd. "So," she continued, "I'm talking about normal women. Now we're going to cover the fine art of complimenting." Tracie stopped for a moment to jot "Compliments" on her Post-it.

"Why can't *I* take notes on this?" Jon whined.

"Because only hosers take notes," Tracie snapped. She ought to tell him about her idea for a feature, but . . . well, maybe later.

"But you're—"

"Look, just concentrate."

"But there's so much."

Tracie had to agree with that. *Oh, I'll never win this bet*, she thought. "Okay, to begin, it's actually easier for us to cover what you *don't* say. So, for a starter, never tell a girl *she* has pretty eyes."

"Why?" Molly asked, and, to Tracie's dismay, she sat down in a booth behind them, preparing to stay.

"*Everyone* tells girls they have pretty eyes," Tracie told Jon. "Who doesn't have pretty eyes? Calves have pretty eyes."

"Yeah, well you don't think about that when you eat veal, do you?" Jon demanded.

"Would you give the veal a rest?" Tracie fumed. "The point is, pick out something small, a tiny detail. *That's* what gets them."

Jon thought for a moment or two. She watched him, holding her breath, hoping for a good one. But his face remained confused. "Like what?" he finally asked.

Tracie exhaled with exasperation. "Be creative. You do it all day at work. It's what you're good at."

"Yeah," Molly interjected. "And didn't you take Creative Complimenting at university?"

Thank goodness Jon ignored Molly and focused on Tracie. She stared right back into his eyes, which were actually a really pretty light brown—and his lashes were *so* long. Tracie wondered, not for the first time, why long lashes were so often wasted on men. Her boyfriend in high school had had lashes just like Jon's. The first time they necked, he had given her butterfly kisses all over her face with them. Funny. She hadn't thought of Gregg or that in years. He'd been so sweet, not at all like Phil.

"Just help me with this a little. Nudge me in a direction," Jon was saying. "Like, should I say, 'Mighty nice pair of incisors you've got there'?"

"And they'll bite the 'and that feeds them, luv," Molly warned.

"That's the general idea, but . . . I don't know." She sighed. "Look, you have to develop a feeling for it. Pick out a single feature. Her eyebrows, her cuticles."

"Cuticles? What's up with that?" he asked.

He watched as Tracie got a kind of dreamy look on her face. "This guy back in high school—my boyfriend Gregg—once told me I had beautiful cuticles. I had no idea what he was talking about. But that he noticed was so . . . so *attentive*." She sort of shook her head, then looked at Jon. "It was hot."

Molly extended her own hands, examined them, and then looked at Tracie's. "You know, I 'ate to admit it," Molly said, "but you *do* 'ave beautiful cuticles." She looked at Jon. "She's good," she admitted. "Sick as a parrot, but good."

Tracie smiled. "That's it. It's time for video."

"At this hour? Tracie, I can't watch movies. I've got a world of work to do."

"It's part of your training," Tracie told him. And she was up and out, leaving him to pay the bill and to follow once again.

Chapter 15

After midnight, the Seattle night was soft. The air felt heavy with moisture, as it so often did, but the mild temperature left it Skin-So-Soft. It was the time of night where you either gave in to fatigue or got a second wind and went out to party. But work loomed. "Come on," she said, and quickened her pace.

"Come on, you," Jon said. In the light that spilled out from the big windows of Java, The Hut, he already looked much improved. She couldn't help but be proud of her handiwork. If you believed the Bible literally, it had taken God six days to make the world. He must have been a man, because look at what a single woman could remake in just a few evening hours: Jon stood, his feet widely spread on the damp pavement, his arms thrust down and out from his body. He might still have the posture of a dork, but not the look of one. Tracie knew Jon was five eleven—and probably the only man in America who was five eleven and didn't cheat and say six feet—but now he looked tall. Her decision on the clothes had made him all vertical lines. His jeans, his chest-hugging T-shirt, the length of his jacket—all moved your eye up as if he were a long dark column. The only horizontal was the line of his shoulders. Thank God he had shoulders. And the jacket's subtle padding gave him a little more shoulder than what he had.

Too bad about the head. Not that he was ugly, but the haircut, the glasses, even the way he sort of hunched his head forward, as if he wanted his face to get somewhere before the rest of his body, spoiled her work. He needed swoopy hair as well as the pants thing. Well, Rome wasn't built in a day, she told herself, giving God a little more credit and herself a little more time. Jon, of course, didn't have a clue that she was admiring him. She'd have to change that about him, too. The man seemed to have no radar receptors at all. What did he think she was doing while she stood on the damp sidewalk staring at him? Meditating? Mentally reviewing a recipe for quiche?

"Come on, you," he repeated. "I'm going home."

"No, no," Tracie said, slightly raising her voice. "Just one more thing."

Jon shook his head. "Tracie, I appreciate all your efforts and I'm really grateful, but I just don't think I can take one more bit of criticism tonight," he told her.

She had to laugh. "Don't worry. We're just going to take a walk, and I'm going to give you your homework assignment."

"More homework?" Jon asked, his voice almost breaking. "Tracie, I left work before seven. I don't think I've done that since I joined Micro/Con. That's considered a half day there. Plus, I usually work for a couple of hours at home. Which I obviously haven't done, but it's waiting for me. A few days ago, in the kindest possible way, you and every salesgirl in the greater Seattle area laughed at my shoes, my hair, my eyeglasses, and my underwear. I spent more money in three hours than I've spent in the last three years, and that *includes* when I bought my condo. And now . . ." There was a quiver in his voice that Tracie couldn't quite figure. Either it was real fatigue, real pique, or a really good put-on. "And now you tell me there's going to be homework?"

Instead of answering him, Tracie began walking down the sidewalk. She figured that before she got to the corner, he'd join up with her, and, sure as death and taxes, he was there—unlike Phil, who was always looking for any opportunity to cut and run, and who probably wouldn't even be home when she called him. In fact, she reflected as Jon somewhat sulkily matched her stride, Phil could absolutely be counted on not to be counted on.

All at once, she was flooded with affection for Jon and his dependability, his doglike devotion. She took his leather-clad arm, squeezed it, and they walked in silence for a few moments. "Are you taking me to be pierced?" he asked in a very small voice. "Please say no."

Tracie laughed and turned them toward the doorway of Downtown Video. "Here we are," she said. "This won't hurt a bit."

"Yeah. When I was a kid, that's what my dentist used to say just before he hit the soft, pulpy nerve. Speaking of which, why are we going in here? Did you just realize Phil can't live without yet another viewing of *Pulp Fiction*?"

"Yeah. I want to freeze-frame poor Marvin's brain splat, like before The Bonnie Situation, the way your nerdy pals do." She disdainfully walked past the usual browsers gathered around the new releases.

Jon, newly energized, caught up with her in front of the suspense section. "Hey, that's not fair. *My* nerds have just gotten into *My Dinner with Andre*. Victor is trying to create a *My Dinner with Andre* video game."

Tracie laughed again and headed to the classics. Downtown Video was no Blockbuster: Here, the classics did not include *Rocky* or even the original *Die Hard*. The collection was as quirky as Mr. Bill, the legend who owned the place. Occasionally, he refused to rent videos to the undeserving. He also prescribed them like medicine, or—in extreme cases—performed interventions. "These are good movies but bad life lessons," he'd said once. "In the book, Holly ends up in the middle of Africa. And the George Peppard character is gay." He'd made her read the novel, and told her she could take out the video only once a year. He also cut her off from her favorite—*Love with the*

Proper Stranger. "She should have had the abortion," he'd said. "Anyway, the Steve McQueen character will abandon her in about eight months and she'll have to raise the kid alone." "How do you know?" she'd asked, angry. "Because I was the Steve McQueen character," Mr. Bill had said more angrily than Tracie was ready for. "Look at me now. A lonely fuck without a family, a son I never met, and a video store." She'd never rented the movie again.

"Tracie, if you rent *GQ's Guide to Debonair Sophisticates,* I'm going to shoot myself right here," Jon said.

"You'd need a gun to do that," she reminded him, then swiftly selected three videos and marched over to the counter. Jon followed her. She reached for his video card. This might be a *long* rental. He handed it to her as meekly as he had handed over his other charges and she passed it on to the clerk.

Mr. Bill, busy with restocking, looked up. "Oh. Someone is having a James Dean retrospective," he said. He looked over at Tracie and Jon. "And it looks like Natalie and James themselves." Tracie smiled. It wasn't a bad thing to be compared to Natalie Wood. Mr. Bill then opened the boxes suspiciously.

"Don't worry," she told him. "*Love with the Proper Stranger* is still on the shelf."

"You're not doing *Out of Africa* again, are you?" Mr. Bill asked sternly. He shook his head and looked over at Jon. "Looks like you found Mr. Trouble anyway," he said disapprovingly.

Tracie looked over at Jon and then couldn't restrain the widest of smiles. What success! Mr. Bill—aging bad boy, font of all wisdom, the purveyor of movies, truths, and practical cosmologies—actually thought that Jon was a troublemaker! "Don't worry about a thing," she said to Mr. Bill as she picked up the bag and led Jon out by the arm.

She was really pleased with her work so far. As they walked back toward Tracie's car and Jon's bicycle, she swung the bag full of the videos. "What was all that about?" Jon asked her.

"Not important," she said, suddenly stopping to survey him. "Okay, stand against that light pole and lean on the bench. Let me take a picture." She pulled out her little camera and peered through the lens. Wow! This would be great in the paper. Was she crazy to think of it as a book cover? "You look pretty good," she told him.

"I do?"

Tracie didn't respond. All of this would be great material for the article. She'd have to remember to jot it all down. "Okay," she said. "Look like you have attitude."

"Any specific attitude?" he asked. "Or is arrogant condescension the entire library?"

"Give it your best shot," she said. Jon posed, his foot up on the bench. Tracie snapped a picture. Just to be safe, she took another. Seen through the viewfinder, he looked even better. You couldn't observe the uncertainty in his eyes, or the irony he wore the clothes with. But, she reminded herself, this project wasn't all for her. He had to figure out how to get himself a girl. All he needed was a little confidence. She threw the camera into her purse and moved closer to him. "Now we're going to practice the look." Tracie indicated the seat. Jon took it and she sat beside him. She stared into his face. "Now, *you* have nice eyes."

"Really? You never told me that."

"Well, you do," she assured him. "But you've got to use them." She waited for a minute, trying to think how to tell him in a way that wouldn't embarrass her but would be effective. "You have to learn how to make them smolder. Remember Al Pacino?"

"I always confuse him and De Niro," Jon admitted. "Look, growing up, my mom and I would watch stuff like *Steel Magnolias*. I missed a lot of the mob films." He paused. "Was Pacino Sonny or the young Don?"

"He was Michael, who had to kill Fredo. God! You are weird. *All* guys know that!" She sighed. "Roger used to watch *The Godfather* every night before he went to sleep. It's kind of a guy's bedtime story." She thought of those nights with Roger while she lay beside him, lonely because he was more involved with the Corleones than he would ever be with her. "Anyway, remember how Pacino used to stare at the Sicilian girl?" Jon probably didn't, but she figured he was afraid to admit it. "You have to look at me, or *any* woman you want, with a single stare that conveys your entire proposal."

"Didn't we already practice that?"

"Yeah, this may be the most important thing you'll learn. So . . ."

"What do you mean? Right here? Right now?"

"Right here, right now. On a greater Seattle transit bench. Just focus and look at me."

Jon stared up at the streetlight. She followed his glance and watched the mist that wavered across its luminous surface, creating a watermark in the very air. I might get old here, she reflected, but I'll never wrinkle. Jon continued staring at the misty light. "I'm asking you to direct this staring at me," she finally reminded him.

"I can't," he told her.

Tracie sighed and handed him the bag. "That's why we rented these James Dean tapes. *Giant, East of Eden, Rebel Without a Cause.* Watch the Ferris wheel scene in *Eden* carefully. Watch his hands. And the way he looks at Natalie Wood in *Rebel.*"

"Tracie, these movies are forty years old!" Jon opened the bag and examined the tapes as if there might be mold on them.

"Yeah, but sex never goes out of style. He was the first great bad boy," she explained. "Meanwhile, just try to hit me with your best shot."

Jon sighed deeply, turned his upper body toward her, and put his brows together. He looked a lot like Superman trying to melt rock with his X-ray vision. She laughed and, immediately offended, he got up. "Come on, Tracie. I can't look at *you* like that."

"I'm sorry. I'm sorry," she apologized. "But I want you to be able to look at hairy bus drivers like that."

Jon tried again and failed again, though this time, they both laughed. "Well, that looked like it might lead to a bodily function," she said. "Though not one I'd want to witness," she added.

"You're disgusting," he said. Then he set his shoulders and tried again. This time, his eyes cleared and the uncertainty was gone. They were dark pools, and the color deepened to the shade of melted chocolate.

"Not bad. But more focus. Project that heat. Look at me as if you've *really* wanted me for years."

Jon figured that wouldn't be hard. He shot her a look that could melt steel from twenty yards. Tracie opened her own eyes wide and felt suddenly uncomfortable. "Uh," she said. "Uh-huh. That's . . . that's pretty good. Uh, maybe that's enough for one night."

Slightly dazed, Tracie stood up. Jon mussed her hair. "Come on, Professor. I'll walk you to your car. But what's my next step?"

"It's time to test the waters," she said. "You couldn't do it at Pike Place Market, so I'll have to find you a date."

Chapter 16

Jon hit the eject button on the VCR and the cassette jumped out of its slot like a Pop-Tart from the toaster. He'd watched *East of Eden* four times. The images of the sensitive, lonely Cal—played by James Dean—didn't strike him as sexy. The guy seemed like a typical bruised loser, not the kind of man women went for. The girl, Aber, going with Cal's brother, played by Julie Harris, didn't seem to go for Cal, either. Why should she? He was neurotic and moody. It seemed to Jon that it was pity that kept drawing her to him. The way he kept going to his father for approval—that whole frozen lettuce episode. Yikes. Why couldn't he accept that his dad was a useless, demented waste? No biggie. Jon's own father was a waste in most ways. And he wasn't even Raymond Massey.

Jon pulled the sweater over his head, shrugged himself into the weird used jacket Tracie had made him buy, and then stood in front of the mirror. It was easy to see himself, because all the clothes that used to hang in the closet, obscuring the mirror, were just about gone.

He had to admit it was a very different Jon who looked out at him. Maybe that's why he was no good at hunting down women. It was hard for him to think about them as scores or one-night stands. Yet, inevitably, some of them would be if he didn't like them enough to be with them permanently. That's where it all got so confusing. He hated rejection. But he'd hate rejecting a woman more. He thought of his mother, and all the women Chuck had rejected. God knew how many, since all Jon knew were the ones he'd actually married.

But Tracie was going to change all that. He was going to out-Phil the Phils and finally use his head to figure out a way to do it. He had followed Tracie's directions—the really tough ones. He hadn't shaved, and his feet, slipped into boots, were killing him now. He was sure he would get blisters the size of kiwis, and probably just as green. Actually, he'd once read about a guy who died from infected blisters. If it happened to him, he hoped it would be after he got to make love with a woman or at least sleep with her. Tracie would feel very, very bad at his funeral. He had to admit that he looked good, but he sure didn't look like himself. He looked like some guy sneering at him. He sneered back, but that just made his reflection worse. Jesus, what am I doing? Next I'll pull a Travis Bickle and ask if I'm talking to myself, he thought.

Jon shook his head. He definitely didn't look like a chocolate Lab anymore. Maybe a weasel or some kind of dark fox. Well, he guessed that was the point. He took out his Samsonite with the broken handle and the wheelies. He was about to open it, when Tracie's tutelage paid off. He could see her perfectly adorable, slightly crooked nose crinkling in disdain. He could almost hear her say, "Wheelies are *definitely* a pucker."

For a moment, Jon wondered what kind of suitcase James Dean would have. But he couldn't remember the guy carrying anything but Sal Mineo in any of the movies. Maybe cool guys didn't take luggage. They traveled light. He sighed. All of this was so complicated.

But now, for his plan to work, he had to have some luggage. After scouring his place for a quarter of an hour, he settled for an old black duffel bag he'd used for laundry back in college. He threw a few pairs of running shoes into it for heft, filling out most of the rest with crumpled *Seattle Times* sheets—being careful to save all the pages with Tracie's features. As he zipped the bag, he hoped this was worth all the trouble. Not that he had much hope.

But despite his usual pessimism, Jon had to acknowledge *something* was undeniably happening. Maybe it was the new clothes. Maybe it was something in his attitude that Tracie's not-so-tender ministrations had changed. Whatever, it was clear that women were definitely behaving differently around him. At work, secretaries, analysts, and even a few of the female executives had started to greet him whenever he walked past them. Even Samantha had volunteered a hello. He was sure that never used to happen, except for a few he was actually friends with. And it wasn't just that. There was something about the way they said hello—something in their voices. It wasn't a come-on, exactly. But Jon was amazed that two simple letters combined, like *h* and *i*, were so musical.

The weirdest thing wasn't that women were noticing him. He guessed that was the point of this whole exercise. The weirdest thing was how he felt about it. Like in the grieving process, there seemed to be multiple phases, three of which he'd already gone through: denial, delight, and pain. Because while at first it had just surprised him, then tickled him, it now hurt his feelings. It had taken him a little while to figure that out. Of course, he knew he should be grateful for even the slightest notice. And he had been. But then some kind of shift had taken place and he had moved from delight at the attention to hurt feelings when even Cindy Biraling, the adorable blond secretary to the CFO, began to greet him (she was notorious for ignoring people, even when they stood with the front of their thighs touching her desk). Over the years, whenever he'd had to drop by or call Cindy, she'd asked not only for his extension but how to spell his name—a sure indication that she hadn't had a clue to what it was. Now she sang out, "Hi, Jonathan." It had started to make him mad. Why hadn't she said hello before? And how come she knew his name now?

But whatever new magic—and the mood that accompanied it—existed, it didn't extend far enough to grant him a date with Cindy—or anyone else at work. He still seemed to be as tongue-tied and moronic as ever with all of the women. Tracie had said that he needed to try himself out in another environment, where no one knew him, but he just couldn't face going into a bar. He'd tried for two nights and couldn't get himself to walk through the doors. All the humiliations of past look-sees and sitting on bar stools, all the past women's put-downs seemed to stand like the angel at the entrance to Eden, barring the way.

And it wasn't just walking into the bar. Somehow, the new attention from women at work had made him feel all his past social-life traumas more acutely. Facing a strange woman that, in Molly's terminology, he was going to try to "chat up" stopped him cold. It wasn't just that the prospect was daunting. He could have done it if it weren't for the Phils, always sitting easily at the bars, seeming to watch his fumbling technique, disdaining his pathetic openers and his feeble attempts at humor. It was as if the Phils of the world could see past his new black sweater and the 501s and the boots he was wearing.

And so he was left with figurative and literal cold feet. Jon had decided that he was going to have to find somewhere to meet women where he wasn't known and he wasn't up against the competition of a bunch of Phils.

Hence the duffel bag.

Jon picked it up. The newspapers partially filled it out, but it was still so light, he'd look strong being able to lift it effortlessly. He shrugged, wished himself good luck, and put on the Tracie-selected lambskin leather jacket. He sighed and tried not to feel guilty. The lambs had already been led off to their slaughter, and now he would probably follow them to his own. It's what he deserved for letting Tracie talk him into the jacket in the first place. His feet were freezing! And it would be drafty at the airport. He wished he could put on a pair of thick gray wool socks, but if God was in the details, his toes would have to freeze.

The buzzer sounded, indicating the taxi was waiting. He grabbed a Huey, Louie, and Dewey Pez dispenser for good luck, picked up the duffel bag, locked the apartment behind him, and rapped down the stairs to the dark street below.

The airport wasn't too crowded, which Jon figured was a good thing. And no one accosted him; plus, today there were no chanting Krishnas. He took those as good signs and immediately rode the escalator down to the baggage claim. He checked out the arriving flights, though he'd already targeted his. Of course, instead of the gambit, he could get an actual ticket and just choose to stand in line behind a pretty woman and chat her up. But he figured people were often nervous before flights. He really would be better off trying to get someone who was getting off a flight. But this was not without risks.

To be less conspicuous, he'd asked the driver to drop him off at the arrivals area, but the driver had said, "No can do. You got to check in and go through security upstairs." Jon considered explaining his mission, then changed his mind. From what he could see from the back of the haircut and the part of the driver's face reflected in the rearview mirror, the guy wasn't quite a Phil, but he could have been a Phil at an earlier time, before he lost a few of those teeth. Jon wasn't telling him anything.

So, walking across the wide baggage claim area, he surreptitiously eyed the group of passengers who'd just arrived on Flight 611 from Tacoma. Tacoma was nice. His uncle and aunt lived there. If a woman had been to Tacoma for business or even to visit her family, he figured she might be very pleasant. Of course, if she lived in Tacoma with her husband and was here to visit her mother, this was not a good thing. He began to scan the crowd. How could you tell? The DC10 held about 280 people. He told himself that at least one had to be female, attractive, and single. But how to tell she was available was another problem. He noticed a blonde, but she was a little too thin, too tall, and too pretty. There was something about the way she swung her head that made her hair move like ten thousand silky strings, and it gave him the feeling she was doing it to be looked at. She was probably considering a move to L.A. Way upmarket for him.

Next, he spotted a redhead with curly hair that seemed so alive, it looked professionally snarled. For all he knew, maybe it was. People probably paid to have that done. Anyway, the woman was cute, and that was enough. Okay. Here I go, he told himself. Instead of throwing his hat into the ring, he threw his bag on the carousel, walked around it as casually as he could, and tried to think of something to say to a total stranger.

It was only when he got right up to her side and saw her in three-quarter view that he realized she was very, very pregnant. Clearly, someone else had thought she was adorable, too. Well, there goes that plan.

With the blonde as too much of a stretch and the redhead about to drop a baby . . . Well, there wasn't a lot left. He eyed the crowd. The usual grandmothers with a toy under their arms didn't excite him, and the harried mothers with children in tow—children wild from the confines of the flight—were also a real stretch. It looked like everyone else was male, except for the person who was far taller than he, wearing silk pajama trousers and a Brooks Brothers–type oxford cloth shirt. It might have been a man or it might have been a woman. Or perhaps someone in the process of changing from one to the other. But since Jon had never had the faintest desire to reenact the famous *Crying Game* scene, he figured he had enough issues of his own to deal with and began to despair.

It was then, as his eyes moved away from the baggage carousel, that he began to fold, the state that for him preceded a complete rout. Then he noticed the young woman standing at the next carousel. He caught his breath. Maybe he wouldn't leave in defeat. A shaft of sunlight—rare in gray Seattle—illuminated her as if she were part of a medieval manuscript. She was perfect. In fact, she reminded him of someone. It wasn't the fine light brown hair cut just below the ears or her profile, which he could see was deserving of the very best cameo maker. It was something in the set of her shoulders and the way she stood that immediately attracted him. Tracie would stand just like that if she was waiting for her luggage. His heart leapt but then fell.

Because the woman—she might have been a year or two older than he, but not more than that—was obviously arriving on the flight from San Francisco. That was a whole different kettle of passenger. If she was *from* San Francisco and just here for a visit, she was probably going to be way too cool for him. If, on the other hand, she was from Seattle and had only *visited* San Francisco for a vacation, there might be a chance. However, if she lived in Seattle now but had originally been raised in San Francisco and had been visiting her family, she would . . .

Jon forced himself to stop the madness. It only proved there was bound to be some way or other that he could think himself out of doing what he feared most. He looked at the woman again. She was lovely. A Lovely Girl. "This is it," he murmured aloud. "Go for it."

He tried to slouch the way James Dean might and, unemcumbered by any packages and without a fanny pack, he stealthily moved toward The Lovely Girl. Completely unaware of him, she was standing with her weight all on her left hip. With her right foot, she was tapping a small tattoo. It wasn't an impatient tap exactly. It was more of a stretching exercise that she was executing with her adorable foot. In fact, as he looked more closely, he realized that all of her was adorable, from the peripatetic toes to the top of her head. Jon simultaneously felt a lustful pull in his loins and a lurch of fear in his stomach. This is dangerous physical work, he told himself, and, before he broke a sweat and ruined the Armani T-shirt Tracie had made him buy, he placed himself directly behind The Lovely Girl. Using all his willpower, he forced himself not to look at her but to stare blankly at the empty conveyor belt, just the way everyone else was.

He tried to count slowly to one hundred, but he only got to sixty-seven. After all, what if her bag came now? He cleared his throat. "Is

• • • • • • • • • • •

it just my misperception, or does it take longer to get your luggage than to fly from San Francisco to Seattle?" he asked aloud. Okay, it wasn't a great opening, but at least he hadn't asked for the time. The Lovely Girl turned her head and he had a look at her profile. Her nose was long and slightly irregular, which, in his opinion, made her cuter. Her skin was luminously pale. This close, Jon could see very fine freckles strewn just across her cheekbones and over the bridge of her aquiline nose. There was something very tender about the tiny constellation. Meanwhile, she looked in his direction for a moment. Then she smiled.

"It does seem to take a long time," she said.

Her voice was water splashing over stones, champagne flutes clinking. Jon allowed himself another brief look at her and then tore his eyes away, remembering not to smile. He shifted his body, pulling in his stomach, thrusting out his pelvis, and crossing his arms over his chest. But then he didn't have a clue what to do or say next. The James Dean pose was a start, but The Lovely Girl had looked at him, was looking at him, with an expectant—or perhaps tolerant—half smile and was clearly becoming restive with the wait.

What came next? He could offer her a ride into town. If only he had a motorcycle. He sighed. Tracie had been right, as always. Oh well. He racked his brain. What could he say?

Just then, a bell rang, and in another moment, the conveyor belt began to move. A young boy, three or four, by the looks of him, began to move, too. He'd been crawling about on the dirty floor and then he'd crawled onto the carousel. For a moment after it began and the horns went off, the little kid was transported—not in a literal sense—but then as the belt lurched him forward and away from his mother, his mood quickly changed. He opened his mouth and a roar of anguish, much louder than a mouth that small seemed to be able to utter, streamed out. Poor kid.

"That's the one from the plane," The Lovely Girl said. Just before the toddler rolled by, Jon swung into action. He bent over and picked the little boy up, swinging him back to his mom's feet. Unfortunately, getting off the wagon train didn't stop the scout from screaming. The little kid's yell got even louder and his face was turning red. The Lovely Girl, as well as Jon's other neighbors, actually backed off. Jon didn't know what to do. He supposed picking the tyke up again was a good idea, but the boy was filthy, and— "Cut the crap, Josh," the boy's mother said, and took the poor kid by the left hand, gave him a yank, and—without thanks to Jon—led the boy away.

The Lovely Girl and the other passengers returned like the tide and she looked up at him. She had gray eyes, Jon's favorite color, and although they were a tiny bit more deep-set than might be considered absolutely perfect, they were more than good enough. But Tracie had told him not to compliment eyes, so he was out of luck there.

"She didn't even thank you," The Lovely Girl said. Surprise more than outrage was outlined on her pretty face.

"No, but later she's going to nominate me for a MacArthur grant," Jon quipped, hoping that those gray eyes wouldn't give him the blank look he usually got back from people when he made those kinds of jokes. Instead, she laughed. She actually laughed! Maybe this was all easier than he'd thought. Maybe it was only a question of showing up at the right place wearing the right kind of used jacket.

Now bags of every description began to slide down the chute and come around the carousel. It was only then that the implications of the fact that his luggage was on the wrong conveyor dawned on Jon. Well, he'd just pretend he'd lost his luggage. That happened all the time. It might make The Lovely Girl sympathetic, although it also might make him look like a schmuck.

Quickly, he thought about what James Dean might do if his luggage was lost, but none of the films gave him a clue whether that would happen or what James would do if it did. For a moment, Jon felt deep bitterness. What good was tutelage if you knew how to react when your lettuces rotted but not when the airline lost your luggage?

Desperate, he tried to think of something else to say to The

Lovely Girl. It was certainly too soon to ask for her name. The luggage coming out of the hatch seemed to be the only thing of interest to anyone. It came in two types—black and indistinguishable from every other piece or one of a motley collection of every kind of bag imaginable, all of which displayed neon yarn, glow-in-the-dark stick-ons, or duct tape so that the owners could distinguish the piece from the myriad others. As if that would be necessary.

So, what to do? Help her with her bag! He looked at The Lovely Girl out of the corner of his eye and tried to imagine her luggage. She would never have a tatty hard-sided avocado green suitcase with pink pearlized nail polish X's along the side. He shook his head as that bag rolled past, and then a miracle happened: *She* spoke. "Isn't it hideous?" she asked. "What people use as luggage, I mean."

In his amazement, he forgot to answer her. He was too busy thinking that she might actually—as Molly might say—"fancy" him. She'd spoken. And she'd spoken a thought he'd had. Maybe there was real possibility here. Well, no sense sending out the wedding invitations if he didn't respond.

"Their bags are as ugly as their travel togs," he said. God! Togs? Who used the word *togs*? Men in smoking jackets. Guys who wore ascots and used cigarette holders. He'd better explain that. . . .

"Oh, I know. My mother said air travel used to be glamorous. That people dressed up for it. Can you imagine? Did you see that getup the mother with the spit-up baby was in?" she asked, then paused. "Oh, probably not. You were in first or business, weren't you?"

It was unbelievable! Here she was, telling him he looked like quality and actually leading him on. Had it always been this easy, even though he hadn't known it and didn't have the tools? Could a leather jacket and the heel blisters make all the difference? Blisters were worth it.

Newly confident, Jon changed his position to what he considered a cooler stance. "I didn't see it, but I smelled something sour," he told her. He reached into his pocket and pulled out Huey, Louie, and Dewey. "Care for a Pez?" he asked.

She chuckled but shook her head. "You're funny. Do you live here, or are you in town on business?"

It was his dream come true, but just how should he answer the question? He'd expected her to ask that. Should he lie and make her believe he was a traveler? Tell her the truth and let her know he was a local? And what should he do about his bag on the other carousel? "I'm here scouting for talent," he said, then thought, What a lame thing to say.

But she didn't seem to think it was odd, or a lie. "You're kidding? I'm just here for a magazine shoot for Micro/Con," she told him. "They want to make their new motherboards look like a mother lode, if you get my meaning."

Holy mackerel! "Do you have any photos you can show me? Maybe I could help you out," he said.

"Let me have your number so that once I unpack I can get you a portfolio."

"Sure." Jon couldn't believe how easy this was. She wanted his number! Okay, so it was under false pretenses, but what the heck. "Do you have a pen and paper?"

The Lovely Girl rummaged through her bag but could only find a pen. "Here," she said, and thrust her hand, palm up, at him. "Write it here."

Wow! What could be better than this? Jon reached out and took her hand. A shiver went through him at the touch of her flesh. Calm down, he told himself. He jotted down the number and folded her fingers up into her palm. "Don't lose it now," he joked as he slowly released his grip on her hand.

"It's about time," she said, and Jon wondered if she meant that he'd been moving too slowly. Then she stepped toward him. Boy, she's aggressive, he thought, but she went right by him and was reaching out her hand when Jon realized she was after her bag.

"Let me get that for you," he said, pouncing on the opportunity. Great. She'd get her bag, leave with his number, and never notice that his bag was on the wrong carousel. He grabbed the bag by the handle, glanced at the name tag, and started to lift it off the rubber mat, then realized he was going completely against the rules. What had Tracie told him? To take, not give. This was old Jon behavior. He quickly let go of the bag as if the strap were burning-hot. The Lovely Girl, Carole Revere if her luggage tag was accurate, looked at him in mild surprise. "Sorry, Carole, I got a cramp in my fingers," he told her lamely. The suitcase was half on and half off the conveyor. It kept moving down the belt. The Lovely Girl gave him a funny look as she went to retrieve the bag herself.

Then she just stood there, holding her bag. What was she waiting for? He had apologized for dropping it. What else was he supposed to do? He must have had a strange look on his face, because The Lovely Girl started talking again. "I have two bags."

"Uh-oh," Jon said, and smiled at her. "I'm beginning to think my bag isn't coming." She'd notice he didn't have a bag. What could he say? The crowd from the Tacoma flight was thinning out. He forced himself to chuckle. "Wouldn't it be a strange coincidence if our bags were lost together?" he asked. "Being together would be our destiny." Oops, Jon thought, I might have gone too far, been too friendly with that comment. Hadn't Tracie told him that he was supposed to make them want him, not show he wanted them? But, based on The Lovely Girl's expression, he figured he was still doing okay. Just don't screw this up, he told himself. But that made him even more nervous. Keep calm, he instructed himself sternly. He looked at her again. She *really* was lovely.

"Maybe our bags have been confiscated. Maybe they'll check them for weapons," he said. God, that sounded crazy. What did she think he was talking about? He was only trying to be funny. "You know, like Ted Kaczynski or something." But she didn't smile. Maybe she didn't know who that was. "You know, the Unabomber." She nodded. He laughed with relief.

"Why would they search our luggage?" she asked, her voice totally reasonable.

Yeah. Why would they? What a stupid comment. He was insane

and he was blowing this. He had to reassure her. He was panicking. "Who knows what they do. Right? But I can guarantee that They definitely won't find a typewriter if They search my luggage. The Unabomber wouldn't travel without that piece of equipment." He tried to laugh. "My bag's guaranteed to be typewriter-free. In fact, it's so light, it could be stuffed with newspaper."

Oh no. Worse and worse. Jon was ready to weep, but he tried to keep his face completely neutral. From the corner of his eyes he again saw his bag, black and ominous, abandoned on the next carousel. The cheese stands alone. He felt sweat breaking out under his arms and on the top of his lip. Great. Now he'd look like Albert Brooks in *Broadcast News*. Flop sweat. He was a flop all right.

Jon glanced back at The Lovely Girl, whose face had sort of come together in the middle, her brows, her nose, her eyes, and her mouth all gathering at the center of her face as if for safety. "Not that my bag is stuffed with newspaper," Jon assured her. "It's the normal weight. I mean, it's even heavier than normal. And it's not like I could be the Unabomber. I mean, they caught *him*. My bag just isn't heavy because I don't have weapons or stuff." He laughed again, because he was dying. Maybe a joke would save him. "This trip, I decided to leave the weapons at home. Just this once."

The Lovely Girl turned her head toward her carousel. She moved away from Jon, and he knew he'd gone way too far with her. Then he saw her reach for her other bag. Miracle of miracles! Once she had it, she came back toward him. Relief flooded him.

But The Lovely Girl's face had changed once again. Now it was closed and aloof, again the face of a stranger. But her eyes darted back and forth, the eyes of a nervous stranger. Yes. He had ruined everything.

"I've got to go," she said coolly. "I'll give you a call when I get settled. And I hope you find your luggage."

Chapter 17

Tears rolled down Tracie's face, but she didn't wipe them off. She just blinked her eyes to try to clear them, then felt one tear glide to the crease beside her nose, tickling her. She reached her tongue up and delicately licked it from the top of her lip. It was just the slightest bit salty.

"How much salt?" she called out to Laura, whose backside was up, while her head had disappeared deep in an under-the-counter cabinet, looking for something. "Do I put in salt?"

Laura grunted and pulled her head out of the cupboard. "Nah. There's a lot of natural sodium in tomatoes. I think that the other seasonings and the natural salt of the tomatoes make additional salt unnecessary."

Tracie nodded, and a tear flew off her chin as she did so. It fell onto the chopping board and moistened an onion slice. She could have thrown the onions into the pot sooner to stop her eyes from smarting, since she had already cut them up as finely as she knew how, but she wanted Laura's approval first.

"You know," Laura said as she stood up, "if you put the onion in the freezer for a few minutes before you slice it, it doesn't make you cry."

"Well, if I had time and could remember things like that, I'd be the type of person who had my panty hose in the freezer, too, so they wouldn't run."

"Does that work?" Laura asked.

Tracie shrugged. "How would I know? I'm not that type of person."

"Thank God!" Phil called from the sofa. "Panty hose are enough of a turnoff. Icy ones would be beyond my tolerance."

Tracie picked up the chopping block and moved it to the skillet, where the butter was already melting. "So I just throw these in?" she asked. Then she saw red bloom against the cutting board and realized she had just cut not an onion but deep into the flesh of her thumb. "Ohmigod!" she said.

Laura was at her shoulder in a moment. Tracie held up her thumb, which was now leaking blood down her hand. A line from one of the Plath poems Laura and Tracie shared with each other came to mind. " 'Trepanned veteran,' " she said aloud.

"Hey, no quoting Sylvia when you're bleeding into the cassoulet," Laura said, and in a moment she had Tracie's thumb under the faucet, then dipped in peroxide, then swabbed with Neosporin and tightly bandaged. By then, Phil had gotten to the counter.

"Hey, girl. Cut yourself?" he asked. Then added, "Why don't you throw in the towel?" before he idly began plucking the strings of his bass. "You were meant for other things." He leered.

"Hey! Be nice. I'm making this for you," Tracie told him, and instead of the towel, she threw the onion into the sizzling butter. The room was immediately filled with a most delicious smell. Tracie felt like Martha Stewart. "Taa-dah!"

Laura nodded, then looked over the onions. "Stir them a couple of times. You want them brown, not burned." She then looked over to Phil and back to Tracie. "Pay some attention to him," she whispered. "He's begging for it."

"Whom am I making this for?" Tracie asked, her voice raised. "I'm working my fingers to the bone for him."

Phil just shrugged. Laura turned to him. "Remember the Partridge Family?" she asked.

"Sure," Phil said. "I hated Keith."

"That's just because you were jealous of him," Laura countered. Tracie almost laughed out loud. "Anyway, did you ever notice that when Danny played the bass, he *strummed* it? Like a lead guitar?" Laura said.

"Get outta town!" Phil replied.

Tracie wondered if he meant it literally. Between her time with Jon and the attention she paid to Laura, not to mention her time at the gym with Beth and the others, she wondered if Phil was getting a bit shortchanged. Well, Tracie decided, that wasn't necessarily a bad thing. Usually, he was the one shortchanging her, stretched between his rehearsals, his writing, and his other, less-defined activities. She looked at the pot of peeled and diced tomatoes already simmering on the other burner.

"You're really going to love this tomato sauce when it's finished," she said.

"Yeah," he agreed. "I'm really gonna love when it's finished."

Tracie turned to Laura. "When do I add the onions to the tomatoes?" she asked.

"When they're nice and brown." Laura paused. "You know, it's my duty to remind you that there are some schools that believe in simmering the tomatoes with the onions. I am of the school that believes that tomato sauce is a tomato sauce and everything is therefore added to *it*. And that browned onions are better."

The only time Laura was dead serious was when she talked about cooking or when she talked about Peter. Luckily, she'd done lots of the former and none of the latter in the last couple of days. "I am of your school," Tracie said, equally serious in tone. "I hope someday to be in your school yearbook and wear your school letter."

"What letter would that be?" Phil asked in his bored voice. "*S* for *slow*?"

"*S* for *sauce*," Tracie told him.

"*S* for *simmer*," Laura added. They both giggled.

"*S* for *stupid*," Phil responded. "Both of you. Or *b* for *boring*." He put down his bass. "God, this is dull."

"I know you are, but what am I?" Tracie dared to sing out. She and Laura used to shout that back at girls in Encino when they'd been called names. Fat and skinny, Jack Spratt, and even lesbos. She hadn't thought of it in years. She danced over to the sofa and put her arms around poor Phil. "Just think, homemade spaghetti sauce anytime you want it." She bent to kiss him, but he pulled away.

"Jesus," he said, "you reek." She put her hands up to her nose, and her eyes began to tear again.

"Phew." She ran over to the kitchen sink and began to wash her hands.

"That won't do any good," Laura told her, picking up a lemon, which she pounded with the handle of a knife and then deftly sliced in half with the business end of the same implement. "Here. Use this."

Tracie squeezed the lemon juice onto her hands and then quickly washed them again with dish detergent. After checking her simmering pot, she made her way back to the sofa and sat beside her simmering boyfriend.

"Come here, you," she said, and pulled him to her, letting his head rest against her chest. He began to pull away, but she captured the top of his head with her chin. "Forget that guitar for a minute and bring those talented fingers over here," she whispered. He turned to look at her and was about to say something, when the phone rang. She reached over. "Hold that thought," she told him, picking up the receiver.

Jon's voice exploded into her ear. "Okay, forget about it," he said. "It's a stupid plan and a stupid idea. Anyway, it's not going to work. I can't do it. . . ."

"Hello, Jon," she said calmly. Phil rolled his eyes and pulled his head away from her. Oh well. She'd just have to warm him up all over again. A woman's work was never done.

"It's not working," Jon said. "I'm not trainable."

"We haven't even started yet, and you're giving up?" Tracie admonished.

"*We're* the ones who never get started," Phil said, while Jon also spoke, but she missed his response. She patted Phil on the knee. There, there.

"What?" she asked Jon. He was babbling, something about the airport and then luggage and that she didn't know he was traveling, and then something about someone pregnant and . . . Phil was getting up to put his jacket on, so she had to grab his hand and pull him back on the sofa to kiss him before he actually left. When she got back to the phone, she heard Jon wrapping it up.

"A madman," he was saying. "She thought I was some kind of terrorist."

"It's a start," she said. It was clear that he'd tried to pick someone up. "Better a terrorist than a dweeb. Much sexier."

"No. It's better to be what I was than a failed Ted Kaczynski."

"I thought Ted Kaczynski was a failure," Tracie said, stroking Phil's arm. "I mean, he got caught, right?" Phil began to pay attention to the conversation.

"The sauce needs stirring," Laura called. "Am I making it or are you?" Tracie knew how seriously Laura took her cooking and she gestured to her that she'd only be a moment.

"Don't joke about this!" Jon was saying. "I mean, you weren't there. You can't imagine the look she gave me."

"Did you ever notice how Ted is a loser name?" Phil inquired aloud. "You know—Ted Kennedy, Ted Kaczynski, Ted Bundy."

"I have a policy not to date any Teds," Laura agreed. "With Eds, I decide on a case-by-case basis."

Jon was still talking, but Tracie hadn't been able to hear much.

She made "hmms" and "mms" to try to comfort Jon. When he paused, she waited a moment and then, to be optimistic, said, "Well, you may get a call from her."

"Get a call from her?" Jon echoed. "I'm lucky if I don't get a call from the police. You don't understand." Even from across town, Tracie could hear his sigh. "You had to be there," he repeated. "I'm hopeless at this. I acted like a madman."

"Girls could like a madman," Tracie said as reassuringly as she could manage. Phil began nibbling her ear and Laura put her hands on her hips to indicate sauce consternation.

"Not ones like this," Jon told her grimly.

"Well, you get an A for effort," she said. "You set your sights too high. It's just too hard to pick someone up cold without some common interest." She pushed Phil off her and got up.

"The sauce needs stirring," Laura repeated. Tracie got over to the stove, and in doing so, she missed something else that Jon had said. "Slow down. Slow down," she told him. Her comfort hadn't helped. From the pitch of his voice, she realized she'd have to take this more seriously. It was obvious he was deeply upset.

". . . because I'd worked it all out. I thought I had it perfect. But you can't work it out. You can't control it. 'Cause when I got to the airport and there was nobody good on that flight—I mean, there was somebody good, but she was too good, and, like I said, the other one was pregnant."

"What other one?" Tracie asked as she took the spoon and stirred the sauce. She felt pulled in too many directions at once. How did women raise two or three children?

"Did Danny really strum his bass?" Phil was asking Laura.

"Absolutely," Laura said. "And did you know Laurie was anorexic?"

"Get out! I had a huge boner for Laurie."

Tracie tried to silence them with her hand motions. Jon was still talking. "So I moved to the next carousel and started talking to Carole, and then my bag was on the wrong carousel, and I guess I pan-

icked and said something stupid, and then she started to act as if I
was—"

"Who is Carole?" Tracie asked as Laura handed her some big
leaves, which Tracie had no idea what to do with.

"This girl I picked up at the airport," Jon said, his voice showing
his exasperation. "Carole."

"I'm listening. I just missed her name." What else did I miss? Tracie wondered. "Where were you going?" she asked.

"Going? I wasn't going anywhere."

"Well, where did you meet this Carole?"

"Tonight. At the airport."

"So why were you at the airport if you weren't going anywhere?
Were you meeting Carole?" Tracie didn't remember that there was
any Carole in Jon's life. Meanwhile, Laura pulled out a leaf from Tracie's hand and threw it into the sauce.

Next, Phil made a gesture with his finger across his throat to say
cut it short, but she couldn't. Laura took back the spoon. Tracie
shrugged an apology. "I don't understand," she told Jon. "What were
you doing at the airport?"

So, while she stirred the pot with one hand and held the phone to
her ear with the other, he told her a long, crazy story that only Jon
could tell. She laughed a couple of times, until she realized that that
might hurt his feelings. Then she managed to keep a straight face
during all the rest of the crazy recitation. Jon was one of a kind.

"So anyway, I wrote my name and number on her hand. Can you
imagine how embarrassing?"

"Well, you'll never see her again."

"I might. I know she's got a gig with Micro/Con." Then he really
lost touch with reality. "Do you think if I track her down, find her
number, and wait a day or two until I call, she might go out with
me?" he asked.

"I think she'd have you arrested," Tracie told him. "Look, you
tried. Forget it. There will be dozens more. Don't sweat it. And you

get an A for originality, as well as extra points for neatness. But it wasn't such a good idea."

"Why not?" he asked. "Just because I panicked? Maybe I could try it again?"

"No. Not that." She sighed and looked down at the sauce, which was thickening nicely. "I mean that the two of you had nothing in common except that you were both at the airport. You weren't even on the same flight. Usually, there has to be some kind of shared *something* to get things started," she explained. "So you were working against yourself there."

Actually, as she thought about it, his idea was pretty neat. Crazy, but so Jon. That he was capable of thinking it up made her smile. The fact that he wasn't capable of carrying it off was because he was Jon. He was nuts, but in a kind of adorable way. He'd eventually make some woman a really great husband. But first, she had to get him a date. She lowered the flame under her sauce. Laura nodded approval.

She tried to think of a place where people gathered—not at a bar or club, because she knew Jon would never be comfortable there, but— It came to her like an avalanche and she smiled at her own analogy. Perfect! Much better than an airport. "Look," she said. "I've got an idea. How about if I take you somewhere where you'll have something to talk about to women?"

"Are you talking to me?" Phil asked, raising his eyebrows. "Because I'm interested." Tracie frowned at him.

"Where?" Jon asked at the same time, his voice suspicious.

"That's for me to know and for you to find out," Tracie announced, again reverting to Encino talk.

"It's time to get serious here," Laura said, interrupting. "We've got some major seasoning that's got to go in." Tracie nodded to her and gave her the "just one minute" sign.

"Trust me on this," she told Jon, and she wondered if she could write about his airport fiasco in her article. It would be really hysterical, but that would be what he might not like. Guiltily, she thought she really ought to tell him about her article idea, but she certainly couldn't do it now, not after his humiliation, and not with Laura and Phil breathing down her neck. "Look, don't lose heart," she told him. "It was great that you took the initiative. Rome wasn't built in a day. The longest journey starts with a single step. . . ."

"Not enough cooks spoil the sauce," Laura said pointedly.

"A stitch in time saves time," Phil added.

"That's not right," Laura said to him.

"I get the idea," Jon told Tracie.

"It's nine," Laura was saying. "Nine."

"It's past ten-thirty," Phil responded.

"The saying is, A stitch in time saves nine," Laura was explaining.

"Nine what?" Phil asked.

Laura ignored him.

"Okay," Tracie told Jon. "So I have a plan. You in?"

"I don't know."

"You promised me I'd pass calculus. I promise you you'll get a date," Tracie assured him.

"Okay," he agreed, but he still sounded pretty demoralized.

"Nine stitches!" Laura shouted.

"I have to go. We'll talk tomorrow," Tracie told Jon.

"Okay." He paused. "Hey, Tracie, thanks."

"*De nada*," she replied.

With relief, Tracie hit the off button and laid the phone on the edge of the stove. "You have to put in the oregano and the rest of the herbs now," Laura instructed. "But I want you to add some more garlic first."

"I have to chop garlic again?" Tracie asked, dismayed. She had started with that even before the onions. She was never going to smell sexy again, unless Neapolitan kitchens were a turn-on for Phil. Remorselessly, Laura handed her the cloves and the chopping board. Tracie shrugged her shoulders and did as she was directed for a few minutes, until the phone rang again. She shrugged at Laura as if to say, Not my fault, and then picked it up. It was Beth.

"I'm going to call him. I'm sitting here alone and he's sitting there alone and there's no reason for me not to call him," Beth said.

"You're *not* going to call him," Tracie told her. "First of all, he's probably not alone. Second, he's made it clear he doesn't want a relationship with you. And, in case you've forgotten, he is your boss. You'll wind up not only losing his respect but your job, too."

"I don't want my job," Beth wailed. "It's torture seeing him every day but not being able to have him."

Tracie shook her head. Her hair fell into her eyes. She *had* to remember to book an appointment with Stefan. Beth groaned. How Beth could manage to get so emotional about a middle-aged, slightly balding, mean guy was beyond her. What Beth needed was a distraction. "You've got more important things to do," Tracie told her. "I want you to go through your closet and figure out what you'd wear on a Friday date."

"Why bother?" asked Beth. "I haven't had a date in months."

"You have one for next Friday," Tracie informed her. "I fixed you up." Laura was tapping her finger against the side of her forehead with the gesture that said, You're crazy. Then she pointed to the sauce.

"With who?" Beth asked, and Tracie could hear the curiosity and interest in her voice, though she was trying to sound disinterested. "Not one of those loser musicians of yours," Beth added. "I don't want to be stuck paying for their beer all night like the last time."

"No, no," Tracie assured her. "This guy's really cool and he's not a musician." Better leave a little mystery. She lied: "I'm not sure exactly what he does, but he's really cute."

"What's his name?" Beth asked.

"Jonny," she lied.

Laura now had both hands on her hips again—not a good sign— and Phil was seriously sulking. "I gotta go," she told Beth. "We'll talk tomorrow at work." At least that will give her something to think about, she figured as she hung up the phone and turned back to Laura.

"You're getting him a date?" Laura asked.

"Well, first I thought I'd take him to a place where he could pick up a girl for himself. But you know, in case it doesn't work out, he needs a date."

"I'll go out with him," Laura said. "I mean, just as a practice."

"Oh, that's all right," Tracie said as offhandedly as possible. "I don't think we should try that. Not after you dissed him at the market." She thought for a moment. "It'll be good for Beth. She's trying to get over Marcus."

"Beth from the gym?" Laura asked. "She's an idiot."

"Well, yes. But she's a cute idiot, and it's just a date."

Laura turned to the sofa as if to ask Phil . . . but Phil wasn't there. "Where did he go?" she asked Tracie.

Tracie shrugged. He must be in the bedroom, sulking. She covered the pot with the only lid in the house, one she had improvised with a plate and aluminum foil. "Can I leave this now?" she asked, feeling as if she were stretched in a half dozen directions. She had to go to Phil and make everything okay with him. And she had to do some work on her article, at least to bring her notes up-to-date.

"Sure," Laura said acidly. "How important is tomato sauce compared to true love?"

Tracie's hands really stank now from the garlic. "Give me a break, will ya?" Tracie asked her. "Also, while you're at it, give me another lemon."

"Sorry. No more lemons," Laura said brightly. "Except for the guy in there." She indicated the bedroom with a tilt of her head.

"Thank you," Tracie told her. "Pete's a great guy, too."

"But Pete is not in my bedroom," Laura pointed out. "I don't have to go in there and give lemon aid."

Phil was lying on her rumpled bed with his guitar next to him. He was breathing deeply, his face stuffed into one of her pillows. But somehow Tracie could tell he was faking. She used to do it herself when she was a kid and her father would check on her. She sat down at the foot of the bed and put a hand gently on his ankle. "Are you sleeping?" she asked.

He immediately picked his head up in an exaggerated start. "No," he said after a moment, rubbing one eye with the back of his hand. "I was just going to try out a few new licks."

There was something very intimate about knowing he was faking his composure, as if she had caught a child in a game of pretend. He was like a child in many ways. Tracie became almost shy. "Look, I'm behind on my meat loaf sampling and I also have to cover the opening act at the EMP for the *Times*. Remember? I thought you might want to go."

"To EMP? Jesus, that place is so lame." Again, Tracie could see that he was covering his disappointment. Bob had talked of the Glands playing at the Experience Music Project through some friend of a friend. But the gig—if it had ever existed at all—had never materialized or fallen through. Since then Phil had had nothing but criticism of the museum that had made news all across the country. Sometimes Tracie thought highly of Phil's iconoclasm and fierce independence but at other times—like this one—she began to believe that he simply rejected things defensively before they rejected him.

"Frank Gehry is going to be there," Tracie coaxed. Gehry was the genius who had created the Experience.

"So what," Phil said. "They spent two hundred and fifty million dollars on something that looks like the wreck of the Partridge Family bus."

"I'm going to try to get an interview with him," Tracie said. "My father knows him from L.A."

"Fine," Phil told her. "Use insider contacts that others don't have. I don't care if that's the only way you can make it, but don't expect me to watch or help."

Tracie shook her head. Why did he have to be so nasty? Sometimes she believed that each time they got close to one another Phil was obliged to spoil it by being what Laura would call an IPP. She shrugged. She wouldn't press him or chase him and after this behavior she certainly didn't feel like bringing him as a companion. Then she remembered that she had yet another agenda. She decided to try one more time.

"Are you sure?" she asked. "We could have fun. We could dance like we used to." When they'd first met, they danced all the time. She'd been impressed with his weird dance moves. They were . . . unique. He didn't dance like a white boy, but he wasn't doing some pathetic imitation of a rapper, either. He moved like a robot ballet dancer. It seemed to Tracie that they hadn't danced together in a long, long time. "Oh, come on," she begged.

Phil fell back onto the mattress. "Nah. I'm really into my playing."

That's such bullshit! Tracie thought. Annoyed and hurt, she tried to cover it. "Okay. I just thought you might want to meet Bob Quinto, the manager. And you know, he's looking for help booking. . . ."

"Are you trying to talk me into taking some kind of straight gig again?" Phil asked, sitting up now.

Uh-oh. Not this argument tonight. "No. I just think . . ."

"I just think you don't have much confidence in me. I don't appreciate that." Phil threw his long legs over the side of the bed and began to push one foot into his boot.

"Look, I'm sorry. I just thought he'd be a good connection for you. Then, afterward, I thought maybe you'd come back here and . . ."

"Forget it, Tracie. I've got a late rehearsal." He put his other boot on.

"Fine," she told him. "I want to work on my article about the makeover anyway."

"Fine," Phil repeated. "Then we're both busy. Too bad I didn't know that before I wasted all this time waiting for you." He stood up and put his guitar in its case. "Good luck with your sow's ear."

"That's not nice," she snapped.

"Oh, I think it's nice," he said. "Nice for you. Nice for your ego." He paused, then cocked his head and raised his voice. "You could be the next Emma Quindlen," Phil said, imitating Jon almost perfectly.

"Anna, not Emma," Tracie snarled at his back as he left.

Chapter 18

Tracie was driving over to Mom's, a diner on the other side of Seattle, where they served things like baked macaroni and home-style chicken potpie. She'd been turned down on the makeover article, but the idea of the best meat loaf in town was worthy. She sighed. After thinking for a while, she'd come up with an angle she liked: Guys in films noir always seem to have a cup of joe and some meat loaf, so she was getting Mr. Bill from the video store to find a few of the restaurant scenes from the thirties and she was going to sample all the meat loaf in town, as Jimmy Cagney or Humphrey Bogart might. Needless to say, Jon had insisted that she include Java, The Hut's, although Tracie didn't feel it was necessary to do any favors for the place. It wasn't as if they gave her good service.

After Mom's, Tracie was going to meet Jon at Java, and over another meat loaf sampling, she'd fit in another lesson. Despite his mission impossible at the airport—she giggled when she thought of it—she could see he was getting close to scoring, or whatever it was that guys called it. The fact that he'd even try on his own was incredible, given what a mess he'd been. But now that he was close, she also knew that Jon needed preparation in one more area. Tracie had thought long and—excusing the pun—hard about discussing sexual etiquette with Jon. She shrank from it, though.

The two of them were really best of friends, but while they talked about virtually everything else, she had never talked to him about sex. Somehow, while she could describe to Laura—or even Beth—the exact dimensions of a man's private parts and any peculiarity thereof, the idea of doing that with Jon gave her the willies. Of course, she didn't *have* to talk to him about willies. He had one and, one presumed, he knew how to use it. But what she knew from sad experience, as well as from the experiences of her friends, was that most men had not read the operating instructions for women's parts. If her work on Jon made him look good and sound good, it still wouldn't be enough, as far as she was concerned, if he couldn't also put them over the top sexually. She told herself she shouldn't expect too much from Jon—after all, she knew he hadn't had that much experience.

Freud had pondered on what women wanted, but he must not have asked his wife, or any of his female patients. Because, based on her own sex life and what she'd heard from her friends, what women wanted was oral sex, and plenty of it. Not that they necessarily liked giving blow jobs, though Tracie herself enjoyed it. The problem was that no matter how good you became at playing the skin flute, men usually left you with a lick and a promise. That is, if they went south of the border at all. Tracie was always deeply offended by men who had an aversion to going down on her but who expected her to look at their own private parts as if they were ice-cream cones with sprinkles. One of the things she loved about Phil was how much he seemed to like all of her body, and her secret place the best. It was also so much easier to have an orgasm if a man knew what he was doing. God, when she thought about the oafs she'd occasionally been with in college who'd thought that pumping away until a girl came passed for good sex! She had to tell Jon about delicacy and teasing, about developing a pattern and then, just when the next touch or stroke or flick was expected, to withhold it and go on to something new until a woman was almost out of her mind.

She crossed her legs, then realized she needed her brake foot. She was so deep in thought that as she was about to pull into the right lane for her exit, she didn't see the blue Maxima to her side. She swerved, got back into the exit lane, and reminded herself to keep her eyes on the road, even if her thoughts were "in the gutter," as her stepmom used to say. As she stopped at the off-ramp light, she thought again of Jon and winced at the idea of leaving him completely unprepared. It wasn't fair to him, or to women. And then there was the question of the real sexual politics: where you slept, whether you slept over, condoms and creams and all the rest. God, she hoped he didn't need help with that, too! She could just imagine having to take him into a pharmacy and asking for ribbed Trojans for him.

As she turned onto the main road, she smiled. She remembered the days back in Encino when she herself was so embarrassed that she couldn't buy tampons if there was a guy anywhere near the pharmacy counter. Instead, she'd have to go into a supermarket and buy Clorox, Ritz crackers, some Oreos, a carton of 2 percent milk, Rice Krispies, a few Lean Cuisines, Wonder bread, and *then* a box of tampons, which would, oh-so-casually, be sandwiched between the sandwich cookies and sandwich bread.

Those days were long gone. She could walk up to any clerk at any convenience store and ask for a dozen lubricated, spermicidal Ramses with reinforced tips. If the guy even raised his eyebrows, she was capable of smiling sweetly and telling him, "Make it two dozen. I'm having a gang bang." As she pulled into the parking lot of Mom's, she smiled at the thought.

A very full belly later, Tracie looked down at the second plate of meat loaf she had to face that day and then glanced up at Jon. "It's not as good as Mom's," she said, gesturing with her fork at the pallid slice.

"It's better," he told her.

What a lie! "Have you ever had Mom's?" she asked, whispering so Molly couldn't hear.

"No," he admitted. "But it couldn't be better than this."

"Oh, how would you know anyway?" she asked. "You're a vegan."

"No I'm not," he said. "You remember? Vegans eat—"

"Caught you!" she said, jumping at the chance. "You're *not* supposed to be talking about your dietary laws to any woman."

"I didn't know this counted," he said, defending himself.

"*Everything* counts. That's the whole point of what I'm trying to teach you." She steeled herself for another bite of meat loaf and an opening for her little planned discussion about the birds and the bees. She needed an opening, but she couldn't really think of one. "Look, we have to talk about . . . seduction," she said, and swallowed hard.

Just then, Molly came over to the table. "Is everything okay 'ere?" she asked, perhaps too sweetly.

Tracie actually had to look up from her plate just to be sure it was really Molly. "Everything's fine. Why do you ask?"

"Just doing my job," Molly said, and refilled their water glasses. Tracie looked at Jon to see if he was curious about this new behavior. But nothing registered on his face. God, now she'd probably hang around, and Tracie could *not* talk about sex with Molly listening. "If you need anything, don't 'esitate to ask," Molly said, and left them their table.

That didn't add up. "You told her didn't you?" Tracie said accusingly.

"Told her what?" Jon asked.

"About my meat loaf assignment! She's never filled our water glasses in all the time we've been coming here. I don't even think she's served us water until today. You rat!"

Jon, his mug at his lips, choked a little bit of coffee back into it. "What do you mean?"

"Well, there are . . . rules. I'm supposed to be treated like an average customer." She felt herself flushing.

"So what if I tipped her off? She's always treated you worse than average. Look at it this way: Molly's finally being nice to you."

"Jon, you aren't allowed to—"

"Hey, it's not a Micro/Con tech breakthrough. It's just meat loaf. Anyway, get back to the seduction. What do you mean by that?"

"Just that there are certain ways you should . . . do things. And certain things you should . . . avoid."

"What do you mean, *things*?"

God, he wasn't making this easy. " 'What do you mean, *things*?' " she imitated. "What I mean is that you need to have a way to get women hot for you." She thought of her afternoon's sexual review, the one that almost made her run off the road. "And the best way is to . . ." She just couldn't get right to the nitty-gritty. She would have to segue into it. "Look, sex is like a dance," she told him. "You know those Fred Astaire movies?"

"Is he another bad boy? Tracie, I don't think I have time for any more videos. I'm getting way behind at work as it is."

"You don't have to watch him. It's just that he was that skinny bald dancer, but he had some kind of sex appeal, because in every movie he'd do this dance with Ginger Rogers or some other woman, but it was always best with Ginger. She'd be angry with him, but when they started to dance, she'd pull away and he would pull her back. Then the moment he let her go, she'd pull away again." Tracie, still sitting, gestered with her arms and shoulders to demonstrate. "But then he'd grasp her hand or her wrist and pull her to him again. And in the end, his persistence and his grace would win her over. And then you'd feel her give in, when her body would melt into his. It was a conquest, sexier than sex."

Tracie felt herself heating up again. She paused, recovering herself. "Anyway, the whole thing about a seduction is that you have to be strong enough, magnetic enough to pull the woman toward you. But then you have to abandon her so that you can replay the seduction. It's that conquest thing that makes women *crazy for you*."

"They want me to conquer them?" he asked. "Didn't that go out with Tarzan? Anyway, that's not what James Dean does."

"Right. James Dean's characters were oblique. They never admitted that they wanted someone, though they yearned. You have to be like that, too. Act like you don't care, but let women *imagine* the yearning. If you actually yearn and they see it, it's kind of a pucker."

"Tracie, I think this is too complicated for me," Jon said, putting down his fork and wiping off his mouth with the napkin.

"Oh, come on. You are the guy who is figuring out Parsifal. You can do anything." She took a deep breath. "Look, it's best if they see you as a tragic figure. And if they feel that they can help you and heal you, that's cool."

"But my life isn't a tragedy," Jon protested.

"No, it's a travesty. That's the problem." She paused. How could she get him to understand? "You have to try and find some secret to tell them and be sure that you tell them you never told anyone. Make them feel as if they're the only ones that could ever understand you. Because you're so complex and they are so sensitive. That will make them feel special and important."

"What kind of secret? I never told anyone that I wet my bed until I was about twelve, but I don't think that's what you have in mind."

"Good thinking, Sherlock." Tracie didn't even want to know if what he'd admitted was true or not. As she leaned back to think for a moment, Molly swooped down on them again and silently collected Jon's plate, wiped up the crumbs off the table, and brought him a fresh napkin and the dessert list.

"Are you still working on yours?" she asked kindly. Tracie couldn't take this sort of treatment. Now she'd be forced to say something good about Molly's meat loaf. She wished she could have her plate taken away. She couldn't eat another bite. Not that it wasn't good, but she was sick to death of meat loaf.

"I'm still working on it," she told the lying limey waitress. As soon as the hypocrite left with the dirty tray, Tracie was ready to continue. "Jon, just make something up. Tell them that you saw your father shoot your mother. Or that you saw your mother shoot your father. Or they both shot each other and you've inherited millions but that you'd never touch the blood money."

"They'd like that?" he asked.

"Only if they believed you. And if you said you never trusted anyone else enough to share that. Then they'll trust you enough to sleep with you." Jon just shook his head.

"Now listen." Tracie continued. "When you *do* sleep with them, it's important that you don't sleep over. No matter how tired you are, or how late it is, you have to get out of bed and go home. Rule Number Five, and the most important: Don't sleep over."

"Never? But Phil sleeps over all the time," he protested.

"Well, he never did at first," Tracie admitted. "The point is, it leaves her wanting more. It's best if you can sneak out while she's sleeping."

"Without even saying good-bye?"

"Leave an elliptical note."

"Like what?"

"Like . . . like . . . 'You made me go.' And don't sign it 'love.' And *don't* leave your phone number." Jon's mouth was hanging open in disbelief.

"They make me come and then I write a note to tell them they made me go? Come on! Am I supposed to seduce masochists exclusively?"

"Look, this is just about hooking 'em. After you're together, you can do whatever you like. But in the beginning, they need to feel that you are special, that they are special, and that they have to be very special to get you. That's why you're not going to call them back."

Jon's eyes almost popped out of his head. "After I finally get someone to sleep with me? What are you talking about? If I don't call them back, how will I get to sleep with them again?"

"You don't need to sleep with them again. Sleep with someone else. Right now, for you, it's about wide experience."

"So I'm supposed to behave like a bastard?" he asked. "That's what women want? Bastards with the right pants?"

"No. Do you think we're stupid? We're complex. What we want is someone who behaves like a bastard but we can tame, or at least we think we can tame. We want someone who's tough—but who has a deeply tender heart we can conquer. A panther who obeys our commands. It's sort of the female equivalent of that old-fashioned guy thing."

"What? Mental illness?"

"No. You know, the thing where men didn't want girls who are easy, 'cause then anyone had them." She paused. "I once liked this guy Earl—"

"You'd like Earl Grey tea?" Molly asked sweetly, coming up behind Tracie. "I'll brew some up fresh." What was with this woman? Tracie actually preferred her as a bitch.

"No, I don't want any tea," Tracie said, and gripped the edge of the table to restrain herself from slapping Molly. "I'll let you know if I want something else." Molly nodded and left them again. Tracie shot Jon a look.

"Oh, let her be," he said. "She just wants you to say something good about this place. Now, who's Earl? I don't remember him."

"That's because it was before I met you. And because he didn't last very long," Tracie said. "Earl was smart, and nice-looking. But he kept telling me how beautiful I was. That I was as beautiful as his ex-fiancée. The fascinating woman who broke his heart."

"Yeah, so?"

"So, after hearing about her and being really jealous, I'm over at his place, and on a bookshelf, lying facedown, is this picture of a fat, ugly girl. I ask him if it's his sister or cousin or something, and he tells me it's Jennifer, his ex-fiancée. If he thought *she* was beautiful, then whatever he thought about me wasn't valid. I broke up with him."

"Tracie, you are crazy. I always suspected it, but now I'm sure."

"Jon, I am imparting secrets to you that men would pay hundreds of thousands of dollars to know. These are the things women discuss in ladies' rooms when they go off together. These are the things that will help you to seduce and abandon beautiful girls all over the country. Maybe all over the world," Tracie told him.

"So you're asking me to hurt women on purpose."

"Oh, Jon, it's just part of the bigger picture," she explained. "It's what they're looking for. Then someday a woman grows up and realizes she wants a man who knows how to treat her well."

Tracie wondered when that time would come for her. Then she thought again about her planned discussion of oral sex and other sensitive things, but she just couldn't go there. This had been enough for her. Who knows? Maybe Jon could be okay in bed. At least he was a sensitive guy. The problem was that he probably hadn't lost his virginity until a few years ago. Maybe she should just ask about that. She took the last forkful of meat loaf. "Umm"—she paused, chewed, and swallowed a final time—"let me ask you something," she said. "Who was your first girlfriend?"

"You mean a real lover or the first girl I liked?"

"A real lover," she explained.

"Myra Fisher."

Now she echoed him. "Myra Fisher? I don't remember any Myra Fisher."

"Well, you didn't know me then. Myra was back in eighth grade."

Her mouth dropped open. "Eighth grade!" He must have misunderstood. "No, I mean the first girl you actually slept with."

"Well, I didn't get to sleep with Myra until the ninth-grade class trip. But we were having sex at her house all through eighth grade. And in the summer between eighth and ninth."

"You never told me about that!"

"Well, I don't think it's appropriate to talk about what *you* might call 'my conquests,' " he said. "It's very personal. I just don't really talk about it."

"Not with anyone?" she asked.

"Not really. I mean, you don't, do you?"

"Uh, not really." She hoped her nose wasn't growing. She looked at Jon and began to wonder about him in a whole new way. "Wait a minute," she said. "That really tall girl back in college, the one with the really long hair . . ."

"Hazel," he said. "Hazel Flagler."

"Yeah. Did you and she . . ."

"Of course," he said.

"You never told me!" Now Tracie was truly shocked.

"Well, what do you think I was doing with her? She wasn't a chess player!" Jon said.

"You never told me," she repeated. Tracie wondered what other relationships he'd had that he'd never spoken to her about.

"Tracie, I grew up listening to women complaining about how badly men behave. I watched my father do it. Do you think after all that I was going to kiss and tell?"

"Kiss and tell? Jon, this isn't some Victorian novel. This is the twenty-first century. Don't you watch *Friends*? Or reruns of *Seinfeld*? People on *Jerry Springer* talk about sleeping with their brothers!"

"I have never been on *Jerry Springer*," Jon said with dignity. And for the first time, Tracie looked at him and imagined that there might be a lot of water running deep under the stillness of his dark brown eyes.

Chapter 19

The next week, Wednesday, Jon met Tracie for the much-discussed haircut. They swung open the salon door, the music blasted from inside, and instinctively Jon stepped back. "Come on," Tracie told him. "Avant-garde hair care is not for the fainthearted." She took his hand and pulled him through the portal. "Don't worry," she said blithely. "Stefan will take care of you."

For the first time in his life, Jon really doubted her. He didn't think so, unless she was implying the mafioso meaning of "taking care of." Well, what the hell. He felt half-dead already.

Was all of this really necessary to get a girl? It took so much time, thought, and energy. Wasn't the relationship supposed to require maintenance, not his wardrobe and hairline? As he was dragged through the reception area—a room filled with bright lights, incredibly loud technorock, and something that seemed like the decor from a very bad game-show set—he felt himself flinch. There was a point at which a man had to put his foot down, and he figured this was it . . . until the woman with endless legs and silvery gold hair down to her waist walked by. She nodded to Tracie and smiled—actually smiled—at him. She was the most beautiful woman he had ever seen. "Hi, Ellen," Tracie said casually, as if the goddess of love had not just walked among them.

"Who is that?" he whispered.

"What?" Tracie asked at higher than full volume, continuing to pull him along.

"Who is that?" he asked, this time shouting. He had fallen deeply in love. She was a dream. She was paradise. If not for the hellish music, he could imagine paradise with her. "Who?" he shouted.

"Ellen? That's Ellen," Tracie repeated, as if that clarified anything.

They'd crossed the reception area, walked through a bustling room of chairs and mirrors, and now Tracie led him down a much emptier hallway, though the music continued full blast. All the walking was taking him farther away from his goddess. Two other women walked by. Neither one was quite up to Ellen's standard, but both were truly, deeply beautiful. Wow! They nodded at either Tracie or him, and on the blind chance that he had been included, he nodded back. Neither one giggled or pointed. It seemed he was expected to nod back, just as they were expected to nod at him. Maybe, he thought, maybe Tracie *did* know something about all this after all. But he would not let Ellen drop. "Who is Ellen?" he repeated once the other two nymphs were safely gone.

"She's Stefan's wife," Tracie shouted casually, as if that didn't mean his entire world had just crumbled. They passed a dozen doors, until Tracie opened yet another one—into what had to be the Holy of Holies in this temple of beauty.

"Isn't Stefan gay?" Jon shouted, still reacting to the technorock. But as the door swung closed behind them, the noise ended abruptly. He was standing in a small, square, perfectly silent white room furnished with only a Star Wars–type barber's chair in the center of it. A tall man stood beside the chair, looking at him.

The guy was tall, six foot five or six, and fair, with very short hair and a scar across one blond eyebrow. Tough-looking. Jon broke the silence. "Hi," he said, his voice almost squeaking. "You must be Stefan."

"You don't realize the sacrifice I'm making here for you," Tracie said as she sat Jon down in a chair. "Just look at me. I'm the one that really needs a haircut, but just remember, you owe me big for this." She stepped back and leaned against the counter. Then Jon was approached by Stefan, who was like Edward Scissorhands crossed with Riverdance. He kept snipping and stamping his feet and jumping. Jon wondered if it was safe for Stefan to move that way with the scissors so close to his eyes, but he guessed Stefan knew what he was doing. After all, Tracie just sat there calmly through all the snips and jumps and didn't seem to notice that there was no mirror, no noise, and no people. Just Stefan and his heavy breathing and his crazy jumping around. It was the strangest haircut Jon had ever experienced.

Jon sat for nearly an hour with a man he had just insulted. Meanwhile, Tracie, who apparently didn't realize the terrible danger he was in, sat on a tiny stool near his feet, chattering away. Jon only wanted to dart out of the seat, out of the room, past the fatal Ellen, wife of this Balkan madman, and perhaps leave Seattle forever. But he was afraid to move because of the very sharp scissors that kept flicking around his head.

". . . and the bicycle," he heard Tracie saying. What was she going on about?

He was afraid to turn his head to Tracie, so he merely twitched his eyes toward her. It hurt to put his eyeballs so far into the corner of his eyes for very long. "What about my bicycle?" he asked. He would have liked to put his hand up to his head, but he was sure that Stefan would snip off a finger. Bits of his hair had been flying around the room for a long time.

"I said we still have to do something about your backpack and the bicycle," Tracie repeated calmly.

"What about my backpack?" he asked. "And nothing's wrong with my bicycle. What do you mean we have to 'do something' about my bicycle?"

"It's just that a bicycle is so uncool," Tracie told him. "I mean, how are you going to take a girl back to your place? Put her on the handlebars?"

"I thought I wasn't supposed to take them back to my place," he said, reminding her of her tutelage.

"Okay. Okay. So how are you going to take them back to *their* place?"

They were going to get into this now, and do it in front of Stefan?

"In their car?" he asked hopefully.

"And how do you get home from there?" She shook her head. "You know, if you didn't have a Schwinn, you'd own a Pacer." Jon didn't know for sure what a Pacer was, but he could tell it wasn't good, because Stefan laughed. "It's hard to date without a car."

"We can go in hers," he said. Jon had to admit he was beginning to see the difficulty, but he pushed on. "Or call a cab?" he asked weakly, knowing it wasn't a good gambit. He heard a little derisive snort behind him and wished that for just one moment he could have those scissors in his own hands. "Look. You know how I feel. A bicycle is safe, convenient, and has very low ecological impact. If I power a bicycle, I don't need to use any nonrenewable fossil fuel to get where I'm going."

"But you're not getting anyvhere. Not vith vomen," Stefan said, speaking for the first time.

Jon tried not to grit his teeth. When he watched *Rebel Without a Cause* and *East of Eden*, he could always see James Dean's jawline stiffen when he got mad. Now he didn't want the Demon Barber of Fleet Street to do him in. Stefan wouldn't hesitate to cut his carotid artery. Jon decided to ignore him. "Are you telling me I have to buy a car to get dates?" he asked, outraged. Tracie knew how opposed to automobiles he was. They were ruining the Pacific Northwest and tearing the hell out of the environment. How could she even propose the idea?

"Then how about reconsidering a motorcycle?" Tracie asked brightly.

"A motorcycle? I already told you that I'd be a danger to myself and others."

"But they're so cool," Tracie said, almost bouncing off the stool in her enthusiasm. "And girls really like guys who ride motorcycles."

"How do they feel about guys who've had an entire side of their face abraded by pavement?" he snapped.

"Temper, temper!" Stefan cautioned.

"We'll talk about this later," Tracie told him.

"No, we won't," Jon answered her sourly, and then he was spun around to face Stefan. Light glinted off the hairdresser's straight razor. For a moment, Jon thought Stefan was going to wield it, Sweeney Todd–like, but this nut was only holding up a mirror.

Jon looked into it. Oh God! He'd become Sonic the Hedgehog. His hair stood in spikes. The Demon Barber should have just killed me, he thought, and he put his hands over his skull protectively. Stefan, the albino Edward Scissorhands, took the last couple of snippets from Jon's new, totally renovated head.

"Unbelievable," Tracie said.

"Transformation," Stefan replied in a self-satisfied tone. But it was Jon who was transformed—but into what?

He continued to stare. Looking behind him, in the mirror's reflection, Jon saw Tracie hug Stefan. Then she danced wildly, full of approval, around Jon's chair. Well, she was his friend. He guessed he liked Sonic the Hedgehog. "Fantastic," she yodeled, and pulled him up from the chair. Maybe it wasn't as bad as he thought. Then Tracie plucked Jon's wallet from his back pocket as she whizzed by and handed Stefan his charge card.

"It's going to be the best two hundred dollars you ever spent!" she told him.

"Two hundred dollars!" Jon gasped. Then he looked at Stefan and the razor and swallowed. He figured it was better than getting mugged, though just as expensive.

Chapter 20

Tracie and Jon pulled up to the entrance of the REI parking lot. He'd been grilling her the whole way, but she'd refused to answer a single question.

Ignoring Jon, Tracie pulled a right, forgot to put on her indicator, and almost got backed into by a passing Saab. Other than that, they had no mishaps. "Let's go." Jon got out of the car, then tripped on the curb as he looked up to read the sign on the door.

"Oh my God! Not here!" Jon protested.

REI was a famous landmark on the outskirts of Seattle, near Interstate 5. It was probably the largest outdoor sports–supply store in the world. It was a gathering place for sports-minded ecoshoppers. Its distinctive architecture and the huge window drew the eye. From the door, he could see aisle upon aisle of mountain gear shining as hundreds of attractive young men and women shopped for equipment.

"Try to pick out a normal girl," Tracie reminded him. "One of these." She pointed at a whole gaggle of them, all willowy, all perfect, with teeth and hair and skin that shone. Jon felt himself growing smaller and darker, a blot on the landscape. Tracie gave him a little shove. "Place yourself near them, but don't come on to them. You have to play hard to get. You have to make *them* want *you*," Tracie told him. She gestured. They had come to an end of an aisle and before them was an enormous rock wall—at least six stories high—enclosed by glass. People were climbing its almost vertical face, visible to everyone in the store, as well as to passing highway traffic.

"Holy shit!" Jon gasped. He hated heights. He'd once told her that he was afraid to look out high windows because it made him feel like jumping.

"Class is in session. You look fierce now, but you have to *act* fierce."

"How? By hanging off a rock? Forget it!"

She'd known he'd balk, but she was prepared. "Come on, Jon. Climbing is the bomb. A real loner's sport. Women love loners. Think James Dean. Think *The Loneliness of the Long Distance Runner*."

"Hey, that guy only broke into a store and stole money. Then he went to London with a girl. I can do *that*. It's heights I don't like."

"Jon, there are a million girls here looking to meet rock climbers."

"I thought they wanted rock singers!" he whined. "You got a rock player. Don't make me."

Tracie decided to ignore him; she took a coil of rope from a shelf on the right and handed it to him, along with a carabiner.

"Try these on. At least *look* like a rock climber," she demanded.

Jon pointed to the space below the indoor rock. "Or like a Rorschach on that floor. Tracie, I watched all those movies. James Dean mostly moped and hung out against a corner of a wall. I can mope. I can rub against corners. James Dean never climbed rocks."

"Don't be so literal. Or so negative. Move with the times," Tracie told him. "I didn't tell you to climb rocks; I only want you to talk about it." She nudged him. A very pretty blonde walked by, and Tracie thought the girl gave Jon the once-over. Good sign. "Anyway, you don't ever have to climb. Just hang out with a piton and talk to a girl."

Jon rolled his eyes. "Talk about what?" He looked up the wall. "I know nothing about this."

"Think positive. They probably don't, either. If they ask you anything, tell them you like Black Diamond stuff. It's the best."

"How would you know?"

"I did an article." It was a lie, but there was no need to tell him about Dan. Tracie drew a black diamond on her yellow Post-it pad, pulled it off, and stuck it on his chin. Even with the Post-it goatee, he looked cute. Absently, he reached up and unpeeled the Post-it. Meanwhile, he kept looking up at the towering faux rock that half a dozen people were climbing. He kept staring as he crumpled the Post-it. It was as good a moment as any to let her little duckling sink or swim, so, quietly, Tracie moved off.

"Why am I thinking Wile E. Coyote? You know the cartoon where he orders the Acme rocket and . . ."

Jon turned back to Tracie, but she'd disappeared. Instead, a long-legged brunette was listening to him.

"A rock etand?" she said. Her voice was as smooth as the rock surface glinting in front of them. "I've never used one. Is it some new piece of equipment?" she asked.

Jon tried to regain his composure. The crumpled yellow note in his hand reminded him of Tracie's advice. And the girl was certainly pretty. "Yeah. Black Diamond. But I stick with the classics, don't you?"

"Absolutely," she agreed. "You climb much?"

"Oh, yeah. Been climbing since I was a kid." God! What men would do to get a girl! His father had once made him limp for a whole afternoon with some woman he was trying to get into the sack. His dad had been real nice to him, and at the end of the day, when the two adults dropped him off, the woman said, "You're a very brave boy." Afterward, Jon asked Chuck why she'd said that, and his father laughed and explained, "I told her you had lost your leg to cancer." And then there was that guy Tracie dated in her first year of graduate school who . . . He pulled himself back to the present and the opportunity that was walking past him on two very nice legs. He turned to look at this woman, who actually seemed interested in him. Her hair was long, and she had it pulled back in some kind of loose braid that started as part of her head on top and became a pigtail that followed her. Behind her, Tracie gave him the "okay" sign. Did that mean it was okay to lie, or that the girl looked okay, or that . . .

"I only got started last year, but climbing is . . . like a way of life," the brunette said, interrupting his moral dilemma.

"Yeah," he agreed, slick as his dad on his best day. "I need it like . . . oxygen. I need to be alone and depend on no one. I need to be a figure, black against a slab of schist." At the corner of the aisle, he pulled a James Dean pose. He hoped she noticed but that she hadn't, by some odd coincidence, been watching *East of Eden* the night before.

Apparently, she hadn't. "I know what you mean," she said with growing enthusiasm. Then, as if reconsidering, she blinked and turned away. Jon immediately felt a knot develop in his stomach. What had he said wrong? Was he going to blow this like he had blown it with The Lovely Girl at the airport? But she turned back to him. "I mean, I don't totally know what you mean because I haven't really climbed alone, but I want to. Do you do aid climbing?"

He didn't even know what it was. "All the time." What the hell, he figured.

She stopped at a section filled with pitons. "It's all so gear-intensive, you know. And everything costs so much. I need a fifi hook and some copperheads. Do you use any?"

"Oh, sure. I never climb without them," he said smoothly. This was scary. The more he lied, the easier it seemed to be. Was this what it had been like for his dad?

The thing was, he wasn't like his dad. He looked at the girl and he liked her. Okay, maybe he couldn't really climb, but he loved the outdoors; he bicycled everywhere. He bet she was as ecologically aware as he was. Maybe she wasn't a vegetarian—it probably took a lot of animal protein to scale a mountain—but as he covertly looked her over, it seemed liked she was the kind of girl he'd want to get to know, that he'd want to do things with.

"What brand do you like?" she asked.

"Black Diamond," he told her, and put his arm against the shelf behind him, trying to look casual. Instead, he almost fell, but luckily, she hadn't seen him falter, because she was lifting some kind of gear off a lower shelf. Jon didn't have a clue. It looked like something a Jew wouldn't welcome seeing coming his way during the Inquisition.

"What about Pika toucans?" she asked. He remembered Tracie's directive, and anyway, he wanted to touch this girl. Her skin was an even color all over—a kind of creamy white, with just the faintest suggestion of pink underneath. Her lips were pink. . . . Then he realized she was waiting for an answer.

"They're okay. I mean, they're not Black Diamond, but . . ."

It's now or never, he told himself. You have to touch her. Jon took her hand as if to look at the gear. "Wow. You've got beautiful cuticles." He could tell the brunette was charmed. She looked down at her own hands, held in his, and he thought she actually blushed.

"I do? Thanks. My name is Ruth, by the way."

"Bytheway. Interesting surname. Are you English?"

Ruth led him toward a line of people and joined them. Jon fell in behind her to keep the conversation going.

"You know, I only have an Edelrid fifi hook," she was saying. For a moment, Jon thought the whole thing was a joke or an elaborate put-on that Tracie had arranged. Toucans, fifis, copperheads. Was this a sport or a circus? But though he'd lost sight of Tracie, he hadn't lost his mind. This girl was enthusiastic and pretty cute and he was going to try to stick it out. "I hope it's okay," she was saying, "because I don't want to have to buy another one."

Jon eyed the checkout line. He guessed he'd have to buy the rope and the belt. He'd consider it just another wardrobe expense. But after another minute, he noticed there was no register ahead. What was this? Then, to his growing horror, he saw a guy at the front of the line throw up a rope and begin to ascend the rock while several other people rappelled down its huge height.

"Is this the checkout line?"

"No. It's a testing line. I always test gear first. Don't you?" Ruth asked.

"Every time I've bought anything here," Jon agreed, truthful for the first time. His mother had always told him not to lie. How in the world has this happened to me? he wondered as he looked with horror at the people at the front of the line. One after the other, they kept swinging themselves cheerfully onto the rock face as if it wasn't a suicidal act. He turned back to Ruth, who seemed to be moving her lips.

"Excuse me?" he asked.

Two more people threw ropes up. He could hear his heart beating against his chest wall. He looked around for Tracie. This has to be a joke, he thought as he and Ruth moved toward the desk. Jon began to panic. He was so very afraid of heights. "I don't have to test this line," he said as casually as he could muster.

"No, but I'm sure you want to try out the carabiner."

An REI expert came up to Jon. "Are you experienced?"

Before he could beg off, Ruth piped up. "He does aid climbing," she assured the guy.

"Then you can tie your own knot," the guy told Jon.

Yeah, around my neck, Jon thought. Or around Tracie's. Jon glanced from left to right, looking for a quick escape. The crowd hanging around to watch all looked like relatives of Madame Defarge at the guillotine. To his increasing nausea, he saw Tracie among them. Jon shot her a desperate look. She shrugged. He looked at Ruth, thought of her creamy skin, then took a deep breath and threw his line up the rock.

"Are you sure you want such a difficult route?" Ruth asked. Jon shook his head, grabbed the rope, and began to climb. Everyone else moved up the face like spider monkeys, but Jon inched along like something melting upward. "Don't worry. I've got you," Ruth called to him. Jon suddenly hated her with his whole heart. He hadn't realized she was a demented sadist bent on his extinction.

"Oh, I'm not worried," he called back, talking to force himself to move up two or three ledges of rock. He was now almost six feet from the ground. He looked over his shoulder and became so terrified that his hands shook and he almost fell. To prevent that, he began to move wildly, pushing himself into the stone while he scrambled up the rope. There was no place to perch, no surface that was anything but vertical. At last, he reached a ledge about twenty feet above the crowd below and grabbed it desperately. He hugged the rock like lichen.

The REI expert pulled out a bullhorn and called up to him. "Are you all right?" Everyone in the huge store stopped to stare. The crowd grew. So this was what people looked like from the ceiling of the Museum of Flight. He watched as Tracie scrambled to the front of the assembly below. Jon could see her, but instead of yelling encouragement, she began to flash pictures of him! No matter how long you know someone, you can't guess their reaction to things, he thought in a detached way. It wasn't a helpful response to his situation, but Jon didn't really mind, since he was going to die right here. "Please answer me," the guy with the bullhorn was calling. "Are you all right?"

Jon knew it was impossible to nod his head or even to move his lips.

"A clinger! We've got a clinger! Would all climbers please get down," the guy with the bullhorn bellowed.

A safety siren went off. People from all over rushed to look. Tracie backed off from the crowd. Meanwhile, Jon tried to make himself one with the rock.

After the humiliation of the paramedics' arrival, Tracie and a pale, disheveled Jon crossed the parking lot to get back to her car. Other people in the lot stared and pointed at Jon.

He's absolutely hopeless, Tracie thought as she pulled the car door open. She'd lose her bet with Phil, but worse, there was no article here. She couldn't make Jon over. He was a lost cause. Worst of all was Jon's future: He'd always be a geek and he'd wind up a bachelor "uncle" to her future children. God, she thought, he'll teach them bad habits.

After a silence that got them onto the highway and halfway back to Jon's house, he spoke. "So, did you see where Ruth went? I risked my life for her. Then she disappears." Tracie said nothing so that she wouldn't explode. "I gave her my number. You think she'll call?"

Is he for real? Tracie thought. "Not after they brought the oxygen for you," she told him.

"That was all totally unnecessary," he said. "I was just hyperventilating. I only needed a paper bag."

"Yeah. To put over your head." She sighed. He was no Sir Edmund Hillary, but, on the other hand, he'd never take advantage of some poor Sherpa. The worst part was his lack of perception. Didn't he know how bad this had been? It was more embarrassing than the airport fiasco. She told herself she shouldn't give up, but she'd definitely have to give him a tutorial before his date with Beth. "We've got to do a little brushup."

"Oh God," Jon groaned. "Not another lesson."

Tracie took her eyes off the road to give him a pointed stare. "You better not complain, mister," she said. "Not after this fiasco."

Jon shrank toward his door handle; then he began to protest. "Look, I can do it. I know I can," he said. "It wasn't like the airport. She was talking to me. She was liking me." He looked at her. She tried not to smile. "Don't give up on me, Tracie," he begged. "I know you're thinking of giving up, but don't."

She couldn't help it—she took her eyes off the road again to smile at him. "I'd never give up on you," she said. "In fact, I've got exciting news."

"I don't think I need any more excitement today," Jon admitted.

"Well, it's not for today. You have an official date. For Friday night."

Jon sat up straighter. When was the last time he'd had a real date? Was it during the present administration? "You're kidding. With who?" he asked.

"Whom," Tracie corrected, though she often made the same mistake. "A girl from my office. Really cute. Beth."

Uh-oh. One of Tracie's losers. Tracie was always reporting on them, but he couldn't keep their names straight. "Wasn't she the one in love with that stock car racer?" he asked suspiciously.

"That was last year," Tracie admitted, as if last year were a century ago. "There's been a club bouncer since then. And a newspaper guy."

Oh God. A Seattle-scene chickie. "She'll never like me."

"She will," Tracie insisted. "We just have a lot of brushup work to do before Friday. Can you meet me tomorrow?"

"I have a planning meeting tomorrow." Jon had been really lax at work. Instead of his usual twelve-hour days, he'd been cutting back, and back. At Micro/Con, a twenty-hour day wasn't enough. This new focus on his social life was going to catch up with him if he didn't put in some time at the office.

"Hey! What's more important—your career or your love life?" Tracie asked. She had a disconcerting way of responding to things he had only thought and not said. Usually, he enjoyed it: It made him feel understood. Now, however, he felt exposed. "No one ever died wishing they'd spent more time in the office," she reminded him.

Yeah, he thought. And no one got to be vice president of development if they had a social life. He sighed. "Okay. Okay. So where do I meet her?"

"Across from the *Seattle Times*. In front of Starbucks. Or inside if it's raining."

"And where do I take her?" he asked. He actually felt himself getting nervous already.

"Take her to a nice restaurant. But not too nice. Now, you remember the rules about ordering."

"Yeah, yeah," he said glumly. "No Cobb salads."

Chapter 21

Tracie walked up the dirty stairs to Phil's apartment on the second floor. The door was open. He always left the door open, which made Tracie nervous. Tracie knew she was a conservative, keep-it-zipped, lock-it-up kind of girl, but this was dangerous. Phil's neighborhood— near Occidental Park—wasn't the best one in Seattle. She didn't even like parking here. Once, her left fender had been scratched badly, and another time, her antenna had been broken off. She actually liked Phil to go to her place, but she refused to have him do it all the time. He almost lived there already. Hence the bet. So here she was, parked in a dangerous spot, climbing the dirty stairs, prepared for dirtier sheets, just to be with him and make her point and keep some kind of balance. She shook her head. Men were so difficult. She knew he'd rather be with her than live like this, but he wouldn't admit it. Tracie figured she'd better win the bet.

She walked in, and the big room—Phil called it that because he thought *living room* was a middle-class term—was in the usual shambles. She stepped delicately around the *objects*. From the doorway of his room, she heard a clicking noise and knew Phil must be writing.

That was so great—he wrote without a deadline, without the

knowledge he'd be published. She could never do that. She hated to interrupt him anytime he was writing, but to do it now and ask for a favor might be really difficult. She tried to figure out how to present what she needed from Phil to make her project happen. What she'd figured, after Jon's failure alone at the airport and the documented failure at REI, was that to get an article out of it, she had to have some success with Jon. She really needed to see him on a date. Maybe she should go with him and coach him. And it wouldn't hurt if she got some success pictures. She jotted a note on a Post-it to remind herself to take her camera along. But Phil wasn't usually interested in going out—unless there was a movie he wanted to see or a gig he was playing—much less in playing duenna to help her. Tracie sighed. She was making progress with Jon. Ruth, or whatever her name was, had really liked him until he had to go freeze on the mountain.

But Phil wouldn't care about that, and he wouldn't care about her article. He'd tell her she shouldn't be writing such middle-class trash anyway. And she guessed he was right, but somehow it didn't seem fair. She paid for the groceries that he ate with the middle-class money she earned. Don't be bitter, she told herself. You respect him because he's an artist, a free spirit. And there was something about him . . . his freedom and his anarchy that made him tremendously alluring. It was too easy to find a dog and domesticate it, especially if the dog was already hungry and weak. When you found a bobcat or a mountain lion and could domesticate it, that was an achievement. Jon was a little Dalmatian or Lab puppy, just looking for a home. But Phil was a wolf, and to get him to eat out of her hand without biting her was an endlessly fascinating task.

For another moment, she thought about the bet she'd made with him. If she won, he'd move in with her. She wondered if that was what she really wanted. Sleeping with him was wonderful, but living with him might present more problems. She loved his longing to be free, but sometimes she wondered why he couldn't mature a little, get a job, and act a little bit more . . . well, middle-class. Tracie wasn't looking for a diamond solitaire and she didn't want to wind up a rich wife in Encino, but everything middle-class wasn't hideous. Marriage and family and a nice place to live and good food—those were all what Martha Stewart would call "good things." Not only were they good, but Phil liked them, too. That's why he spent so much time at her place.

She moved closer to his door and stepped on the lid of a pizza box.

"That you, Tracie?" Phil asked without looking up.

"Yeah," she said, trying to imitate him. "I got home late from rehearsal."

Phil turned from the computer screen and rubbed his eyes as if he'd been typing a long time. "Hey, you don't have rehearsals."

"You win the prize," she said, and went up behind him to put her hands on his shoulders. They were so wide. "Hey, I need help."

"Got an itch that needs to be scratched?" he asked, stretching.

"Not now. I'm talking about my project with Jonny."

"Jonny? You mean Jon? The so-called sexless savant?"

He'd been reading her notes for the article! Tracie blushed and crossed to the bed, away from him. She was careful to respect *his* privacy. He'd obviously been looking at her notes and Post-its. Well, she admitted to herself, she did stick them all over. But it still annoyed her that he was snooping. He'd be sorry. She moved a half-filled bottle of Evian. "That's just it. He doesn't look like a Techno-Nerd anymore. He's really coming along. Want to check him out?"

Phil turned back to the screen. "No."

She'd known that one wouldn't work. "I've got a date set up for him on Friday," she told Phil.

"Is Chelsea Clinton that desperate?" Phil asked. "And how will Mr. Techno-Nerd cope with all the Secret Service agents watching his every move? Not that he has any," Phil added.

"He's got moves. I taught him moves," Tracie said in Jon's defense. She hoped that despite her chickening out on her sex lecture, he did have a couple of his own. She paused. She'd have to try now to slip this in gently. "Look, I fixed him up with Beth from work." Maybe if she just made it sound casual and fun. "For Friday." She paused again. "So won't it be a hoot? We need to go out with them. Like a double date."

" 'Like a double date'? Now I know I'm dreaming. Or is this a nightmare?" Phil asked, his voice heavy with sarcasm. "Tracie, I don't date. I certainly don't double-date. And, if I did, it wouldn't be with that Techno-Nerd. Or your little friend Beth."

Well, there was nothing left but begging. "Come on, Phil. We don't have to be with them. I just have to watch him. Like a coach. I have to be able to help him if things go wrong. It's the first time." She paused. "And for reportage, I have to observe."

"That doesn't mean that I have to be subjected to it."

Sometimes he was so selfish and predictable that she wanted to kill him. "Phil, I swear to God. If you don't do this for me . . ."

"I don't want you helping him anymore," Phil said suddenly. He took her hand, put down the water, and pulled her to him. He cradled her between his legs. "This is taking up too much of your time," he said, nuzzling her neck. "You were gone almost all night. Plus, if you win, then . . ."

His moves gave her a shiver of pleasure down her back. "Then we're sharing laundry duties," she said, finishing the sentence for him. "You'd look so good over a box of Tide."

He pushed her away and stood up abruptly. "See," he said. "See! I told you! This is not what I wanted. And you want me the way I am. That's why you picked me. You don't want me in an apron, dusting the living room. Domesticating the outlaw is a lose-lose." He threw himself onto the bed. "I wish you'd just drop this stupid project of yours."

Tracie sat at the edge of his bed and put her arms around him. "Maybe my dad wants you as an in-law," she said, fibbing, "but that's not on *my* mind. Besides, Phil, I really want to write this piece." If child psychology didn't work, maybe teen psychology would. "You're just afraid I'm going to win the bet, right? And that you were wrong about Jonny."

"What's with this Jonny stuff?" he asked. "Anyway, I wasn't wrong. You can't turn that guy cool."

"Then come see," she said as he rolled her on her back and kissed her deeply. "Will you come?" she whispered, and he nodded his head in a silent promise.

Friday morning at work, Tracie was frantically typing at her PC when the phone rang. Without a missed keystroke, she reached over and pushed the headset button.

"Tracie Higgins here."

"I know that. I called you," Laura said.

"Are you going out to look for a job today?" Tracie asked her. She loved having Laura there, and she certainly didn't want Laura to go back to Peter, but she couldn't stay cooped up in Tracie's apartment.

"I have an interview at three o'clock," Laura said proudly. "And I thought I'd stop by afterward so we could have a drink."

"Great," Tracie told her. "That's great, Laura." Then she remembered that tonight Beth was going out with Jon and that she was coaching. "I can have a quick drink," she said, because she didn't want to let Laura down after her interview.

"Fine," Laura said.

"But it'll have to be quick, because I have to go out." There was a pause.

"Do I have to baby-sit Phil again?" Laura asked.

"Nope. He's going out with me."

"Wow! Congratulations," Laura said. "What's the event?"

"Jon's coming-out party."

"Why? Is he gay? It didn't seem as if he was gay."

"Don't be ridiculous," Tracie snapped. "He's going out with Beth."

"Oh, so tonight's the night. Circuithead meets Airhead."

Tracie was about to protest to defend both of her friends, but then her phone flashed. "I've got to go. I'll see you around five," she said. Then there was a call interrupt.

"Tracie Higgins," she announced.

"Are we still on for tonight?" she heard Jon ask.

● ● ● ● ● ● ● ● ● ● ●

She rolled her eyes. "Yes, you're still on. Why wouldn't you be on?"

"You know," he said, "I've had a lot of last-minute cancellations in my career. Plus, I really ought to work. I mean, I've slacked off lately and I'm so far behind. . . ."

He was impossible. He'd worked twenty-four/seven for years. He was using work as an excuse, when, in fact, he had no self-confidence. Beth hadn't even met him yet, and he still figured he was striking out. "Forget about the past," she told him. "You're a new man. You look bad, you act bad, and you are bad. You are a bad boy, a chick magnet. Think of Beth as nothing more than an iron filing."

"Hey, did you have those little games when you were a kid?" he asked. "The ones that had the face of a bald-headed guy and a bunch of iron filings in a plastic bubble? You could make them into hair or a beard by using the magnet?"

Tracie drew her eyes away from her screen and stared into the phone. "Jonny, don't ask any questions like that tonight, okay?" she suggested. "No Mr. Potato Heads, none of your imitations of Cartman from *South Park*. And don't sing the entire *Gilligan's Island* theme song. When in doubt, be silent."

"Silent. Right," he agreed from his end of the phone. "But do you have to call me Jonny? It's so . . . weird."

She thought his voice sounded a little hurt, but she told herself it was for his own good. "Yes. Get used to it." She tried to think of what he could do to guarantee Beth's interest. She paused. The best trick would be to be unavailable. But how? She remembered a fight with Phil and smiled. Yes! "Jonny, there's something I want you to be sure to do," she told him. "Some time after you flirt with the waitress, I want you to excuse yourself and go over to the bar and talk to a woman."

"A different woman? But I . . ."

The light for line two on Tracie's phone went on. "Jonny, hold on a second, will you?" She was liking his new name, she realized as she pressed down the button for line two. "Hello, this is Tracie Higgins. May I help you?"

"What I want from you is a little more than help," Phil said.

"Hold that thought, and hold for a second." Tracie pushed line one and continued with Jon—uh, Jonny. "Where were we? Oh, yeah. You're at the bar talking to a woman. . . ."

"Trace. For tonight, I already have a date. I couldn't get one girl. I can't simultaneously pick *two* women up."

"That's not the point," she said. "Think of it as a magic trick. It's illusion." She remembered Phil on the other line. "Hold a minute," she said, then punched her other button. "Phil, I'll be right with you." She punched line one again. "So, Jonny, just ask her what time it is. Or the best road to take to Olympia. Anyway, then I want you to write a phone number in pen on your hand."

"Whose phone number?" Jon asked.

"Just *any* phone number," she told him, exasperated. "Then go back to the table and don't say anything about it. Just make sure Beth sees your hand."

"Let her see it?" he whined. "Tracie, you're getting me nuts. This is cruel and unusual punishment. Maybe we should cancel this. I'm so behind on my work. And I'm not feeling well all of a sudden."

"Don't even think about getting sick," she warned him, "or it's back to airports for you. Anyway, she'll love you over this. It will make you seem like a conqueror. You can have anyone, but you picked her."

"But I might also be picking up someone else," he whined. He still didn't get it.

Tracie rolled her eyes. " Jonny, this is what dating in the new millennium is all about: cruel and unusual punishment. Now do you get it?"

"I got it. So I'm going to meet her in front of your building at five-thirty."

"But be sure not to come until about quarter to six," she said.

"But . . . ah. Okay," he agreed.

"See ya. Wouldn't wanna be ya!" Tracie sang out, using Encino-speak again. Only after she had hung up and gone back to work did she notice that the light for line two had gone out. Phil! She shrugged. She didn't know where to reach him, but Phil would call back.

Beth was primping while Tracie, Laura, and Sara watched the operation. "You ought to brush out your hair," Sara suggested. Tracie handed her a blusher and straightened up her collar.

"I already have, Sara. Thanks. God, I'll probably sweat like a nervous pig," Beth said. "I wish I'd brought my perfume."

"You want to borrow some of my Giorgio?" Laura asked, rummaging through her bag.

"Thanks, but no," Beth said. "I already put on White Shoulders this morning. Together, they might curdle. Is he really cute, Trace?"

"Yeah. He's cute . . . in a kind of James Dean way." Tracie figured she could plant that in Beth's mind.

But Beth asked, "Who's James Dean?"

"Some dead guy. An actor, right, who made sausages?" Sara said.

"You're so lucky, Beth. I haven't been on a date in four months. Tracie, why don't you ever fix me up with somebody? Doesn't Jonny have friends?" Sara asked.

"Tracie never used to know anybody good," Beth said. "Laura, where did she find this guy? I'd never heard of him," Beth pointed out as she applied some mascara.

"She's manufactured him," Laura told the girls, then grinned over their heads at Tracie. Tracie gave Laura a warning look, then looked at her watch. "You're going to be late," she told Beth. "And Laura and I are going out for a drink."

Beth panicked. "You're kidding! I still have to tweeze my left eyebrow. Who has a pair of tweezers?" she asked. "I look like Gorilla Girl." Laura handed her the tweezers while Tracie sneaked a peek out the window. Whatever time Beth got there, Jon had to be a little later. God, she hoped Beth wouldn't be too disappointed or diss him too badly.

"It's already twenty to six," Tracie announced. "You were supposed to be there ten minutes ago."

"Make him wait. They're always late for us," Sara said.

Beth plucked two invisible hairs from her eyebrows, returned the tweezers, picked up her bag, and was ready to run. "Hey, if we go to the elevator bank, we can see them meet across the street," Sara said.

"Let's go," Laura agreed.

So Laura, Tracie, Beth, and Sara wove around the homeward-bound stragglers in the hall. They got to the elevator and Beth pushed the button. "Wish me luck!" she cried.

Before they could answer, the doors opened and she got in the elevator. Just then, the disgustingly beautiful Allison dashed into the hallway. "Hold the elevator!" she called. "I'm late."

"As if I give a shit," Sara murmured, but of course one of the men in the car hit the open button, hoping that for just a few moments he could stand beside Allison and drink in her aura. Beth was standing beside Allison, and her glow faded, but Tracie refused to acknowledge that.

"Have fun," Tracie said. "He's a dreamboat."

The three remaining women watched the door close on her hopeful face. First Sara, then Laura, and finally Tracie drifted over to the window. They waited a few minutes, looking out onto the street. Soon enough, Beth was below them. They watched as she crossed the street and stood alone in the twilight.

"If that son of a bitch doesn't show . . ." Sara said under her breath. "You know, Beth's had it so rough."

"He'll show," Tracie said grimly, hoping she was right.

"She looks really great," Laura said a little wistfully, her nose almost pressed to the window. "So thin."

"Ha! I hope he comes at her from the front and doesn't see her ass first," Sara said.

"Sara!" both Laura and Tracie cried.

"Just joking," Sara said.

Below them, Beth stood there, shifting from one leg to another, trying to lean against a light pole nonchalantly. The girls all watched in silence for a few more minutes. Despite her nerves, or because of them, her face had that first-date brightness that turns into a glow when women fall in love.

"If he doesn't show, I'll kill you, Tracie," Laura said.

"If he does and he's good-looking, I'll kill you for setting up Beth before you thought of me," Sara grumbled.

"Hey, hey!" Tracie soothed. "Don't get so excited. You probably won't even like his looks."

Just then, Tracie saw him chaining his bike to a railing just around the corner. God! She hoped they hadn't noticed him yet. Like an idiot, he had the motorcycle helmet lashed to the handlebars. She had to tell him everything, including not to take the Schwinn to the date. It was amazing that he didn't get arrested for public lameness. Tracie watched as he grabbed the helmet, ran down the street, and then slowed at the corner. She saw him check his reflection in the drugstore window. Luckily, Sara and Laura still hadn't spotted him. So that when he made the turn and swaggered across the street, there was nothing to link him to the Schwinn.

"There he is," Laura said. Down below, Jonny crossed the street and approached Beth. Clearly, they'd made contact and were introducing themselves. Tracie stepped back from the two girls and surveyed their reaction.

"Oh God. He looks great!" Sara was saying. She put her face up closer to the window and cupped her hands around the side of her head to cut down the reflection and get a better view.

"Nice sweater," Laura commented.

"Nice jacket. I saw one like that last year in Ralph Lauren," Sara continued. "Looks like the guy's got some bucks. Not to mention a nice set of pecs."

"He's got a helmet! Does he have a motorcycle?" Laura asked. Tracie remembered that Peter had a motorcycle.

"Where's his bike?" Sara asked.

"He probably parked it around the block," Tracie said truthfully; then, to distract them, she added, "You know, he just broke up with someone."

From the window, they watched Jonny and Beth talking. Jon put his hand in his pocket and pulled something out, putting it right in front of Beth's face.

"Is that a lighter?" Sara asked. "But Beth doesn't smoke."

Tracie rolled her eyes as Jon put the Pez dispenser back in his pocket. She'd have to kill him later. Then he reached out and touched the end of Beth's hair. The two of them laughed over something. And, in the silence by the elevator bay, loneliness began to envelop the three women. Tracie couldn't help but remember how excited she used to get when she'd first met Phil—how she'd spend an hour trying on every possible outfit. She remembered how happy she'd get just seeing him. That reminded her. "Laura, come on. We've got to go," Tracie said. "I've got only twenty minutes for a drink and then I've got to meet Phil."

"Yeah, and I've got a story due." Sara sighed.

"I guess I'll get to work on my résumé tonight," Laura said. "That, and read the want ads."

The three women all sighed as one and then each turned her back on the window and walked away.

Chapter 22

A waitress stood at the table and looked expectantly at Jon and Beth. She looked at least a hundred and ten years old, one of those women who would work until the day she died.

They were at the Merchants Café, the oldest restaurant in Seattle, and their waitress was probably even older. Jon was nervous, but so far, he hadn't blown it. Before he'd left work, he had called and had another quick review session with Tracie. She was going to show up and observe from a distance, to help him through. He was determined to do this perfectly: remember the lines he was supposed to say, compliment the appropriate odd thing, and avoid any mention of his dietary habits. He would carry no luggage, and he wouldn't hang off any rock walls.

But somehow, as he looked across at Beth's pretty face, all the tutoring became a mishmash in his head. For a moment, he felt sad and wondered why all the charade was necessary. It just increased the gulf between them. But he had to admit that Beth was really cute and she was looking at him with more interest than he'd gotten from a woman in a long, long time. He told himself he was going to have to tough it out. He was absolutely committed to making all the right plays.

By now, the waitress was tapping her foot, impatient for their order. Jon remembered that there was something he was supposed to do when Beth selected her meal. He tried to think quickly, reviewing what it was. Something about veal? No. For a moment, he panicked. Then he remembered. He'd have to wait until she selected her choice.

"I'll have the Dover sole," Beth said to the waitress.

"Are you sure you want to order that?" Jon asked, proud that he'd remembered in time.

"Why? Isn't it fresh here?" Beth asked him.

Wait. That wasn't part of his tutorial. He realized, too late, that in Tracie's scenario, his date ordered something very fattening.

"All of our fish is fresh daily," the waitress said hostilely, as if any discussion of the fish reflected on her honor.

"I'm sorry. I'm sure it is," Jon said apologetically. He hadn't meant to insult the Merchants Café. How could he explain? Thinking quickly, he said, "Uh, I'll have the sole, too." He didn't particularly like sole, but it was a good peacemaking gesture. At least he hoped so.

"It comes with salad. You want potatoes or rice?" The waitress took the rest of their order without comment and then left, shaking her head. Meanwhile, Beth was staring at him, a half smile on her face.

"You're weird. You warn me not to have the fish and then you order it, too?"

Jon shrugged. Okay. He'd screwed that up, but he wouldn't screw up anything else. He tried to think of what James Dean might do. He probably wouldn't have ordered the sole. What had Tracie taught him? He looked across at Beth. She did have pretty eyes, dark, with a fringe of darker lashes, but he knew he wasn't supposed to say that. So when the waitress returned to the table and put two salads down, Jon took the old woman's hand to stop her. He looked at Beth.

"Doesn't she have the most beautiful eyes you've ever seen?" he asked his date.

But, even as the words were out of his mouth, he realized with a sinking feeling that it was very clear that the waitress's eyes were not beautiful. In fact, they were hardly visible, buried as they were in the folds of her wrinkled face.

"Oh, yeah. She absolutely does," Beth agreed, probably to make the woman feel good. Or because she thought Jon was trying to be sweet.

"Thank you," the waitress responded. Well, he hadn't made Beth jealous, but at least he'd made up for his fish insult. What next? This was so difficult. He sighed. Once the waitress left, he began to fiddle with his salad, afraid to speak and afraid of the silence.

"That was considerate," Beth said, using the voice that he'd heard all his life. "You're a sweet guy."

"No I'm not," Jon said with more force than he meant to use. Beth blinked the eyes he was not supposed to comment on. Great. Next he'd start babbling about his luggage and the Unabomber. She'd run screaming from the restaurant. Get a grip, he told himself. Beth was saying something about the place and he had to get out of his head and respond. "Are you from Seattle?" he managed to ask. God, that was lame, but at least it got her going. She began talking about each of the places she'd lived. But he got distracted. Because out of the corner of his eye, he saw Tracie enter the place with Phil and take a table on the other side of the restaurant. Oh, no. She had told him she would be there for him, but somehow he hadn't imagined Phil along with her.

Of course, she wouldn't be coming alone and he supposed that Phil—odious as he was—was better than Laura. In case he blew this, he didn't want the woman he'd accidentally tried to pick up to watch him go down in flames.

Tracie surveyed the room, caught his eye, and then waved to him discreetly. She slipped into a chair with her back to Beth and Jon. Then Jon realized that Beth was asking him a question.

"Huh?" he asked like a lunkhead.

"What kind of bike do you ride?" she repeated.

"A Schwinn . . . uh . . . Could you excuse me a minute?" he asked as she laughed.

"Yeah, sure, Jonny," she told him. He gritted his teeth. He hated that stupid name. He got up and started to walk toward Tracie's table, but Beth interrupted him. "I think the men's room is that way," she said.

"Oh, thanks. Yeah, right." He walked off in the direction that Beth pointed in, then managed to hide himself for a moment in the hallway and doubled back. He crouched, then ran to Tracie's table. He stuck his head up between Tracie and Phil. He'd just blank Phil out. Phil, and all the smooth Phils of the world. Jon focused on Tracie.

But he couldn't blank Phil out, because when he raised his head to Phil's eye level, Phil did a complete double take. If he'd had something in his mouth, it would have been a spit take. Though he was in no mood for jokes, Jon readied himself for the insult.

"Whoa, little dude! Is that Jonny?" Jon didn't bother to respond, but Phil continued. "Tracie, he looks good. I mean for him, he looks really good!"

Jon just decided to ignore him. "It's going all wrong," he told Tracie.

"Oh, really?" she said sarcastically. "Could it have been when you flicked your Bic at her?"

"It wasn't a Bic it was a Pez."

"Well, that makes all the difference," Tracie told him, but the sarcasm was lost on him.

"Okay, okay. I screwed up but how do I fix it?"

"How do you know you have to?"

"She's already told me she thought I was a nice guy."

Phil laughed. "Uh-oh," he said. "You can take the dweeb out of Nerdland, but you can't take the nerd out of the dweeb."

"Thanks, Yoda," Jon snapped.

"What were her words exactly?" Tracie asked.

"She said I was 'a sweet guy.'"

Phil laughed. "Shit!" Tracie said. She rarely used expletives, so Jon knew it was as bad as he thought it was. He'd tried to do his part. He'd tried to do everything she told him to. He'd tried to follow directions, he really had. The hair, the clothes, the restaurant, the things he was supposed to say, and not supposed to say, but it still wasn't working. Maybe he should consider a career in a monastery.

Despite his nervousness, he realized he was babbling, but he couldn't stop. "And she didn't order veal Parmesan, the waitress is older than my grannie, and when I pulled the beautiful eyes bit, she thought I was being sweet." He banged the table with his fist. "Why do they always think I'm sweet?"

Tracie tried to reassure him. "Calm down. Don't worry. They'll feel you're heartless enough eventually. This is only your first try. Just think of this as a practice. Did you do the phone number trick?"

"What trick?" he asked.

Tracie glanced over at Phil, then glanced back at Jon. "The one I told you about," she said. She took his hand and wrote on it with her finger.

"Oh, yeah," Jon said. "Yeah, I mean, no, but I will." Despite himself, he turned his head toward Phil, who, if he had to witness this humiliation, could at least be useful. "By the way, Phil, do you ride a Yamaha?"

Phil looked at him with disgust. "No, I play a Yamaha. I ride a Suzuki."

Jon had to get back and had no time to be as snotty as he would have liked. "Great. Thanks," was all he had time to say before he scurried back to the hallway. There he stood up, looking around for a woman to talk to before he wrote on his hand. But there wasn't a woman around, and even if there had been, Beth couldn't see him. He had to do *something*, so he just took out a pen and scribbled a phone number on his hand. Walking the way James Dean did in *Giant*, he swaggered back to the table, where their fish had already been served.

"I started without you," Beth told him. "I hope you don't think that's rude."

"No. Not at all." He put his hand out to reach for the tartar sauce and almost knocked it over. Beth caught it and held his hand for a minute. "Oh. Thanks," he said.

Beth colored and looked down. She noticed his hand. "Isn't that Tracie's phone number?" she asked him.

Goddamn it! "Uuh . . . yeah. Sometimes I forget it," he said as smoothly as he could. He figured he'd better change the subject. "So, to answer your question, I ride a Suzuki."

"A 750?" she asked as she put a piece of endive in her mouth.

Her mouth was very sexy. It was pouty, or whatever word women's magazines used when talking about fluffy lips. She had a very red lipstick on, and for some reason, it gave Jon a real tug in his lap. "Uh, yeah."

"I didn't know Suzuki made a 750. My brother rode a Harley." She finished her fish. "He said Japanese bikes were all crap."

"Well, that seems kind of ethnocentric."

He looked down at his own fish. It was cold, and he'd never wanted it in the first place.

"Don't you like your fish, Jonny?"

God! Every time she called him that, he thought she was talking to someone else. "Uh, yeah. Well, no. Not really," he admitted. "I just ordered it because you ordered it. But I'm not a vegetarian or anything," he assured her. There was a silence for a moment. He had to say *something*. "You have very nice earlobes," he said at last. "Very shapely."

Beth laughed. "You are too weird." She laughed again. They talked for a while. "I like your jacket. Where did you get it?" she asked.

"My girlfriend—I mean a girl who's a friend of mine—I mean a friend of mine who's a girl—she thought it would—"

She interrupted him. "Are you seeing somebody? I mean in a serious way?"

Had Tracie told him what to answer to that? If she had, he couldn't remember. "No. No. I—"

"You're not living with her, are you?" Beth asked.

He remembered his line for that. "No. I live alone. But you can't come over."

"Well then, let's go to my place," Beth said.

Jon put down his fork. Had he heard right? He almost asked Beth to repeat it but, with his heart and other parts of him leaping, he figured he shouldn't press his luck. He gestured for the check and left cash on the table as soon as it was handed to him. (Tracie had told him not to use a charge card, and anyway, he wanted to be quick just in case Beth changed her mind.) Now he just had to get her out the door before she noticed Tracie and Phil at the other side of the restaurant.

Out of anxiety, he took her by the shoulder and gently but firmly pushed her toward the door, turning her body so that she'd be angled toward the bar and not the other dining room.

She turned her head over her shoulder. "That's sexy," she said.

Jon couldn't believe it. As he was opening the door and about to disappear through it, he only had time to give Tracie a fleeting glance. She had her neck craned and, though he couldn't be sure, the expression on her face looked a little bewildered.

Chapter 23

Tracie lay in the dark, staring up at the ceiling, with both her dinner and Phil's leg pressing heavily on her. He was sprawled across more than his share of the bed, making the little groaning sound he made at irregular intervals just before he fell asleep. She tried to extricate her leg from under his without disturbing him, but it wasn't possible.

After Jon and Beth's quick departure from the Merchants Café, she and Phil had finished their dinner. Phil had also finished the entire bread basket, most of the second one—except for the piece she couldn't resist—along with a large salad with blue cheese dressing, and then a very rich dessert. She thought of one of the Encino sayings she and Laura had used when they were learning the times tables: "I ate and ate and got sick on the floor. So eight times eight is sixty-four." He had finished up with brandy and two double espressos. Just to keep him company, she'd had one. It must be the espresso, mixed with my natural anxiety for Jon, that's keeping me awake now, she told herself.

They had come in more than forty-five minutes ago and collapsed on the bed. Since then, Tracie had had trouble sleeping. She wasn't used to such a rich meal at that time of night, and she never ate bread and desserts. But she'd been so nervous, expecting an emergency call on her cell phone to explain what had gone wrong at the restaurant.

It hadn't been going well. She could tell that from Jon's feverish questions and his report on Beth's comments. Beth, of all her friends, wasn't going to like a nice boy. What went wrong? she wondered. She supposed it wasn't possible to change Jon, and his true-blue color had shown, despite the camouflage they had tried. Well, Beth's loss. She just hoped that Jon wasn't too decimated. She had done this to build his self-confidence, but it seemed it was working the opposite way.

She shifted her weight. Phil's long leg still hung over hers. Her right foot was going to sleep. She would have to nudge him to get out from under. He was such a bed hog, she wondered why she even wanted to win her bet. He'd been awful at the restaurant, imitating Jon and making fun of both of them. He ate like a pig, he never had any money, and though he was undeniably good-looking, he looked at other girls. Sex was great, but sleeping with him certainly wasn't easy.

But that didn't cause her insomnia. What she couldn't understand was why they'd left the restaurant so soon, why Jon hadn't called her, and why he didn't answer when she rang his phone. Of course, she'd told him that he'd have to work at being unavailable, but she hadn't meant unavailable to her. Knowing Jon, he just didn't want to bother her with yet more bad news. Still, she'd called four times already and let it ring, hoping he hadn't turned the phone off and that he would pick up so she could comfort him.

She decided to try one more time. As gently as she could, she pushed Phil's hip with her hand while she tried to wriggle her leg free. She had extricated her knee when he lifted his head. "What time is it?" he asked.

"Sleepy-sleep time," she told him. "Roll over." He did, and Tracie got up and looked over his shoulder at the clock. She picked up the phone, dialed Jon's number, and, when there was still no answer, decided to dial Beth. What the hell. Beth might ream her for setting her up, or for waking her up, but she could always pretend she was upset over Phil. She'd gotten enough calls from Beth over Marcus to make that all right.

But there was no answer at Beth's, either. "It's almost two A.M. Where are they?" she murmured to herself. Phil grunted. Worry now mixed with her curiosity. Maybe . . .

"Downloading recipes, for all I know," Phil said. He sounded incredibly cranky. He always did if he was awakened. "Come on, go to sleep. You're nobody's mother," he reminded her. "What's it to you?"

"Well . . . I just hope they're all right," Tracie told him, then sat back down on her side of the bed. She imagined Jon finally giving up and hanging himself in his new, pared-down closet. Or snapping, and attacking Beth like a sex-crazed weasel.

Phil turned over, but Tracie continued to stare into the darkness. In a moment, she heard his snores.

She was sitting on the sofa in the dark, trying to think of what she'd do next, when Laura got up from her futon and stealthily walked to the side table and lifted up the phone. "What are you doing?" Tracie asked.

Laura jumped in surprise and strangled a scream. "Oh my God! Tracie! I didn't know you were there."

"Obviously not," Tracie said. "Who were you about to call? No one in Encino," she said accusingly.

"I wasn't going to call anyone," Laura said.

"No," Tracie agreed, her voice mockingly sarcastic. "You just woke up in the middle of the night with a phenomenal need to dust the phone." Tracie narrowed her eyes, although in the dark she could barely see Laura's white shape. Has she been doing this all along, while I thought she was getting over it? Tracie wondered. "Since no 900 numbers have shown up on my bill, I have to think that you've been calling Peter," she said bitterly.

"No, Tracie. I swear I haven't been. This was the first time. It was just that I . . ." Laura sat down beside Tracie. She picked up one of the throw pillows and pulled it to her chest. There, together in their nightgowns in the darkness, Tracie was suddenly flooded with tremendous affection for her friend. It wasn't easy being Laura. Who could understand a big, funny, smart, wisecracking girl with a passion for cooking? Who would want to be with her, to love her as much as she deserved to be? Well, Tracie would, and any man who wouldn't was losing out. And not just on great dinners.

"I don't know. I watched Beth get ready for her date, and then you had to rush off to Phil, and it seemed like everyone had someone but me. And I thought of Peter. I know I shouldn't even think about him," Laura admitted, her voice full of pain. "I know that. But . . ."

"I know," Tracie echoed, putting her arm across Laura's shoulder. "It's hard to be alone in a world of couples. I hope that Phil and I don't make you feel left out. I'd hate that."

"No. No. You never make me feel like the third wheel. It's so nice that you'd even have me here." She paused. "It got really bad in Sacramento." Laura made a little choking noise. "You know, I don't want Peter back. It was just hearing Phil's snore that somehow made me so lonely." She paused, and Tracie could see a single tear roll down Laura's cheek. "I wanted to be next to my own snorer," Laura said, then sniffed. "So sue me."

"I won't sue you this time," Tracie told her, "but I am going to tell you that you have to give up the reruns of *Quincy*. Jack's a bad influence on you. You know, Mr. Bill at my video store won't let me watch *Love with the Proper Stranger* anymore."

"He won't?"

"Nope. And that's a good thing. You have to get out there again. Oddly enough, you're not likely to meet anybody in front of my TV or in my kitchen."

"You may have a point there," Laura admitted.

Tracie moved her hand to Laura's two and rubbed them. They were big and warm and capable, just like Laura. "Come on," Tracie said. "Don't you think it's time you decided to stay up here? Look for a job?"

"Well, I already went to one interview," Laura said hopefully.

"It's a start," Tracie told her. "And let me make you an appointment with Stefan to add some streaks to your hair. It'll be fun."

"Hey, what do you say if just this once we make farm cakes? I know how you love them." She took one look at Tracie's expression and backed off. "Okay. Okay. Just a pan of brownies from a box."

"I ate and ate and got sick on the floor. So eight times eight is sixty-four," Tracie sang as she got up to go to the kitchen. "And then we sit here on the sofa together and watch *Barnaby Jones* or whatever else is on."

"Really?" Laura asked, her voice full of enthusiasm again.

"Sure. Maybe you could wean yourself off Klugman with Buddy Ebsen," Tracie told her. "Think of Buddy as the patch. Did I tell you Jon wanted his nickname to be Bud?" Tracie asked, then wondered again for a minute what Jon was doing at that moment.

"Bud? You're dreaming, right?" Laura asked, and they both giggled in the darkness.

Chapter 24

Jon sat in one of his beanbag chairs, his helmet in his lap and with what he knew was a dopey look on his face. He couldn't get the half smile off his face, despite the fact there was a big Parsifal project meeting that afternoon—unprecedented for a Saturday—and he wasn't prepared to lead it. Instead of focusing on the next steps he and his staff had to take on Parsifal, he was replaying moments from the night before over and over.

Beth had been an enthusiastic partner, but a little too athletic and fast-tempoed. Jon had put his hands on her and slowed her down the way you would with a nervous dog. Every time she wanted to jump to some new position, he'd reminded her with his hands and his tongue—and sometimes by pressing his chest against her—to take it slower. He wanted her to savor each stroke, each caress, each flick of the tongue.

And, once she relaxed, she seemed to enjoy herself. He could tell that she'd had plenty of experience, but he thought she was probably more practiced at pleasing men than at taking her own pleasure. The first time they'd made love, he'd come far too quickly. But that had given him the advantage when they made love the second time, and using his hand as well as long, slow strokes, he'd been able to make her come.

At least he thought so. Jon sighed. The night with Beth had given him a new attitude. He was surprised that it didn't really bother him that he didn't know her very well and didn't think that he'd like her too much when he did. What they had done had just been healthy and fun, but the only thing he didn't like about sex with an almost stranger was that you could never be sure if your partner had come or not. With his last girlfriend, they had had an agreement that she wouldn't fake it. He hoped Beth hadn't, but he couldn't know for sure. Jon looked around the table in his office, imagining the faces of his department staff, who in the next half hour would all be sitting there looking at him. Not one of them, he guessed, would feel as good, as relaxed, as he did at that moment. Or as unmotivated. Or as unprepared. He hoped that they had not been goofing off as much as he had.

As the meeting time approached, he couldn't keep his mind on the matters at hand. Visions from the previous night kept coming back to him: his hand moving down Beth's back into the hollow right above the swell of her hips; the way her eyelids flickered when he moved his hand slowly from her neck to her breast. He moved his tongue against his top lip and then thought about her nipples and how they'd felt against his lips. He felt a stirring in his trousers and realized he better focus on Parsifal, since he'd have to stand up for a good part of the meeting.

Beth was nice enough, but kind of silly. If he wasn't playing the game by Tracie's rules, he didn't know what they would talk about. Yet he felt a tug toward the phone. He wanted to call her. No, he didn't want to talk to her; he just wanted to meet her somewhere for an instant replay.

More and more, he was coming to understand that all was fair in love and war. It wasn't that his father or Phil didn't like the women they hooked up with. They just didn't like them enough. Sex with a stranger—and Jon knew that Beth was a virtual stranger—could be a lot of fun, but afterward there wouldn't be much to say.

His phone rang again, but, as Tracie had warned him, he didn't answer it. That was really putting a crimp in his professional life, but, remembering the previous night, he knew it was worth it. Jon grinned. The thought that he could do it again gave him a little thrill. He thought of the women that were coming to the meeting today: Elizabeth, Cindy, and Susan. He certainly wouldn't mess with anyone who worked for him, but Samantha—she was a different story. Jon wondered if his new look might work on Samantha. His phone rang again, but again he ignored it. His assistant was calling everyone to remind them about the meeting. Again the phone rang. Annoyed, he got up to check the caller ID and realized it was Tracie.

He reached out to pick up the receiver and then stopped. He was embarrassed. He knew Tracie. She wasn't a reporter for nothing. She'd question him on every detail, and somehow it would feel bad to tell Tracie how much he'd enjoyed her friend Beth. It would, however, be equally wrong to pretend that he hadn't enjoyed being with her. He sat back down on the beanbag, and as it gave a sigh of escaping air, so did he. In a way, he owed last night to Tracie and many nights to come. Somehow, though, he really didn't want to talk about it with her.

He'd left Beth's apartment, just as he'd been instructed to do, but shouldn't he eventually call her? Tracie was going too far with that. Still, what she had prescribed had worked. And if he was honest with himself, he knew he didn't actually want a relationship with Beth. So what was he going to do? Tell Beth he'd like to see her again just for sex? Lie to Tracie and pretend the sex hadn't happened? Betray Beth and tell her it did?

Lauren, his assistant, stuck her head into the office. "George says he doesn't have the time line ready," she told him. Jon was out of the chair in a minute. "Goddamn it! How can we schedule each work step without the time line?" he asked. "We're counting on it."

Lauren shrugged. "He says he tried to call you but that he didn't get you."

"Well, he didn't leave a message," Jon said. What he didn't say was that he had rigged his voice mail so that it would always say his message box was full. Lauren shrugged again and disappeared. Shit, Jon thought. While he was getting laid, Parsifal was getting screwed.

He had to review his E-mail, get a copy of the database report, and check his new voice mail messages. Even though Tracie had told him to get rid of voice mail, he couldn't do it at work. Since he was used to getting half a dozen phone calls at home from Micro/Con people, just aborting his home system was traumatic. And using the filled-mailbox ploy was dangerous. Look at what had happened with George and the time line. He got on the phone and began to listen, a pen ready. "You have twenty-seven new messages." Jon groaned. It would take him until the meeting just to clear the messages.

The first message was from Tracie. "I called you at home, but you didn't pick up. Are you depressed? How did it go? Call me."

The second one was also from Tracie. "I've tried you about four times at home again. I'm dying to know how it went. Look, she's not worth getting upset over. There will be others."

Jon had to smile at that, though he felt a little guilty for not having called her. The third call was from his mother. "Hi, Jonathan. I know you must be working very hard, but I wanted to talk to you. It's not very important, but if you have a spare moment, give me a call."

Oooh. He hadn't seen or talked to his mom since Mother's Day. Of course, she thought he was busy with work, as he usually was. He told himself he'd call her back that evening.

The fourth call was also from Tracie, but it was from that morning. "Where are you?" she said. "Come on. Call me. I'm at work. I haven't heard from Beth yet. I hope you didn't murder her." The next call was really breathy, and for a moment he thought it was Tracie again, fooling around. Then he realized it was Beth.

"Hi," she whispered. "Last night was . . . well, you know what last night was. Where did you go? Thanks for leaving your number. Call me." Jon hunched his shoulders guiltily. Tracie had been very clear that he shouldn't reveal where he worked or give out his number, but when he'd snuck out of Beth's bedroom, he'd felt so guilty that he had left his Micro/Con number and he'd rigged the phone so that anyone calling in wouldn't necessarily know that it was Micro/Con. He sighed. This was all so much more complicated than he had imagined.

Jon repressed a grin and listened to the rest of his messages. There were four more from Tracie, each one making him feel more guilty, and two more from Beth. He wasn't the only one who called over and over again. Obviously, women did it, too; it was just that they had never done it to him until now.

His other messages were from George and some of his own staff members. All the news was bad. Jon was almost finished with the lot when there was a new woman's voice on the phone. "Hi, this is Ruth. We met at REI. Remember?"

Jon's eyes widened as he stared at the machine. How could I for-get? he thought. "I hope you're okay," she was saying. "You know, I panicked on a climb myself. Anyway, if you'd like to get together and have a cup of coffee or something, I'd like to see you. I hope you don't mind if I don't leave my number. I'll just call you back later."

Holy shit! Jon was too shocked to listen to the rest of his messages. He couldn't believe it. Tracie wasn't just smart; she was the Goddess of Love. He would have to call her, despite his embarrassment, and he'd have to ask her what to do about Beth and Ruth. Maybe he didn't have to see Beth again. He could just move on to Ruth. After all, she'd called him. That might make it even easier. Of course, he didn't want to hurt Beth, but he figured he didn't have much in common with a Seattle club girl. Not that there was going to be much in common between him and an REI mountain climber girl. But who knew?

Jon dialed Tracie, but her line was busy and he didn't want to leave a message. What would he say? Mission accomplished? Lafayette, I was there? Best to see her in person, but when the beep sounded, he panicked and started rambling. "Tracie, I need to cancel our Sunday brunch. I'm swamped at work but I do have a progress report to turn in. Can you see me Monday night after work?"

He hung up the phone and went over to his terminal, trying to pull the Parsifal project together. He was whipping up E-mails in a frenzy when Samantha appeared in the doorway behind him. He saw her reflection in the terminal.

"Jon, do you have a minute?"

Jon allowed himself to look up at her, but only for a moment. "Actually, not right now," he said. "I'm kind of busy." He bowed his head, trying to hide a little smile. Did a man's luck just change completely with the roll of dice or a roll in the hay? It couldn't be, could it?

"I . . . I just wanted to apologize again for that mix-up."

"What mix-up would that be?" he asked. The phone rang. Yes! "Excuse me for a second, Sam." He picked up the phone. When he heard the voice again, he felt it was too good to be true. "Oh, hi, Ruth. Sure. I remember you." Unbelievable! How could he be so lucky? He could talk to Ruth while Sam watched. There *was* a God. "Well, actually, I haven't been climbing since," he told Ruth while he watched Sam's reflection. "No. I'd like to. With you. That'd be great. See you then, Ruth." He hung up the phone.

"Sorry," he said, turning to Sam, but then remembered he wasn't supposed to apologize for anything.

"That's okay," she said, and took a tentative step into his office. "Anyway, you know that Saturday we were supposed to get together?"

"When was that?" he asked, vividly remembering the night he'd stood in the rain.

"Oh, it's not important." He thought she blushed. Was it possible? Had *he* made the beautiful Samantha, homecoming queen of the marketing group, blush? "Well, what I mean," she continued, "is maybe we could get together tonight."

Jon looked up cheerfully, then gave her a slight frown. "Hey, I'd really like to. Maybe some other time. I've just made a climbing date." He paused. He was loving this. "You're not a rock climber, are you?"

"No. Not really." Now Sam paused. "But I'd like to try it."

"Well, maybe sometime," he said vaguely.

"Great, Jon. Are you going to have lunch in the cafeteria?"

"I think so," he told her. Then he said nothing. Absolutely nothing. He watched as she tried to leave. Just as she began to move, he spoke again. "Oh, and Samantha . . . my friends call me Jonny."

"Great, Jonny," she said. "Uh, do you still have my number?"

He nodded, but just barely. Then Jon watched Samantha walk out the door and down the hall. He got up, calmly closed his office door, and then did a huge freakin' victory dance around his desk.

It wasn't until late afternoon—after the Parsifal meeting and long overdue phone calls—that Jon got a chance to gobble a quick sandwich, leave his mother a message, and get to the toilet. He was in a stall, just finishing, when he heard Ron and Donald.

"I don't know," Ron was saying. "I mean, it seemed like he was totally in the dark."

"In the dark? It was Helen Keller night in the black hole of Calcutta," Donald answered.

Ron and Donald were probably two of his smartest staff members, but Ron had a head of unfortunate red hair—the kind that looked pink and thinned early—while Donald might have been five foot two if he stood up straight. Both of them were brilliant, but neither one was what Miss Manners might call "a social success." They constantly hung together, and everyone at Micro/Con called them "RonDon." Now Jon had a sinking feeling in his stomach that they were talking about him.

"Hey, George," Donald said. Someone else had joined them. "What was with Jon in the meeting today?"

"I don't know, but I don't think he had all his burners going. He didn't know anything about the database project," George said. "And it wasn't my fault about the time line."

Jon gulped. It was true. He'd missed all of George's calls.

There was flushing, and Jon almost thought they had left, then realized their conversation was continuing. "Something about Jon has definitely changed," Ron—or Don—said.

"You mean like he's not as supportive of off-loading to the database as he used to be?" George inquired.

"No. Not about work," Don—or Ron—said. "I noticed it, too. He looks different."

"Yeah. And . . . and I think the pets are noticing him," Ron—or Don—said. "Jennifer smiled when she gave him that FedEx this morning."

"Jenny Pet smiled at a lowly mortal?" George asked. "Inconceivable!"

Jennifer was undeniably cute, but probably only eighteen. She worked in the mail room, and when she made her rounds, all business activity stopped.

"You know, I think you're right. When he left the meeting to get the marketing data, the women followed him with their eyes," Don—or Ron—said.

"You mean like in those holograms of Jesus?" Ron asked, his voice cracking.

"Kind of like that, but with sex," Don said. There was a pause, and for a moment Jon again thought they might have left. Then Don continued. He'd obviously been reflecting, because when he spoke, it was slowly, with great deliberation. "I think Jon is . . . hot."

"Homo! Homo!" the other two chanted.

In his stall, Jon shook his head. They were worse than Potsie and Ralph. He couldn't believe they made six figures a year.

"Shut up, shut up," Don yelled at them. "Don't you see the important implications here?"

"What implications?" George asked.

"Jon's done something to change himself. Something that works with the pets."

"Yeah?" George said. "So?"

"Well, if Jon can do it, we can do it," Don declared triumphantly. Then someone entered the stall next to Jon, water ran at one of the sinks, and Jon figured it was time to sneak out.

Chapter 25

When Tracie finally fell asleep, she had troubling dreams. At twenty-two after six, one of them made her wake up in an anxiety sweat. She was with her old dog Tippy and she was surprised and happy to realize he was alive again. Then for some dream reason, she started painting him blue. The little cocker spaniel stood there patiently as she rolled paint on with a fluffy roller, blue, all blue, until only his eyes remained, looking up at her in a sad but unsure way. At last, she finished, and taking the last bit of paint from the can, she upturned it on his head, covering his eyes as well. Tippy began to run in circles, yapping the way he did, and then he began to attack her ankles. He was biting her over and over again, and her red blood was mixing with the blue paint when she screamed and awoke. It was a horrible dream and she didn't want to go back to sleep after it. Maybe it was anxiety from not seeing Jon Sunday night. God, the waiting around for his so-called progress report was driving her crazy. So, she took a long shower and extra time to blow-dry her hair—it was too long and she needed a cut. On her way out the door, she snagged two more of the brownies she and Laura had baked on the weekend, ate one, and put the other in her bag for later. After all, it was a Monday.

Mondays were always a bitch because Marcus met with the brass in the morning. Then he passed the joy along at the afternoon editorial meeting. But this Monday, Tracie didn't have the regular knot in her belly. She was eager to get the scoop from Beth. Jon's social life was going to be good for her career in several ways, she realized as Marcus walked by her cubicle and raised his brows in surprise when he saw her. She smiled at him as obnoxiously as she knew how and sang out, "Good morning."

After he was safely gone, she took out the brownie and coffee that she had brought and put it down on her desk. At least it wasn't a farm cake. Between Laura's cooking and Jon's love life, she was eating a lot more than usual. The sessions at the gym weren't going to be enough to keep up with these calories. But she was ravenous.

She was also more concerned and curious than she could bear. Where was Beth? She jumped up on her chair and scanned the floor to see if Beth was around. She wasn't, so Tracie jumped down just in time to miss Marcus as he doubled back for something or other. This time, she ducked so that he wouldn't pick on her too much later. No sense making it worse at the editorial meeting than it had to be.

Without Beth to debrief, she dialed Jon's work number. She didn't get him, so she tried Beth's extension. No answer. She drank her coffee, nibbling guiltily at the brownie until the coffee got too cold to drink and there was nothing left but crumbs. It was only then that she saw Beth's curls bobbing two aisles away.

Tracie was out of her chair in a minute and at Beth's cubicle before Beth even sat down. When Beth made the turn, she smiled at Tracie. Tracie followed Beth into her work space. "Well? Aren't you going to say anything?" she asked. She couldn't tell if Beth was angry at her for the fix-up or if she had to be angry at Beth for blowing Jon off.

"Oh, I knew you were going to do this," Beth said. "I thought about it this morning, showering. Okay, okay," she agreed, then sat down and ran a brush through her hair.

"Okay, what?" Tracie asked.

* * * * * * * * * * *

"Okay, okay, you were right. About everything."

Tracie paused, really confused now. "Which everything would that be?" she asked.

"Everything about Marcus," Beth said. "He's boring and fat and way too old. Plus, he's selfish in bed. You've been right all along."

"You spent the night with Marcus?" Tracie asked, her heart sinking. "I can't believe it."

"Not with *Marcus*. With *Jonny*," Beth said. She took out a compact and looked into the mirror.

"With Jonny?" Tracie echoed. "You slept with Jon—Jonny?"

"Ohmigod," Beth said. "He is *so* good. And he's so great-looking. I mean, I didn't really like him, not like him like him, but then I just figured it would be a good thing to do to get over Marcus. Jon was sweet, you know. But then he kissed me, and it became a lot more than distraction sex. I mean, the way he touched me. He's got the most incredible hands."

"You're talking about Jonny?" Tracie asked. She was stunned. "Jon Delano? You slept with him?" Tracie felt dizzy. Somehow, the idea of Beth and Jon . . . This was more information than she required. She realized then that she'd never thought about Jon as a sexual partner. She'd even failed to talk to him about it. Tracie, Beth, Sara, and Laura talked about sex frequently. Laura once described how Peter's peter took a decided turn toward the left and the benefits and problems that presented. When Sara slept with the guy who wasn't circumcised, she had rushed in the next morning to describe the whole thing—as it were—in complete detail. She called it a shar-pei. But this was different. This was far too personal.

Beth was hanging up her coat. "You know, I guess I was getting used to Marcus. He's smart and everything. I mean, you can't deny that, but he's kinda"—she paused and Tracie realized she had no idea what was coming next—"kinda tired, I guess. Or maybe just so experienced that he's not so into it, you know what I mean?"

"Maybe *selfish* is the word you're looking for," Tracie suggested. And for a fraction of a moment, she thought of Phil.

"Yeah," Beth agreed. "Selfish."

Tracie didn't need to be told that Jon was anything but. For some reason, she had never really considered how that aspect of his personality would manifest itself in his sexuality. Silly of her. Of course he was generous and considerate in bed, as in all things. He had a great relationship with a warm and considerate mother.

"I had a hard time figuring out what type of guy he is," Beth said. "I mean, at first he looked like a tough guy—you know, a kind of Matt Damon in *Good Will Hunting*. But then he was more like an eccentric, kinda like Johnny Depp in *What's Eating Gilbert Grape*. Once we got talking, I saw he had this really sensitive, sweet side, like Leonardo DiCaprio in *Titanic*. . . ."

"Is there any movie star he doesn't resemble?" Tracie burst out.

"He's not like Ben Stiller," Beth said, missing the sarcasm, as usual. "I slept with Jonny not because he seemed like trouble but because he was different. He really likes women." Then she put her purse away, opened a drawer, and took out a flacon of perfume. "Thank you so much for setting us up. I like him. I mean I *really* like him," she said. "And the sex was just so—"

"Please, please," Tracie said, putting her hands up in surrender. "I don't need to hear this."

Beth looked up from the mirror at her friend. "You're acting like you're mad at me for having sex with him or something," Beth said. "How come? We're both adults. We took precautions." She paused. "Did you ever sleep with him?" Beth asked. Tracie shook her head no. "He was just so unbelievable."

It had been a hellish editorial meeting. But she couldn't get over the bombshell that Beth had dropped. And after she'd reached Jon, the bombshell had been followed by a barrage. "It was great," Jon had babbled. "So much fun. Beth's a real good kid. Your advice worked liked a charm. God, it was great to have sex again. Tracie, I'll always be grateful to you. It's like giving me the words *open sesame*."

"Fine, Aladdin," she had snapped. "Just don't expect a thousand and one nights."

"Why not?" he had asked. "I think I'm on a roll. You know what happened?" She'd shaken her head, wordless at this turn of events. "Ruth from REI called this weekend. She called again this morning, and we're going to see each other. I'll tell you more when I see you."

Tracie had been speechless. She'd gone to the editorial meeting in a state of suspended animation. All during the meeting, she couldn't help but look at Beth and imagine her and Jon in bed. She didn't know if she was disgusted with Beth, angry at Jon, or just mad at herself. She'd barely flinched when Marcus abused Tim and mocked Sara. She didn't remember to shrink down in her chair. She didn't need to look at either of them and wonder why they hadn't quit. If they were self-respecting, they would have, but she supposed if that was the case, she wouldn't be here, either. Allison was the only one who had escaped unscathed, and Tracie would almost swear that that meant Marcus was sleeping with her now. But that wasn't certain reasoning, because when he had been sleeping with Beth, he had felt free to make mincemeat of her whenever it suited his fancy.

Mincemeat brought her back to what she had just finished: the article on the best meat loaf in Seattle. Stupid. She shook her head. "Now," Marcus had said. "I have been truly pleased by the work done for this fine establishment by the late—no, make that the lately early—Tracie Higgins. Putting on a little weight lately, Miss Higgins? Perhaps it was in the line of duty. Fine coverage of the meat loaf crisis." He showed his teeth to the table. "So, onward and upward. I understand there is a new trend toward designer cupcakes. Little tiny things with really good frostings and new kinds of toppings. The days of the multicolored jimmies are dead and we at the *Times* will cover it." He looked directly at Tracie. "A cupcake story, my little cupcake. And get in all the bakeries that advertise."

"You are kidding," she'd said.

"Afraid not. We'll put it in a Wednesday food section." Then he'd turned to Beth, who had done, Tracie had to note, an excellent job of getting through the meeting. "Are you listening?" Marcus asked her.

"No," she said. "Is it my turn?" Tim laughed into his hand and disguised it as a cough. Allison tossed her perfect hair. Tracie decided once and for all that she would write her article for some other publication and do her best to get the hell out of Dodge.

Photos and Post-its were taped all over the inside of her desk. All of her ideas about nerds, cool guys, and the differences between the two were jotted on charts and graphs. Jon before and Jonny after were immortalized in photos. Each step of his progress was minutely detailed. But somehow, the date with Beth changed things.

She had called around to all of her journalistic contacts, verbally pitched the story to a couple of them, typed several query letters, and faxed them in a flurry of activity that made her look as if she was truly dedicated to the *Seattle Times* and Marcus. Too bad for the *Times* that all of it was motivated by her need to get away from him. It was too soon to tell, of course, but it seemed as if *Seattle Magazine* or a laptop publication in Olympia might bite.

But what was she going to do next? Add another Post-it that said "Jon fucks Beth"? Would Marcus like to have the article now? In fact, her wall looked like it was yellow, with a bad case of peeling. You could hardly see the green wall under all the Post-its. She sighed. Lots of notes, but no writing.

When the phone rang, Tracie was glad for the distraction. But before she could answer it, Beth scurried across to the phone. As Tracie reached for it, Beth put her hand on the receiver.

"Can I answer that for you?" Beth asked.

"No," Tracie told her. "Not since you didn't answer all weekend. Anyway, since when do you want to answer *my* phone? Just since your date with Jonny."

"Yeah? So?" Beth sat down. "Did you talk to him? What did he say about me? Does he like me?"

"If you let me answer it, I might find out." Tracie finally picked up the receiver. "Hello," she snapped into the mouthpiece. Beth watched her as if she were performing surgery instead of talking on the phone. "No, I can't. I have a deadline for this stupid cupcake article. No, the food, not the musician. Well, maybe what I do is as important to me as what you do is to you. No. Maybe tomorrow night." Tracie placed the receiver in the cradle.

"That wasn't Jonny," Beth said, and Tracie figured she should get the Nobel Prize for that one. Beth's eyes were open wide. "You just blew off Phil?"

"Yeah." Tracie had the strongest impulse to smack Beth, though she didn't know why. It was just her face. She had never really noticed just how annoying it was. "He's so self-centered. He wanted to have dinner."

"When you see Jonny again, can I come, too?" Beth begged.

"No!" Tracie told her, then realized she was almost shouting. She calmed down. "Look," she said slowly, as if she were talking to a child, "Jonny knows your name and number. You know his. As you said, you're both adults." Tracie felt exhausted, as if she'd run a marathon or climbed the rock face at REI a dozen times. She wanted to go home, crawl under the blankets, and have Laura serve her anything but meat loaf instead of sitting here, looking at a glowing Beth and writing about cupcakes. "You two work it out from here on in," Tracie said. "Call him if you want to see him so much."

"I already called him three times," Beth admitted. Again Tracie really felt like slapping her, and she put one hand over the other, just in case. "You know," Beth continued, "he doesn't have an answering machine or voice mail at home. Isn't that weird?" Tracie just shrugged. "He's not married, right?"

"Would I set you up with someone who was married?" Tracie asked, and shook her head. What had Laura called Beth? An airhead?

"Well, do you think he has a steady girlfriend?" Beth the Relentless asked. "Do you think he lives with her?"

"I *know* he doesn't." If Tracie told Beth the truth about the lack of other options Jon—or Jonny—had, Beth would probably drop him like a hot potato. "At least he didn't," she admitted.

"I'll just try him again," Beth said.

"Don't you think it's a good idea to just give it a rest?" she asked. She realized, with an unpleasant start of surprise, that she didn't like Beth or Jon very much at all.

Chapter 26

Phil and Laura sat at Tracie's dining table playing cards. They were playing for peanuts: not low stakes, but actual peanuts, because, to Phil's disgust, Tracie had no chips. Tracie was looking over her notes and photos, but the laughter from the other room kept distracting her. Perhaps it was something else: She still hadn't really talked to Jon. It was odd: The article sucked, but the makeover seemed to be progressing nicely. Despite not knowing Jon's take on his date, Tracie was determined not to obsess over it. After all, this turn of events gave her an ending for her article. In fact, it justified the piece. She knew she should be grateful and just get on with writing it.

But the truth was, she couldn't get very far with it. Without a deadline, she was having trouble focusing. Right now, she wanted to eat something, or to call Jon, or to put on the TV, or to lie down just for a minute and close her eyes. To be honest, she wanted to join in the card game. It sounded like fun.

Tracie heard Laura slap her hand down on the table. "Gin!" Laura exclaimed. On her bed, Tracie shook her head in pity for Phil. All their girlhood card playing in Encino had taught her that no one could beat Laura at gin. She'd once stripped their entire Girl Scout troop of money, jewelry, and Barbie dolls.

Tracie smiled at the memory, then forced herself to look back down at the makeover piece. She sighed and decided she couldn't concentrate on the article until she talked with Jon and found out what was really going on with Beth.

Had Jon become so unavailable? Was he avoiding her? Stranger things had happened. Maybe Jon really liked Beth. Tracie knew that would be delicate to talk about, because she truly didn't think that Beth was nearly good enough for him, certainly not smart enough. But since Jon hadn't had anyone for so long, he might confuse sex with love. Tracie decided she'd have to try gently to guide him out of that idea, but she'd have to be sure that he didn't hurt or insult Beth in any way when he did it.

But who knew? Maybe it would work and she should just keep her nose out of it. After all, there were a lot of friendships that broke up when people fell in love and got married. She thought it had happened with the Beatles, but she wasn't sure which ones. Maybe when Paul married Linda.

Marriage! The idea of Jon marrying Beth was so ridiculous that Tracie didn't know whether to laugh or to shudder. God, what am I doing, sitting here wasting my time over the idea? she thought. She told herself again that the incident was probably just a momentary attraction and would burn itself out in a few weeks.

Tracie looked at her Post-it notes stuck on the door frame, the window, and flapping off of pages of printout notes. She sighed at the thought of gathering them up and putting them away. Nah. She'd leave them where they were.

Meanwhile, she could hear Laura rattling the peanuts as she pulled them to her side of the table while Phil was shuffling the cards. "Have you lost weight?" she heard Phil ask Laura. Surprisingly, the two of them seemed to be getting along lately, but that was sweet of Phil anyhow. Tracie smiled—he could be thoughtful if he tried.

"Maybe a little," Laura told him, obviously concentrating on her

game. There was a very brief silence. Tracie sniggered. If Phil was try-
ing to distract her from her game, his attempt would be useless.
Laura was the only girl Tracie knew who didn't care about her weight.
"Gin," Laura said.

"Shit!" Phil exclaimed. "You can't have gin. We only drew one
card."

"Gin," Laura repeated, implacable.

"Misdeal!" Phil cried.

Ha! Tracie snickered. She knew that route was futile.

"You dealt," Laura told him.

Tracie could hear Phil complaining and gathering up the cards.
The two of them argued for a while as Tracie tried to tune them out,
knowing the irrevocable outcome. How long until Jon arrives? she
wondered. What will he say? What's going on with him? She
stretched out on her bed and might have dozed off for a few minutes. Then she heard her name drift into the bedroom. "So you
know, I'm trying to follow some of your advice, but I don't think Tracie is noticing."

"Oh, I'm sure she is," Laura said in the distracted voice she used
when she was counting cards.

Tracie immediately wondered what the advice was, why Laura
hadn't mentioned it to her, and whether Phil had asked for it or if
Laura had volunteered it. Phil was speaking again. She moved to the
end of the bed.

"I think you're right. I think I used to . . . take her for granted or
something," he was saying, "but you know, now I think she might be
doing the same to me." Laura murmured something Tracie couldn't
hear. Then Phil must have gotten up from the table, because she
heard the refrigerator door opening. She snuck to the bedroom door
and peeked out. Phil had pulled open the vegetable drawer and was
removing a head of iceberg lettuce. How had that gotten in there?
Tracie hadn't been grocery shopping, and Laura despised iceberg
lettuce.

Phil proceeded to cut the greens in half, then into quarters, and put the pieces on three plates. He took them to the table. "You wanna eat?" he asked Laura. Phil put out three place mats and three folded paper napkins. Then he lighted a candle, but once he'd done that, he obviously didn't know where to put it. He looked around for a candlestick, then, not seeing one, he stuffed the lit taper into the top of an empty beer bottle, Chianti-style. What in the world was he up to?

"You know, women want different things at different times of their life," Laura was now telling him as she put away the cards, gathered up her peanut winnings, and turned to Phil. "I was going out with that nitwit in Sacramento because he was exciting. But when you get old—I mean, I'll be thirty in just two years—you want something more stable. Someone with a job. Someone who can give back."

Phil nodded as if he'd take this as gospel. Tracie felt her jaw hang open. She could hardly believe it, or what he did next, which was lifting an already-opened can of Chef Boyardee ravioli and dumping the contents into a waiting pot. She couldn't believe it. He was trying to make dinner!

Of course, his attempt was laughable, but he was trying. It was so cute, like Peter Pan trying to stick back his shadow with soap. He was about to turn up the flame, when Tracie left her room. She couldn't stand it any longer. Laura was still sitting at the coffee table, eating her winnings. Phil now had his back to her and was stirring the ravioli with a fork. Just then, the intercom rang. Jon had arrived at last. Tracie ran to press the intercom to buzz Jon in.

"Are we expecting someone?" Phil asked.

"Jon's just dropping by for a minute," Tracie told him.

"From what I hear, Beth says nothing Jon does takes a minute," Laura said, wagging her eyebrows.

"When did you talk to Beth?" Tracie asked Laura. It seemed as if Little Miss Busybody was talking to everyone behind her back.

"Most of this afternoon," Laura admitted, sweeping peanut shells into a wastebasket. "She kept waiting for Jon to call her back, which he hadn't, and she had to talk to someone about him in the mean-time." Laura shrugged. "I was an obsession recipient."

Tracie shook her head. "Don't mention her," she warned Laura.

"Hey, I don't have dinner for four here," Phil announced as Tracie crossed the room to open the door.

"Oh, don't worry," Laura told both of them. "I don't have to join you."

"Don't be silly," Tracie told her. "This'll just take a couple of minutes. We're going for a walk; then just the three of us will have dinner."

Tracie opened the door, and as usual, they hugged. She was interested to see what Phil's reaction to the new Jon would be. So when Jon entered the living room, Tracie was behind him. Looking over Jon's shoulder, Tracie watched as Phil eyed him from the top of his black-and-blue spiked-up hair down to the soles of his new boots. The expression on Phil's face was one of surprise, quickly followed by dismay, and then replaced by false nonchalance. Watching the changes was like watching the three seasons bloom and fade in time-lapse photography, like they always did on the Disney Channel.

But when Tracie turned again to Laura, her friend's reaction—though a little more subtle—was more interesting and more of a tribute. Laura gazed unblinking at Jon and, for just a moment, her eyes had that longing, the expression that men got when they admired sports cars too fast or too expensive for them.

"Hi, Jon," Laura said in the voice that she used only when she was trying to be cute.

"I don't believe it," Phil blurted as Tracie and Jon walked into the room. Suddenly, she realized there was no way they could talk about what had happened in front of Phil and Laura.

Phil stood up, put down the empty Chef Boyardee can, and walked halfway around Jon. "You didn't buy this stuff," Phil said. "Tracie bought this stuff." He turned to Tracie. "Where'd you get that jacket?" he asked. "It's just like the one I used to have. I want a jacket like that."

"We got it at—" Jon started to say, but Tracie interrupted him.

"Never reveal your sources," she told him, touching his shoulder. "We're going for a walk," she told Phil and Laura, then grabbed her coat.

"What did you do to your hair?" Phil asked Jon as Tracie began to push him from behind. She had her hand in the spot between his shoulder blades, and before he could talk to Phil, she'd pushed him out the door.

"Be back in a half an hour," she called over her shoulder.

They walked down the stairs and out to the street before she let herself say another word. "You know, I just don't get you," she said once they were on the wet sidewalk.

"What?" he asked, but she could tell he was uncomfortable. He matched his stride to hers.

"I work with you day and night for weeks. I set you up with a date. I even coach you while you're on it. Then you don't even call me to tell me how it went. And I have to find out from my girlfriend that you slept with her!"

Jon looked down at the pavement and winced. "Was that information you required?" he asked. "I mean, I guess it was the point. Anyway, now you know. So, in a way, I guess I can say the experiment is over. It worked."

"That's *not* the point!" Tracie exclaimed. "I mean, why did you sleep with Beth?"

"Isn't that what you expected me to do?" Jon asked. "Wasn't that the whole point? Date 'em, do 'em, and drop 'em. *I* certainly didn't make that up."

"I don't think I ever put it that way," Tracie said.

"Well, it may not have been how you put it, but as I recall, we were working at ending my celibacy."

Tracie narrowed her eyes. "But not with my friend," she told him. "And don't feel so good about it. Beth is so desperate."

"And you don't think I was desperate after a yearlong dry spell?" He was whining like a Borscht Belt comic.

Tracie shook her head. She felt like slapping him. "Do you know how thoughtless this was?" she asked. "Not just doing it but doing it with Beth? We talk about our personal lives, and now I'm going to have to hear more than I would ever want to know about your sex life."

"Excuse me?" Jon said. "You two talk about your sex lives? I'm not making you talk about it. And anyway, if you didn't want me to sleep with her, why did you set me up with her? You made the date for me."

He was being utterly exasperating. "I didn't mean for you to sleep with her," Tracie explained. "It was just a practice date."

"You mean I was supposed to strike out?" Jon asked. "You were setting me up for failure? Another no-hitter for the guy who was batting zero?"

"You're not a batter and Beth isn't a ball," Tracie snapped. "She's been terribly hurt by Marcus, and I didn't mean—"

"Marcus, your boss?" Jon asked. "She was going out with Marcus?" He rolled his eyes and leaned against a mailbox until he realized how wet it was.

"I'm the one who has to hear about Marcus a hundred times a day. I know how disgusting he is."

"Beth was going out with your boss and you set me up with her? That's the kind of taste she has and yet you thought she'd be right for me?"

"I thought she'd be *wrong* for you," Tracie said. "Remember? You were supposed to be bad."

"Then you did mean for me to date her, do her, and drop her," Jon cried, triumphant.

"Don't tell me what I meant!" Tracie snapped.

They walked along the sidewalk in silence for almost an entire block. Then Jon stopped, took her by the shoulders, and turned her to him. For a moment, Tracie thought that he might be about to kiss her. "Tracie, you're my best friend. Why are we fighting? You told me what to do, and then who to do it with. And I did it. So why are you mad? If you don't want me to see Beth, I won't see her again. Just please don't be angry at me."

Tracie looked at him. Despite all the changes she had wrought, he was still Jon. His eyes were warm and pleading. She loved Jon. "I guess I was just hurt," she admitted. "I expected you'd call me right away."

"I was embarrassed," he said. "Plus, it was very late." He stopped. "I . . . I don't think guys talk about sex the same way women do."

"Okay." She sighed deeply. "The whole thing was ridiculous," she said. "I don't even know what I was aggravated about. It's just that Beth talked about nothing but you all day, and it drove me absolutely bonkers."

"She did?" he asked.

Just how sexually confident is he? she wondered. And how justified is his confidence? Looking at him now in his new clothes, at his new hair and his unshaven jaw, she realized for the first time that he might be very, very good indeed. She turned away so he wouldn't see her blush. It was weird to think about him in a sexual way—a little like thinking of your brother in that way. When he took her arm, she actually jumped.

"You're not still mad?" he asked.

"No, I'm not mad," she said. Once again, she thought this would be a good time to tell him about her idea for the article. Maybe if she told him, she wouldn't have so much trouble writing it.

When she got back to the apartment, all she wanted was a beer and a hug, but when she opened the door and looked in the refrigerator, then back at Phil's pouty face, she realized she probably wasn't going to get either one.

"Did you get any beers?" she asked him.

"No. If it's not here, I won't drink it," Phil said. "I'm trying to cut back."

Typical. He always thought of himself. "Speaking of cut, I have to get a haircut. You want a cut, Laura?"

"Yeah. But what I really need are streaks."

"Stefan is great with streaks. Jon goes to him."

"You know, that guy ought to be paying you tuition," Phil told her.

"And you oughta be paying me rent!" Tracie said, slamming the refrigerator door. Phil, oblivious, stirred the ravioli, picked up a bottle of Kraft French dressing, crossed to the table, and poured it on the lettuce halves with a flourish. "Dinner is served."

"You made dinner, Phil?" She looked at the pot. "Gee. I'm sorry. I'm just not hungry."

"But . . . I did it for you."

"Why don't you eat with Laura while I take a bath?" she suggested. "All I want to do is crawl into bed." Tracie went into the bathroom. Phil followed her.

"Tracie, this is important," he said. "I wanted to talk to you over dinner. I thought I might . . . There was this job—" He stopped talking. She was looking under the sink for her Vitabath.

"You mean with another band? Leave the Glands?" Tracie asked, shaking her head.

"No. I mean a real job," Phil said. "Well, it's like a trainee job. Can you imagine me in semiconductors?"

Tracie stopped rummaging under the bathroom sink and stared at him. "Did I just hear you say something about getting a job as a train conductor?" she asked him.

"That is *not* what I said. Jesus, if you paid half the attention to me that you're giving to the nerd and that article, you'd know what I'm talking about." He turned and walked out the door.

Fine. He could go home. All she wanted was a hot soak in her tub.

Chapter 27

Low conversation filled the Malaysian restaurant. Waiters and waitresses glided back and forth between the kitchen and the dining room with huge serving trays. Jon sat at a table in the corner with Samantha. He was in his James Dean/*Rebel Without a Cause* pose, just ending an intense story.

"I've never told anyone before," Jon said, then paused. Jon was nervously playing with the Goofy Pez dispenser. The ears were flipping around in circles. What now? he thought. For brevity's sake, he'd decided to combine two of Tracie's directives: He'd made up a tragedy and simultaneously told it as a secret imparted only to Samantha.

Samantha's sympathy, an altogether appropriate reaction to his story, filled him with contempt. He supposed it was because he'd made a sucker out of her with the lie. But if he told a stranger he was Mormon, or an orphan, or that his birthday was on Independence Day—it was actually on December 3—there would be no reason for them not to believe him. Lying to Samantha was no big trick. So why did it make him feel superior?

Something else troubled him: The more he lied, the easier it became. And the more it made him wonder if anything anyone said was the truth. How about his father? Had he also lied to Jon all those years like he lied to his mother? He paused and stared down at the table.

"I just can't get over how I misjudged you," Samantha was saying. "I mean, I'd noticed you, but somehow I thought you were . . ." She paused, and Jon wondered what version of the word *nerd* she was thinking of using. "Well, I just imagined you as very different," she said.

He nodded, then executed a perfect James Dean shrug. "Yeah. A lot of people don't see the real me." He sighed and looked down at the Pez dispenser. "My brother really loved Pez." He'd already figured out it was best if he didn't talk too much. If he did, he'd only screw things up or have to lie and remember what he'd said. Maybe that was why men like his father moved on: The lies got too complicated and the truth was unacceptable, so you just started over.

Samantha heard the sigh and reacted with greater attention. "What are you thinking?" she asked. "You can tell me." Her eyes were pleading. Lie to me, they said. Tell me something dramatic, something that makes me privy to the drama. "What happened then?" Sam asked, leaning toward him.

"He was on the back of my motorcycle . . . and I wiped out. There wasn't a scratch on me, but he"—Jon paused for effect—"he died." He let silence reign again for a few moments while he looked out toward the kitchen and worked his jaw muscle as visibly as he could. God, I'll wind up with a jaw like Jay Leno's by the time I'm done. He figured he'd better finish the story. "I've always felt responsible, but since then, I just don't get frightened."

Sam nodded her head. "I think I understand," she said, which was a good thing, because Jon certainly didn't. What bullshit! Women actually liked this crap.

The cute young Asian waitress came over to their table. Jon looked up from Sam and, in apparent surprise, took the waitress's arm. "Doesn't she have the most beautiful eyes?" he asked Sam as he smiled up at the girl. When he saw the reaction on Samantha's face, he knew he was golden.

The next morning, Jon was walking down the hallway at Micro/Con, feeling pretty cocky. He had his radar on for Samantha, when he spotted a familiar-looking woman in the distance. He'd all but slept over at Sam's the night before, and although they hadn't gone the entire distance, Jon felt that an excellent blow job was nothing to sneeze at. And somehow he knew that oral sex was Samantha's prelude to the real thing. It was her way of showing him she wasn't the kind of girl who went all the way on the first date.

Sam had been very sweet and giving—surprising in a woman who was so successful and assertive in the office—but perhaps he shouldn't be surprised. He was finding out that a woman's sexual personality wasn't necessarily obvious from her public personality. While he pondered this, he kept his eye on the woman he'd clocked in the distance. Until he realized who it was. "Carole!" he yelled. It was The Lovely Girl from the airport! Hadn't she said something about having Micro/Con as a client?

She turned around and, once she did, Jon did everything he could to recover his cool. He certainly shouldn't have yelled her name. Now he wouldn't run to catch up to her or anything. If she waited for him, maybe he'd just pretend to walk by her. No begging girls to turn around and look at him. It was a bad slip.

Sometimes he thought he'd never learn. But The Lovely Girl, Carole, once she saw him, approached slowly and, as she did, he watched recognition dawn across her face. He had assumed another one of his James Dean poses; this time it was the defiant one from *Rebel Without a Cause*. He hated the idea that she would remember him as a geek, that he had called out to her, and that she must realize he worked here, but he wanted to conquer. Maybe he could make his early gaffe of seeming as close to a serial killer as possible without DNA evidence work for him. Being dangerous yet respectable enough to work here actually might make him a more acceptable candidate. Maybe it was all for the best.

Carole eyed him up and down. "The plane, right?" she asked. He kept his face blank. Could it be that easy? No. Because then, her eyes flickered and she said, "Oh, the luggage."

Well, a good offense was the best defense. He managed a laugh. "Yeah. I lost my luggage and you misplaced your sense of humor." He paused. "Man, you completely missed my madman riff," he said, making a gesture with his hand over his head to indicate the joke had gone over hers.

To his surprise, she blushed. "Sorry. I was probably a little tense. I don't like lying. But . . . you look . . . different."

He shrugged. "Maybe it's the boots," he said, and she looked down at his feet.

"You work here?" Carole asked. "I didn't realize you worked here. Did you tell me that?"

He could see her relax. She smiled. Clearly, she was deciding he wasn't a maniac living in the woods, waiting for his next victim. Or if he was, he was a maniac who at least had excellent health coverage. "Sometimes I'm here," Jon said truthfully. For once, having been exposed as a guy with a day job would work for him. He smiled. He had to admit he was starting to get it. All you had to do was try to anticipate a woman's thoughts. "What is it that *you* do here?" he asked.

Carole smiled. "I can't tell you that," she said.

He shrugged. By asking, he'd lost a few points, but he didn't really care. After all, he had a date with Ruth tomorrow, one on the weekend with Samantha, and Beth kept calling. If she didn't stop soon, he guessed he'd have to sleep with her again just to keep his phone line open. He almost smiled to himself at the thought, but instead he looked at Carole. She wasn't just pretty; she was smart. And she was working at Micro/Con. They would probably have a lot in common. Jon wondered what it would be like to be with a woman who understood his work and the implications of it. Even Tracie didn't get it.

He smiled more broadly at Carole. "Can you tell me if you eat?" he asked.

"Eat?" she said. "Of course I eat."

"Can you tell me if you'll eat with me?"

She smiled back at him. "Of course I'll eat with you."

And afterward, you'll kiss me and then probably sleep with me, too, he thought hopefully. Jon grinned. This was a lot more interesting than Parsifal.

"Where?" she asked.

"I can't tell you that," he said, and she laughed. "If I told you that, they'd find me and they'd kill me."

"Don't you hate that when it happens?" she asked, and he realized she was flirting with him. Ah, flirting. He looked Carole over. She was funnier than Sam, and probably funnier than Ruth would be. And she was very, very lovely. But not quite as lovely as he'd remembered.

Jon was at a corner table at Vito's on Ninth and Madison with Ruth, the mountain climber. The room was dimly lighted and candles burned in tiny glass lamps at each table. He had just led her up to his obligatory drama/secret/I've-told-only-you story. "What happened?" Ruth asked breathlessly.

"I was a twin," he said. "But my brother killed himself. I was better at school, better at sports, better with girls. To me, it was never a contest, but I guess he just couldn't . . . compete. I always felt responsible." He paused for a moment, surprised to actually feel a bit of the pain of his lost imaginary twin. He shrugged. "Well, since then, I just don't get frightened."

"Really?" Ruth said, and he could see the sympathy blossom across her face.

When their chubby blond waitress approached the table, Jon stopped her from taking away his plate by putting his hand on her elbow. "Doesn't she have the most beautiful eyes?" he asked Ruth.

* * *

Jon leaned back against the banquette. He had gotten a corner booth at Java, The Hut, but he wasn't alone, waiting for Tracie. He was with Doris, the Asian-American waitress he'd met while out with Samantha. "What happened?" the girl asked him, as if her total existence depended on his next words.

"We were fooling around at target practice," he told her. "I'm a great shot, and he dared me to shoot a cigarette out of his mouth. You know, even though I was only fourteen and he was my dad, I said no. He got belligerent, but even so, I said no." He took out a Casper-the-Friendly-Ghost Pez, and offered it to her as if it was the Legion of Honor. Jon continued, "Then he bragged to all the guys, his pals, about my aim and bet them I could do it. It was a big pot. After he shot his mouth off like that . . . well, I had to try . . . and I shot his mouth off. Literally. It was an accident, of course." He sighed deeply. "But I always felt responsible. Since then, I just don't get frightened." He heaved another deep sigh, then turned his head toward the window, as if his dad was out there in the dark parking lot.

Molly came up to the table to give them their dinners. After she slid the hot plate across the table and handed each of them a plate, Jon grabbed her hand. He looked up into Molly's face. "Doesn't she have the most beautiful eyes?" he asked his date.

Chapter 28

Tracie sat at her desk, grumpy and resentful. She should be working, but since the morning editorial meeting, she'd lost all motivation. Instead of beginning a new draft, she picked up the phone and dialed Jon. She hadn't heard from him in days. Not only was she curious as to what was going on with him, but she needed to vent.

Nobody was as good to complain to as Jon. Laura only made jokes and tried to cheer her up. Phil tried to distract her. But Jon knew how to empathize.

Even before Tom Brokaw had written *The Greatest Generation*, Tracie had been deeply fascinated by Pearl Harbor and World War II. Her mother's father had died in the Pacific, and her paternal grandfather had served there. One of the few things she'd enjoyed in Encino were visits from Papa, and each time she'd ask him for stories from the long-ago war. So it came as a deeply unpleasant shock when, at that morning's meeting, Marcus had assigned a follow-up piece about local World War II vets to Allison.

"Marcus, I'm prepared to cover that. I have some material I didn't use in my Memorial Day story," Tracie had said.

"Thank you for that spirit of volunteerism and cooperation,"

Marcus had told her, "but I feel certain Allison will be able to meet the challenge."

It was so unfair. Tracie had been stuck with a lot of stupid topics for almost a year, and now a story that held real interest had been wrested from her. Her disappointment was so sharp that she couldn't even look at Allison without imagining what Marcus had made her do to get the assignment. In the meeting, Allison had glanced over at her, shrugged her shoulders, and given her a sorry-what-can-I-do? smile. Tracie would have enjoyed wiping the smile off her face with steel wool and a little muriatic acid. To add insult to injury, Marcus had assigned her a Father's Day feature. As if she didn't have a serious father issue, along with most of America. "Can I do deadbeat dads?" she'd asked, but Marcus had merely laughed dismissively.

She lifted the phone and punched in the Micro/Con number again. Not only was Jon still not available, but his voice mail was full and Tracie couldn't even leave a message.

"Have you heard from Jonny?" Beth asked from the doorway.

Startled, Tracie looked up. "No," she snapped. "And even if I had, I wouldn't tell you."

"Oooh," Beth cooed as she stepped away. "I guess it's best not to speak to you until the end of the day."

Tracie could hardly believe that Beth seemed to shrug off Tracie's mood as she went back to her cubicle. Usually, she was good for at least half an hour of obsessive pestering. Tracie was getting so tired of Beth's inquiries about Jon that she wished she'd never set them up together. *How was I to know that it would go this far?* Tracie asked herself. But with any luck, the whole situation would go away soon.

At least she'd made progress with the makeover article. It needed a good rewrite and an ending, but she thought it was funny and pithy, and even the photos looked good. She wondered if she had the courage to send the draft to *Seattle Magazine*. Then she thought big. They had seemed interested. Why not try *Esquire*? She had never been published in a national magazine. She knew she ought to look at some magazines and see who was on their masthead and what they were publishing.

Which reminded her: She'd finally gotten another appointment with Stefan, and if she didn't leave soon, she wouldn't be there in time for the haircut she so desperately needed.

Screw Marcus, Allison, and the *Times*. She'd be taking a long lunch today.

Music blared in the shop as Laura, with her hair in a hundred strips of aluminum foil, waited for her process to work. Meanwhile, Tracie was finally getting her hair cut by Stefan. "Not too short," Tracie instructed him. Stefan had granted a special dispensation and was allowing Laura to watch him while her hair was being processed.

"I know," Stefan said. "Never too short." He sighed heavily, as if he was tired of every hair on every head in Seattle. Tracie hoped he wasn't in a bad mood. Stefan in a bad mood was not a good thing. "How is your little experiment vorking?" Stefan asked, and for a moment, she didn't have a clue as to what he was talking about. Then Stefan continued: "He's some cute cookie boy." Tracie knew he was talking about Jon. "He vas in two days ago. I liked the blue. It vorked on him," Stefan said.

"Jon was in?" Tracie asked. "Jon came in here by himself?"

"Yes, two days ago," Stefan told her.

Tracie could hardly believe it. First of all, Jon had gotten a haircut just recently, and second . . . "How did he get an appointment before me?" she asked.

Stefan smiled, not at her, but to himself. He shrugged. Tracie just managed to catch the movement from the corner of her eye. "He is most persuasive, your cookie boy."

Laura giggled. "Cookie Boy?" she asked. "That's worse than Kissy Face. Do you really call him that?"

"No," Tracie snapped. "The only thing I've called him lately is ungrateful."

Tracie couldn't believe he'd made an appointment. Nor could she believe he had time for things like that but had no time to call her. Just then, the door opened and Beth, her hair plastered to her head in some kind of mud pack of color, stuck her head into the all-white sanctum, then walked in.

"No interruptions," Stefan said, holding up his scissors hand.

"Not too short," Tracie reminded him. "Beth, what are you doing here?" How many people could ditch work without the *Times* shutting down, and could they all be here? Was Allison getting a facial while Sara had a pedicure and Marcus got a perm?

Beth ignored Stefan and walked over. "Obviously, I'm not having root canal." She smiled. It was a big cheery smile. Tracie braced herself for the next question, sure to be about Jon, but Beth merely took a seat on the floor.

"No spectators, please," Stefan said, brandishing his scissors and then taking another snip off the top. Tracie looked nervously from Laura to Beth. If he was taking off too much, they would tell her. At least she hoped they would. Calm yourself, she thought. Stefan is the only man in Seattle you can truly trust. That's why you come here, put up with his idiosyncrasies, and pay his outrageous price. But she wished she had a mirror.

"Beth, you better go," she told her friend nervously.

"That's okay," Beth said. "Stefan doesn't really mind."

"So, how is job on Cookie going now?" Stefan asked.

"Just great. Almost too great," Tracie told him. "My friend Jon needed a lot of help, but he's looking good."

"Way too good," Beth agreed.

"You can be too rich or too thin, but you can't look too good," Stefan intoned.

"He's right." Beth groaned.

"I thought you hated him," Tracie told her. "Isn't he the guy who never calls you back?"

"He called me back just after I talked to you," Beth said with a triumphant but guilty little smile. "That's why I'm here. It's an emergency."

"I hope you told him to stick it," Tracie said, but she felt her heart dropping in her chest, because if Jon had called, and if he'd asked her out, Beth was going to go.

"I told him I'd love to see him tonight," Beth gushed.

"Tonight? He didn't call you for days and then he asks you out for tonight and you say yes? You are hopeless," Tracie told her.

"I figured it out," she said. "Jonny's a very sensitive guy. I just think he's afraid he felt too much for me. It scared him."

Tracie and Laura exchanged a look. Behind Beth's back, Laura rolled her eyes.

"He was afraid of his feelings. It happens with guys."

"Beth, sweetie," Tracie said in a kind voice, "you didn't scare him."

"Please vould the psychology convention convene at the university? Or in the insane asylum? Just not here. No speaking here," Stefan said firmly.

Beth paid no attention. "You know, he's just traumatized because of his brother's death," Beth told Tracie.

"What brother? Jon—Jonny's an only child," Tracie said.

"No," Beth said, shaking her head. "He doesn't like to talk about it. Except to me."

"Oh God!" Tracie groaned.

Laura rolled her eyes again and snorted. Tracie couldn't believe it. She'd taught him that trick—to come up with something dramatic—but that he'd actually done it, and succeeded! Even with Beth—not exactly a polygraph.

"What?" Beth asked, staring at Tracie. "Oh, don't be hurt. A lot of guys will confide things in me that they don't tell anyone else." She waved. "I gotta go. I don't want to be late for him."

"Get out of here," Stefan said, and Tracie didn't know if this was in response to Beth's comment or if he was trying to maintain creative control.

She ran out of the room, and Stefan, with a noise somewhere between a sigh and a moan, took two more snips at Tracie's hair.

Laura squinted her eyes and shrugged, then pointed wordlessly to Tracie's head. Tracie felt a tug of terror. "Remember, not too short, okay?" Tracie told Stefan again. "Isn't that unbelievable about Beth?" she said to Laura.

"Oh, yeah, that'll keep her going for another three months of obsessing," Laura said. "But I have to say, I think I'm over Peter."

"Great!" Tracie exclaimed.

"And I think I want to stay here in Seattle." She paused. "I'm looking for an apartment."

"Terrific!" Tracie told her, and she meant it.

"Yeah. I figured that would be good news," Laura said. "I've been a pain in the ass with my moping. Plus, I know it's been a strain to have me at your place. I know I'm kinda getting in the way of your thing with Phil," she added.

Tracie shook her head to say no, then heard Stefan's quick intake of breath and realized she had moved at a critical moment. "Sorry," she said to Stefan. "No problem," she told Laura, but Tracie felt guilty, since she'd so recently thought the same thing.

"I know you didn't mean to have me move in permanently. . . ."

"You're always welcome," Tracie said.

"In my country, ve say guests, like fish, stink in three days," Stefan said, and took another slice at her hair.

"So anyway, I can't afford a place without a job, and I can't set up as a caterer without capital, but they need a cook at a brunch place and—"

"You got a job?" Tracie asked, surprised and delighted.

"Yeah. I talked to the owner. It's a done deal."

"Do I get a discount if I go there?" Tracie asked.

"No, but as an incentive, I promise I won't spit in your food," Laura assured her.

"Great!" Tracie said. She tried to put her hand up to her ears to see if they were still covered, but Stefan hissed and pushed her hands away.

"Well, congratulations." For a while, they sat in silence except for the ominous sound of Stefan's scissors. "I really can't believe Beth," Tracie said after a moment or two to break the silence. "How could she have said yes to Jon after he'd dissed her so badly?"

"How could she say no when she likes him so much?" Laura responded, shrugging.

"You know, he told me he'd made a date with Ruth, that girl from REI. He's probably seeing other women, too. And he hasn't told me anything," Tracie complained.

"What does it matter to you what he does? I think you are obsessed with him."

"I'm not obsessed with him," Tracie protested. "I just need to keep my information straight for my article." She heard Stefan sniff. He was taking a very long time. He never took this long.

"That is so ridiculous. You can't get me with that crap, Higgins," Laura told her. "I think you're in love with Jon."

"Laura!" Tracie jerked her head to turn toward Laura and Stefan's scissors narrowly missed her ear.

"Stop it! Stop it! Stop it!" he cried. "This is about my head, not your heart."

"*My* head," Tracie corrected him. "And my heart has nothing to do with it. I love Phil. Jon is just my friend. He's always been my friend." Laura began to hum, as if listening to Tracie was a waste of time. "Come on. You know that, Laura," Tracie protested. "I'm just trying to do a job, that's all. I'm not obsessed with him."

"That's what you think," Laura said. "We always deny we're obsessed in the beginning."

Stefan made a frightening noise somewhere between the hiss of a radiator and the rattle of a snake. He stomped over to Laura, and for a moment, Tracie thought he was going to hit her. Instead, he unfolded a piece of foil. "Ya. That is true," he said. "You are finished." Tracie wasn't sure if he meant Laura was done with her streaking or that Tracie was in emotional trouble. Whatever, he returned and snipped again, this time at her bangs.

"Not too short," she repeated. "And I'm *not* obsessed," she told Laura.

"Yeah. And Marcus is a nice guy. Look, I live and breathe on Obsession Street. I own a place there. You just rent. And I got to tell you, Tracie, you *are* obsessed."

"No. I'm . . . annoyed. I'm . . . regretful," she protested. "The piece is really coming along, but Jon's . . . changed. He's not behaving like a good friend. He's hurt Beth and he's probably hurting other women. I just hate that."

"Maybe he needs someone to give him his comeuppance," Laura said.

"Can you believe it?" Tracie asked Laura.

Laura shrugged. "You have tampered with the rules of the universe. Now prepare to meet the consequences of your karma," she said in her most annoying Buddha tone.

Tracie moaned. "Oh God! I *have* to destroy this man's confidence."

"Yes," Laura agreed. "Return balance to the universe."

"Leave him alone. He is like cook in a candy store," Stefan said.

"A cook?" Laura asked, but Tracie raised her brows in warning. Never correct a hairdresser with scissors in his hand was the basic belief in her universe.

"I have to have him taken down by a real man-killer," Tracie said. "Have the hunter become the prey."

"Too bad you don't know a man-killer," Laura said. "Except for me, of course, but now I have a job. Maybe Sharon Stone is available."

"Laura, you're a genius!" Tracie exclaimed.

"I know, but do you think these streaks are going to suit me?" Laura asked.

Stefan took one last snip at Tracie's hair and spun the chair around. "Finished!" he said, pulling out a mirror.

"Oh my God!" Tracie moaned as she looked at her reflection. Her hair was *way* too short.

✳ ✳ ✳

Tracie lay on the sofa, her shorn head wrapped in a towel turban, while Phil and Laura, who were cleaning up the lunch dishes, bickered, as usual.

"Oh, come on," Phil was saying. "Next you'll be telling me there's a special order for washing dishes."

"There is," Laura told him. "Don't you know that?"

"I know when you're pulling my chain," Phil responded.

"I wouldn't touch your chain with a dish brush," Laura said, brandishing the dish brush and tossing her beautifully highlighted mane of hair. "But I can't believe you don't know the order in which you're supposed to wash dishes."

"Bullshit. There's no order. You wash them when you run out of clean dishes, right, Baldy?"

Tracie murmured something from her fog of short-hair blues. But they didn't need a response.

"It's *not* arbitrary," Laura was saying. "It's based on what goes in your mouth first."

"What are you talking about? Is this some kind of dirty joke?" Phil asked.

"Get your mind into the detergent, where it belongs," Laura said with a scowl. "Mrs. Ogg always taught us that we have to begin with silverware, because we put silverware into our mouths. You wash them first, when the water is cleanest. Right, Tracie?" Tracie murmured again. "See. Then you put them aside and wash glasses, because you put glasses up to your lips."

"You're not fuckin' with me!" Phil said, and his face had a look of amazement, as if she was revealing the secrets of getting published or how he could actually play his bass guitar. "I'm going to write a poem about this," he announced. "Wouldn't that be a great piece, 'Chrome Dome'? Come play in the water with me," Phil said.

Tracie rolled over and groaned. Laura just shook her head. "Just let her be, would you? Look, pay attention. Next come the plates, because they don't get touched by your mouth."

"Well, my plate does when you do the cooking, because I usually lick it."

"Well, isn't that cute?" Laura said in her toughest voice. "Like that's going to get me to cook more often for you." But she blushed a little. "Anyway, the last thing you wash are the pots and pans, which even you don't lick." She handed him the pad of steel wool.

Tracie wished they'd just disappear. She wanted Phil to go home and leave her to dwell in her own misery. At least Laura was trying to help out by keeping him busy. Tracie had been on the sofa for a few days. She'd even called in sick at work. She tried to work on her next article for Marcus, but all she could think about was getting Allison to take Jon down a peg. But just how could she get Allison to agree to a blind date?

"I might not lick pans, but my roommates do," he said, and began scrubbing the pot without any protest.

"Aren't you too old for roommates?" Laura asked.

"Look who's talking," he taunted. "Hey, Tracie, come out from under those blankets." Tracie moaned as a response.

"Hey, I'm looking for a place," Laura said.

"You are?" he asked. "You going back to that dipshit in Sacramento?"

"No," she said as she peeled off her rubber gloves. She began to rub some cream over her hands, concentrating on the knuckles and cuticles.

"Why do you do that?" Phil asked.

"To keep my hands soft."

He reached out and took her right hand. "Yeah," he said. "They are soft." He paused for a moment. Then he looked back at the pot and began to scrub harder, looking away from Laura. "So, you really trying to move out? You found a place and everything?"

"You know," Laura told him, "I think Tracie might pay a little more attention to you if she could take you a bit more seriously. If you had your own place, and a real job and some kind of game plan."

"I have a game plan," Phil said, and scowled into the Farberware.

"And that would be living off the six dollars a year you make from your writing?" Laura asked. "Or would it be living off the free beers you make at your gigs?"

"It would be none of your business," Phil told her.

Laura shrugged. "Suit yourself," she said. "But you know nobody's adolescence lasts forever. Except Warren Beatty's."

"Who's that?" Phil asked.

"It's irrelevant. His job's taken," Laura told him. "Anyway, Seattle is full of jobs. All kinds of them. There's no reason why you couldn't find something you'd like to do that actually pays. It's not like you do anything during the day except sleep and mooch."

Phil put down the pot. "Well, fuck you, too," he said. "And fuck the horse you rode in on."

"Oh, leave Trigger out of this," Laura said in a good-natured voice.

"I need the free time to create," Phil said, sounding like a petulant child. "I need empty days to write."

"Oh, come on. You might be able to get Tracie to buy that crap, but not me, buddy. My dad was a writer. You know what he did?"

Phil shook his head.

"He wrote. That's what writers do." She stopped a moment and then patted his arm in a sisterly way. "Look, I didn't mean to hurt your feelings. It's just that I think you're not really happy."

"Who said you're supposed to be happy?" Phil asked as he slipped into his jacket. "Who said life is about being happy?"

"Nobody in Encino," Laura agreed. "But that's why I got the hell out. And I don't think it's about being happy, but I don't think it's about being stuck, either. I think you—I mean everyone—just moves toward what they enjoy and away from what they don't enjoy. That's all that you can do. And I don't think you enjoy sitting around all day and being fairly useless. Not to mention getting humiliated by rejections from pretentious magazines and imbeciles like Bob." She shrugged her big shoulders. "I just think the scene's gotten old for you. But hey, call me an optimist."

For a heart-stopping moment, the room was very still. Tracie winced, expecting Phil's screams to begin at any second. She heard him clear his throat. Then there was silence again. Maybe he'd hit Laura, or break something before he stormed out of the apartment. Instead, he cleared his throat again. "You know," he said in a very gentle voice, "I've been starting to think the same thing."

Chapter 29

Tracie sat in their usual spot at Java, The Hut, waiting impatiently for Jon. She fiddled with the tiny ends of her hair. She'd never had a cut this short. She *really* hated it, and hated Stefan, who'd cut it; Phil, who made fun of it; and Laura, who had just told her not to worry about it, that hair grew back. At least she could count on Jon for support. She looked at her wristwatch. She'd been here almost twenty minutes late, but he still hadn't shown up. It was unlike him.

Molly strolled over, and Tracie winced in advance. This wouldn't be pretty. "Bloody 'ell! You've joined a nunnery? I didn't even know you were Catholic. Plus, you're 'ere on time and 'e's late. It's the end of the world."

"I'm not *always* late."

Molly leaned against the chair. "Not if fifty-one weeks a year three years running doesn't mean 'always.'" Molly took out her order pad. "Shall we go through the usual pantheon until you settle for your scrambled eggs?" she asked. "Or are you just going to sit there pulling on the ends of your 'air as if that will 'elp them grow?"

Tracie dropped her hands to her lap. "Molly, underneath that nasty English exterior, you really don't like me, do you?" Tracie asked.

"No, actually, I don't," Molly agreed cheerfully.

Tracie was taken aback. She hadn't actually expected to hear that Molly hated her. For a minute, she didn't know what to say. "But why? I've never hurt you."

"I guess I just don't like fools," Molly said. "I'm the daughter of one and an ex-wife of another. Call me oversensitive, but it's given me an aversion to them." She shrugged.

"I'm not a fool," Tracie protested.

"Yeah, and I'm not a waitress." Molly pointed to the plastic name tag pinned on her chest. "Read the card." Then she pointed at Tracie. "Yours says 'Tracie 'iggins—part-time journalist, full-time fool'!"

"What did I do?" Tracie asked, and, for some reason, she thought of the dream she'd had where she was painting her cocker spaniel blue.

"What 'aven't you done?" Molly asked angrily. "You date jerks. One useless git after another, and you don't know enough to get over it." Molly slid into the seat across from Tracie. "And, since you asked, mind you, if that isn't enough, you're turning the only nice guy in the great Northwest into a jerk."

"Jon! He's not a jerk. He's just . . . a little more stylish," Tracie said. "And he feels better about himself," she added.

"At the expense of others?" Molly asked. "I know what's going on. 'e brings them 'ere for coffee before going 'ome. It's like my Moggy bringing 'is mousies to me before 'e finishes them off. Three different women last week! And 'e bragged to me 'e 'ad *two* dates on Saturday." Molly leaned closer to Tracie. "You took a warm, sensitive guy, a guy who knows 'ow to listen to a woman, a guy who knows 'ow to please—who actually *wants* to please—and gave 'im all the tricks of the trade that the cold bastards use on us. 'e's a full member of the Guild of Guys now. Do you know what you've done?"

Tracie stopped protesting, sat there a moment, and thought about it. "Something very, very, bad?" she asked tentatively. Molly stared at her, and everything the waitress had said came together in Tracie's mind with her dream, Phil's jealousy, and Laura's warning. She'd need a little help and a little luck, but she thought she could undo the damage she'd done. "Molly, you're right," she said. The waitress nodded. Tracie swallowed her pride. "Will you help me stop him being a jerk?"

" 'ow?" Molly demanded.

"Get me two tickets to Radiohead. You've got the connections." Though Molly had stopped traveling with the rock-and-roll bands, they still called and visited when they were playing Seattle. She knew—and had probably slept with—every roadie, not to mention most rhythm guitarists in the business.

Molly made a face that showed she doubted Tracie's motives. "What do I get out of it?"

"You get your nicest guy in the Northwest back."

"I'll think on it," Molly said, but Tracie could see by her expression she was sold.

"Thank you, Molly."

"Mind you, I'm not sure I can do it. And don't take 'im back all the way to where 'e was. I liked what you did when you just made 'im look better—let's face it, 'e needed a visit from the fashion police." It was the first time Tracie could remember Molly approving of anything she'd done. "But don't you see that changing 'ow 'e *acts* is altogether different from changing 'ow 'e *looks*?"

"I guess it is."

"You've betrayed women everywhere," Molly hissed. " 'e used to be gifted, now 'e thinks 'e's God's gift. There's a big difference." She gestured with her chin over her shoulder. "Take a look."

Tracie turned. Jon was entering the coffee shop. He had a new swagger, a new persona. "I really did wrong," Tracie agreed. Then Molly nodded her head and disappeared into the kitchen.

"Here I am! Your star pupil," Jon said as he slid into the booth, taking Molly's place. Tracie looked him over. She could see he not only looked good but felt good, too. She wondered how good Beth felt right now. "Hey, what's with your hair?" Jon asked.

"What about it?" Tracie asked, forcibly restraining her own hands from covering it. She couldn't believe that Jon was being critical of her.

"I don't know," he said, and shrugged. "Who did it? You probably shouldn't try anyone new. *I* just went back to Stefan."

"Well, good for you," Tracie said. "It was Stefan who gave me this cut."

"Oh, well. It's nice." He almost closed his eyes in a kind of wince. "Yeah," he said. "It suits you."

"And how does your life suit you?" Tracie asked coldly. "Is it time for a few more lessons?" She was about to tell him he needed lessons in courtesy and thoughtfulness and remembering old friends. But before she had a chance to begin, he agreed with her.

"Absolutely," he said. "But I guess it's the advanced class now."

She couldn't get over him, and he obviously couldn't get over himself. "Oh, really?" she asked, trying not to show her pique. "And what would that consist of? Orgies? Menages à trois?"

He laughed, as if all of this was a big joke. She wondered for a moment if Molly was right about *everything*. She didn't think so, but it looked as if she was right about Jon.

Then Jon's face got serious. Maybe there was a chance he, too, wanted to change back. "Well, to tell you the truth, I really do need help." He looked at her with his old expression, a kind of tell-me-how-please look. "Uh, Tracie, I don't quite know if I should ask this, but . . . how do I get rid of them?"

"Rid of whom?"

"Well, say"—he paused, as if trying to pull up an example— "Beth. She calls at least four times a day. I finally saw her just to get rid of her, but you can't get rid of her. No matter what you say, she doesn't give up. I mean, I know she's your friend, and I don't mean to be disrespectful, but I think she needs to work on her self-esteem. Meanwhile, I don't know what to do."

Tracie took a deep breath. This was the Jon she knew. Maybe he wasn't an insensitive prick bastard. Maybe he was merely inexperienced, a little stupid. And, apparently, very, very good in bed. She blushed.

"Oh, don't be mad," he said, mistaking her reddening face for anger. "She's nice and all, but she's . . ."

Tracie told herself she had never expected Jon and Beth to be a permanent thing. She'd expected Beth to be cruel or bored by Jon. She had miscalculated, and that was an error of judgment on her part, not his moral wrong. And she supposed that it was no worse for Beth to be obsessed with an disinterested Jonny than a disinterested Marcus. In fact, maybe it was better because Jon couldn't fire her. Tracie took a deep breath. "Look, if you have to blow someone off, always use the INYIM line."

"What's that?"

Tracie spelled the initials on the damp tabletop between them. "INYIM. 'It's not you, it's me.' You know . . ."

"I've heard that from women!" Jon exclaimed.

"Yeah," she agreed. "We use it all the time, too. But it's sexier, somehow, from men. You know, 'I can't settle down. I'm a rambling man.' " She paused. "When I was teenager, every time I heard that song 'The Wanderer,' I'd get furious."

"The guy that went from town to town?" Jon asked.

"Yeah. You know, the kind of guy who could never settle down. When you're that kind of guy—"

"You're like James Dean!" Jon said.

"Yeah. The type of guy who says, 'You're the kind of girl I could love but . . .' "

"I got it, I got it," Jon said, excited and enthusiastic again. Then he leaned forward, so close that she could count the tiny wires of beard on his cheek and chin. "Hey, listen to this: I bagged Samantha."

Tracie recoiled as if she'd been bitten. "Why don't you shut up?" She asked him, and rose. Without thinking, she swung her arm as if to hit him. Jon put both of his hands in the air to ward her off.

"Wow! What's that about?" he asked. "I thought you'd be pleased with my progress."

"Progress? You don't call me back. You date Carole and Ruth and don't call Beth, except to break up with her! Then, out of boredom, or weakness, you see her instead—and you sleep with her to keep her hooked?" She had to stop to catch her breath. "You tell me that you 'bagged' Sam. *Bagged?* You really liked Sam. That's the way you tell me you had sex with her?"

"Hey, don't be mad. It was safe sex," he protested.

This was too much. Tracie got out of the booth, grabbed her jacket, and started to walk to the door.

Jon caught up with her and grabbed her hand. "Isn't this what you trained me for?" he asked. "I figured you'd be impressed with all I've done. I swear, Beth and Sam and Ruth all liked it."

"Ruth! You slept with Ruth, too?"

"Ruth and I didn't do much sleeping." Jon grinned. Tracie couldn't get angry again—she couldn't get over it. Had he always been a weasel in sheep's clothing? He was looking at her dazed face. "Hey, we had fun," he told her. "It means you've taught me well, Yoda. Wasn't that the point? Do you realize I even got it on with Enid from my building? Enid, the personal trainer."

"Enid?" she asked, her voice raised. Most of the people in the restaurant looked up. "*Enid?* She . . . she . . ." Tracie knew she was sputtering, but there were times you got beyond words. "She's ten years older than you, and a drunk. And a slut!"

"I'm not going to marry her, Trace," Jon said, his voice lowered. "It was a casual thing."

"I can't believe you slept with her. She's nuts, and you should be ashamed."

Molly came over to them. "We don't do take-away," she said, and led them back to the table. Putting both her hands on their shoulders, she sat them down, pulled out a pad, and looked ready to take their orders. "You 'ave some talking to do. Meanwhile, the usual?"

"No," Jon said matter-of-factly. "New man. New menu. Waffles."

"You want 'am with that?" Molly asked.

Tracie couldn't believe it. As if she would eat with him, as if all of this was okay. "No," she said. "He doesn't eat pigs—he fucks them."

Molly smirked. That only made Tracie more furious. "You are disgusting," she said to Jon. "I don't want to eat with you, I don't want to sit with you, I don't even want to talk with you."

Tracie looked at Molly. "Forget brunch," she told the waitress. "He's too busy for brunch with me." She got up and stomped away.

Chapter 30

Tracie was a woman with a mission, a female on a quest. Unfortunately, as she passed people, they said, "Hi," usually followed by "Some haircut!" Or "Ears lowered, huh?" or just "Tracie?" This was not the look she'd choose for walking into the enemy camp, but she imagined herself as Saint Joan. Her voices were telling her, Jon must be taken down. The fact that she'd have to use another enemy of women to achieve her goal didn't bother her.

She paused at Allison's cubicle. There was no denying the girl was gorgeous. She was looking over some work and her hair fell straight as a plumb line from the crown of her head across her pale cheek to the surface of the desk. She was so involved in what she was looking at that she didn't notice Tracie, so, without invitation, Tracie moved toward her desk.

"Hey, Allison. I wonder if you could do me a favor?" Tracie asked.

Allison looked up with a not very favor-oriented expression. Her perfect cerulean blue eyes blinded. Tracie automatically touched her tiny twigs of hair. "I know. My hair's too short," she said, precluding a first strike by Allison.

"Oh. Have you changed your hair?" Allison asked, and Tracie felt more insulted even than when Tim told her it was a bad Sinéad O'Connor impersonation. But as she stood there and looked at Allison, she realized that Allison was the kind of girl who probably didn't notice anything different about another woman.

"Anyway, I got free tickets, including a backstage pass, to the Radiohead concert and I told a friend of mine he could go, but my boyfriend is really freaking. So I wondered if . . . well, would you mind going with my friend?"

It was the first time Tracie had ever seen Allison look anything but bored. "You're kidding, right?" she asked, and her eyes—if possible—got even bigger. "I tried to get press passes for two weeks. I mean, I did *everything*." Tracie thought of the way Allison played up to Marcus and wondered whether *"everything"* included sexual favors. But somehow, Tracie thought that Allison was the type of woman who liked to tempt but not deliver. With her, men lived on the promise of sex, not the reality. "I'm dying to go," Allison added.

"Great! So you'll go out with my friend Jonny."

Suddenly, Allison's flawless eyes narrowed into Siamese-cat slits. "Hey, wait a minute! I mean, this isn't some dorky cousin you're fixing me up with or something?" she asked.

Tracie had a feeling that Allison liked only men who were the possession of other women. "Ha." Tracie laughed. "No. No blood relation. If he was, our dates would be incest. Actually, this is the guy Beth dropped Marcus for."

"Really?" Allison asked. "I didn't know that Beth had dated Marcus. Anyway, I thought he dropped her," Allison said, exposing herself as both a liar and an idiot at the same time.

Tracie shrugged. "I don't really know the details," she said as casually as she could manage, although the impulse to pull out a Remington and shave Allison's perfect locks suddenly became incredibly strong. "All I know is that he briefly dated Beth and that all the girls in the newsroom want him. But I've started going out with him, although my boyfriend doesn't know. So just go to the concert, keep my seat warm, and he'll take you out to dinner first, if you want to."

* * * * * * * * * *

She watched as a light as small as a struck match began to glow behind the turquoise pools of Allison's pupils. Actually, her whole face began to glow with the perfect light of a smooth glass lantern. If her forehead were transparent, Tracie was sure she could have seen little wheels and gears grinding away as Allison compared the thought of stealing a man from Tracie with the risk of being found out by Marcus. "Okay. Sure."

As if her own thought had conjured him up, Tracie heard a gurgling noise behind her. She turned and found Marcus standing in the doorway of the cubicle. *How long has he been there?* Tracie wondered. Maybe it was she and not Allison who was risking her job. "So, speaking of the man that half the girls in the newsroom want," Tracie said in a bantering tone. Marcus didn't smile. Tracie felt a flutter in her stomach, and both women looked at him silently.

"Tracie, can I talk to you a moment?" Marcus asked, then turned on his heel after he gestured for her to follow him. She walked behind him down the hall. Had he heard everything she'd said? Even the fiction about Beth dumping him? Tracie decided that if he fired her, she would sue. She didn't know for what, but the guy was a hound.

The walk across the newsroom seemed endless, and when she got to his office, she was almost shaking. A lot of heads followed her perambulation, but nobody said anything.

"I heard a rumor," he said as he sat down in his chair and threw his feet up on the desk. Tracie wasn't sure if she should sit down or not, but she decided to. God, was he going to talk to her about how she'd fixed up Beth with Jon? Or was he going to yell at her for her idea to use Allison as a tonic? Or had he overheard her complaining about losing the Memorial Day follow-up piece and her theory on how Allison had gotten it? She held one hand with the other in her lap and had to use all of her self-control not to let one of them rise and pull at the pathetic stubble of her hair. "I hear you're thinking of freelancing," he said.

"Freelancing?" she repeated like an idiot, but his comment had come out of left field, or someplace further away, if there was someplace further away than that. How could he know? Had someone from *Seattle Magazine* snitched on her? Did they all run in the same pack at Seattle's toniest parties?

"As a full-time employee here, you are strictly forbidden to offer work that has not been presented for publication here to other outlets."

Tracie couldn't believe it. He was bothering her about the piece he'd turned down? For the first time, instead of being frightened of Marcus, she noticed something—nervousness, or fear?—behind Marcus's bravado. But what could he be afraid of? And how did he know about her query letters?

"I'm not sure that I'm going to freelance anything," Tracie said as truthfully and calmly as she could. "But if I do freelance an article, I would always hope that it would be published here." She paused and tried a smile, although what she really felt like doing was taking a bite right through the end of his shoe and into his big toe. "Anyway, Marcus, the only thing I've been working on—aside from your assignments, of course—is the makeover piece you rejected."

"What makeover?" he asked, and stood up. He began to pace back and forth along the windowed wall behind his desk. She could see that in profile he was still quite handsome, although the beginnings of a double chin weakened his otherwise-strong face. He crossed his arms, then turned and caught her looking at him appraisingly. It was his turn to smile and, probably to make her more uncomfortable, he passed the desk and began pacing behind her.

"Oh," he said. "Are you talking about that technotransformation, 'Mild One into Wild One' by the inversion of a single letter?" Tracie craned her neck, but each time he came into view, he turned and walked in the other direction. She decided to ignore his pacing and stared out the window instead. She kept quiet. "Maybe I was a little bit premature," he said. "I'd like to take another look at it."

Tracie knew that she should say no, that what she needed was an article to run somewhere else and without his butchering, but she wasn't sure if she could stand up to him. "It's just in draft form," she informed him, listening to his restless footsteps.

"I don't mind," he said and, from behind her, he put his hands lightly on her shoulders. She jumped in her seat and he took them away.

"Okay," she said, sounding to herself like the old Mary Tyler Moore character when she was startled by Mr. Grant. "I'll give you a draft right away." Then she was up and out of his office in a heartbeat.

"Tracie, can I talk to you a moment?" Marcus asked her again late that afternoon. Do I have a choice? she wondered. He stepped into her cubicle. "I read the draft of the dweeb makeover. I'm deeply surprised. It's actually pretty good. You're wasted on these stupid holiday pieces. There are some other assignments I'd like to see you working on."

Is he serious? What's going on? she thought.

"Come on with me," he said. She thought that he'd leered, but with Marcus, almost every expression was that unpleasant.

"Really?" she asked, and then wanted to bite her tongue. She had to learn not to react to either his praise or his criticism. What am I? His puppy? She followed him down the long hall that ran in the back of the building. Her thoughts kept her from noticing that Marcus had stopped, and she almost bumped into his back. He turned to face her. The hall was momentarily deserted, and he leaned against the wall, crossing his arms in that gesture of self-sufficiency she had come to know and dislike.

"Do we have a release from this guy?" Marcus asked.

"Uh. Sort of."

"What does that mean?"

"It means not yet, but I can get one. He's a friend."

"Not after this piece comes out." He laughed, then looked around. Tracie couldn't help it—she, too, turned her head, as if the enemy were listening. That was why she was so surprised when she

turned back and saw he was leaning in, inches from her. He pushed
Tracie against the wall and stretched both arms to either side so that
she was backed against the wall, penned in by his arms and only
inches from his smirking face. She could feel his breath on her forehead. "How about we edit it tonight . . . together?"

She couldn't believe it. He was actually putting a move on *her*.
She thought of bringing her knee up between his legs, but she
needed the job. "Marcus . . ." she began. He leaned closer, his mouth
almost on hers. She squirmed down the wall. "I don't think so."

"Come on. Don't play shy with me. I know how you look at me in
those editorial meetings." He was about to try to kiss her, when Tracie gave him a really big push, big enough to throw him off balance.
He stumbled, and she couldn't help it—she pushed him again. Then
she saw Tim and Beth standing just behind him. How much had
they witnessed? Marcus fell to the floor. Beth stopped and stared at
him. Tim, reluctantly it seemed, bent to give him a hand up. Embarrassed, Marcus slapped it away and stood.

"By the way, I'll need that Father's Day piece by the end of the
day."

"But you said—"

"Your mistake," Marcus told her, and turned and left her alone in
the hall.

Later on in the afternoon, when Tracie was finishing the Father's Day
piece, the Radiohead tickets arrived. Wow! Molly had come through
for her. She'd have to leave bigger tips. She had to get this article
turned in. She'd called Jon over and over. She had to reach him, or
she'd be stuck giving these tickets to Allison for nothing. Just then,
the phone rang. It rang a second time, then a third. She needed a
distraction, so she took the call. "Hello, Tracie Higgins here," she
whispered into the receiver.

"Hello there, alchemist. What's up?" Jon asked her.

"Hey, I'm glad you called. Boy, have I got a girl for you tonight!"

"I can't tonight. I'm going out with Ruth."

"Well, cancel Ruth, because this girl is *really* something."

"I guess it won't hurt Ruth to be on hold a little longer, right?" Jon asked. "She's a climber. She likes to hang around." He paused and then laughed. "If I blow her off for tonight, I'd be Ruthless."

"Right." Tracie half-chuckled at the lame joke just for him. He'd be punished for it all tonight. "Come by here at six-thirty. I've got tickets to the Radiohead concert. Come to my office and I'll brief you."

"Okay. See you later, then."

Chapter 31

Jon had felt so bad after Tracie walked out on him at Java, The Hut that he couldn't concentrate on anything and so he had gone to visit his mother. He told himself that he owed her a visit, but it was for him, not her, that he'd gone. She'd made him chicken and noodles, one of his favorite comfort dinners, without even being asked. "Honey," she'd said, running her hands through his new haircut, "you look so tired. Working hard?" He hadn't said "hardly working," though that was closer to the truth. He'd only nodded. "Jonathan dear, why don't you get yourself a dog?" she had asked. It was the kind of crazy question only mothers would ask. But there was something sweet and even right about the question. All at once, Jon felt a yearning for something true and loyal and warm. He almost told his mother about the fight with Tracie, but he was too ashamed of the rest of his behavior.

So, expecting not to hear from Tracie at all, he'd called her, needing to apologize. He'd been delighted that she seemed happy to hear from him, and even more delighted about the date she'd set him up with. He had thought Tracie was really mad at him, and he'd been ready to do whatever it took to make peace. Although he'd loved this whirl of sexual activity, and had no intention of giving it up, he knew that he needed Tracie as a friend. In fact, she was his only close friend. She was also the only one who knew who he really was right now. And this Chick of the Universe sounded too good to be true, but Jon wasn't even nervous. He had the concert tickets in his pocket, one of his new Armani shirts on, and the magic jacket, which seemed to do the trick. He hadn't shaved since Monday, and he knew he looked good, because, although he still didn't have the confidence to sit at the bar, he'd walked past it and several women had turned their heads to check him out.

Anyway, with Tracie back on board, he had his confidence back. She'd seemed so angry at Java, The Hut, but, though he still wasn't sure exactly why, seeing her at her office had reassured him. She hadn't apologized or anything, but maybe setting up this date was her way of making peace. Tracie wasn't good at being wrong. And he didn't need her to say "Sorry about that PMS episode" or "Too bad I took out my anger at Marcus on you" to make up. She'd acted normal—no, even nicer than normal—when he picked up the tickets. She'd even approved of his outfit and straightened his collar before she sent him on his way. So that was all right.

He didn't have much interest in Radiohead—in fact, aside from *Karma Police*, he couldn't remember ever listening to anything they'd recorded. But Tracie had briefed him on the Chick of the Universe's passion for Thom Yorke, and Jon's only regret was that he hadn't had a chance to watch MTV to get a few of Yorke's moves down. If he could copy James Dean, he could surely imitate Thom Yorke. This girl—for a frightening moment he couldn't remember if she was Alexandra or Allison, but then he figured he'd call her Ali and be safe—would just have to settle for James Dean, the way the other ones had. He smiled slyly and shook his head. In a way, it was lucky he hadn't known it was this easy; if he had, he probably would have flunked out of high school.

He sat at a bistro table, ordered a beer, and when it arrived, he began swigging it and waiting. He didn't have a watch to check, but he was sure he was late. How late was she going to be? He wondered for a moment if he had the wrong restaurant, or if he'd been given the wrong information by Tracie. But no, this was the place, and what the hell: If Ali didn't show up, he'd just call Ruth, or even Beth, and tell her he'd copped a couple of great tickets and ask her to go with him. And if he couldn't reach one of them, he might actually approach the bar. There might be other girls there in love with Thom Yorke.

Bored, he picked up the menu. It was the usual bistro fare: fancy burgers, *pommes frites*, chicken paillard. He was just putting the menu down when he saw her. She was standing across the room, looking around. She wasn't the Chick of the Universe. She was much more: She was an angel. Jon knew immediately that this was the woman Tracie had set him up with, and he blessed her in his heart. Every man and woman in the dining room paused to look at her. And then, as if in a dream, but also as inexorably as his own death, she moved slowly toward him. She was tall, and aside from her shoulders, she was very wispy. Her legs began at the floor and went on forever. Her hair was an indescribable silvery blond, and he would give his life to stroke it.

Be cool, he told himself. Neither Thom Yorke nor James Dean would even blink were she to join one of them. All of Tracie's training flashed through his mind. He tightened his hand around his glass and forced himself to take another slow sip to steady himself.

"You must be Ali," he said to her as she reached the table.

"Allison," she said. Her eyes flicked up and down over him and he could feel her sizing him up. "You must be Jonny."

He nodded, because it was best not to talk again until he had control of his vocal chords. She was breathtaking, and there was something about her skin that reminded him of the perfectly smooth sheen of the screen on his new laptop. What do you talk about to a goddess? He found himself as tongue-tied as he'd ever been in the Micro/Con hallway with Samantha. God, he couldn't afford a relapse now, not when the Chick of the Universe was sitting across from him. He was about to really fuck up and ask her how she liked working at the *Times*, or whether she'd majored in journalism, or what her horoscope sign was, when he remembered that he was not supposed to talk too much. He moved his jaw in the approved James Dean manner, picked up his beer, and sipped it again. He'd wait this one out.

And it was a good thing he did. Because although Allison must have been used to dozens—no, hundreds—of men trying to impress her and entertain her, she wasn't used to silences except for those that she maintained. He was white-knuckled by the time she spoke, but that gave him time to slow his breathing and get himself back with the program.

"What do you do?" she asked.

"About what?" he responded, and her eyes blinked. Then she almost smiled. Her lips, which had been perfect in repose, were even more desirable when they opened. And her teeth! Ten thousand orthodontists dreamed of making a cast of teeth like that to show future clients.

They talked a little bit, and she wanted to know about his job, his family, what kind of car he drove, and a bunch of other desultory stuff. But while they talked, he realized he'd learned to play the stupid game so that he could graduate permanently to a woman like Allison. Why would you need any other woman if she wanted to wrap her arms around you, to put those lips against yours, to let you touch a square inch of her perfection?

As Jon sat across from Allison in the dim light of the bistro, he fielded her questions successfully but couldn't get over how beautiful she was. This was the best score he'd had so far.

And then the waitress came over to get their dinner order. For a moment, Jon thought he'd just ignore the girl, who was only a dim shadow of Allison's beauty. But something inside him spoke. He hadn't planned it; it just happened. He was on automatic pilot! Jon found himself doing a double take and turning to Allison. "Doesn't she have the most beautiful eyes you've ever seen?" he asked.

Chapter 32

The next morning, Tracie found herself humming as she walked down the corridor at the *Times*. She was early again, still in her coat and holding a paper bag with a cup of coffee and a muffin. Beth was in her cubicle, and she looked up. "Hi, Tracie," she said as her friend breezed by, but Tracie knew she wouldn't get off that easily. She stopped humming, aware that she was being followed down to her desk by Beth. She sighed. Well, soon all this would be over. Beth could become obsessed with someone else; soon she'd have her friend back, and things with Phil would go back to normal.

"Have you heard from him? Did she shoot him down?" Beth asked.

Tracie shrugged, though she knew that wouldn't end the questioning.

"She shot him down, didn't she? She's such a fool!" Beth cried.

"Beth, I have more important things to do than track every blip in the love life of my friends," Tracie told her. She took off her coat, hung it up, and sat down. Sara entered the room.

"Did you hear?" she asked.

"Hear what?" Tracie wanted to know.

"It's about Allison. It's something about Allison," Beth said breathlessly.

And then Sara smiled with the superior look of a person who has heard office gossip a minute before anyone else. Tracie shook her head and turned away, opening up her breakfast bag.

"Well, guess who just called in sick?" Sara asked.

"Marcus?" Tracie inquired. "Gee, I hope it isn't hysticular cancer," she said.

"Allison! Allison called in sick? On an editorial meeting day?" Beth asked.

"Marcus will kill her," Sara said.

"She's fearless. She probably iced Jon," Tracie said confidently, then smiled. She opened the bag and took out the farm cake and her coffee. "Beth, I thought you were getting help to get over these obsessions. What does your therapist say?"

"He's just interested in prescribing new meds for me. We don't really talk. He's more of a mental bartender. Speaking of obsessions, I thought you were through with those chocolate cream cheese muffins. You know, they're addictive."

"I haven't had one in awhile. Just this once . . ." Tracie began.

"You're worried about something," Sara said.

"No I'm not!" Tracie answered a little too quickly.

"Okay. So tell us what Jonny said about Allison, then," Beth insisted.

Tracie turned away from them. "He didn't say anything. He didn't call," she admitted.

"He didn't call? Oh my God! He always calls. Oh my God! Tracie, she's got him. She's got him, just like she got the others. He's just a fish on her hook, another pike on her lure, a trout," Beth ranted.

"Would you please cut the fish talk? I can't take fish analogies on an empty stomach."

"Poor Jonny," Beth said, shaking her head. "He deserves better." Tracie knew that as far as Beth was concerned, Beth was the only thing better. Oh well, everyone had their blind spots. Then Tracie's phone rang. "It's him! I bet it's him. I'll get it," Beth exclaimed, going for the receiver.

"Excuse me! I think this is *my* phone and *my* office," Tracie reminded her.

"Well, it's definitely your *cubicle*," Sara quipped. The phone rang again.

"Please let me pick it up," Beth begged. "I'll give you fifty dollars next payday." The phone rang once more and Tracie tried to reach it, but Beth blocked her way. Tracie, too, was dying to hear what had happened, but she wouldn't reveal that for fifty dollars, a hundred, or even for a farm cake. How many rings before it kicked into voice mail? Usually three, but sometimes four. She tried to reach past her friend, but, like a goalie on speed, Beth blocked her again.

"Beth, stop it!" Tracie said. "Have some self-respect."

"God! This is better than *The Young and the Restless*," Sara joked.

Feinting to the right, Tracie grabbed the receiver from Beth's left side before Beth could pick it up. "Would you guys grow up?" she said as she placed the receiver to her ear. "Hello."

"Tracie? It's Allison." Ha. Tracie could torture Sara and Beth now, payback for their harassment. Plus, she'd get to hear how Allison had leveled Jon, and she'd savor every minute of the story. She didn't like to think of herself as a bitch, but he really deserved it, and he'd be glad of it in the end.

"Oh, hey, Allison," Tracie said smoothly. As she expected, her words galvanized Beth and Sara. Sara's eyes opened so wide, they might have popped, while Beth's curls actually looked as if they were standing on end. Sara jumped up from the desk and came to Tracie's side, motioning to get at the receiver, while Beth immediately did the same on the other side. Tracie tried to wave the two of them off while she listened to Allison.

"I've got this problem, Tracie. I can't get out of bed." Tracie thought that's what she heard, but Allison's voice was getting even lower. She sounded awful.

"Is it the flu?" Tracie asked.

"No. I just can't get out of bed." Beth gave Tracie a sharp elbow in the ribs, not because she'd heard what Allison said but because she couldn't. Tracie had the phone pressed tightly against her ear.

"Well, there's a lot of virus going around. And you have laryngitis for sure."

"No I don't. I'm not sick," she said in a whisper that sounded annoyed. There was a pause. "I can't get out of bed because I don't *want* to. I'm here with Jonny and . . ." Tracie fell into her chair, nearly knocking Sara over.

"Oh shit," Sara said. "This'll look great for Marcus."

Beth and Sara tried again to listen in, but then they noticed that Tracie's expression had changed from her superior smile to a grimace. She turned her back to the two girls, who were watching her intently. She felt as if her head was spinning. She'd missed something that Allison had said. ". . . I just can't get out of bed. I don't want to ever again. And I'm exhausted."

"But . . . but . . ." What could she say? He's not really that good in bed; he's just my friend? Don't believe what you see and feel; he's really a dweeb? Don't be nice to him; punish him because he deserves it? "But . . . the editorial meeting," she said lamely.

"The hell with Marcus and the meeting. This is just too good."

"It is?" Tracie asked before she could stop herself. After all, she was a girl who had blown off work for a bad haircut. "It is?" she asked again.

"The best!" Allison whispered in a knowing voice.

Well, if anyone knew, it would be Allison, Tracie thought bitterly. What was wrong with this picture? Beth was pushing her on one side and Sara on the other, but Allison was talking again.

"Tracie, I owe you an apology. I never thought you liked me very much, but I guess I was wrong."

No you weren't, Tracie thought. But you're wrong now.

"What?" Beth said. "What did she do to him?" Tracie elbowed Beth and covered the phone with her hand.

"I guess I just want to say thank you," Allison continued. "Jonny told me what close friends you are and . . . I'm just really grateful to you for the best night of my life." Allison's voice sounded teary and she stopped as if to catch her breath. "Thanks," she said.

"You're welcome," Tracie replied.

"Oh, he's waking up. I have to go," Allison informed her. "Thanks again, Tracie." And then the phone went dead.

Tracie put the receiver down and slowly turned back to her two friends. "She spent the night with Jonny."

Beth groaned. "I can't stand it. It's just not fair."

"She's in bed with him now," Tracie said, shocked to feel tears rising in her eyes. She suddenly felt incredibly lonely. "I don't get it. I mean, how good *is* he?"

"*Really* good," Beth told her, then got up slowly and turned to leave. "Maybe I should go back to Marcus," she said as she walked out of the cubicle.

Sara looked at Tracie. "What are you going to do?"

Tracie forced herself to sit upright in her chair, picked up her farm cake, and took a huge bite. "Wait till Sunday's brunch," she said with her mouth full. "I'll *kill* him."

Chapter 33

Jon lay against Allison, dozing, his legs against her silky backside. Her skin was one of the wonders of the world. He moved against her, freshly aroused, his cock bumping gently against the small of her back. For a moment, he thought of Parsifal. If there were a way to build *this* into a virtual reality game, he could buy Bill Gates out in a matter of months.

Jon smiled. Last night, like the previous two nights with Allison, had been incredible, but it topped a whole series of successful nights. If he wanted to think of his recent sexual successes as conquests, Allison was Waterloo and he was the Iron Duke.

His cock moved again. He supposed there would never be a more perfect moment in his life. Yet something was missing. He thought, for some reason, about the Bible: not because Allison was a blessing, though she was very angelic in appearance, but because of the way the Bible described sex. In the Bible, when men slept with women, they "knew them." In a way, he could understand that, because the act of mounting Allison, of seeing her beauty naked and open beneath him, was an act of knowledge. And when he entered her, there was a thrill of possession and of a deeper, more forbidden knowledge.

But he did not know Allison. Not in any real way. Perhaps someday he would, but he had no idea what he would find. All he knew right now was that she was exquisite and that moving on her and in her and over her had become a pas de deux, more erotic and beautiful than any ballet. But he also knew that he was lying next to a stranger. And he was worse than a stranger to her: He was an imposter.

Jon's eyelids fluttered. He sat up and stretched. Allison rolled onto her back, exposing not only her lovely face and the aureole of wheat-light hair on the pillow but also her absolutely perfect breasts. It was amazing, but he felt himself stand up for her again, as if three times hadn't been enough.

Actually, to be honest, the sex, though good, hadn't been terrific. Allison was used to being pleased, and she was nowhere near as good a lover as, say, Beth, but just looking at her had given him enough of a thrill to make up for the difference. So he was thinking about another attempt, when his phone rang.

He had taken her to his place—breaking the rules, which Tracie would not have approved of, and here was his punishment. He thought for a moment of just ignoring the phone, but he didn't want Allison to think she was that important to him, or he'd never get another shot at her. He hoped it wasn't Beth. So, on the second ring, he reached over and picked up the receiver.

"Hey, Jon. Do you know what day this is?" a male voice asked, and he nearly dropped the phone.

"Dad?" he said, but then he didn't know what else to say. He hadn't heard from his father for at least two years, except for one postcard he had gotten from Puerto Rico, and then a letter from San Francisco begging him to invest $100,000 in a new venture that his dad and two other losers were trying to start. He had barely been able to understand the prospectus, but he had sent his father a money order for a thousand dollars and a note that wished him luck. He hadn't heard from him since then.

"Dad . . ." he repeated. Beside him, Allison turned and lifted her head, leaning it against her arm so she could look at him. But he didn't want to be looked at right now. He sat up and threw his legs over the side of the bed, turning his back on her.

"It's my day, Jon. It's Father's Day. Remember? And I *am* your father."

There was a defensive yet pleading tone to his voice that made Jon very uncomfortable. Had he been drinking this early? Jon still didn't have a watch, but it was early—*very* early for drinking. Of course, he didn't know what time zone Chuck was in—or even what hemisphere. Maybe it was cocktail hour in Singapore.

"I wondered if you'd have the time to meet me?" his father was saying. "I came a long way, son, to see you."

Jon shrugged a little. If his father was calling him "son," it was definitely a sign that something was wrong. His father never liked to admit that he was older than thirty-five, which made it awkward to have a son Jon's age. As he aged, his women hadn't, though there'd been a frightening decline in quality. Jon sighed and hoped his father didn't hear it. "Sure," Jon said. "Sure I can meet you."

"Shit! Shit," Tracie said as she looked at the papers spread out on her living room floor.

"Come on, his eggs aren't that bad," Laura said. They were having a late breakfast, prepared—oddly enough—by Phil. He had insisted. Though the eggs were cooked until they were brown and the pota-toes were uncooked, so that they were unpleasantly crunchy, Tracie had hardly noticed. Instead, she was mourning the abortion Marcus had made of her feature on Father's Day. It hadn't been easy to think of an original angle, but she'd been pleased with the piece, since what she'd managed to do was a piece about alternative fathers. A priest who had helped raise a dozen orphan boys, a Yuppie who was Big Brother to a wheelchair-bound fatherless nine-year-old, a guy who had run a summer camp and served in loco parentis for dozens of boys, as well as a couple of grandfathers who were raising their grandsons.

It had run four full columns in length, but it had been cut to less than a column, mentioning only the grandfathers in detail, with the others given barely a sentence. And someone else had supplied the usual crap about where "normal" kids were bringing "normal" dads to celebrate, along with a list of restaurants serving special brunches. Enraged, she glanced at the byline and found that while her name was on it at the bottom, it did add "With special reporting by Allison Atwood." "Goddamn it!" Tracie said, and threw the paper halfway across the living room.

Oblivious to her pain, Phil chose that moment to ask, "How do you like the eggs?"

She could hear Laura stifling a laugh behind her, but she managed to suppress her own rage at the paper long enough to turn to Phil with a tight smile. "Really good. Thanks." What she thought was that she'd cooked him probably a hundred breakfasts without any fuss, and, usually, without any thanks. But if a guy fried up one goddamn egg, he expected the Nobel Prize.

"Really? You like the eggs?" Phil asked, probably because they hadn't praised him enough, and Tracie wondered, not for the first time, if she could perhaps somehow manage to live without sex.

Tearing himself away from Allison had not been as painful as the apprehension of what little treat Chuck Delano had waiting for him.

Jon didn't hate his father. It would be easier if he did. Instead, what he felt was a kind of indignation cut with pity. It was the pity that had gotten him out of his bed, into his clothes, and into a taxi. He wondered again what was waiting for him.

When Jon was just a teen, his father had made him go with him on several of his little excursions. Chuck—he didn't want to be called Dad—would sit across from some young woman but direct conversation to Jon. "Now, son, I want you to meet my new girl. Isn't she a pip?"

There had been a lot of those, because, though Jon hated to acknowledge it, his father was a good-looking and sometimes charming guy. But when Jon was in his early teens, Chuck had been at the top of his game. As his career had ebbed, so had his looks, and he'd found more solace in Southern Comfort than the entire Confederacy had. And more and more frequently, Chuck had used him as a prop to help with the women. He hadn't had a choice—his father had visiting privileges—and a part of him had wanted to see his dad. What kid didn't? As Jon hit maturity, Chuck certainly still hadn't. Just before he'd left Seattle for parts largely unknown, he'd taken Jon out for the last time. Another one of his jobs had ended in disaster, and after a few drinks and a lot of self-pity, Chuck had become maudlin. "Gotta start again somewhere," he'd said. "Got it all planned out. And I want you to be a part of it. You're my flesh and blood." Jon had been working at Micro/Con for a few years, but his father told him to quit. "You'll never get rich working for someone else," he said. "Take it from me. I'm striking out on my own." Striking out was more like it.

Jon hadn't noticed a very young woman peering at them from the bar until his father pointed her out. She looked like a ninth grader. Jon had almost thought she was interested in him, but he'd been sure the proof she carried was fake. "I was thinking of asking her," Jon's father had said. "Asking her what? How she scored on her PSATs?" Jon had asked. "No. No. To marry me," his father had answered matter-of-factly.

Jon had the taxi drop him at the corner near where he was meeting his father. The neighborhood was getting seedy, not far from the bus station. What in the world could he get his dad? A pint of Southern Comfort? A one-way ticket to South America? He entered the drugstore in the middle of the block.

He settled on some aftershave, the classic, stupid Father's Day gift. While the clerk gift wrapped it, he remembered that Phil lived somewhere around here, and that Laura had considered a place in the neighborhood until Tracie warned her off. Despite the wind that was making his eyes tear, he smiled. He'd have an earful for Tracie tonight.

His father had given him an address just a few blocks north of where he was now, a restaurant called Howdies. In another block, Jon could see it, the kind of big, grim, noisy place that people who took long-distance buses stopped at to eat.

As he swung the door open, an automated voice shouted, "Howdy." But that was about it as far as the theme went. The place was a grim collection of Formica-topped tables and molded plastic chairs. It was cavernous, and along one long wall ran a food service where hot tables offered up yesterday's meat loaf, macaroni and cheese, mixed carrots and peas. Jon felt as forlorn as the bowls of browning iceberg lettuce that sat, unwanted, in a row across the top of the salad section. From the entrance, he saw the ghostly glimmer of a white face under a cap and an equally white hand beckoning. Jon walked down the long aisle toward his dad.

He tried not to make a noise or stare once he saw him clearly, but it would have been equally cruel to avert his eyes. Chuck seemed to have aged two decades in the two years or so since Jon had last seen him. His father began to struggle to his feet, but Jon waved him back and took the chair opposite. He didn't kiss or hug him, but he did hold out his hand. His father's was thin and his skin was amazingly papery. Jon was too shocked by his appearance to say anything. "Hello, Jon," Chuck said. "You're looking well." It wasn't the best opening, since Jon couldn't give the standard "Yes, so are you." He fumbled in his pocket and then silently handed Chuck his gift. Chuck took it and looked at it blankly, as if it were a meteorite or a ball of buffalo mozzarella. "What's this?" Chuck asked.

"It's . . . it's . . . it's a present. You know, Father's Day."

Chuck stared at it and but didn't move to open it. Then he shook his head a couple of times. "You're a really good boy, Jonathan. You take after your mother's side of the family." Involuntarily, Jon nodded. "You're looking good. Still crazy after all these years, huh?"

It was a song that his mom and Chuck used to sing together when they were in a good mood. Jon remembered driving to Vancouver, with them singing happily in the front seat while he chimed in from the back. "Still can't afford a car?" his father asked, and when Jon was about to protest, Chuck raised his bony white hand to stop him. "I'm only joking," he said. "I know how well you're doing."

"You do?" Jon asked.

"Your mother keeps me up-to-date. On the Internet. Thanks for coming to see me, son," Chuck said, and Jon felt his heart tighten in his chest. The "son" business was usually the beginning of the financial requests. But it didn't materialize this time. Chuck talked about his place in Nevada, gardening, and the Seahawks, Donald Trump, the upcoming election, and an episode of *Frasier* where Niles and his father both seemed to want to date Daphne. None of it added up to anything, and Jon kept waiting for the touch, the angle, until his father lifted up the brim of his cap and ran his hand over the stubble of his shiny head. "It itches like hell," Chuck said. "They told me that was normal after chemo." It was only then that all the pieces fell into place. Before Jon could say anything, Chuck leaned forward and looked him in the eyes for the first time. "I've got a good chance," he said. "It hasn't metastasized. I have some radiation treatments to go through and then, with luck, I'll be right as rain."

"Good," Jon managed to choke out; he didn't feel strong enough to ask a single question about what kind of tumor, whether it had been operable, what the percentage of success was. . . . It all flashed through his mind, but he looked across at the shriveled shell of his father and didn't ask a thing. "You look good, Chuck," he said, and for the first time, his father laughed.

"You're too fucking much," Chuck said, shaking his fragile-looking head. He'd always been so vain. Jon wondered if he cared anymore about his looks or was only focused on survival. Again, he thought it was too personal a question to ask.

In fact, he didn't have much to say. "Good luck," he murmured at last. "If there's anything I can—"

"Well, I did wonder if there was any chance I could be put on your medical plan?" Chuck said. "That would be a big help. I don't really have the kind of benefits that give you priority seating in the waiting room."

"Hey, don't worry about that," Jon said. "I can talk to my benefits coordinator tomorrow." He doubted he could get his father, a man with a preexisting condition, who he hadn't lived with for fifteen years, any coverage, but he could certainly pay for whatever treatment might cure or comfort Chuck.

"Or maybe your mother could get me reinstated," Chuck added. "I thought about going over to see her while I'm here. Is she hooked up with anyone now?"

"Yes." Jon lied as smoothly as if he'd been doing it all his life. The last thing his mom needed now was to nurse her dying ex-husband. "You'd like him. He's a professional wrestler."

"I never should have left your mother," Chuck admitted.

"You never should have cheated on her, either," Jon said, and then regretted letting that slip, but his father merely nodded his head.

"Don't make my mistakes, Jon," he said. "Find a good woman. Stick with her. You'll never regret it."

Chapter 34

Molly was talking to a customer and didn't notice when Tracie walked in, which was a relief to Tracie. Phil had been really talkative all evening and kept trying to keep her from leaving. But she was here on time, despite Phil, and proceeded to go to her usual spot to wait for Jon. Just as she was slipping out of her raincoat, Molly approached her with two steaming mugs of coffee. "You 'ave no one to blame but yourself for this little turn of events," Molly said as she placed the two cups on the table and slid opposite Tracie in the booth.

"Excuse me? I don't remember inviting you to join me."

"Well, if I don't, you're going to be 'ere alone this time," Molly said as she pushed the sugar holder toward Tracie's hand. "We're making some doughnuts in the kitchen. You'll be able to dunk them. In your tears," she added. "I take it the tickets didn't work. And I 'ad to fuck a roadie to get them. Waste of a good favor, I call it."

"I think you're being a little overdramatic," Tracie said with as much dignity as she could muster. "Anyway, I have nothing to cry about."

"Being stood up by your friend after all these years won't upset you then?"

"What are you talking about? I'm early and Jon's a little late. What's the big deal?"

"No, luv. 'e was late *last* week. And a *little* late the week before. My bet is that this is the week 'e doesn't show at all, Radiohead tickets or no."

"Don't be ridiculous. We meet for this late brunch every Sunday, no matter what. Except for the time he had his appendectomy," Tracie told Molly, as if she didn't know. "I'm his best friend."

"You're a lot more than that." Molly stood up and looked deep into Tracie's eyes. "Face it: You're a scrambled egg girl who thinks she should like something different. You don't even know what you feel about 'im, do you? 'e was at your beck and call and you were too stupid to appreciate it."

"I did that?"

"Yes, Dr. 'iggins." In disgust, Molly got up from her seat and walked toward the kitchen.

Tracie sat alone in the booth, staring out the window. Bored with the lack of activity outside, she started to fiddle with the packets of Sweet 'n Low. There were eleven—a very unsatisfactory number. She tried to arrange them in three rows of four, but the last, short row annoyed her. So she reorganized them into two rows, the top with five and the bottom with six, but that looked like a pyramid without a top. So she did one at the top, a row of two under that, a row of three beneath that, and a row of four underneath. But then she had one left. What the fuck? she thought, then tore it into a star shape and put it at the top of the triangle that now became a Christmas tree. She got the Sweet 'n Low all over everything. The powder that spilled all over could be snow. Too bad it's mid-June instead of Christmas, she thought sourly.

" 'aving fun?" Molly asked on her way by the table.

Tracie sighed. Maybe Molly was right about her. Maybe she was a scrambled eggs kind of girl, a person who liked to work under deadlines, have assignments, and didn't know when she loved somebody. After all, Laura had said the same thing a week ago. She glanced down at her watch—only another nine minutes had passed. Where the hell is he? she thought. She'd always taken his promptness for granted. But he'd come early because . . . he loved her best. She felt water rise up to the bottom of her lids. Somehow, she'd counted on that. Who did he prefer now? Who was he with? Ten minutes passed. Tracie couldn't take the waiting any longer. She got up and went to the phone booth at the back of the coffee shop. She punched in Jon's number, but there was no answer. "Damn it!" She hung up the receiver and dialed his work number—he might have fallen asleep over his terminal—but all she got was the same recording saying his mailbox was full. "Goddamn it!"

She marched back to the booth, passing Molly, who was taking another customer's order. Molly looked up and smiled at her with an unbearable I-told-you-so grin. Tracie gathered up her raincoat and bag, stalked across the floor, pushed the door open, and stormed out.

She put her bag over her head to shield her hair from the rain and walked quickly to her car, fumbled with the keys to unlock her door, and finally managed to get inside. Why the fuck do I live in a city where it always rains? What's wrong with me? She drove like Mario Andretti through the wet, deserted streets of downtown Seattle. The rain was coming down so hard, it was like a sheet sliding down the windshield. She glanced at the console clock, which told her Jon was now—wherever he was—forty-eight minutes late for his date with her.

Tracie squealed up to his downtown building, parked illegally in front of it, and left the emergency flashers blinking. She hustled out of the car and ran up the stairs to his loft. Ridiculous! His rent was exorbitant, but he had no elevator, no amenities. So like Jon!

Her hair—what there was left—was glued to her head from the rain. What does it matter anyway? she thought, and she took her right hand and slid it across the top of her head to try to get rid of the excess moisture. When she got to his door, she was panting, but it didn't stop her from banging loudly. If he was in bed, she'd pull him out and drag him into the rain and let him hang there by his collar like a wet puppy. But there was no response. Despite the clear reality that no one was going to answer, she kept hammering. Well, she had to do something. She rooted through her handbag, found a pen, but couldn't find any paper. She was reduced to using a pad of small Post-it notes. She began to write on the first one "I can't believe that" and she smashed it onto the door with her fist. The words were smeared from the dampness of the rain, but it was still legible. Then she wrote, "after all these years you'd" and, running out of room, she tore off the page and also stuck it onto the door. She continued to write another: "completely forget about our" and she squished the Post-it against the door beside the other two. There was plenty more to say. Luckily, she had two pads of Post-its. "Ungrateful." "Thoughtless." "Rude."

She wrote, tore off another, and wrote again. The only sounds she could hear were the rain hitting the hall window, her own heavy breathing, and the scratch of her felt-tip pen on the tiny yellow papers.

By the end, Tracie had twenty-three Post-it notes stuck all the way down Jon's door, telling him what a pig he was and how she would never see him again.

Then the wave of anger receded and left only sadness behind. She looked at his door. It was ridiculous, just as she was. No dignity at all, just like her. He'd probably see them and laugh. Maybe he'd see them with Allison beside him. For a moment, she was tempted to tear all of the smeared notes down off the door. She chucked the remains of the pad into her purse and left.

Tracie got back in her car and tried to drive herself home, though the tears were making her vision cloudy. By the time she got to North Street, she was sobbing so hard that she was gasping for air. She pulled the car over to the side of the road, yanked her sweater partway off so that her arms were free but her head was covered. She used her free hands to wipe her covered face.

When she took her hands away from her face, she caught a watery glimpse of a bicycle whizzing by her. What a city! Rain all the time and nuts out in it. Her tears kept falling, and she kept making moans and hiccups. But finally, unlike the rain, her tears stopped. She wiped her swollen face, put her car in gear, and accelerated to get back on the road. She drove past the bike that had just gone by her. "You idiot!" she said aloud. "Haven't you heard of mass transit?" she asked into her rearview mirror as she drove away from the bicyclist.

It was a short ride on empty streets, but it felt as if it took a week to get home. She was exhausted, as if she had run all the way. When she finally reached her house, she parked quickly and got out of the car, slammed the door, and ran through the rain to her building entrance.

Chapter 35

Jon had gotten back to his place after he left his father waiting for the bus. He had hardly been able to climb the stairs to his loft, his knees had been so weak. If he had never liked the image of his father as a carefree womanizer, the image of him as a pathetic, regretful, sick man was no better. Jon had managed to walk in the door without crying, only to find Allison still lying on his sofa in nothing but his one remaining Micro/Con T-shirt. She was watching TV. He had to cover his shock, because he had completely forgotten she'd still be at his place.

"Where have you been?" she asked unreproachfully. And he had to endure chitchat and a bunch of questions about his job, how long he'd been at Micro/Con, whether he had stock options, and what his relationship with the founders was. He wasn't even able to lie, based on Tracie's rules. He just tried his best to be civil until she moved toward the bedroom. Then, when she bent over to pick up a shoe, he felt himself rising to the occasion, and he went to her for the only comfort she knew how to offer.

"I thought you'd never ask," Allison said with a smirk.

Well, maybe once for the road, Jon thought, and looked at his wrist. He still didn't have a watch, so he glanced at the clock on the other side of the bed. Shamefully, the reality of his father was erased by the drug of Allison's body and he used it hard, losing himself in an exhausting encounter. It blanked out everything, and for that, he was grateful. Shakespeare had gotten it wrong: It wasn't music that had the charms to soothe the savage breast. It was the horizontal two-step. But once he awoke from the postcoital drowse, the image of his father lifting his hat to scratch his bristled scalp came right back. Some Father's Day. And then he remembered that it was Sunday night and tomorrow he had Parsifal and the progress meeting to— My God! Tracie! He sat up as if powered by a 1K-megahertz chip. He was almost forty minutes late already.

He jumped from the bed and began to dress in a frenzy.

"Where are you going?" Allison asked in a sleepy voice.

"I . . . uh . . . I just remembered," he began. What could he say? I just remembered I forgot my friend? I just remembered I have to meet another woman? I just remembered I don't want to make love to you? "I . . . uh . . . left my clothes in the dryer," he told her lamely as he slid his right foot into his shoe and grabbed his sweater. He ran for the door.

"Wait!" Allison called out. "When will . . ."

He was jiggling with the lock and the chain that was across the door, so he couldn't hear what she'd said. Tracie would be enraged! He couldn't believe it. In seven years, he hadn't missed one time . . . nor had she. Well, except for his emergency appendectomy. He threw the dead bolt, turned the knob the other way, and finally got the door open.

"When will I see you again?" Allison asked from the bedroom door. She had the sheet wrapped loosely around her, one pink nipple just peeking over the top, her hair a tumbled blond sheet over her shoulders. Allison stopped and put her hands on her waist. "You're such a dick," she said.

Jon blinked, once, twice, then three full times as he let the words sink in. "I am?" he asked, his voice delighted with enthusiasm. She

looked like a goddess. A goddess he had worshiped with his body. Jon
shook his head. Amazing! Amazing!

"I'll call you," he said. Tracie was waiting; he really had to go. He
was out the door, down the stairs, and out in the wet in a moment.

He was lucky. Unbelievably, a cab was passing. He hailed it. He
was already damp, but he settled into the backseat. "Java, The Hut,
on Canal," he told the driver. "Hurry!"

There was a clock on the dashboard. It was even later than he
thought. What would he do if Tracie had already left? Well, he had
left his bike in the alley back at Java, The Hut. He'd take it, bike over
to her apartment, or, failing that, bike up and down the streets until
he found her and apologized.

Somehow, he thought that might not work. Not because he
wouldn't be able to find her, but because she wouldn't accept the
apology. She'd probably been subjected to forty-six solid minutes of
taunting from Molly, the Manchester Menace. He cringed, thinking
of what Molly might say to Tracie if she had the opportunity to get
her alone.

He had a feeling she might be enraged, and he wouldn't have
been surprised if she'd torched Java, The Hut as well as anything
else that annoyed her right now. When the cab slowed down near
the coffee shop, Jon didn't wait for the car to come to a complete
stop. He threw money on the front seat and thanked the driver as he
jumped from the moving vehicle. He ran around the back of the taxi
and flung open the door. He looked toward the table that he and Tracie always sat at. As he glanced around the room, he saw Laura in the
kitchen doorway and Molly sitting down at a booth.

What was Laura doing here? Was Tracie so angry at him that
she'd refused to come? Maybe he wasn't late; maybe he was being
stood up by Tracie. Or, a best-case scenario, she was in the bathroom
or checking up on Phil on the phone. He approached Molly, who was
picking at a plate of scrambled eggs. He grabbed her arm. She looked
up at him, her face expressionless, but he knew immediately what
had happened.

"She was here, right?" he asked Molly, his heart dropping.

"Right," Molly said, and went back to her plate of scrambled eggs.

He couldn't believe it. He'd broken years of tradition. He felt sick to his stomach and more than a little frantic. "Molly, I'm a jerk and I know it," he admitted. "You know it. But please, do you know if she went to my house or back to hers?"

Molly shrugged. "Actually, I don't know," she told him. "She doesn't really confide in me."

Laura had ambled over from the kitchen. He turned to her. "Please, Laura," was all he said.

"I didn't see her go, but I'd guess she headed toward your place," Laura offered. "And she borrowed a knife," she added.

Jon didn't know if she was joking or not, but he didn't care. "I'm getting my bike," he told Molly, and turned and ran through the restaurant, literally jumping over backs of empty booths. He ran through the kitchen, almost upsetting a tray of scones. Outside the back door, his bike was leaning against the railing, where he had locked it up. He dropped the key in his haste and then fumbled with the padlock. When he finally got it off, he turned the bike around and pedaled down the wet cobblestones of the alley and out into the street. The rain hit him full then and he hunched his head against it as he turned toward his building.

It was a long, cold ride, and without his poncho, he was drenched to the skin long before he got home. But he wasn't cold. He was actually sweating, both from fear and exertion. He *had* to catch her before she left. When he pulled up to the front of his building, he was short of breath, but he had to manage the fucking stairs. So he galloped up them two at a time to get to Tracie faster. He was gasping as he opened the fire door to his hallway and his heart was thumping hard against his chest wall. It felt as if it skipped a beat when he saw the hallway was empty. She was gone, and if he could find her, she'd be even more furious. As he approached his door, he realized she was furious already. He saw the Post-it spectacular and, without reading it, spun around and ran down the stairs.

At the foot of the staircase, he grabbed his bicycle, cursed himself for not having a car, and maneuvered it through the doorway and back out into the rain.

He began hating everything about himself and his life. Why did he have to be born in Seattle and still live there, a place where it always rained? And why was he so stubborn? How come he had never bought a car? Adults have cars. And how could he be so stupid as to have forgotten his appointment with Tracie?

He always felt as if Tracie were an orphan. He was her family. Her mother was dead and her father was as good as. She had been waiting for him while he had been lying beside a naked stranger. In all the years and with all the boyfriends that Tracie had had, she had never—not once—skipped their Sunday appointment. What would he do if she hadn't gone home? Would she have gone to Phil's? Did he know Phil's exact address? He couldn't remember it, if he had ever known it.

The rain was dripping down his face, falling off his chin and onto his chest. The downpour had gotten more intense, and the visibility had worsened. He was only a block from her house. He pedaled harder and then saw the brake lights of a car only a few feet in front of him. He swerved to avoid it, realizing that it had pulled over to the curb because of the downpour. That was close, he thought. I'd better be more careful. He couldn't afford not to make it to Tracie's.

Just as he came around the corner of Tracie's street, he saw her car pulling into the parking space and he watched her get out. He threw his bike down. It splashed into a puddle, but he didn't care. He began to run toward her. "Tracie! Tracie!" he shouted, but either she didn't hear or she was purposely ignoring him.

Chapter 36

Tracie had run into her building, but she'd still gotten drenched. Now she shivered as she stood in front of her door, fumbling with her keys. She had to hurry. She'd heard Jon call out to her and she'd seen him out of the corner of her eye as she'd run into the lobby, but she didn't want to see him like this—or maybe ever. She just wanted to get into her place, lock the door behind her, crawl into bed, and never get out. But her hands were shaking, and Jon stepped off the elevator and came up behind her before she could get in.

"Tracie . . ." he said, but she ignored him and continued to try to get the door unlocked. Jon moved closer to her. He was even wetter than she was, but she would not turn around, even when she felt his chest pushing against her back. He reached out for her hand, but she slapped him away. How dare he touch her?

She got the door open and tried to push herself in, leaving him out in the hall, but he was too fast for her and managed to get his shoulder into the doorway. "Go away," Tracie said, still keeping her puffy red face averted. "Get out!"

"Tracie, you have every right to be angry, but you have to—"

"I don't have to do anything," Tracie said.

"But I—"

She turned to face him. What did she care? Let him see how bad she looked. He meant nothing to her. "Did you have your appendix out again?" she asked him as viciously as she could. "That would be the only acceptable excuse."

"Don't you think that's a little harsh?" he asked.

"No," she said, and tried to close the door on his shoulder.

"Ouch!" He sucked air in through his teeth and pushed the door open.

"Don't come in here," she warned him. "You're not welcome." She looked around behind her. Where were Laura and Phil when she needed them? "You hurt me. Really hurt me," Tracie said.

"I'm sorry. I never meant to," Jon said, trying to console her.

"Who was with you?" she asked. "Beth? Was it another pity fuck? Or was it Ruth? If you were Ruthless, it must have been Carole in from San Francisco." She turned her back on him and walked toward the sink. She was still hiccuping. A woman had no dignity when she was hiccuping. "Oh, or maybe you were doing Enid. I'm sure it was very aerobic." She hiccuped again, filled a glass with water at the sink, and was about to gulp it down, when he answered her.

"It was Allison, actually," he said, "but I saw my—" Before she could even think about it, she had thrown the water across the kitchen and into his already-drenched face. Jon choked and put a hand up as if warding off a blow. They both stood there, frozen for a moment. "I deserve that," he said. "I know I've behaved badly. But don't act as if you have no part in it."

"Oh, go ahead and blame me," she said. "Next, you'll rape someone and tell them that they asked for it." He grabbed her by the shoulders. "Let go of me," she said as she tried to pull away.

"Not until you talk to me. Not until you calm down and listen and talk to me."

"Go talk to Allison," Tracie spat out at him. She tried to pull away, but his hands were too strong. She just couldn't bear it. She was so disappointed, and so angry, and so ashamed that she turned her head away, covered her face, and began to cry.

Then Jon softened his grip and cradled her in his arms and—at last—as if he had been waiting for years to do it, he kissed her gently and then wildly, passionately. At first, momentarily shocked, Tracie struggled, but then she kissed him back. It was heaven. It was . . . everything. She began to shiver. Jon left her mouth and kissed her face, then licked the tears that still clung to her lashes. His own lashes were wet with rain, and at last she felt them against her cheek and brushing her lips and her brow. Then he found her mouth again with his own.

Her shivering increased and she couldn't tell if it was from the cold or the heat. His wet clothes were pressed against hers, but she could feel the heat of his body through them. She couldn't think, only feel, and this felt so natural, and at the same time so extraordinary, so unexpected. Then anything resembling thought was completely gone. "You're cold," he said, holding her face in both his hands. "Don't you know enough to come in out of the rain?"

"I don't know anything," she whispered, and nestled her head against his chest. She was surprised but grateful when he picked her up, carried her to the bedroom, and took off her wet jacket and shirt. Tenderly, he wrapped the coverlet around her shoulders. "You're shaking, too," she said.

"Not from the cold," he told her.

"Come here," she said, and he took off all of his wet clothes, right down to his shorts, and climbed into bed next to her. She wrapped her arms around him and for a moment they lay still under the blanket. She could feel his hipbone against her thigh. His breathing was shallow; then she realized it matched her own. As if on cue, as if the moment was preordained, they turned toward each other. She felt him hard against her and shivered again.

"Are you still cold?" he asked, and in answer, she kissed him.

* * *

Tracie awoke, the afterglow of wonderful sex still surrounding her like an aura. She turned her head on the pillow. Jon was awake beside her, looking at her face with love and wonder. "You are so beautiful," he told her.

"Oh, come on. I—"

He covered her mouth with his hand. "You are so beautiful. So beautiful," he repeated, and though she had thought she didn't have any tears left in her, they filled her eyes again. With wonder, he ran his hand from a rib to her waist and then around the swell of her hip. "You're so . . . beautiful," he said. "Your breasts are perfect, so soft, so vulnerable. They make me think of new puppies—blind, but so alive and responsive."

"Puppies!" She laughed. "Where did you get that idea?"

"I don't know. My mother said I should get a dog." They both laughed; then he kissed her again, long and hard. She pulled away.

"Jon, I've been really stupid."

"You're adorable." He said it in a way she had been hungry to hear all her life.

But she had to tell him. She had to apologize for how ridiculous she'd been. How blind and foolish "No. No. I didn't know what I wanted. Molly told me . . . scrambled eggs. . . ." Oh, how could she explain? "I just didn't see—"

Jon kissed her. It was another perfect kiss. Then he looked at her. "Did you major in cute at school? Or do you still take lessons?" he asked. "Did you know I love your earlobes? I've always loved them." He bit one gently and she shivered. "They're adorable."

He stretched out, luxuriating in the bed. "I feel like we're the only two people in the world. Like Adam and Eve on a raft." He paused and lifted himself up on one elbow. "Will you let me eat poached eggs now?"

"Right this minute?" Tracie asked. She thought she was pretty cute, but he was gorgeous.

"Well, not right this minute," Jon said. "There's something else I want to eat first."

"Again?" she asked, and hugged him. She was so happy, her chest hurt. The strangest thought flitted into her head. She wanted to die right then so that she would always be this happy. "You can eat anything you like," she told Jon. "Just promise you'll never leave me." She looked deep into his eyes.

Very seriously, Jon looked back at her. "I have to leave you," he said. "I have to pee."

She laughed, relieved. "Okay, but just this once. And hurry."

Jon got up and walked past her desk. He crossed to the bathroom, but on his way, he noticed all the Polaroids Tracie had tacked up. They were arranged in a before-and-after format. Tracie's eyes opened wide. She sat up. Oh my God! Did I ever begin to tell him . . . to ask him . . . Her mind raced to everything she had there, every stupid, shallow observation, every silly adjective, and, worst of all, the bet. She closed her eyes and made a futile prayer that he would just turn and keep heading to the bathroom, but he didn't. He read a few of the Post-its. Then he saw the printout of the article. Again, she breathed a silent prayer that he wouldn't pick it up, but he did. His face dropped.

Tracie couldn't believe that she could go from such total joy to such complete misery in less than a minute. She wanted to cry out, to tell Jon to drop the article, to ignore it. Oh, she knew she should have told him about it so long ago.

Jon's face had gone white and he put the draft back down on her desk. He walked over to the damp pile of clothes beside the bed and began to fumble with his shorts, then his jeans.

"Jon, don't," she said stupidly.

"I have to go," he told her, his voice dead. Then he looked up at her for the first time since he'd seen the snapshots. "I don't like to stay over," he said. "I like to sleep alone."

She recognized the words she had taught him. She jumped up, wrapped the sheet around herself, and stood up. "Are you using the bad-boy treatment on *me*?" she asked. Then it occurred to her that maybe all of this—standing her up, following her, seducing her—

could have just been an elaborate part of his new persona. God, was that it? Had all of this been just an act, a taste of her own medicine? She began to shiver again. "What am I? Just another notch on your floppy disc?" she asked him.

He was already pulling his shirt on. "And what am I? Your chance at being the next Anna Quindlen?" Jon snapped at her. He thrust his arms into his jacket, snatched up the article, and threw it in front of her. "You did this to me so you could get a big byline?" he asked.

"Of course not. I did it because you asked me." How could he think that? And even if part of it was true, hadn't what they just shared transcended all that went before? "I began the article because—"

Jon turned his back on Tracie and walked out of the bedroom. She ran behind him, clutching the sheet around her. "Jon! Wait."

He was at the door, but he turned to her. "I can't believe it. I'm a photo op. A story? 'A nerd.' That's how you saw me? 'A corporate weenie'? Very complimentary."

"Jon, once I began writing it, I knew I could never submit the thing."

"But this is the way you once saw me," Jon said, looking at one of the photos he still clutched in his hand. He shook his head, crushed the photo, and threw it onto the floor. "You know, I was a little afraid when we made love that you might be doing it for the wrong reason. But until now, I never thought I was just a career opportunity." He smiled, but it was a mean smile, one she had never seen. "What was this going to be? The climax of the piece?"

"Jon, I—"

He shook his head. "You say you love me, but you mocked me and used me in this stupid newspaper piece. You and Marcus must have had some good laughs over this. How about Beth—was she in on it? And Laura? Did she see it? Did you and Phil read it in bed together?"

"Jon, when I started, I thought it was a good idea. I put a lot of you and a lot of my love for you into it. And it's good. But I'll just tear it up. I always meant to ask your permission, and then, somehow, it all got too sensitive and—"

"Sensitive! Ha, that's a laugh," he said. "There will be a special on *Nightline* the day you become sensitive. You're the one who taught me to hurt people," he reminded her. "You're the one who taught me the fun of being Mr. If-I-Tell-You-a-Lie-I-Can-Fuck-You-and-Forget-You. Sensitive?"

"Forget the piece."

"Forget *you!*" He turned to go.

"Wait! Five minutes ago, you promised never to leave me. You've been my friend for seven years. I told you the article was a mistake. I was going to dump it. But you treat me like this now?"

Jon moved to the door. "Hey, it's how you like to be treated. Didn't you teach me that? All the tricks. Women seek pain, right? They want to be treated badly. I'm a good student, even if you didn't let *me* take notes."

"Please. Jon, I love you."

"What does love mean to you? Betrayal? Forget this. This is . . . nothing." He opened the door, then turned back to face her. "Are you going to tell Phil about this?"

"About what? Nothing happened, right?"

Jon turned and closed the door behind him. Tracie could only manage to wait until he'd safely gotten out of range before she burst into sobs.

Chapter 37

Tracie hadn't slept all night, but she looked as if she hadn't slept for a week. She'd been caught coming in late—real late—and she hadn't even been able to duck her head in the traditional gesture of apology. So, an hour or so later when Marcus called her into his office, she knew the news wouldn't be good. She'd also heard from Beth, who'd heard from Sara, who'd overheard Allison talking to Marcus, that he was furious because Allison had dropped him. That wouldn't sweeten his mood. He was such an ass.

But as ridiculous as Marcus and his romantic life was, hers was worse, and she knew she was in no position to judge. Molly had been right about everything: She was a fool, and it was depressing to think of how she'd hurt Jon, been hurt by him, ruined the most important friendship she had, as well as all chances for true love.

Because she did love Jon. And it wasn't because he looked good now, or that she'd finally discovered what a thoughtful and gifted lover he was. It was because she'd always loved him. She had simply been too stupid to know that she did. And for that, she'd be punished, probably for the rest of her life. She'd called Jon more than a dozen times, in an imitation of Beth. The irony wasn't lost on her.

Jon hadn't called her back and wouldn't take her calls at the office. She wasn't sure that she could get him to forgive her.

Now, however, she had to see Marcus and probably get another lousy assignment. Marcus sat at his desk with his sleeves rolled up. He looked like he was in the middle of some major editing job. His blue pencil had already slashed veins and arteries on whatever story corpse he was working on. He was slashing so energetically, he even had a streak of blue along the side of his mouth, as if he might have been editing what he said, though Tracie knew better than to believe that.

She looked at him and suddenly felt that she couldn't bear one more snotty remark, one more insult. She took a single step into the room. "Yes?" she asked.

"That Father's Day article was pretty good," Marcus admitted. "With Allison's help," he added. She just stood there. It's odd, Tracie thought; once the worst thing has happened, other things that frightened you before no longer have any power. She remembered feeling this way just once before, after her mother died. The two girls who used to tease her mercilessly, her teacher, who frightened her, and even the Rottweiler at the end of her block in Encino had no longer held any terror for her at all. Let them all do their worst; she didn't care. In a way, the desolation then had been peaceful, just as it was now. She looked at Marcus calmly. There wasn't anything he couldn't do to her.

"Yup. Couldn't have done it without her. But it's too bad it was cut down so much," she told him calmly. "Maybe on my next assignments, they can be longer. But just try not to make them holiday pieces."

"That's a deal," he said rather affably. He picked up the papers he was working on and tossed them onto the credenza. "Sit down," he said.

"No thanks," she told him, and leaned against the doorway. There was a time when she would have done that to be insolent, but now she just didn't care.

"Well, I'm going to run the nerd makeover. It's actually pretty funny," he said. "I thought we might also run a sidebar with Ted Waite; Steve Balmer, the new head of Microsoft; and maybe Marc Grayson— you know, the head of Netscape. And maybe Kevin Mitnick, the hacker that just got out of jail. I thought we'd show him in his orange jumpsuit as a before and then I'd have the photo department do a montage on all of them after. Mitnick has got to find some girl to support him, since they won't even let him work at a McDonald's. Poor bastard. Live by the computer, die by the computer."

At that moment, Tracie wished Marcus would die by his computer. Her equilibrium, her dead calmness, had disappeared as he spoke. Jon might never forgive her for what she had done, but he'd certainly kill her or himself if the article was published. "You can't run the article," she said.

"Look," he told her, "I know all about your little talks with *Seattle Magazine*. But you can't publish there if I put in a first claim. We have the option, and I'm sure you did this on company time."

"Marcus, you can't publish it," she repeated.

He picked up the pile of papers off the credenza and waved them at her. "After all the time you put into that? And the time *I* put into it? It's the only good thing you've done."

"Marcus, you can't run it. . . ." How could she explain? Why would she explain to an idiot like him? "It . . . it will hurt people," she said.

"Oh. Well," he intoned, deeply sarcastic. "Well, if it will hurt people . . ."

She looked at him and knew that she couldn't stand him for one more minute. He was an egotistical, self-important, bullying hack and she was sick and tired of it.

"Look, if you run it, I quit," she told him.

"Really?" Marcus said with that same sophomoric tone. "I have a better idea. You're fired."

"Great," she told him. Her calmness returned. Sometimes complete desolation, a totally empty landscape, was best. "I'll go clear out my desk," she said.

To any observer, it would have been clear from the detritus on the bed that Tracie had been lying there for several days. There were the remains of a take-out pizza, empty ice-cream containers, half-full cereal boxes, magazines, rumpled newspapers, and books. She couldn't read much. Mostly, she cried, slept, and watched *Ricki Lake*. Sometimes she watched *Jerry Springer*, but it made it her feel worse about herself. Today, Ricki had brothers and sisters who slept with each other and who wanted the world to recognize their love. Either the show or the mud-pie ice cream she had eaten along with some Ritz crackers was making her queasy. So she hit the remote, turned on her side, and pulled a blanket up over her head. The phone rang and she listened to see who was leaving a message, but it wasn't Jon, so she didn't take the call.

She must have dozed for a while, but she woke when she heard the rattle of her lock. By the time she came out from under the blankets, Laura had entered the bedroom and was looking around. "Wow. Worse than I thought. I bought everything you asked for but the cookie-dough ice cream. That was too decadent."

"Yours is not to reason why, yours is but to shop and die," Tracie said.

Laura sat down at the foot of the bed, got up to remove a plate with toast crusts, and then sat down again. "You're the one who looks like you're going to die. Look, I know you feel really bad. Maybe you even fucked things up permanently with Jon, though I think you two may work it out," she told Tracie. Tracie merely groaned. "Still, you have to get out of bed eventually," Laura said.

"No I don't," Tracie contradicted. "I have no job, so I'm not going to the office. And I'm not going to the gym ever again. It'll take at least two years before I need another haircut. This is it."

Laura looked into the bag of groceries, pulled out a package of

Goldfish, and opened them, popping a handful into her mouth and passing the rest to Tracie. "But what will happen to you?" she asked.

"As long as there's pizza delivery and cash to pay for it, I've hit the mattress and I'm staying right here," Tracie declared. "I've ruined my life. Molly was right. I'm such a fool."

Laura got up, went over to the dresser, and took bread, cream cheese, and a jar of Welch's grape jelly decorated with the Spirits of Mickey Mouse from the bag. Laura opened both spreads, laid out the bread, and, using her finger as a knife, began to make two sandwiches. "Molly's a wise woman. And a nice boss." She handed a sandwich to Tracie.

"Ummm." The soft white bread, the creamy cheese, and the sweetness of the jelly comforted her. Before she swallowed, she pulled herself up into a sitting position. She wanted to die, but not the way Mama Cass had.

Laura sat down beside her and took a bite of her own sandwich. "So what did Molly say?"

Tracie dripped a glob of jelly onto the blanket, smeared it up with her forefinger, then licked it. "She told me I was wasting my time with idiots, when Jon loved me. Jon was right there in front of me all the time. And I couldn't appreciate him." She took another bite of the sandwich. If she kept focused on her regret that soon it was going to be gone, she couldn't think about her regrets over Jon. "Why do women go for bad boys?" Tracie asked Laura. "Why do we make ourselves suffer when there are nice men around? Why don't we see them?"

Laura shrugged. "Because God is a sadist?" Laura asked, getting up to make another pair of sandwiches.

Tracie ignored her flippancy. "Why did you think you loved Peter and I thought I loved Phil and Beth thought Marcus was worth obsessing over?"

Laura handed her another sandwich, sat back on the bed, and crossed her legs. "I figure it's just one of nature's ugly little jokes on women. A phase we have to go through, like menopause or bloating."

She took a bite of her second sandwich. "The worst irony is that in about five years, we're going to start looking around for nice guys to marry. And all the ones we blew off in high school and college and in our early dating years will be taken—you know, the nerds like Bill Gates and Steven Spielberg and Woody Allen. The guys who couldn't get laid for two decades and now get to sleep with movie stars and models because they're so smart and powerful."

Tracie threw herself back down onto her rumpled pillows and let her cream cheese and jelly sandwich rest on her chest. "I've messed up my whole life. I'll die miserable and alone."

Laura shrugged. "What about Phil? You don't have to be alone. You could probably stay with Phil, even if he is unpublished, unemployed, and has an unrealistic sense of his self-worth."

Tracie listened to Phil's description. "Wait, I think I'm falling in love with him all over again." She paused for a moment and then shook her head. "Phil! He's bored me for a long time. I just didn't notice."

"Oh, I don't know," Laura said. "He's not so bad. I kinda—"

Tracie interrupted her by sitting up. The two sandwich halves flew down the length of the bed and hit Laura's arm, flopping onto the blanket again. "You know what really bothers me? I can't believe I didn't notice Jon until I dolled him up and got all the other girls interested." She shook her head. "I didn't see who he was until I ruined him."

Laura picked up the two sandwich halves and handed them to Tracie, who shook her head. If she ate anything else, she'd vomit, and since she wasn't going to get out of bed, she didn't like to think of the consequences. "I love him, but I deserve to be alone here the rest of my life." She flopped back down. "Believe me, it will be better for the world this way," she said, staring up at the ceiling.

"Well, look on the bright side," Laura said cheerfully. "You've finally realized you love him. I've known it for at least a year."

"Great, be like that. Be the smart one. If you had told me that then, I could have had him. Now I have to get in line behind Allison, Beth, Samantha, Enid, and Ruth."

"Wow!" said Laura. "They're all hooked, huh? It's a good thing he never slept with me." She paused for a moment, as if considering whether or not she should say what she had on her mind. As always, she decided against discretion. "Was he as good in bed as Beth said he was?"

"Better." Tracie groaned, began to cry, and pulled the blankets over her head. A few minutes later, she controlled herself and wiped her eyes and nose on the blanket, then looked out from under it. Laura still sat at the side of the bed.

"Tracie, I don't think this is healthy," she said in what had to have been a whopper of an understatement. "Are you sure it's over with Jon? You're never coming out of your apartment again?" she asked.

Tracie nodded. "This is not a negotiation, Laura. I've taken myself hostage and nobody gets out of this place alive."

Laura nodded and shrugged. "Then it won't bother you that something else really bad has happened. Something worse than your fight with Jon."

"What? What could possibly be worse than this?" Tracie asked.

"The article ran."

Tracie jumped up as if hit with an electrical current. "Get out! It didn't!" she said. "Marcus fired me, but he wouldn't—"

Laura took the newspaper out of the paper bag and threw it on the bed. "It did. And he would." She grabbed the paper and began riffling through it. "Page one of the Living section," Laura told her.

Tracie got to it, surveyed the damage, and moaned. The article took up the whole front page, and it continued on the third and fourth pages. It also carried the ridiculous makeovers of the hacker and the high-tech CEOs. Tracie moaned again. "Oh God. I'll never make up with Jon now. He'll never speak to me. Fuck Marcus! That lying scumball." She began to scan the piece. "Oh no. The best man on the planet, and I've made a laughingstock of him."

Just then, Tracie heard the door locks as they started to be released one by one. For a minute, she thought it was Jon, then realized who it had to be. "Oh God! Phil's here." Tracie heard the last lock release; then the door opened and Phil's footsteps crossed the living room.

He entered the bedroom. But he was a different Phil. He looked like the subject of some makeover from hell. He'd had his hair cut and his act was cleaned up significantly, but in all the wrong ways. He still wore jeans, but he had a lamé sports jacket on. He carried a briefcase, as well. He approached the bed, yet he didn't notice Tracie's condition or the junk all over. He just swept a spot clear and sat down next to her. Tracie was too exhausted to comment. Laura, however, did a double take. "Phil, is that you?" she asked.

"Hi, Laura," he said cheerfully. "Hey, Trace, notice anything different?"

"You got a haircut?" she asked. "Yours is too short, too."

He smiled. "You'll get used to it. And that's not the only change. I got a job."

Laura stood up. "Hey, guys. I'd better go. I've got the evening shift at Java, The Hut. Trace, call me later." She reached down and rubbed Tracie's foot, then left the room.

Alone in a dirty bed with Phil, Tracie felt unbelievably claustrophobic.

Phil smiled at her, as if she looked as pretty as a picture with her butchered, greasy hair, her oldest nightgown, and the dirty coverlet. "Tracie, you won the bet," he said. "I saw the article. And I'm ready to be committed."

"We look like we both are," was all Tracie could manage to say.

"Great. You got me. Fair and square. I got my stuff packed to come here."

Tracie groaned and rolled over in bed. "That's all right, Phil. The bet idea was stupid. You shouldn't play with people's lives to win a bet."

"Well, stupid or not, I'm ready to move in," Phil said.

Tracie didn't respond. Her life was a nightmare. She just lay under the covers, promising herself she would never move or speak again.

"Hey. You sick or something?" Phil asked. Tracie knew he was self-involved, but she'd never thought he was an imbecile until now. Phil pulled the blankets down from her head, and though she tried to catch at them, he was too fast for her. He reached into his briefcase and took out a paper bag and a black velvet jewelry box. He handed it to Tracie. "This will make you feel better."

Tracie rolled her eyes. "Phil, I gave up farm cakes and I don't need another guitar pick right now."

"It's not a guitar pick," he promised. "Open the box." Tracie did. There was a tiny diamond in a traditional engagement setting. She tried not to let her jaw drop. No wonder Phil had never been able to succeed as a bass player. He had the worst timing in the world.

"Marry me, Tracie," Phil said. "I love you."

Tracie looked at the ring, then back at Phil, and burst into tears. She was so frustrated with her own stupidity that if she could have, she would have torn her own head off.

Lovingly, Phil took Tracie in his arms. "Oh, baby. I know. I love you, too," he told her. "I'm sorry I put you through such hell. I guess I just had to grow up a little. You know, start thinking of other people." Tracie sobbed louder. He held her tighter. "It's okay," he said. But of course it wasn't. "Thanks for putting up with me and going the distance." He patted her back. Tracie hated to be patted.

"You know, Laura helped me think this through. I've set new priorities, Tracie, and you're my number one." She sobbed harder, but he didn't seem to notice.

"Your article was really good. You're better than Emma Quindlen."

"Anna," Tracie sobbed, dangerously out of control.

Phil looked at her with concern. "Honey, calm down. You got to try on the ring."

She couldn't. She'd rather cut off her hand. The man that she'd thought she desired for so long, the man that she'd tricked herself into thinking she cared about was not only ridiculous but also a stranger to her. "I . . . I . . ." She tried to stop crying, wiped her eyes and her nose with her fingers, and looked at him. "Phil, do you think my earlobes are adorable?"

He shrugged. "I don't know. I never noticed."

Tracie began to wail again. Phil stood up, reached over to her bureau, and handed her a Kleenex. Then he turned his back to the bed and took off his sports jacket. He laid it carefully on the chair beside the bed, then patted it as if it were a good dog. "I got to take care of this baby," he said. "I think it was the jacket that got me the job."

"What job?" Tracie managed to ask.

Phil turned back to her, and for the first time, she saw the T-shirt he'd been wearing under the jacket. It had a huge Micro/Con logo on it. Wordlessly, she pointed at it and began to scramble off the bed in horror. "What? How?" she managed to say. "Why . . . are you . . ."

Phil looked proudly down at his chest. "Oh, yeah," he told her. "They didn't just give me the job. They gave me the T-shirt and a thousand dollars' worth of stock. Isn't that neat?"

Chapter 38

Jon was sweating. He was moving as fast as he possibly could. The last time he'd felt this kind of panic was when he was being chased by the neighborhood dog, notorious for biting anyone that got within fifty yards of his owner's yard. But this time, Jon was trying to escape himself. He had managed to get into the Micro/Con building undetected early enough that morning and get himself set up on the treadmill in the workout room. Now, however, people were starting to come in, and he knew it wasn't his imagination—he was the focus of everyone in the room. Usually, people would stare blankly while they pedaled a bike, pulled on the weight bars of the bench press equipment, and walked on the treadmills. But this morning, it was the stare of wonderment, of recognition, of celebrity. That's what happens when your best friend splashes you all over a section of the local newspaper, he thought.

He couldn't believe that Tracie had been so spiteful as to publish the article because of their fight. But he guessed he'd just never really known her. He'd been so upset, he'd had to spend the night at his mother's, and that hadn't been easy, either. She hadn't approved of the article, but she'd kept urging Jon, "Call Tracie. I don't know why this all happened, but I do know that a friendship like yours and Tracie's shouldn't end like this. Call her." Then she'd talked a lot about forgiveness, and visiting his dad in the hospital. Jon had been upset enough to think—but not say—that it was a lot easier to forgive someone who had ruined her life than it was to forgive someone who had ruined his.

He still hadn't actually taken in his visit with his father. After he'd gotten over his pity, he thought he was angry at Chuck, too. What was this Mother's Day and Father's Day about anyway? Why wasn't there a children's day? Chuck had just used the holiday as a wedge, as a way to get Jon to see him without having to actually apologize directly for all of his childishness and thoughtlessness over the years. It was easy enough for his mother to preach forgiveness: Grandpa had been a really good father and a really nice guy. He'd filled in for Chuck more times than Jon liked to remember. Next Father's Day, Jon decided, he was going to go to his grandpa's grave and thank him. Maybe, that is, if he didn't die of embarrassment between now and then.

Jon tried to avert his eyes from the other employees who had come in to work out—or to gawk at him—but it wasn't an easy thing to do. What he wanted so desperately to do was to hit the stop button, jump off the rubber track, and tell them exactly what Tracie had done to him. How she had violated him. How she had exposed him as the town clown. How she had made him the Micro/Con mascot. But Jon opted for jogging on the treadmill. His head was pounding with every step he took. How could she do this to me? he thought. He couldn't remember having this feeling of pain in his chest since his father left him and his mother so long ago. Sure he had felt badly for all the other women his father had been with and dumped, but this hurt was something that Jon couldn't get past.

He wiped the beads of sweat from his forehead before they could roll into his eyes and sting. Though that wouldn't be so bad, he

thought. Then my vision would be impaired and I couldn't see everyone looking at me. He wondered if the hurt he felt was what he had
inflicted on all the women he had slept with since this whole transformation started. Especially Beth—she was the most persistent of
all of them. Well, he was definitely his father's son, thanks to Miss
Higgins.

Why had Tracie decided to sleep with him only after he had been
with all the others? Was she jealous of them? Had she wanted him all
this time? Or did she want to see if he was doing the sex thing right
and take notes on that, too? Jon couldn't take the pressure of the
room any longer, so he stepped off the treadmill and left the gym.
He used his towel as a shield, pretending to wipe down his wet face
and neck.

At least the changing room was empty and he was given a moment to gain his composure before having to step out into the hallway. He had managed to get halfway down the hall on his way to his
office, when he was met by Samantha. Jon almost wished for the
time when it was only a daydream to have her come up to him. But
what she did to him was beyond even his own wildest dreams. "You
rotten little bastard!" Sam spat in his face, and before Jon could respond, she had slapped him across the face.

Great, if all the other women at Micro/Con had this reaction, he
would be black and blue by noon. He put his hand up to his face and
continued down the hall. He couldn't help but look into the door-
ways of the offices along the way. Luckily, most were empty, so he was
fortunate enough to get down to the main room, where all the cubicles were located in his department. All that came to his mind
was the possibility of a reenactment of the scene in *Jerry Maguire*
when Tom Cruise goes to leave his job and everyone stands up and
watches him go to the elevator. If only he were leaving, Jon thought.
He thought that he could stand up to them and say that the article
Tracie had written for the paper was not his mission statement, that
he'd had nothing to do with it. Then everyone would go back to what

they were doing and never give any of it another thought. He stopped at the entrance to the big room. Everyone was working away and no one really looked up at him; they were doing what they usually did every morning when he came into his office. Could be worse, he thought as he entered his office.

He decided he'd shut the door on the rest of his staff today. That way, anyone wanting entry would have to be announced first. As he turned from the door to head to his desk, he was taken aback by Carole, who had perched herself on a beanbag chair.

"Good morning, Mr. Bad Boy," she said with a sheepish grin on her face. "You're the talk of the commissary today."

Jesus! He didn't need this, not after all he'd been through already. "Good morning," he said quietly, and went to sit in his chair. "Can I help you with something?"

"I'm going home today and I wanted to say it's been a pleasure having met the 'Sexless Savant' of Seattle." She grinned again.

"I didn't have—" he began, but she got up from the chair and put her finger up to her mouth to signal him to be quiet.

"You don't have to explain anything to me, Jonny," she said in a snotty voice. "A boy's gotta do what a boy's gotta do. You'll manage." Then she stepped closer to his desk and pointed to a memo. "Based on what this says, you should have spent a lot more time on Parsifal than on me and all the others."

Jon looked down at the paper. Shit! It was from Dave, his division supervisor. He scanned the words and the word *failed* was in bold capitals in the second paragraph. He pushed his chair back from the desk and Carole went to the door. "Good luck," she said. "Maybe we'll meet at Carousel B again sometime."

Finally, his day was over. Jon walked out of the office building and headed toward his bike. Tracie stood beside it, her hand on the seat. When he saw her, he stopped for a moment, then turned back toward the Micro/Con entrance and began to walk away. "Jon, please,"

Tracie called, and came up beside him. "Just let me explain and apologize."

He shook his head. "I didn't know you were a liar."

"Jon, I swear. I was going to ask your permission before I—"

"Permission to humiliate me?" he asked, interrupting her. "I don't think I would have granted that, even for you."

"Listen! Marcus had rejected the idea months ago. I was—"

"But when he changed his mind, you stepped up to the plate, huh?"

"Marcus promised he wouldn't run it. . . ."

"Who do you think you are?" he asked. "*Who?* What gives you the right to play God?" He couldn't believe how callous she had been, how she had used him as a pawn to get closer to Phil. For a moment, his anger rose so high, he could understand how men hit women. "Interfering with people's lives. Changing them altogether."

"But you asked me to," she reminded him.

That was true. What had he been thinking of? Jon thought of his father and all that he had put his mother and stepmothers through, as well as the pain he had caused. Jon shook his head to snap himself out of his reverie.

"You know," Jon said to Tracie, "maybe Molly is right. For a smart girl, you're really dumb. Maybe I was asking you something different. Maybe I was asking you a more important question than why I got blown off by Samantha."

"What? What were you asking me?" she demanded.

Jon turned his back on her and walked away. He wanted her to melt, to disappear. Instead, she followed him. Christ! He didn't need anyone watching more drama in his life. But Jon couldn't keep silent. "After being my best friend for more than seven years, maybe you should have known what I was asking. And why," he spat out at her.

"If you wanted me, why didn't you say so? Why didn't you tell me, or make a move on me?" she demanded. "I'm not a mind reader."

The unfairness of that stung him. "Why should I? So I could hear that you loved me but you just didn't love me in 'that way'?" He felt a pain and a rage he hadn't known was there. "Do you know how insulting that is? Do you think I needed to hear that said aloud by you?" he asked. "You were smart enough to pull off this charade so that women would fall for me. You were smart enough to turn me into a newer, better version of my dad. You were smart enough to write an article that makes me look like the jerk I am. But you're not smart enough to know about subtext? What kind of writer are you?"

Now tears were actually rolling down her cheeks, the cheeks he'd covered with kisses. "Jon, I love you. I made love to you. . . ."

"But not until you changed me. Not until half of the women in Seattle had slept with me first." He finally got his fucking bike chain. Tracie came up beside Jon and gently touched his arm. He pulled away from her so violently that she stepped back. "I wasn't good enough for you before. You didn't notice me, or you took me for granted or . . . something. Anyway, you didn't want to make love to me then."

Tracie put her head down and her hands up to her head. He wouldn't let himself care how pathetic she looked. He'd seen her look this sad over morons she'd dated once. When she did answer, it was a whisper. "I think I always did want to make love to you. You were the only one who really knew me, Jon. But I was stupid. And I think I was afraid. Jon, do you know how much our night together meant to me? Do you know how much I loved it, how much I love you?" she asked.

Jon turned to her. "And you weren't afraid of Phil?" he asked. Tracie raised her head and gave him a guilty look. And then his hope was smashed, because he knew her well enough to know she'd done something very wrong. Despite his accusation, she wasn't a liar. Maybe the article had been a mistake. So what was it that she had now disclosed with that look? What had she done in the last twenty-four hours that she shouldn't have? . . . "Who did you sleep with last night, Tracie?" he asked.

Tracie lowered her gaze, but not before he saw her blush. Now he knew he was right. "Phil, but I . . . but he had just . . . we didn't . . ." she stammered.

He didn't want to hear another word. He actually got sick to his stomach and thought he might throw up right there on the macadam. "I was alone, Tracie. And that's what I'd like to be now," Jon said abruptly, then mounted his bike and rode off.

Chapter 39

Jon's mother kept giving him two pieces of useless advice. "Call Tracie, Jonathan," she said. "And get yourself a dog. A nice golden retriever maybe."

"I don't want to call her. I want her to be struck by lightning," he muttered, his mouth full.

"Why, Jonathan Delano!" she exclaimed, but then she backed off.

The problem was that he couldn't find anything that assuaged the pain. He wasn't so humiliated anymore—people were such jerks that having his picture in the paper had made him a celebrity on campus and some geeks had taken it seriously enough to try to emulate his "style." He put an end to that by stopping at the Micro/Con shop on campus and going back to his usual T-shirts and khakis. The hell with the pants thing.

But he couldn't seem to snap out of the pain he was in. One night, in total desperation, he picked up the phone. But he didn't call Tracie. He called Allison.

She seemed delighted to hear from him when he called. He'd tried not to—for both of their sakes—but in the end, he couldn't face another long night alone. By the time he picked up the phone, it was too late even to pretend to meet for dinner, so Jon asked if she wanted to join him for a drink, which he guessed was Bad Boy Talk for wanting to fuck. Or maybe Bad Boy Talk for wanting to fuck was asking her if she wanted to fuck. He wasn't sure. But he knew he needed a drink or two, or six, and some company.

He met her at Rico's, and he had already had a couple of shots of Southern Comfort before she got there. First, he'd asked for Dewar's and it was harsh, but now he was drinking in memory of his father—even if his father wasn't dead yet. Jon couldn't understand how anyone could like the taste, but after three drinks, he had to admit there was a certain logic to his father's drug of choice. It tasted like paint remover, but it was effective. He wasn't drunk, though. Tracie's betrayal and the bet she'd made with Phil would take at least a bottle of Southern Comfort—or paint remover itself—to erase.

He stared into his glass and wondered if he'd ever known her. He couldn't believe the Tracie he knew would make love to him the way she had when all along she was angling to get Phil to move in with her.

Phil! Jon ordered another drink, and the bartender was only too happy to oblige. Jon wanted to put the cold glass up against his forehead, but he took a sip instead. Maybe if Tracie's choice hadn't been Phil, he could have lived with it. Maybe. But Phil was a true idiot, pretentious and self-involved and—Hey, let's face it, he thought—not too smart. Jon had already vowed that he'd never see Tracie again, but earlier that day, he could swear he'd seen Phil walking across the Micro/Con campus. It couldn't have been true, but if he did see him anytime soon, Jon promised himself he'd do everything he could to beat the living crap out of the stupid bastard.

Just when he felt drunk enough to want to get drunker, he looked up from the bottom of his Southern Comfort glass and saw Allison walking along the bar toward him. All of the men turned their heads to follow her progress. She was beautiful; he knew that. Prettier than

Tracie. Definitely prettier than Tracie, he repeated to himself. Taller, and her breasts were bigger.

Every man at the bar wanted a chance to touch those breasts, but he was the only one who would be able to tonight. That is, if he didn't drink too much more Southern Comfort.

"Hi," she said, draping one arm around his shoulder. Every other guy, all the Phils and all the losers, tasted disappointment along with their booze. He knew what that felt like. The problem was, he didn't care that he'd triumphed over all of them.

"What's your poison?" he asked her, just the way his dad did. She ordered an Absolut on the rocks, and Jon hoped she wouldn't drink too much, because she had to drive them both to his place, manage to get up the stairs with him, take off her clothes and then his. Sorry, boys, he almost said aloud. He'd take this one home. Fuck Tracie.

For a minute, he thought about fucking Tracie. He closed his eyes, not because he wanted to make the memory more vivid but because he wanted to push it away. He would sleep with Allison; he would rub his body against hers and it would feel good to both of them, and he hoped that on the other side of Seattle, where Phil and Tracie were rubbing their bodies together, she'd be thinking of him.

Allison moaned and Jon moved his hand to her shoulders, lifting himself up so that he could improve his thrust into her. "Oh, Jonny," she moaned again. He stopped, and then after a moment, when he didn't continue, she opened her eyes.

"Not Jonny," he said. "My name is Jon," but he'd already lost his erection and his desire to pump himself into her a second time. The first one had been enough, anyway: It had been an anger fuck, a fuck for the boys at the bar, all sound and fury, signifying nothing. In his bitterness and anger, it was pleasurable in a sickening way. The worst part was that she seemed to have liked it, too. He rolled off of her.

He was ashamed of himself. He was worse than his father—his father didn't, as far as he knew, sleep with women to punish them. He couldn't move from the bed, and it wasn't sexual exhaustion that kept him there.

Allison walked around his apartment as he lay there. Now he understood the wisdom of Tracie's rule to go to the woman's place. Could he ask her to leave? It seemed very harsh indeed. "So you've been with Micro/Con almost since the beginning," she was saying.

"Not really," he said. "I mean, I wasn't a founder or anything. I came in after the first IPO."

"But you must have a lot of stock by now," Allison said. "And a lot of options."

"Yeah," he answered, and wondered if he could tell her he was feeling sick. It wouldn't be a lie. But would it be enough to make her leave?

"You know, Marcus isn't even vested yet," Allison told him. "And he's not an officer of the company."

Was she talking about the slimeball at Tracie's office? "Really?" he asked, as if he cared. "The guy who harasses Tracie?"

Allison shot him a look. "Does he harass her, too?" she asked. "I swear, I'm ready to put in a grievance. But I figure now that Marcus knows Tracie's engaged, he'll probably lay off her. He doesn't seem to go for married women."

"Engaged?" Jon asked. He could swear he felt his heart stop. Maybe it was just his lungs. He couldn't breathe. "Tracie's engaged?"

"Oh, didn't you know?" Allison said casually. "I thought the two of you were such good friends."

Allison came back to the bed and put her hand gently over his crotch. Nothing happened. "I don't mind about that," she said gently. "You know, I don't think sex is the most important thing." She lay down next to him and put an arm across his chest. He could feel her perfect left breast against his shoulder, but it could just as well have been a throw cushion or a rubber duck. When she moved her hand between his legs again, he lay limp under her hand.

Tracie was engaged to Phil. The bass player wasn't just an idiot she'd outgrow. He was going to be, at the very least, her bad first marriage, and possibly the father of her children. With that thought, Jon could no longer control himself. He rolled away from Allison, out from under her hand, over to the side of his bed, and vomited onto the floor.

Chapter 40

Tracie stared out the window at the Seattle sky. As almost always, there was a gray cloud cover, but just now, as she looked, a hole had appeared and silvery light was shining through in that pattern that made the sky look magical. There must have been a lot of turbulence, because as she watched, the torn clouds began to come together again, first in shreds of mist and then, like a tissue over a healing wound, they covered the brightness and closed out the sun.

Tracie didn't allow herself to sigh—Laura noticed those and commented on every one she made—so she just took her eyes from the window, crouched down again, and dipped her roller in the pan of paint that she and Laura were slapping on the wall.

Laura's new apartment was going to be nice, but Tracie thought the mauve paint was hideous. She'd been too pleased at Laura's enthusiasm to comment on her paint selection—Laura had really gotten into DIY decorating. Home Depot was now her preferred singles' meet market. She'd already dated a cop she'd met there, as well as a sales rep and the supervisor of the paint department. She'd kissed him in the jacuzzi department. "You just love him for his discount," Tracie had joked, until Laura found out the guy wasn't divorced but only separated. She had dropped him like a hot portable grill. Tracie rolled the paint across the wall in the letter X that Laura had instructed her to do, then wrinkled her nose when she noticed the ten thousand tiny freckles of mauve paint that had sprung up on her arm.

"Too much paint on the roller," Laura told her as she rolled the adjoining wall. Laura looked at her and shook her head. "You'll never be a Kandinsky," Laura told her.

"So what?" Tracie responded. "I never wanted to play the violin." She rolled her eyes as well as more of the paint, and this time most of it stayed on the wall. The light that filtered in through the window reflected the mauve color on both of them and made Laura's complexion hideously sallow. This is not a color to paint a bedroom, Tracie thought, unless the next man Laura finds at Home Depot is not only legally single but also color-blind. It would make both of them look like hepatitis sufferers.

"You know, I've been thinking about it, and you're going to have to get a job," Laura said. She kept her back to Tracie and kept staring at the wall as she rolled up and down, up and down.

"I'm trying to write a novel," Tracie reminded her. "Believe me, it's work." Like a baby writer taking tiny steps, Tracie was learning a new schedule of writing in the morning, editing in the afternoon. She was writing about a girl growing up in a place like Encino, overcoming the death of her mother. It wasn't exactly autobiographical, but at least she could say the research came easily to her.

"I know. And I'm proud of you. It's not that I think you're lazy," her friend said. "It's because you have to get out."

"Next, you're going to tell me to run a personal ad," Tracie snapped, and when she put the roller back into the pan, she used a little too much energy and splashed the mauve paint onto the woodwork. "Oops," she said, and wiped up with one of the paper towels. Luckily, it was latex. It would take only an hour, instead of two days, to clean up.

Laura turned to her, ignoring the spilled paint. "Look, I've left you alone to mourn," she told Tracie. "Have I interfered? Have I told you you couldn't lie alone in your apartment every night like a dead salmon after the spawning season?"

Laura had been surprisingly good, or merely busy. Tracie had spent days, maybe even weeks, trying both to remember and forget every detail, every moment of the perfect time with Jon. When he'd told her he loved her, that he'd always loved her, it had been like a magical dance, the kind of thing that only happened in dreams—where you put on toe shoes and realize not only that you can effortlessly dance en pointe but that you also know every bit of choreography to the *Swan Lake* pas de deux. She and Jon had moved as one. Each touch had been so expected, yet so spontaneous, so new that Tracie had been able to hold the memory fresh for weeks.

Somewhere, she had read that women couldn't remember the pain of childbirth, because if they did, they would never go through it a second time. She didn't know if that was true, but she couldn't remember the joy, the perfection of her union with Jon because the pain of knowing that she would never have it again would be too much to bear. She had spent as much time as she needed berating herself, hating Marcus, blaming Phil, and every other wasteful, unfair emotion. But eventually, she had to give it up and more and more of her time became focused on the present, rather than the past. She didn't regret losing her job at the *Times*. She didn't regret her minuscule income. She didn't even regret going into the capital of the tiny trust fund her mother had left her. In fact, it was the first time she'd appreciated this money.

"I don't need a job, and I can't write if I take one," Tracie reminded Laura. "Anyway, if I budget my money, I can manage to take off the rest of the year, and I ought to have it written by then."

"Yeah, but if you have a job that doesn't require any mental energy, you'll be able to write better and you'll be able to hold out for *two* years," Laura pointed out. "Just in case it takes you a little longer than you thought to produce this." She grinned, picked up a brush, and began to cut a line along the ceiling. Tracie marveled at her steadiness. She was tall enough—or the ceilings were low enough—for her to do it without getting up on a ladder. "I think you better clean up now, anyway," Laura said.

"Why? My painting's not that bad," Tracie protested.

"Yeah, but Phil's coming over, and I don't think either of you wants to see the other one."

"Good point."

Laura had been seeing a lot of Phil. At least it seemed that way to Tracie, who never saw anyone except Laura. Of course, Laura didn't have too many other friends or even acquaintances in Seattle yet. But still, she seemed to be settling in. The apartment would be cute—aside from the mauve bedroom—and Laura seemed happy with her job at Java, The Hut. Tracie hadn't been there since her breakup with Jon, but Laura gave her detailed reports about the denizens regularly. Apparently, Jon had quit going there, too. That, or he had been edited out of Laura's running commentaries. Anyway, Tracie was glad about Phil, partly because she felt guilty about him and also because she was delighted to put down the mauve roller. "You know, if you want to date him, I don't have any objection. It's over."

"No, we're just bad friends," Laura wisecracked. "We meet once a week or so to bitch about our lives. It took him a little while, but he's starting to get good at it."

"You know, Jon and I started out as friends."

For a moment, Tracie allowed herself to think about the bitch sessions she used to have with Jon, but she pushed him from her mind, as she now forced herself to do several dozen times a day.

"Anyway," Laura said, "I really do think you should get a job as a waitress. They're looking for one at the restaurant. It's only part-time. It'll get you out. It gives you more material. And the tips aren't bad."

"Tips!" Tracie snorted. "What? Buy Micro/Con before it splits again? Plant my corn early? Come on, Laura, I'm not in college anymore. I'm not going to work for tips."

Laura pushed Tracie into the bathroom and handed her some soap. "Here's a tip," she said. "Wash those speckles off before they dry. And do everything else I tell you. I'm always right."

Tracie snorted again.

Tracie, upset and disheveled, was pushed into Java, The Hut by Laura. She forced her to approach Molly. Tracie was clearly reluctant. "Do you need another waitress?" Tracie asked.

"Yeah, like I need a wider arse," Molly told her. Then she looked Tracie up and down. "Why? You need work?"

"Well, I was sort of fired, but my boss says I quit, so I'm not sure if I'm getting unemployment. . . ."

Molly put up her right hand as if she didn't want to hear any more. With her left, she handed Tracie a Java, The Hut T-shirt. "At least you know the menu by 'eart," she said.

"See, I told you," Laura said to Tracie.

"See what?" Tracie asked.

"Will you hire Tracie?" Laura asked.

"I may do," Molly answered; then she sighed. "This probably will end my dream of becoming the next Starbucks, but what the 'ey."

Molly could hire her? "Don't I have to talk to the manager? Or someone?" Tracie asked. "I mean, I have no experience."

"Don't worry, you'll be punished for it, too, my lamb. I 'ope people tip you like you used to tip me," Molly said with a bit of sarcasm. "Isn't it obvious to you that this place 'as no manager?" she asked.

"So you own this place? I didn't know—"

" 'oney, there's a world of things you didn't know. But I think you're starting to learn." Molly paused. "It's over with Jon, then?"

Silently, Tracie nodded. "We kind of—"

"Say no more." Molly turned her attention to Laura. "You're late. The kitchen calls. And we're out of tomatoes."

"No problem." Laura flashed Molly a smile, then gave Tracie a thumbs-up sign.

Tracie looked toward the front window; the tree outside had gone from bud to full leaf and she had not even noticed. She was still working for Molly when the tree turned orange, dropped its leaves, and then spent close to a month covered with ice. It was the winter of her discontent.

Chapter 41

Jon walked with Lucky through the Pike Place Market. It was the first springlike day. People were out, and Lucky sniffed the air as if there was something new in it. Jon didn't even notice women who turned their heads to look at him. His last night with Allison had been his last night with anyone. He hadn't responded to Sam or Ruth. Even Beth had finally stopped calling. He had thrown himself into his work, but it was too late to save Parsifal. Alone, he weathered his first professional failure. He tied Lucky's leash to a railing beside some outdoor tables. Not that he had to: The dog would wait all day and night for him, leashed or not. He went into a shop to buy coffee.

Standing in line, he saw that the labels beneath the buns and cookies were Post-it notes. He stroked one with his finger, then shook his head. He didn't allow himself to think of Tracie at all. He had enough discipline now to enforce that rule. His loneliness at first had closed in on him as dense as a fog over Puget Sound. He didn't like to admit how many nights he had spent at his mother's trying to get himself through this little crisis. She hadn't said anything about it, always greeting him cheerfully, never asking questions. The only thing she did do was make one suggestion: "Why don't you go over to the pound?" He'd never thought of himself as a pet lover, but, at the same time, he felt like a dog at the pound: lonely, locked up—emotionally anyway—and seeking companionship. As he'd looked in the cages, there were all the canine losers in love's game: puppies too exuberant, dogs that had grown too big or not been cute enough or smart enough or lucky enough.

Jon got his coffee and a sticky bun he'd split with Lucky. The dog greeted him with exaggerated gestures of joy, waving her butt and tail. As he untied her leash and turned to go, he saw Beth sitting alone. He could duck her, but at that moment, despite Lucky, his loneliness was so great that he walked over to her. "May I?" Jon asked.

She looked up. "Oh, sure. How are you, Jonny?"

"Jon. Just Jon," he told her. "And this is Lucky."

"I didn't know you had a dog."

"Just got her awhile ago. As for me, I'm okay. How are you?"

"Oh, same old, same old," Beth said. She picked up her coffee and sipped it. She was also consuming a Milky Way. "It's not much fun at the paper. Marcus got sued for harassment by Allison, and without Tracie—"

"Tracie's not at the paper?" Jon asked. He'd forced himself not to read the features, to avoid looking for her name.

"Didn't you know she quit?" Beth asked.

"No." He tried really hard not to ask her anything more; he used all his willpower and yet failed. "When is she getting married?" he asked Beth, shamed and frightened by his lack of control. He couldn't allow himself to go back to the misery he had suffered these last months.

"Allison?"

"No, Tracie," he forced himself to say. He hadn't spoken her name since the last time he'd seen her, and he had promised himself he never would again. His mother had stopped asking how she was, though she hadn't ever asked what had happened between them. "I knew she and Phil were engaged."

"For about a minute," Beth said, making a face. "They broke up."

Jon tried hard not to show any reaction. But he felt dizzy. He didn't hear Beth's next words until she was up to ". . . and Tracie's working at Java, The Hut. At least she was the last time I saw her."

It was too much information to take in. He thought he must have heard wrong. "As what?" Jon asked. Perhaps this was some kind of bizarre joke.

"I'm not sure," Beth told him. "But I think you should check it out. I know how she feels about you."

"You do?"

"Come on. She's been in love with you for years. She just didn't know it," Beth told him. "You know, about some things, I'm not completely stupid."

"She loves me?" Jon asked.

"You don't hang out with a guy for seven years if you don't love him," Beth told him. "And you still love her. Don't you think it's time to end the fight and tie the knot?"

"Only to hang myself," he told her.

Chapter 42

Jon sat in a window booth, a menu covering his face. Outside Lucky lay under a bench to avoid the passersby. Jon couldn't help but notice that on the menu were half a dozen Post-it notes with specials listed on them. Beth must be right. The fluttering yellow tags on the menu were more beautiful to him than daffodils on a spring hillside. His heart was racing in his chest. He watched Tracie from a distance as she took an order, poured more coffee, then wiped up a table.

It was hard for him to watch her waitressing. In all the years he'd known Tracie, he'd never even seen her fold a napkin. Now, looking at her, he was experiencing something he thought therapists called "cognitive dissonance." But he'd had a lot of confusion over the last forty-eight hours about what he saw and what he thought he knew.

After he'd spoken to Beth, he had gone home and tried to work out what had really happened—not what he had thought had happened—between him and Tracie. As best as he could reconstruct it, Allison had lied to him about Tracie's engagement. And whether she had done it on purpose to alienate him from Tracie or for some other reason, he didn't know and probably never would. He'd searched out

Phil, and though it had caused him some loss of pride, he was sure it had caused Phil just as much.

Phil sat in the tiny cubicle in the department he'd been assigned to and probably felt humiliated while heads turned to see why such a junior employee was being visited by one of the honchos. Phil had bitterly confirmed Beth's story.

Tracie approached the table. "Can I take your order?" Jon lowered the menu and stared at her. Tracie started with surprise and could barely stand to look back at him. But bravely, she did. Their eyes locked and all that she felt for him was there in her facial expression. "What are you doing here?"

"What are *you* doing here?"

"I work here," she said. "Things at the paper didn't pan out."

"I heard you were engaged to Phil."

"That didn't pan out, either. I wouldn't marry a guy on the rebound." Then she bit her lower lip, as if she were punishing it for talking too much. She looked down at her order pad. He could see her try to pull herself together. "Can I have your order please?" she asked.

"Adam and Eve on a raft," he told her.

Tracie looked stricken. She teared up and had to turn her head away for a minute. Jon could hardly believe it. When she turned back, she was angry. "This isn't fair!" she said. "I know I hurt you, but I have to work here. Teasing me is—"

"I'm not teasing," Jon said, his voice as gentle as he could make it. "Who are you on the rebound from?"

"Who do you think?" she snapped and threw down the pad. She began to walk away. Jon leaped out of his seat at the booth and caught her hand. She tried to pull away. He turned her to him. Tracie hung her head to avoid eye contact. Tears fell. Jon looked over at Molly.

"Doesn't she have the most beautiful eyes you've ever seen?" he asked Molly.

"Oh! Don't tease me," Tracie cried, and tears formed in her beautiful eyes. She tried again to pull away.

"Play nice!" Molly warned him. "No rough stuff."

"So when are you getting married?" Jon asked. Molly gestured to Laura who came out of the kitchen to watch, her eyes opening wide, her mouth agape.

Tracie turned to him. "I told you: I'm not marrying Phil."

"Right," he agreed. "You're marrying me."

Then she stood still and Jon had a moment to think about how beautiful, how perfect every line of her was. If he had sculpted her himself he wouldn't alter a single line. "You're marrying me," he repeated, this time with all the love he felt for her.

"I am?" she asked, and he watched her expression begin to change, as if blood was flowing into marble and enlivening it.

" 'Course you are, stupid," Laura said from her doorway.

"You're all mad, the lot of you," Molly told them, pretending to scold. "Well, I suppose you two better get together. There's no one else in the greater Seattle metropolitan area who would 'ave either one of you." She shook her head in a mock reprimand.

"I'm marrying you?" Tracie asked him again. She blinked. "Why?"

"Because you love me," he told her. "And you have for a long time. It's only now that you really know that," he said, explaining it to her and himself at the same time.

Tracie wiped her face, covered with tears, with the back of her hand.

Jon handed her a napkin and continued. "And because we'll have beautiful children. Because I'll be a great dad and you'll be a great mom. And because we both love Seattle and want to live here forever. And because you could use a part-time mother, and mine wants the job. Plus, she wants grandchildren."

Tracie swallowed, mopped off her face again, and threw her arms around him. "Those are enough reasons," Tracie said. She pushed herself against Jon's chest, and he breathed in the scent of her warm skin, her clean hair. She looked up at him, then sighed and nestled her head against his chest. It fit perfectly.

Jon put his arms around her. The fit was even better.

"I love you, Jonathan," Tracie said.

"I've always loved you," Jon told her. "And I always will."

And he was right.